Sister
Mother
Warrior

Sister Mother Warrior

A NOVEL

VANESSA RILEY

wm

WILLIAM MORROW
An Imprint of HarperCollins*Publishers*

SISTER MOTHER WARRIOR. Copyright © 2022 by Vanessa Riley. All rights reserved. Printed in the United States of America. No part of this book may be used or reproduced in any manner whatsoever without written permission except in the case of brief quotations embodied in critical articles and reviews. For information, address HarperCollins Publishers, 195 Broadway, New York, NY 10007.

HarperCollins books may be purchased for educational, business, or sales promotional use. For information, please email the Special Markets Department at SPsales@harpercollins.com.

A hardcover edition of this book was published in 2022 by William Morrow, an imprint of HarperCollins Publishers.

FIRST WILLIAM MORROW PAPERBACK EDITION PUBLISHED IN 2023.

Designed by Elina Cohen
Map by Nick Springer, copyright © 2022 Springer Cartographics LLC
Part Opener art courtesy of Shutterstock / annamyslivets
Chapter opener art courtesy of Shutterstock / Jena_Velour

Library of Congress Cataloging-in-Publication Data

Names: Riley, Vanessa, author.
Title: Sister mother warrior : a novel / Vanessa Riley.
Description: First edition. | New York, NY : William Morrow, [2022] |
    Includes bibliographical references.
Identifiers: LCCN 2021054914 | ISBN 9780063073548 (hardcover) | ISBN
9780063073562 (ebook)
Subjects: LCSH: Haiti—History—Revolution, 1791–1804—Fiction. |
    Marie-Claire Heureuse Félicité Bonheur, Empress of Haiti,
    1758–1858—Fiction. | Montou, Victoria, approximately
    1739-1805—Fiction. | LCGFT: Historical fiction. | Novels.
Classification: LCC PS3618.I533 S57 2022 | DDC 813/.6—dc23
LC record available at https://lccn.loc.gov/2021054914

ISBN 978-0-06-307355-5 (pbk.)

23 24 25 26 27 LBC 5 4 3 2 1

For mothers in Africa,
For sisters in the Caribbean,
For the women warriors of Haiti,
For girls everywhere,
Like the mountains rise.

UNITED STATES OF AMERICA

LUISIANA

GULF OF MEXICO

Tropic of Cancer

NORTH ATLANTIC OCEAN

BAHAMAS (BRITAIN)

CUBA (SPAIN)

HAYTI

JAMAICA (BRITAIN)

VICE ROYALTY OF NEW SPAIN

CARIBBEAN SEA

NORTH PACIFIC OCEAN

VICE ROYALTY OF NEW GRANADA

CAICOS ISLANDS

Cap-Français

Barrière-Bouteille

Vertières

Bois Caïman

Fort Bréda

Fort La Fin du Monde
Fort Madame
Fort Innocent
Marchand
Habitation Frère

TORTUGA

Fort Pierre Michel

Cap-Français

Cormier Habitation

Gonaïves

Petite Rivière

Crête-à-Pierrot

Marchand

Saint-Marc

Petite Rivière

GONAVE IS.

HAYTI

Jérémie

Léogâne

Port-au-Prince

Miragoâne

Petit-Goâve

Grand-Goâve

Jacmel

BAY OF JACMEL

0   20   40
Miles

Map copyright © MMXXII Springer Cartographics LLC

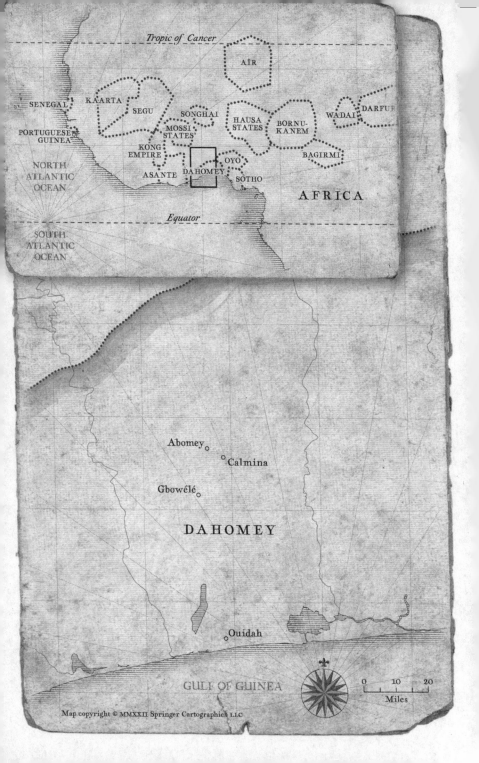

Tropic of Cancer

AÏR

SENEGAL
KAARTA
SEGU
SONGHAI
MOSSI
STATES
HAUSA
STATES
BORNU-
KANEM
WADAI
DARFUR

PORTUGUESE
GUINEA

KONG
EMPIRE

BAGIRMI

NORTH
ATLANTIC
OCEAN

ASANTE
DAHOMEY
OYO
SOTHO

AFRICA

Equator

SOUTH
ATLANTIC
OCEAN

Abomey
Calmina

Gbowélé

DAHOMEY

Ouidah

GULF OF GUINEA

0   10   20
Miles

Map copyright © MMXXII Springer Cartographics LLC

Fort Madame

June 8, 1805

It's on my heels again, making me pace, tripping my feet. I fall against the freshly whitewashed wall and allow Death's passage.

The dark angel won't stay away from my life. From the beginning, it pursued my bloodline, everyone of African descent, swiping at the harbors, huts, and homes. Now it stretches a wing to a protected fort high atop a mountain.

I'm filled with fear, not merely for me but for the emperor and the new nation.

The bright red-and-blue madras scarf wrapping my braids has come loose. My hair drops to my shoulders. I focus on the wrinkles in my yellow muslin dress and smooth the pleated train falling at my back. I don't look the image of a dutiful wife, a regal empress, or anyone's proud sister or friend. What prayer does one offer the Virgin Mary for intercession or St. Louise for energy, when the heart is full of regret?

Wanting to be anchored, wanting to be right, I embrace the wall. My fingers feel the roughness of the joints the plaster tries to hide.

The truth always reveals itself and demands its pound of flesh. And I'm tired of being left to scrape the bottom of the soup pot and lifting an empty ladle.

Can't pretend anymore.

Can't forget the sins of others, or mine.

A large window in the outer wall of my fort allows the air to enter. The breeze is scented with pine and fresh earth excavated for the last fort to be built, La Fin du Monde, the End of the World.

Calming, I force my eyes to acknowledge it's not a thick window but a large loophole for firing a cannon. The sixteen-pounder that's been brought here mirrors the many that lie about the island I'd known as Saint-Domingue. Forged in bronze, the long barrel uses its strong shoulders, the trunnions, to balance on a cartwright's carriage. The wooden structure must be strong to bear a ton of weight. It's under-appreciated how it helps the weapon aim and perform its calling.

Craning my head in the direction of the cannon's bore, I wonder what it targets. This high in the sky, will its lead balls or grapeshot blast clouds or ghosts?

Finding my strength, I move to the barrel and let my fingers thumb its worn cast crest.

Can't read the Latin. I'm unsure which king could claim it or if his army tried to seize our land. Regal men rose and fell or changed alliances too quickly to remember, too quickly to trust.

Grasping the knob at the back, the rings that reinforce the heavy trunnions, I understand better that with all its power, the costs to maintain its strength overwhelm the soul.

The scent of gunpowder lingers in the empty chamber. If I close my eyes, Death will remind me of the faces lost, those I've tended and fed and still lost.

It could all start again—sin, war, murder—that's the prophecy the duchess will use to coerce my agreement.

I don't think she's wrong, but I'm loath to promise anything.

"Ma'am." My servant, my friend, has found me in the hall. "Ma'am, are you well?"

"Yes, just a little warm."

Turning away from her clear eyes, I step closer to the loophole and see the Artibonite Valley below. Houses on the hillside look small, even happy with their coconut palm roofs. It's not Le Cap or Léogâne or any of the places I've known. Still, this valley has a quiet dignity, a unique peace.

My husband's Marchand palace is below, with a smooth, tiled

roof, gingerbread in color. He's not here. Another part of the country needs him.

He named this abode Fort Madame. It's a gift to me. I've made this instrument of war my palace—my refuge . . . from him.

My friend taps my shoulder. "Madame, the duchess is worse. She's asking for you."

For me?

The battles we've endured say it's not me. I'm not her first choice. She's looking for repayment, a pound of flesh—mine.

Remembering my station, my duties, I tie up my braids. "Let us go to her."

The young woman with her straight posture leads me down the hall. It's a passageway heading in the direction of the powder magazine. Tallow candles sit in sconces along the wall, burning their good fire to show me the way. Each step draws me nearer to the barracks, the duchess's quarters.

A servant running fast like a musket ball intercepts us. His dark face holds a frown that could block the sun even atop this high hill.

I squint at his uniform, the rich red and the bleached white, and take pity. Journeying to the top of the mountain can wind the greatest athlete.

"The emperor is delayed in Le Cap, madame. I sent soldiers to hurry him."

Delayed.

Another euphemism. "He'll find his way home."

Head shaking, I dismiss the officer and refuse to think of what excuse my husband will have this time—politics, another widow to woo?

This wasn't how things used to be. We once had no doubts about each other.

Unwilling to turn the corner, I clasp my sleeves right at the gathers of the cuffs. "Perhaps we should try again to get the duchess something to drink. Fetch some asowosi tea with a pinch of salt. That will cut the harshness. Then she'll not say it's the bitter alomo broth her king refused."

"Asowosi? Oh, the crawling ivy with berries. Your knowledge of plants amazes, madame. Oui to the salt. The duchess hates pungent taste, no matter how tough she is. I'll get the tea at once."

My friend nods and runs toward the building with the kitchen.

She disappears around a corner like smoke from a dying flame.

Now that I'm alone, the cloven hand of Death grabs my ankles. I can't shake free. Nor can I lead the dark angel to the duchess. Toya deserves better.

Singing hymns, my aunt's songs, renews my peace. Freed, I float to the barracks with the grace of my grand-mère and hum all the way to Toya's bedchamber. Like my maman, I'll see what I want and pretend that Death is not coming, not now.

All will be well. The sands of time should be infinite for us—the duchess and me. Our grains in the hourglass should fall forever, not be measured and wasted and soon gone.

My chest gongs beneath my airy bodice. The soft soles of these lilac slippers slap the stone floor in my retreat.

"Marie-Claire? That you?"

I stop and turn back. The duchess's voice is low. The vinegary smell of medicine reaches the doorway.

Lying on the mattress, Toya has her eyes closed. Sheets rustle about her diminished form. Her lungs struggle with noisy breaths.

"Asowosi tea will let the good air in." That's what my botanist prisoner once said. "I'm having some made."

"Come in, my empress," she says. "I have something to ask, something to say. There's little time."

Non. Stalling, I trace an imagined line on the floor. "When the tea comes, it will have a little salt. Just for you, Duchess."

Nothing but a groan is uttered.

She knows I haven't crossed her door. Like a coward, I stand at the ready, clutching the frame that separates her side from mine.

The tall woman looks small with her spine curled, shoulders hunched, head low. I miss the days when she stood erect and swung a cutlass with abandon. Toya twirled a bayonet better than any man.

Her brown eyes stir. She waggles her index finger. "A mango. Find me a mango. Slice it for us. Let's share and agree. Like sowing a seed."

Us agree? The jealous part of my broken heart wonders if my sleep will ease when her soul leaves and Death wins again.

"A mango, Marie-Claire."

"If that is what you wish."

Her lips are drawn, and she nods, then turns deeper into the pillow.

"Get up. Reign again. Claim the power. I won't fight."

Hands lifted in prayer, I beg the Virgin Mary and St. Louise for her life, then whisper to the duchess, "Don't leave him—not now. He needs you."

Toya's movements still, but her yellowing eyes are on me.

I'm ashamed but draw upon the strength of my blood and vow to break its curse. "I'll get the mango, Duchess, even if I have to yank it from the tree myself."

With all the peace I can muster, I search for a glimpse, a sparkle, the tiniest *oui*—an agreement that an offering of fruit *will* pay my debts.

The Prophecy

One day gods from heaven came down.

The earth shook, dancing from the sound.

All knew they arrived to loose the bound,

And this hope made the world feel new.

—ANONYMOUS, STYLED IN THE FORM OF UTENZI

1

Adbara

1750

The Outskirts of Gbowélé

The strange warriors looked at me as I stood on the side of the road. Their harsh gazes burned into my chest, searing holes into my soul, which had already escaped. Everything I knew, everything I wanted was dead.

The day was overcast. The air felt hot and dry. Dipping my chin, I glanced at the ground, the thick red clay beneath my feet. The oppressive afternoon sun that hardened this mud must surely dry my tears.

The enemy had destroyed peaceful Gbowélé—all the huts burned, our growing grounds trampled. All the villagers, my neighbors . . .

My father had led us from the north to Gbowélé two years before. He wove baskets. My mother made medicine. When he died in a hunt during the last rainy season, the elders asked us to stay. In our mourning, we found home. Now it was gone again.

Nose wrinkling from the haze lingering in the air, I wished it smelled of the seasoned stew my mother, my iya, had started before dawn. She'd cook down sweet yams and onion with bush meat, letting it simmer all day. In the evening each morsel melted on the tongue.

We didn't make it to dinner. The Dahomey came. Like my iya, the kettle burned, the hut became ash, all the food and our dreams dissolved to soot.

Foreign words surrounded me. Different and angry and impatient commands echoed. They rumbled in my head like my iya's last moans. Why did she let the fire take her? Why didn't she fight?

Movement, fast and precise, fluttered in the distance. When I lifted my gaze, I saw guards draw spears and force crying girls down the red road. Some I knew. Some were younger than my twelve years. Why were they going? Why was I not with them?

Soldiers carrying muskets looked in my direction, toward me and the young ladies who stood nearby. Ashamed of the dirt on my bared bosom, the blood staining the kente silk of my wrap, I let a shiver overtake my limbs.

Leave me to mourn.

Don't say another foreign word to my face.

Yet what was I to do if they did? Nothing but comply, like I had as I watched them rape Gbowélé of her treasures.

I wanted the tongue of my mother. I wanted her. Wish she had wanted me, wanted me enough to fight.

Heavy tears tracked dirt down my thin cheeks. I sniffled, then held my breath, as if that could subdue the pain swirling inside. These people had stolen enough, even ripped away my beads, my family's generational wealth, from my neck.

Sinking to the ground, I wrapped my arms about my bosom. My wrists crossed where strings and strings of carnelian beads had once hidden me.

Was it not a week ago when they were given as part of my purification ceremony? I was pristine. My mother had sung to me. Her little Adbara, she said as she made my skin soft with her special creams. Didn't she know her daughter couldn't live without her?

The pots she labored over for her medicines combusted when the fire started. All my years on this earth, I'd been jealous of her work, everything she did for others. I watched the fire destroy them. I cried as she chose to burn with her jars instead of hiding with me in the woods.

My eyes grew weak again, then the tallest woman I'd ever seen stopped in front of me. She wrenched me up by my shoulders and bellowed more stiff-sounding words. With her spear, she knocked my knee and made me bow.

My palms covered my face. My bony arms rattled like wind chimes.

"Axɔsu! Axɔsu!" She pointed to a man in rich royal robes. "Axɔsu Tegbesu!"

Their king? The Dahomey's leader, Tegbesu, was here and coming my way. The warrior woman jerked my chin lower. She wanted me to greet this man, this king of the killers.

The Dahomey army gathered the remaining Gbowélé men, the young and strong, the ones who weren't wounded, and made them march along this red clay in the same direction as the crying children. The rumors must be true. The Dahomey sold their vanquished enemies to the white devils. This was under the direction of Axɔsu Tegbesu.

I wanted to fight. I was twelve, but I'd performed the blessing ceremony with the white strips of calico on my head, with the leaf pressed between my lips. The elders had sanctified me as an adult, a woman.

The girl behind me grabbed me and kept me kneeling. "You must submit," she said. "It's the only way to live."

The tall warrior, with cockle shells dripping from her hat and a glorious jet tunic covering her, nodded and moved to the next girl.

I tried to turn to see who whispered at me, but she slapped my cheek forward.

"Sorry," she said. "But don't get me in trouble. I'm only trying to keep you from being sent to Ouidah. All those not wanted are sent there. They'll be boarded on boats and sold."

This language was not Kwa or Yoruba, but close. I understood what the girl meant and was happy it wasn't what the Dahomey spoke. I made my voice slow. "Tell me what is to happen to us if we're not sold?"

Silence was my answer and then the small sound of teeth chattering. She was scared, too. She didn't know our fate.

"Move them out," a commander, a thick-muscled man, shouted in my language at their prisoners, then waved his large hands. "Lead them forward!"

He and other armed men drove what was left of the people of

Gbowélé down the red clay road, right past me and the girls kneeling. I was glad our heads were bowed, offering a parting sign of respect.

When I looked up, I saw that the last person in the line was the son of a neighbor whose father had been beheaded hours ago. This young fellow with hands tied with jute rope about his wrists locked his black eyes to mine. This look was more than fear, more than loss or even grief.

It had no name, this feeling, but I knew it in my soul. It had visited me watching my mother die.

The chief warrior woman, with her bulging limbs, poked at me with a spear. "Sit up straight. Raise your chin now."

Her tight voice enunciated my language. It rang with authority. She dropped the weapon in front of me as if I'd be stupid enough to grab it.

The warrior drew her cutlass to my chin. "I said lift your face. Axɔsu Tegbesu, the king, is coming."

This woman was in charge. My iya would say her shiny cowrie shells were of great value. She was the only warrior to wear such beading.

Pebbles I had scooped from the clay swirled in my palm. If I tossed them at her, she'd cut off my head. Then I'd join my mother and my father.

Yet Death was fickle. It might not unite us. It might send me somewhere angry orphaned girls, girls with fury at their mothers, spent eternity.

I lifted my face. My vision became soggy. The sobbing wouldn't quit.

"Stop it, stupid girl. Stop it, for your own good. Smile so he'll choose you. Then you'll know life." Her tone wasn't as angry as before. It almost sounded kind.

Six more warriors, all women, all dressed in dark tunics with off-white sashes from which hung weapons—cutlasses and muskets—led a man in purple robes. A turban of dark blue topped his head. His jaw was strong, and his eyes were as dark as the black stones I'd fished from the rivulet. I smelled the sweet perfume of his clothes, saw his shiny onyx skin.

The woman chanted. "Axɔsu ɔ, tɔ mì ton wɛ, togun ɔ bi sin tɔ."

The commander translated. "The king is our father, father of the people. He is to choose if you'll become wives, first wives, or warrior wives."

The soldier women parted, bending in low bows, and the king approached us where we knelt on the road that led to banishment.

In the point of his chin, the straightness of his carriage, I saw dignity and strength. He was beautiful, different than any man of my village.

The king made a broad circle around us. Then he stopped, looked up to the sky with his hands held wide. Time slowed until he moved. This time he extended his palm over one girl.

She looked relieved and fell on her face, kissing at his feet.

He passed over the next young woman. His palms remained flat at his sides. When he did this, two of his female guards led her away.

"No!! Please!" The girl struggled, but they hit at her legs and forced her to walk.

She screamed even after I'd lost sight of her.

That wouldn't be me.

The courage I didn't have to save my mother would come. I rallied and wiped my eyes. If I were led away, it would be with a dry face. I owed no man my tears.

The head warrior bowed again to the king. "Axɔsu Tegbesu . . ." Whatever she said sounded pleasant. The king nodded as if he were immune to the chaos and continued his process of selecting and discarding, until only I was left.

I didn't lower my eyes. I waited and looked forward to my fate. He stopped in front of me. Readying to be skipped and join the castoffs, I stared at the king.

Different and powerful his features—his broad nose, his strong thick lips—the beauty and symmetry of his countenance became shaded. His hand hovered above my head.

He'd selected me. I was chosen.

For the first time in my life, I wasn't left behind. An unexpected sob welled. My chest loosened. I took a deeper breath and bowed low, lower than all.

When I arose, the king had departed.

The head warrior gathered me and the eighteen others the king had spared. "Congratulations," she said. "You'll be tested to see if you stay and become Dahomey."

Turn into one of them?

My brow rose. Being picked didn't change what had happened. They slaughtered Gbowélé.

A big woman with arms that looked as if she could crush coconuts smiled the smile of a green mamba snake readying to strike. "The process to become Dahomey, the Minos, the brides of King Tegbesu, begins in the morning."

"It's just training? We have nothing to fear?"

The lead warrior shook her head, then gathered up her discarded spear. "If you fail in your training, you'll be executed or sent to Ouidah. The Dahomey want only the best to serve the king."

The girls to my left and right looked frightened. My cheeks felt fevered. I, the one Iya had left behind, had been selected to train as a killer and to destroy villages.

The warriors moved us along the red clay road, walking us in the direction opposite the slave coast. Though my gait was even, my insides spun. Like the whirly bone toy my father made twirl faster and faster on a vibrating leather strip, I became dizzy. Tomorrow things had to slow, then I'd find my way. At least I'd been promised the morning.

The smell of fiery ash, Gbowélé's ash, was in the air. We'd passed the burned elder's hut. A pile of embers and brokenness was all that remained.

For a moment, I'd allowed myself to be flattered, but it was impossible to serve the Dahomey, the men and women who'd doomed my home and given my mother her chance to die.

THE SUN BEAT DOWN ON MY SWEAT-DRENCHED BROW AS I MARCHED with the soldiers across the dry plain. For the past three months the

Minos, the fierce warrior women of the Dahomey, had tested me, me and all the girls the king had chosen.

The trials, the repetition of tasks, wore down my soul. I simply looked forward to morning. Yet many disappeared each time the light came. Only ten of us girls had survived.

At first, I hated everything. Then after weeks of training something changed. The fifth night of being left alone in the Lama Forest with only a cutlass for protection, I gave myself to the experience. I found a new me. The thrill of learning my strengths made my heart leap.

The Dahomey feats of endurance pushed me to demand excellence. The thorns of the vine-laden hill knew my flesh. They pierced every limb until I no longer winced, until I cheered the exertion.

Gaou Hangbé, the lead woman, said it was good to feel nothing, to shed no tears for torn skin. Soon I stopped remembering the pain of Gbowélé or even missing my mother.

"Take positions along the ridge." Gaou waved her hand, rushing us. "Today we study the battlefield."

As trained, I unhitched my cutlass. The metal gleamed; the leather wrapping the handle felt hard but supple. Within my palm, it gave me power and control.

Creeping in the finger grass with emerald blades cushioning my knees, I found a spot, then looked to the valley below.

"What do you see?" Gaou asked. "Notice everything."

In the distance a naboom tree grew. Its skinny trunk held a weighty canopy that curled like a baby boy's rich, thick hair. On the other side of the plain, elephants surrounded an umbrella acacia. Its thorns, both the straight ones and the hooked ones, held yellow-orange seedpods.

The breeze scattered them, sending the bright colors to the ground. Such a contradiction for the acacia to have great weaponry and still lose its treasure.

But then, then I remembered my iya gathering bark from these trees to fight swelling. In a glimpse, I saw her making teas for the sick. I caught myself looking back, thinking of the old. I made a heavy blink and chanted, *nothing came before.*

That was what Gaou taught us to do, and I promised never to fail myself or the Minos. With them I belonged. Awkward and gangly me had forced a place as a warrior. They were my home.

"You see the trees and the five elephants, but do you see the lion in the distance?" Gaou's voice was strong. I doubted she feared anything.

"If we were the elephants," she said, "what would we do, Minos?"

Many yelled, "Hold your ground," others, "Attack."

I . . . we all revered animals. They were the gods' handiwork. I couldn't think of attacking one, but I focused on Gaou calling us Minos, like we were all equals. I didn't know one could hunger to belong, not until now.

"You would attack the elephants and then the lion?" Her tone was lower. Though she asked everyone—the tilt of her head, the angle of her face with the slight jiggle of those glossy shells on her helmet—her question seemed directed at me.

With a shy cough, I shook my head. "We do not have them surrounded. The elephants will escape if we charge. The lions are powerful. They cannot be ignored."

"Good. And we wait for one or the other to make a mistake. Every battle is a strategy." Gaou half smiled, then turned and looked away.

My friend—the young woman captured the same day as me, one with whom I'd secretly shared a sweet ogbono in the depths of the Lama Forest—winked at me. We survived hunger because of the fruit. We outlasted training because of our bond.

"All animals are beautiful, but we must think of them as a threat. Study *our* prey, Minos. Elephants are big, but they have weaknesses." Gaou tightened her grip around her spear. "We must face the enemy without fear. It's the same as facing a man on the field of battle. We must not give an inch, no deference because they are male. To win, we will not accept their terror."

Terror.

My iya's . . . she had stayed inside the burning hut until the thatch of the roof glowed. She was yelling at me to run, but I refused to leave her. She and her beloved pots burned before my eyes.

Did Iya know the Dahomey would take me? Did she want me to go with them?

The earth trembled. Three young elephants trampled near, kicking up dirt. Dust rolled up to our ridge. When the fog lessened, I saw a fast-moving lion. It prowled and attempted to cut a stray from the pack.

Swatting their long trunks, two big elephants approached. They trumpeted and charged until the lion backed up. The young elephants rushed to the herd. The older gathered around them and formed a protective ring.

Gaou moved her hand through the air as if she were wafting the fragrance of a hot stew set before us. "Smell the honey in the breeze?"

Faint as it was, the sweetness tickled my nose.

"The young calves are male. They give off that scent to let the older know they are no threat."

"One would think their size would do that." I covered my mouth. I shouldn't be free with my tongue, but thoughts that burned needed to be said . . . especially goodbye and sorry.

I knew that now.

"Soldiers who serve other kings first think Minos are weak because we are women. Then they meet us in battle. One taste of our cutlasses, they die knowing the truth." Gaou rose from her crouched position and pointed below. "The lion sees the strength of the battle line. The elephants protect what's important. They've forestalled the attack."

A horn shrieked. A medium-sized elephant in the far distance was being chased by another lion. The defeated one joined in and the two big creatures pushed the loner toward our ridge.

Pouncing on his back, clawing from behind, the lions took down the elephant. Dust and raw honey scent came at us.

As the beasts struggled, Gaou made a gesture sending six of the fleetest, strongest Minos forward. She counted down, lowering fingers until her hand was balled.

The warriors raised weapons, ran into the fray, and chased the lions away. The hunted elephant stood anew, but like the other predators, the Minos attacked from the rear, jabbing with spears. Wrapping its hind legs with ropes, our women brought him down.

The earth shook. I coughed at the dust clouds gathering, but the smell, the sweet smell, turned ferrous.

Gaou snapped her fingers. A second wave of Minos climbed down to the beast and finished sending the elephant to eternity.

Cutlasses dripping with blood, the women returned, displaying pieces of dismembered flesh stabbed on their spears. Two returned with the trunk, the tenderest morsel on an elephant.

Tonight, like the seed of the ogbono, the meat would be roasted. Our warriors would give thanks and cook the kill on a spit and flame.

We, the new recruits, stood still. Not quite in control of my thoughts, my body started to quiver. I wanted the honey, not the blood.

King Tegbesu would be proud," Gaou said, then led us to camp chanting, "Axɔsu Tegbesu wɛ ɖÓ acɛ daxÓ é è nan ɖɔ lé é mì nan nɔn gbon é nu mì."

The Fon language they'd taught us sounded like music. The words meant King Tegbesu had the divine right to dictate the way we shall go. He'd chosen me for this.

I closed my eyes and I saw those words scribbled on my lids. My iya was a healer. I would have followed in her path, but now I was a hunter. I had to let go of my fears and be one with this path.

My friend brushed my shoulder of dust. She smiled at me and I watched her mouth the Fon words.

My thoughts stilled and I drank in the dust and the perfume of killing. "Axɔsu Tegbesu wɛ ɖÓ acɛ daxÓ é è nan ɖɔ lé é mì nan nɔn gbon é nu mì." I said this, and meant it, more than I had ever before.

"Being set apart is lonely, until you find purpose." Gaou's voice—strong, bold, and assured—penetrated my skull. It pierced my heart.

"Whatever happens," my friend said, "we'll survive together. We're twins, becoming Minos the same day. I stand with you."

We had no names yet. When we finished training, the fire ceremony would give us one. I couldn't wait to say hers and to hear mine.

"They say a mature elephant is only good for a hungry man."

"Keep talking." I let my whisper kiss her ear. "All will be well. There's nothing to fear anymore."

"Always something. We're giving up everything to belong." A frown dulled her brown eyes, eyes I found hooded in shame.

"We aren't alone in this, not anymore." I pumped my spear into the air. "Together and belonging is better."

"Freedom is better . . ." She looked away, not finishing her thoughts.

I decided not to dwell. If I was to be a warrior, that meant I had to become comfortable with bloodshed and destruction.

At camp, the steaks of our kill sizzled and spat bubbling fat. My gut forgot the honey and succumbed to the fragrance of charred meat and spice.

2

Adbaraya

1758

Calmina, Dahomey Kingdom

If Gaou Hangbé looked down from her place with the ancestors and saw what I was doing—shirking my duties, running around the walls of the city looking for my friend—shame would fall from the skies like balls of fire.

Eight years I'd served at her side, learning from the great Gaou every movement and strategy, until she fell in battle to the Oyo three rainy seasons ago.

"Toya? Adbaraya Toya?"

Hearing that name, garbled and low as if it came from the waters of the rivulet, made me stop.

Made me remember.

Gaou Hangbé led me to the babbling stream at the center of camp. My sisters, my soon-to-be sisters, danced and ate of the feast, the roasted fruits and hearty stew that scented the air.

Creamy white carnelian beads straddled my hips, forming an apron that protected my womanhood from the spitting ash.

"The fire will greet you," she said. The beading of her hat, of her breastplate, jingled when she leaned forward, warming her hands over flames that glowed red, red like blood. "Take the leaf from your mouth, Adbara," she said. "Give it to the flames. Then we shall know your new name."

Holding my breath, praying to retain a bit of the old, I did as she asked.

In seconds, the leaf ignited, licked away to nothing. Sparks hissed as the logs offered mournful crackles, then all dulled. Silence.

Had the gods rejected my offering?

Everything, everyone celebrating the completion of our training, of becoming Minos, stilled. It felt like the world ended before Gaou raised her arms.

"You shall be called Adbar . . . aya. Adbaraya Toya."

My leader's voice sounded strangled, but my cheeks began to burst. I had something of the old. I would keep my name, most of it. "Thank you, Gaou. Thank you."

Dancing and singing began anew, but the woman I idealized frowned as if the sky had fallen. "Do not be thankful for a curse. Adbaraya means torn apart, torn away. You will be torn away from all you know."

No. "That's already happened. It's why I'm here."

She put her hand to my chin. "Again, judgment comes for you. Toya means water. The water will take you. You will be set apart for betrayal."

"Toya? Adbaraya Toya?"

My face fevered.

"Adbaraya Toya, are you all right?"

Eghosa's voice. Blinking, I came to myself, turned from the rivulet then began searching for her.

Made a warrior the same day as I, my friend was given the name Eghosa, which translated to god's servant. Yet, when I saw her grinning at me like a Guinea baboon and reaching for an ogbono instead of manning Calmina's western gate, I suspected her god was mischief.

"Come down, Eghosa."

"Who's to catch me?" She'd scurried to the highest part of the bowing tree. "Our troops are away and the new Gaou is my friend, my champion."

My hands felt damp curled about my spear. I feared less about Eghosa falling and more that we'd be caught, and I'd disappoint my king.

Sweat dampened my brow under my bronzed hat with feathers and cowrie shells—Gaou's helmet. "Down, now. You're to guard the gates of Calmina. The palace can't be unprotected."

"Adbara, with most of the Minos away training new recruits in the Lama Forest, no one is around to catch us."

My forces were woefully diminished. It would be easy to attack the city. I couldn't let that happen, but the pleasure on her face . . . "Be quick."

"A concession? Perhaps I should continue to call you by your old name, Adbara. Then you'll pay attention to me. You don't. Not that much anymore. I'm not as important to you, now that you're Gaou."

"That's not true or fair." I slapped at the trunk. My strong arms could shake it down, knocking her from her perch, but my patience had grown. Summoning my authority, I craned my neck toward her. "Come down, Eghosa, now."

"Afraid King Tegbesu would see and know you aren't perfect? Or would think you remembered a friend?" Her voice mocked, but she wore her begging smile that made me feel guilty about upholding my responsibilities.

"Why not be a first wife, Adbara, to justify your being away from me? Don't you ever yearn to be more than a glimmer in the king's eye? I'd want that for you."

At twenty, I knew my mind and what contentment was. "I advise the king. Nothing more."

Eghosa still pouted and remained high in the tree. "Maybe I have things to tell you, too. But you're busy. I don't make you red in your cheeks. Not anymore."

Her voice was bitter, as if I'd purposely been aloof. Eghosa and I . . . we'd always been close, but I had responsibilities. Those came first. "You can't be away from the gate. It's a breach."

She stripped off her beaded headband, tossing aside the precious leather adorned with yellow-orange cowrie shells, one of the many treasures bestowed to the warrior women by Tegbesu.

Her shiny braids glistened and fell upon her shoulders. "You're a good leader, but I'm a better friend." She clasped the elusive ogbono and shook it. "You need more pleasure."

"Gaou Hangbé would want—"

"You're Gaou, Gaou Adbaraya Toya. Don't walk upon her shoulders. Choose your own path." Eghosa's words were lyrical. With a kiss to its skin, she held up the fruit, and I imagined the tangy taste of the ogbono, the way the slick flesh settled on my tongue and dripped tart and sweet juice. "This is not ripe enough. Must get one worthy of us."

"No, Eghosa. Come down. Stand in front of Calmina's high walls and guard the gate. Let's have no more foolishness."

Her eyes became small. "Did becoming Gaou mean losing us?"

"Eghosa—"

"Remember how you'd dip in the water to cool your heels every time we ended patrol. Then you'd clasp my hand and say, 'Together we win.'"

"That was early on. We had to mature." I had to outgrow the prophecy.

"Do it now." She pointed to the water. "Show me our proper Gaou can be fun."

With the sand beneath my bared feet burning of the day's scorching heat, the draw to be carefree and reckless like Eghosa was magnetic. If I turned to the western gate and splashed my thorn-scarred soles in the glistening waters, who would know? Who would suspect that the new Gaou was human? And no longer fighting the past.

"Adbara . . . ya. You look as if you're going to pass out. It's just water. The king won't see his favorite misbehaving."

My cheeks felt flushed. She knew my heart and my unrequited feelings . . . but voiced it to the wind.

The breeze made leaves rustle, even those of the nearby baobab. "You sound boisterous, but do be careful not to play with temptation and pride. The god, Cagn, might hear and flip you upside down like he did those trees. Till this day the baobabs look as if their roots are growing to the sky, and their trunks remain fat and stunted."

Eghosa did a flip out of the tree and landed. "I'll take care after pleasure." She wrapped her arm around mine. "Come to the grassy knoll and share in friendship and ogbonos." My friend, my temptress, pointed to one in a neighboring tree.

Then she leapt like a scurrying mongoose, twirled between the acacia's branches until she swooped into the green canopy that held our jewels, yellowed ripe ogbonos. Arms stretched wide, she balanced on the knurled limb and seized the one. "For you, my Gaou."

"What has come over you, Eghosa? You seem rebellious."

"Maybe I am. Maybe I'm remembering the old, all we gave up . . . when we were forced to live as Minos. You and I would be married women now with children, something of our own to love." She hung upside down. The shells of her bracelets rattled. The breastplate of her tunic slipped, sending the biblike grass cloth to her chin.

"Come down, my Minos. Stop looking to the past."

Eghosa swung by her knees. "I had a lovely village. A happy home. A mother and father who were proud of me. I liked the neighbor's son. He was nice. And I dream of a man's eyes looking at me like I'm a woman, a lover, not a soldier, not a killer."

She'd never talked of the time before. I didn't understand why she sounded hurt about our duties. "Eghosa, what has happened? What is this about?"

"Nothing, not that you'd notice, not unless the king said it."

Pounding my spear along the ground, I stood up straight. "Come tell me your troubles." I pointed over my shoulder at the red walls of reinforced brick and thatch. "Behind those proud gates that we've polished with palm oil until our hands are numb, that we've lined with the skulls of every transgressor who has come against us, our king sleeps at ease. We stand at the ready against attack. We must always be ready. There is pride in being fierce and prepared."

"Ready for what? The next war? What about what I want? What about freedom?"

"We are not enslaved, Eghosa."

"Are you sure? We can't go and come as we please. We cannot love and be loved. We must think and do for a king who can have what he wants, and that means keeping us servile. We are slaves. We've just been trained not to care."

Heresy.

Temptation be gone. "King Tegbesu cares for us. Axɔsu Tegbesu wɛ ɖÓ acɛ daxÓ é è nan ɖɔ lé é mì nan nɔn gbon é nu mì." I chanted this over and over and waited for her to repeat it.

She didn't. Instead, she bit an ogbono, devouring it with its juice dripping down her plump lips.

Thinking of what Gaou Hangbé would do, of Cagn's wrath, I clasped my palms about the spear instead of shaking Eghosa. "I've been made the leader. I have to protect the king, us, all our ways."

"But they're not truly our ways. They've been drilled into our skulls." She held an ogbono to me. When I refused, she took a big bite. Her purr of pleasure was loud enough to wake the dead. "You have forgotten too much, Adbara."

"And you've awakened at the wrong time. This should've been said before."

"To say this and be sent to Ouidah. I was frightened of the un-known. No one ever returns. But I thought I could bear this life." She shook her head. Then licked juice from her fingers.

"We pledged and trained together. We are of one mind. What has made you question our fate?"

Eghosa looked off into the distance. "The king's not here. I've heard no gong. No wives are coming. You can be truthful, or has becoming Gaou stolen the rest of your will?"

Something had bewitched her. Eghosa had the humblest of spirits. "You've never spoken—"

"Never said. I remember my home and I hate being here every moment. I hate what we've been forced to become." Her low voice sounded wet. "Forced to forget."

"Please say no more, Eghosa. Just come down."

"Maybe I don't want my only friend to become the same unfeeling killer as Hangbé."

The woman was jealous or drunk on palm wine or both. My boldness returned. The soft feelings of my heart for her, for what we'd endured, I banished. "Enough foolish talk. Man your gate. You're a Dahomey. You're a Minos. Duty first. It must always come first."

"I'm a Minos, but I'm still Igbo of Guinea." Eghosa let go and dropped upon her thick-muscled legs. "Come with me into the grove of kapok trees and palms. Maybe we will find one of the lise trees that bear the red fruit. We can bring some back to the king, since his do not bloom."

These weren't my friend's thoughts. "Who's telling you this? Who's making you speak against our king?"

"No one. Forget I've said anything. Watch this." She plucked a close ogbono from a branch, then flung it into the air. It pitched higher than the two-story roof of the palace.

Whooping, the sound she made during an attack, she flung her cutlass. It sailed over my head and went end over end toward the fruit. Eghosa followed, running with the speed of an antelope.

The sharp cutlass in midair swept through the falling ogbono, slicing it in two.

As she'd done in defensive training, Eghosa leaped and stretched for the pieces. One hand caught half, but she missed the other piece.

Thwack.

The gleaming blade smote Eghosa's outstretched arm.

Cowrie shells exploded like gunshots. My rebellious friend dropped face-first into the rivulet.

NO. NOT ANOTHER WOMAN I LOVED . . . SHE COULDN'T DIE IN FRONT of me. Outside the walls of Calmina, Eghosa's rigid body was half in, half out of the deep stream. Furious and frightened and forgetting my own breath, I ran to the showy fool and pulled her head from the waters.

I touched her stilled face.

Her eyes didn't open. The years of us being together, the battles we'd fought, slid past me. She was why I'd survived.

"Eghosa, do you hear me? Don't die. Not dishonored like this. In battle like Gaou Hangbé—that was right. Or tired and old with all the work done. Don't choose this way to leave me."

Grasping her wrist, I saw nothing but a scratch. The bracelet had taken the brunt of the cutlass's bite. I pushed on her chest and spittle spurted.

Then I heard her gasp. She jerked up and shook off water like an elephant frolicking in mud. Rocking her, I held her to my bosom.

Her arms fell around me. "Sorry."

Crouched beside her, not letting her go. "Your folly almost killed you. These weapons aren't for show."

"I know. Just wanted your attention." She rubbed her wrist. "I misjudged things." She took a deep breath. "Only broke my bracelet."

It took more than a minute for my arms to unwind from her shoulders. "Could've been your neck. You could've sliced through your arm and bled out."

Slowly standing, I remembered how to refill my lungs, but that pulse of mine refused to slow. "You made me see your death." Like my iya. "That's not right. Friends don't do that."

"Adbaraya, I'm not dead. But my cowrie beads are flung everywhere."

When I helped her up, the somber sweet gaze that was ours returned. I saw the twelve-year-old girl who encouraged me, who helped me become strong. I needed to be as good a friend to save her from this bewitchment. "What's your secret, Eghosa? What has happened?"

She pressed her arm to her stomach. "Who's asking, Gaou or my sister-friend, my twin who found time for me?"

I took off my helmet and laid it on the short grasses carpeting this patch by the rivulet. "Tell me."

"I'm in love, Adbaraya."

"With the king?" I said this hoping it to be, for Minos were brides to the king. There could be no other man.

Eghosa swallowed and looked down. "Yes." She poked at the nick on her wrist. "And I'm jealous that you are spending so much time with him that now I see neither of you."

Lifting her chin, I stroked the soft flesh with my thumb. "I'm a third-rank ahosi wife, like you. I'm celibate. My body is given to the battle, to keeping our king and our world safe. My duty is demanding, but there's nothing else."

"I never see you unless you're doing your rounds. I could be bursting with news and you're not here. This is not like we used to be." She didn't hold my gaze.

Something had happened. Eghosa didn't trust me enough to confess. "Our world is at risk. The Oyo almost defeated us. We must be ready for the next battle. I have to study and prepare plans. I need my dearest friend to understand. I need her support."

She hugged me, crushing me in a tight embrace. "I get confused, sometimes, thinking of all we gave up. I'm bitter—"

I put my pinkie to her full, plump lips. "We were redeemed by the Dahomey. We are Tegbesu's. We serve him and only him. The past is gone."

A river poured from her eyes, and she gave an ugly and throaty sob. "I want it gone, but the loneliness of my heart brings it all back. I want the life I would've had, the one with real love."

In the quiet of the night, I knew this restlessness. But my vows meant everything. Despite the curse of my name, I'd never separate myself from the Dahomey or the will of my king.

When I rocked her, she quieted. "The unease will pass. Go put aloe tincture on this cut to make it heal. You were saved by a bracelet. You're the luckiest of fools."

"I saved the seed, too. Well, this half anyway. It's a promise." Her infectious smile blossomed. "Good to know you still care. You'll protect me, even if I do stupid things? Even if I'm weak?"

Her low, seductive voice returned, and she nudged me, offering the piece she'd caught. "For you. Adbaraya. The fullness of the ogbono is like your face, except you're ripe and ebony, not pale. Please, have the ogbono. It will be our secret."

She put the fruit into my palm. And greedily my fist closed about it. I could imagine—the taste, the sweet-and-sourness of it; the flesh, tender with nips of firmness about the skin. I could even smell the seed roasting in our quarters. Eghosa would cook it. She did it the best.

Ogbono.

All pleasure.

All sin.

"No." I tossed it into the water. "This is temptation. It's wrong."

"You're scared of feeling anything more, Adbara, aren't you?"

"It's Adbaraya Toya. Look how you've let your soul grow discontent. Lamenting the past has done it."

"Adbara . . . aya, that is a waste of good fruit."

How could she be sweet one minute, then manipulative or joking the next? "Eghosa, do you think me naïve? Are we not the same age and lived the same life since Gbowélé?"

She didn't answer, merely picked up the cutlass and swung it around. "Forget what I said. Let's go back to marching and protecting Calmina. Duty demands we be alert. Raiders could be in the area."

I went back to the grove and claimed Eghosa's spear and offered it to her. "Don't let the enemy catch you off guard. With our Minos training in Lama Forest, we could easily be overrun. It's three days of constant running to go from Lama to here."

She stuck the spear's staff under her arm. "Raiders trade with our king. He allows the French to flatter him to sell them slaves. He likes their money."

I searched her guilty eyes. "Who has said these things? Who's corrupting you?"

"No one. I hear poachers sometimes. Their guides speak our Fon language. They say all the whites war for Black flesh and Tegbesu doesn't care. As long as they pay, he'll sell people . . . our people."

She made the king's divine right to choose who lives or dies or who's driven down the red clay road all about money. That was wrong.

Eghosa stepped away from me and went closer to the grove, searching the leaves, the trunks, as if another ogbono was near. "What if the king is wrong, Adbaraya? What if his choice to war with the Oyo is merely to get more people to sell? What if all perished in your Gbowélé for silver?"

"King Tegbesu has the god-given right to dictate the way we shall

go. Axɔsu Tegbesu wɛ ɖÓ acɛ daxÓ é è nan ɖɔ lé é mì nan nɔn gbon
é nu mì." I said it slowly and raised my voice until Eghosa repeated it
with me. "We have to believe in what we've been taught. We have to
trust our king."

She put her warm palm on my forearm. "You're right. I'm resentful.
I miss my friend, my Gaou. And if he'd made you a first wife, I'd never
see you. We'd be separated unless a gong rang and the Minos had to
escort the royal women on walks. What type of life is that for me, never
seeing my friend?"

A lump rumbled down my throat and trampled my stomach like a
herd of elephants. "Eghosa, I haven't forgotten you. I never will."

A tear fell onto my hand. She cried, "Everything feels like I'm lost.
I'm losing you and me."

A noise came from the grove, a call that sounded like a hoarse
hadeda, a brown ibis, opening its long beak to screech songs.

Her gaze switched to the grove. Was something there? The thing
that captivated her, dancing her to the edge of betrayal?

"Let me go back to my post, Gaou Toya, unless you feel I must be
punished."

"No. Take your place."

She nodded and went to her station at the western gate beside the
babbling water as if nothing had changed.

Warring with myself, but needing to complete my rounds, I stopped
beside her at the entrance to the city. "Eghosa, I love you, but my duty
is to the king. I find no fault in Tegbesu's divinity or his right to make
laws or to judge. I'll not question his decisions."

"Even when it's unfair?"

I turned back and took the thin bracelet of cowrie beads from my
wrist and put it on hers.

"No, Adbaraya. That is yours. The king gave it to you."

"Keep this to remember that you're Tegbesu's wife, too, as much as
my friend. We fight together. We die together." I stared at her until she
looked up at me. "Tell me the problem. Let me help."

The rapid beating vessel at the side of her neck shifted the bib of her uniform. "The ogbono is my sin. I enjoy one every night. I leave my post to go get one."

That wasn't it. The proud tones she'd had before disappeared. These humble words hid the truth. My iya had been humble, but she pushed for what she wanted.

A pain hit my chest, harder than a fist. I forgot to breathe again. Iya chose her death. And my friend might have done the same. With a nod, I left her guarding the western gate. I had to speak with the king to learn if I could save her. I didn't know how I could watch Tegbesu use his infallible right to sentence my friend to death.

The Prophecy

One day gods from heaven came down.

The earth shook, dancing from the sound.

All knew they arrived to loose the bound,

And this hope made the world feel new.

The ones they chose had to obey

Virgin wombs bore warriors tway.

Darkness, light, they battled always.

Yet how were sins paid by just two?

—ANONYMOUS, STYLED IN THE FORM OF UTENZI

3

Sainte

1758

Cap-Français, Saint-Domingue

On the steps of her father's town house, Sainte listened to her little sister sing a solemn hymn. The words sent peace and soothed, at least for a moment, the agony of fleeing the capital.

> *Let all that dwell above the sky,*
> *And air and earth and seas,*
> *Conspire to lift Thy glories high.*

Five-year-old Elise possessed a voice that sounded very adult. Watts's lyrics made her tone ring pure like crystal, like the white sand found along the shores of Cap-Français, the city everyone affectionately called Le Cap.

Sainte, who'd celebrated a solemn sixteenth birthday a month ago, walked there every day to see the fishing ships and to smell the sea air. Often, she'd scoop some of the beach silt and watch bits of quartz sparkle. The grains reflected the pinks and reds of a dusky morn.

She should've kept a pinch or two in a pot. Then she'd have something to remind her of the good, every little dusting of joy that they'd miss when they abandoned the home and city she loved.

"Marie-Sainte?" Her mother's sharp tone echoed. "Why are you dawdling? Get moving. There's much to do."

Standing at the threshold, Sainte hesitated. One slipper remained inside her old world, one of little cares—of fine linens and dresses imported from Paris. Her other foot tapped the limestone step, where she readied to carry another bundle.

Hoisting the linen parcel to her shoulder, she moved to the back of the dray and dropped it beside her singing sister. The little girl looked small and helpless sitting in a pile of their worldly goods—the few things they were allowed to take to their new lives.

"Souer, my sis," Elise said, "I didn't know we'd lose everything if Père died. Sorry."

Their father should be alive and using his position on the council to help calm everyone. Yesterday, at the market square, vendors, Black, Blanc, and Colored, seemed nervous. They expected a rebellion. That happened often, every few months, because of an assembly ruling or some wicked punishment of an enslaved by a planter.

"I didn't, either, Elise." Without François Lobelot, his daughters and his wife were reduced to nothings. Sainte made a fist. It wasn't fair. Weren't they like all the other families of Grand Blancs, the wealthiest men of the highest tier of Saint-Domingue society? Sainte and Elise were educated and expected to enjoy the finest.

Except they weren't like all the others. If they were white like their father, then they could claim every privilege.

They weren't.

Their skin held a slight tan, lighter than their mulatta mother's. Their maman's, Madame Lobelot's, Negro blood could be traced to West African shores. She had been enslaved by Monsieur Lobelot until he married her. The colony of Saint-Domingue would never see her as a Grand Blanc but as a Colored Affranchi. Other than remaining free, as his widow she wasn't due his lands or much of the marital possessions they shared in this town house.

"Sainte, you're not moving fast enough." Tall, thin, proud Maman rubbed her brow with an embroidered lacy handkerchief. "What . . . what's going on?"

Her gaze pointed to the end of the street at the town square, Place d'Armes. Though a few blocks away on Rue Sainte Marie, the crowds and the flames couldn't be missed. This was the central point in Le

Cap where important decrees were read, where the Colonial Assembly led celebrations for King Louis XV.

Sainte covered her mouth. Hadn't she told Maman to burn the town, then none of Father's brothers could have anything? "A rebellion, Maman? That's what Père said would happen if the massa poisonings continued."

Her mother looked as if she wanted to slap Sainte's words from the air. The woman grimaced and waved her crumpled handkerchief. "Go inside and get the last of our things. Say your goodbye to this place. It's not safe to stay."

"But the crowds, Maman—"

"Sainte, please. Whatever it is, we need to be away from here. Then you can focus on a fiancé, the proper one. Everything is precarious. You must wed to save us."

There was only one man Sainte cared for, and he wasn't the Blanc Maman had picked. This past month, the arguing between mother and daughter had become old and staid, and more hurtful than a man left to die, a father begging to be saved.

Filled with bitterness, Sainte stormed into the house. She wouldn't be bound to a marriage to keep her mother in handkerchiefs. She wouldn't be a wife to a Petit Blanc, some man with a little business in trade hoping to make a fortune and become a Grand Blanc. Neither would she be a rich man's mistress, which was common for light-skinned Affranchi. Her uncles, Père's brothers, said Sainte and Elise were *stained with a little bit of color* and would do well as concubines. Working as prostitutes was what they suggested should be the daughters' fate when Père needed help with his debts.

From the window, Sainte watched Maman tug on her satin jacket and flip up its rose-embroidered hood. With her matching petticoat of white silk, Maman intended to flee in her most expensive outfit. She looked good and proud, though everything was in ruins. That persistence or stubbornness spoke to Sainte.

With a shake of her head, she went to the last of the dishes. They were stacked on the floor where the mahogany table once sat. Maman

had sold it yesterday. Kneeling, Sainte ran her thumb along the edge of
the fine porcelain plates. They once held perfect sauces. The matching
bowls offered savory soups. She counted it lucky none of her uncles'
wives wanted to eat from anything Black lips had touched. It would be
childish to kiss everything that remained, every piece of furniture, every
curtain. Yet it was a greater shame that Maman planned to sell these
treasures tomorrow for fast money. Three mouths to feed without Père
seemed impossible.

Stuffing napkins between the plates, she stopped and traced the
stitches of the Lobelot crest embellished on the linen. In her head,
she heard her father's chuckles as he sat by the fireplace. Turning
to the mantel, she remembered the nutty scent of the pine logs burning, her father's pipe, and the fragrance of cherry ash that filled the
room for his special Sunday smoke.

Then she saw him die in front of her. He jerked back and forth in
the rocking chair, gasping, choking, turning colors—green, then purple, then gray.

"Sainte! Sainte! We have to hurry."

Hearing the panic in her mother's voice, she picked up the dishes
and ran.

Outside, the crowd in Place d'Armes had tripled. They yelled curses.
They sounded angry. It had to be a rebellion.

Maman stared at the commotion. "Sainte, the world is in chaos.
Can't you see this? All the rights of the Affranchi will be taken away
because of this."

"How does the enslaved uprising affect free Coloreds? The large
habitations with the sugarcane fields, that's where most of the poisonings occurred. *Most*." Sainte hinted at what she'd come to believe. Père
had been murdered.

"The Blancs don't think the Blacks are smart enough to plot rebellion. They will blame the free Colored. We will lose more rights."

"We are running from our home. What rights do we have?"

Sighing and looking to the cloudy sky, Maman took the dishes and set them down. "Listen, Sainte. We need protection. Your marriage will provide this."

"If you'd helped Père to breathe, he could've protected us."

Maman's guilty fingers trembled. "There was nothing to be done. But you have much to do. Agree to the betrothal, merely to get us more time. Who knows? You might find Monsieur Havans engaging. And if not, I can make sure he never hurts you."

No one could ensure that. Marriage took away parental rights. Women were property of their husbands. "Non, Maman. Father would never have me settle. He wanted the best for me."

"He wanted to sell you . . . to settle you with one of his rich friends. The son of a Grand Blanc wanted a plaything. Lobelot's debts—"

"Non. That has to be a lie, and a dead man can't correct it." Sainte lowered her voice, lifting her hands to beg. "Maman, I love someone else. Guillaume Bonheur, the fisherman."

"The poor, Black fisherman, the one whose skin could make him the next one executed in Place d'Armes." The cold look in her light brown eyes burned straight through Sainte's chest. "Non. I've sacrificed too much to keep you two safe and free. Non."

Maman had turned on her . . . like she had on Père.

Monsieur Joseph, a homme serviteur, one of her father's formerly enslaved men made free by Père's will, lumbered from Place d'Armes. "It will be bad tonight. You must hurry."

Her mother's false smile appeared. "We'll discuss this later, Sainte. Joseph, there you are."

"Oui, m'dame." He wiped moisture from his big balding head. "The trouble tonight, mesdames, is bad, but at least your youngest can find sleep."

Elise had flopped onto the bedding and snored.

Chanting sounded from the square.

"Burn the poisoner!"

"Brûlez l'empoisonneur!"

"Brûlez! Brûlez!"

Sainte squinted and saw a man at the center of the mob. His voice overtook the crowd. It was deep and dark and proud and soon silenced everyone else.

> *One day gods from heaven came down.*
> *The earth shook, dancing from the sound.*
> *All knew they arrived to loose the bound,*
> *And this hope made the world feel new.*

People pushed past the rows of elms that bordered the square and then spilled onto the surrounding rues.

"It's not a rebellion?" Maman said, even as she offered Sainte mad eyes. "Monsieur Joseph, is it slaves or Affranchi to be executed?"

"Neither. A maroon. A runaway who's been caught. They're going to make an example of him once they finish their questioning."

Maman cupped her hands to her olive-brown face. "Joseph, is the scaffold up to hang him?"

"Non, Madame Lobelot," Joseph said, "The Blancs have formed a mob. They will—"

"Burn him," Sainte said and took a few steps to gain a better look. "The Grands and the Petits have joined together for this killing?"

"When have they not been together?" Joseph, the old hulk of a man, shoved things into the back of the dray. "They'll join forces to kill Blacks and to murder a few Coloreds they don't like tonight."

That was Saint-Domingue.

Skin separated everyone until it was convenient to inflict pain or to put someone else in their place. Grands hated the common Blancs that made up the Petit class. The Petits and the Coloreds wanted everything the Grand Blancs had—education, respectability, representation in the assembly, and riches. The Blacks, the poor Blacks, were kicked by everyone. They, for the most part, weren't free and had no money or education.

Her Guillaume was an exception. He was sable skinned, darker than Joseph. He had a little education, but life had blessed him with wisdom. He made money fishing, but he was freer than Sainte.

Elise stretched and kicked at the wall made of bundles. One flopped onto Père's rocking chair. Weathered and tired from too many years of harsh service, Joseph moved slowly and tied down the last of the goods. "Madame Lobelot, you and les demoiselles need to stay away from Le Cap until the fury settles."

Maman tugged at her reticule, which was stuck on the dray's rough sidewall. "We're going to Marmelade. That's where we'll start over."

Well-to-do Coloreds lived there. And they weren't that, not anymore. Sainte freed the reticule. "What will we have in common with those rich people? Have they too lost their father?"

Her mother groaned and clutched the satin bag to her chest. It jingled with the table money.

Sainte pointed to Place d'Armes. "Père wouldn't allow them to burn the place. He'd stop them and remind everyone that Le Cap is the Paris of the West Indies. It's always meant to be beautiful."

Joseph offered a bitter laugh. "Beau pour certain, but the Blancs do not care. Grands or Petits. They'll break everyone they think a threat. They'll make their *Paris* a bonfire if it will rid them of a pest."

He put dining room chairs into the spot where Elise had lain. Three were all that were left of Maman's beautiful set.

"Thank you for staying, Joseph. I don't—"

"You owe me nothing, m'dame. You'll always be my sister. There's nothing I wouldn't do for you."

The shouts, the curses picked up again. Someone had cut away a few trees and set them on fire in a pile by the great fountain.

Enslaved men with bare feet, in simple shirts and pants, were lined up. The white men—finely dressed Grand Blancs with top hats and coats gathered with Petit Blancs, men with shirtsleeves rolled up and nary a cap or coat of any type—were all howling to burn the maroon. They dragged a big Black man in chains closer to the fire.

"Are they going to hurt him?" Elise sounded small, lost. She didn't understand the power of skin. Blancs were never punished for hurting Blacks or Browns.

Joseph shrugged and sucked his teeth. "This is not for show.

Mademoiselle, you'll hear of the troubles tomorrow. Let's get you goin'."

"It's wrong." Sainte looked straight into his eyes. She wanted him to know her light skin hadn't given her airs or made her untrustworthy or a schemer. She hated the lustful attention her complexion brought from the Blancs. It was probably why she loved Guillaume even more; every inch of him was jet like a black pearl.

Maman was olive-brown. She was the schemer. She was the one who should be under suspicion. She was the one . . . *Oh, Père, I miss you.*

"Brûlez! Brûlez!" Voices boomed like cannons.

Guillaume could be there. Sainte's stomach turned and flipped, then slammed against her spine. He could be taken by men who didn't like the look of a free Black man. "I need to see what's happening."

Face wet, with rouge-red eyes, Maman wiped at her small nose. "Daughter, keep still."

Joseph grunted and shoved the last portmanteau against the rocker. "Madame Lobelot, you leave. I'll bar the door."

"Not leaving you here, Joseph. No one needs to protect a house that's going to be sold off in the morning."

"The crowd is chanting *Mackandal, Mackandal.*" Elise sort of sang it, too.

Joseph's eyes bulged. "I didn't see him." He stretched and squinted, then nodded. "It's Mackandal. It's his turn. Oh, Lord. They dragged him to the fire."

Maman paled, and her warm skin became ashen. "Non. Not him. They couldn't have caught him. He's too clever." She made the sign of the cross, called out to Mary then to St. Michael the Archangel for protection.

"They've got him, Madame Lobelot. The Vodun priest must've poisoned one too many Blancs."

"Poor Mackandal." This affectionate whisper crossed Maman's quivering lips. The singing man—the one about to be slain in the center of town—was dear to her.

Sainte gripped her elbows until her skin reddened. Why should it shock her that Maman was in league with a man who'd burn as a murderer?

"Get into the dray," Joseph said. Maman took a seat up front and Sainte climbed in the back and sat in Père's chair.

Creature of habit, Joseph drove up Rue Saint Marie to catch the quickest route to leave Le Cap, but this took us toward Place d'Armes.

Up high, Sainte gained an unwanted view of the mob and the flames.

"Turn us around!" Maman sounded panicked and pushed Elise's head down. The child shouldn't see the violence, but Sainte couldn't look away.

"We're stuck, Madame Lobelot. There's too many people to go any-where."

"Keep trying, Joseph, s'il vous plaît."

The mob railed at Mackandal and pushed the big Black maroon closer to the fire. The priest said something that made the crowds part.

The sour scent of ash reached Sainte when his lyrics struck her ear. "He's chanting a prophecy. Can't you hear it, Maman? We shall be judged for what happened to Père."

She didn't answer, but the priest's indictment would haunt.

> *One day gods from heaven came down.*
> *The earth shook, dancing from the sound.*
> *All knew they arrived to loose the bound,*
> *And this hope made the world feel new.*
>
> *The ones they chose had to obey*
> *Virgin wombs bore warriors tway.*
> *Darkness, light, they battled always.*
> *Yet how were sins paid by just two?*

Those lyrics seared into Sainte's mind like a fiery iron brand. "How will us two, me and you, Maman, pay for my father? Isn't losing every-thing enough?"

Her mother winced. "Joseph, get us out of here."

"I can't, madame. The crowd is too thick."

With his arms tied behind him, Mackandal bucked and ran at the Blancs. Yelling people parted like Moses's Red Sea.

"Justice!" someone cried out.

"This is wrong. There's no trial." Maman's whispers grew louder. "No justice. He only helped women in bad situations."

Joseph laughed. "You've been the woman of a Grand Blanc too long. Madame Lobelot, you forget how things are for Blacks and Coloreds. There's no justice. That's why Mackandal taught poisons."

Poison. Sainte remembered her father's last minutes, the gasping. Her mother, the healer, stood by and did nothing. "Maman, who is this priest to you?"

Hand covering her face, dabbing her eyes, her mother waved the handkerchief she sported. "He gave women a way to fight back, to rebel and stop harsh treatment." She looked at Sainte. "Sometimes a woman has no other way out. Mackandal helped many."

Was this a confession? Did the priest help with Père's death?

Elise pointed straight ahead. "They're dragging your friend toward the flames."

"Don't say that, child." Their mother caught Elise's hand and lowered it to the dray's wall.

Mackandal cried out, "Stop!"

The crowd obeyed as if he'd entranced them, then he sang louder than a church bell.

> *Plague and black death were on each head.*
> *The blood of kin paints the land red.*
> *Violation claimed every bed.*
> *Judgment only escaped a few.*

Men pulled Mackandal back to the stake. Maman made the sign of the cross again. Then she swilled rum from a flask hidden in her reticule. "My fault they execute him. It has to be."

"Hush, femme. Hush." Joseph grasped Maman's fingers. "Quiet and be sober. We haven't reached safety."

How was this her mother's fault?

"Burning is a terrible way to die." Joseph tried to ease the dray to the left. "The flame, it starts slow at the feet, then makes the body a candle. The flesh becomes a slow-burning wick."

Gagging, Sainte coughed and hung over the side.

Elise kissed her hand. "Don't be sick like Père."

The mob of whites shouted over the priest.

"He poisoned four on my estate."

"Brûlez l'empoisonneur!"

"Brûlez! Brûlez! Make his last moments hell."

Her mother reached back and caressed Sainte's cheek. "Burning isn't justice. This has to change."

"How do you know a poisoner?" Sainte looked up and caught her mother's gaze. "Did he help you kill?"

"No. He escaped your father's habitation years ago, went to the mountains, and became a houngan poison man. He never forgave your father for an accident that claimed his arm."

Maman took another drink. Sainte had spent fifteen years on this earth watching in her shadow. Her mother spoke partial truths when her eyes were rimmed red.

Accident meant stolen, done on purpose. Père or one of his slave drivers must have sawed it off.

The white gold of sugarcane made the slavers crazed. They'd do anything, even chop limbs, to possess a bigger harvest. Sainte hoped Père wasn't like that, but the threats he'd mouthed about her engagement to Guillaume, the words he used . . . she was no longer sure.

The condemned man lunged forward and broke free of the ropes that bound him. "Thousands of thousands died on your land. Does the blood of the enslaved mean anything to you? Haven't you stolen enough bodies from Africa to fulfill your lusts for flesh and sugar?"

A distant church bell rang. The shallow, dull sound fell into Sainte's bosom, squeezing her heart. She understood Mackandal's words. "Maman. He's cursing them."

Hammers pounded a stake into the ground. Men dragged the priest to it.

"Sainte, I need you to save the family. Choose us. The Blanc landowner should be your fiancé, not the Black fisherman. He'll be at the house I've rented tomorrow. His money is the only way. We need to stay safe and free. All is at risk because your father is gone."

Non.

Never.

The man Sainte loved was darkness, and she was light. They were twins in their spirits. And yes, so in love.

She wouldn't sacrifice her life because of Maman or even her sister. She'd save Elise another way and began singing Mackandal's lyrics.

"Stop, young lady. Marie-Sainte Lobelot, you will listen this time."

Sainte wouldn't.

Instead, she stayed transfixed by the priest. Flames leapt all around him. Minutes later, it licked at his knees.

The priest screamed, then said, "There's no god but mine. Twin messengers will come from the divine. They'll usher in liberty. Liberty!"

Again, the martyr began his strange tune.

Under Joseph's hand, the mule turned, but there was no way to leave Place d'Armes. They'd have to wait for the crowds to thin before they could reach the Chemin du Nord, the way to Marmelade.

So Sainte kept watching and singing with Mackandal until the priest was consumed.

4

Adbaraya

1758

Calmina, Dahomey Kingdom

At the western gate, I prepared to review my Minos. Only nine stood with me. In six to eight weeks the new recruits training in the Lama Forest would come. I prayed the Oyo would stay away until then.

The royal advisers approached. It was rare to see them without the king. I dipped my chin to the three. "Counselors."

"Gaou Adbaraya Toya." Taller than the rest, with mahogany skin, like a polished conophor nut, the king's nephew, Nosakhere, greeted me. He had a reputation of being a skilled metal artisan, gifted in working with molten iron. "We must speak to you."

"We're about to drill before returning to our positions at the city gates."

"It is a matter of importance, Gaou Toya," Nosakhere said, asserting himself. "I'm concerned about the diminished force of Minos. I hear the kinsmen of our enemy Gaou Guinon are organizing."

Allada was over a hundred miles away. We'd be warned if there was movement. "Gentlemen, be at ease. We are training new Minos in the Lama Forest. We must wait until they arrive before we consider any actions."

Even as I answered him, the man glared at me with wide haughty eyes, then at my Minos.

"Are you sure, Gaou Toya? Your forces look scant. Only nine to protect the king?" He spread his arms. His purple tunic exposed a well-muscled form and a hint at the royal scars on his chest, like Tegbesu's.

"We should head back to the capital. Abomey is not far. It's also a change of scenery. You know the king does not like to sit still."

Abomey was seven miles from Calmina. A short route but one that could lead to exposure. Poachers and traders in the area were continual threats. "Counselor Nosakhere, we have everything well in hand. When our strength is restored, we can entertain moving the king's party."

Frowning, the fellow wandered between my thin columns of Minos. His stately posture was erect. His locks were thick and pulled tightly into braids falling to his back. The open brass helmet atop his head shined like golden cowrie shells.

Each of the other advisers was dressed in a robe of garnet and gold, but Nosakhere's royal purple had beading and appliqués of elephants. He must be Tegbesu's favorite.

My eyes went to the bracelet Eghosa wore, the one the king had given to me. She hadn't given it back. And at this moment I doubted she noticed. Her eyes were on Nosakhere.

With shoulders broader than the others', this man was rumored to be the successor to the king. Our Dahomey process was not like that of the whites, who gave the crown to the eldest son. Our next king could be any man of royal blood who claimed the throne first. Tegbesu had avoided several assassination attempts, outwitted his brothers, and claimed his father's royal stool, the Dahomey throne, before he could be thwarted.

An odd twist trembled my gut. Why would Nosakhere encourage travel when it could endanger our king and his wives . . . Did he have plans of an early ascension?

Growing angry, I stared at him like Gaou Hangbé would, with confidence in my abilities and suspicion of his. "The Oyo still rage, waiting for us to make a mistake. I'll not rush into any decision."

"You mean you won't make another mistake."

"What do you mean, Nosakhere?"

He stopped his review and returned to the other advisers, who stood near me. Then he stepped closer. "Some wonder about the last battle against our enemies. Gaou Hangbé made terrible mistakes. Some wonder if her replacement is up to the task. You're not born Dahomey. You're from the conquered people of Gbowélé."

How did he know?

Many women from many places had been chosen to be Minos. "I'm Dahomey in every way that matters."

"Of course you are." He folded his arms behind him. "And we wouldn't want another failure or heavier casualties."

His rebuke of the late Gaou's battle plans was misplaced. We'd been given bad intelligence of the size of the Oyo forces. She had paid with her life. And I'd killed ten to save Tegbesu from certain slaughter. I gawked at Nosakhere's haughty eyes. "The king's safety and that of his wives comes first. I'll explain to him, personally, why we must delay."

The counselor stormed away, towing the other advisers to the shade of a lise tree. Animated and heated, their hands whipped the air. Was he upset that I'd not do his bidding?

Eghosa left her spot in line and came to me. "Handsome, Adbaraya." A purr left her lips. "He's . . . they say he's very smart. Speaks the traders' tongue."

Which tongue? The French, the Portuguese, the British? "Get back in line, Eghosa. We need to take up our positions before these men find fault."

With a nod, she reclaimed her place in the last row. She bounced her spear up and seized the shaft, ready to attack.

Nosakhere returned. "May I inspect your troops one last time?"

His mouth was pressed into a snarl; his eyes, tigerlike, squinted at me as if I were in the wrong, as if he knew one of mine . . . had sinned.

Eghosa?

Did he know she'd been absent from her post? Did my failure to discipline her taint his judgment of me? Or, worse, was he trying to expose her?

"Gaou Adbaraya Toya, I asked to inspect your Minos again."

I bowed my head and waved him forward.

He passed me and went among my women, examining each, looking for a flaw, a thread missing on their striped tunics, something to use against my leadership.

He circled Eghosa. His hands went to her spear, rubbing the sharp metal point. His face shifted from blank to something different.

Her deep brown cheeks seemed brighter.

I hadn't seen her look like that before.

"Counselors, we welcome your scrutiny, but hurry," I said. "We must return to our positions around the city."

Nosakhere stepped to me. "Thank you, Gaou. Please continue to consider my request. Abomey is where we should be. It's safe. It's best for all."

The counselor fingered the raw edge of his robe, even fluttered the beads. His linen fell and exposed more of his shoulder and the scarifications, the basket-weave design of royal men.

"I will." I made a deep bow. "Thank you for visiting."

He left, taking the other advisers and his innuendo with him. Yet I stayed suspicious. I wouldn't breathe easier until these men had returned within Calmina's walls.

My forces needed to be replenished before Tegbesu's favorite counselor attempted an assassination.

THE OPEN DOOR LET TWILIGHT ENTER THE BARRACKS. THE GLOW of the full blood moon kept sleep from my eyes. Tossing, then turning on my bedroll, I stilled. Nightmares of Gbowélé, of my iya, of Gaou Hangbé's death haunted me.

Pulling my knees to my chin, I glanced at two Minos slumbering on grass cloth mats, their heads bobbing, their mouths leaking snores.

This room should house sixteen, not three. If Nosakhere knew of Eghosa's dereliction, he'd get her punished or killed. The loss of another Minos would further threaten our forces. The loss of my friend threatened my heart.

It had been days since the royal counselor questioned both my aptitude and my loyalty. Why would Nosakhere bring up my old home? Did he desire me to be distracted and tormented?

Or had he, like Eghosa, wanted me to question Tegbesu's authority? True, a part of me did. The king had authorized the attack on peaceful Gbowélé, and he permitted my neighbors to be sold to slavers.

Eghosa said I chose not to remember, and she was right. Belonging mattered more to a girl of twelve than a Minos of twenty.

Eghosa and I hadn't been the same since I became Gaou. Hangbé said I'd be set apart. Was this estrangement what she meant?

I swept the feather of the helmet over my thumb. Strumming its line of beads and sleek shells, I began to chant.

> *Axɔsu Tegbesu wɛ ɖÓ acɛ daxÓ é è nan ɖɔ lé é mì nan nɔn gbon é nu mì.*
> *King Tegbesu has the divine right to dictate the way we shall go.*

Going to Tegbesu was the answer. He'd make things clear.

I prayed to Gaou Hangbé for wisdom, then to Ayaba and Loko, the sister goddesses, to protect all my Minos, and then I called upon Zinsu and Zinsi. I needed the twins' magic to make my way clear.

When I rose, I dressed in my favorite tunic of gold. The hem had painted red palm fronds. I took great care and fastened my iron cuff, then anchored the leader's helmet to my head, before wrapping my bosom with my cowrie-adorned breastplate like I was going to war.

Along the barrack walls, oiled to a mirror's shine, I glanced at the plume of red and speckled blue feathers of my helmet. One of my braids poked from the brim. Pushing it under the bronzed and cotton-formed cap, I looked ready to battle. I'd have answers tonight.

Exhaling, I sampled the sweet still air. Night let birds rest, except for the raspy, throaty moans of the black-crowned thrush. One scampered on top of the barracks and lighted on the skulls lining the roof.

These bones that had been reduced to perches were a symbol of Dahomey dominance. I wondered how many men of Gbowélé's skulls had become a part of the fabric of this city.

Walking down the geometric streets of Calmina, I smelled the pitch.

Every street corner had lamps—some of clay, others of bone—fueled with palm oil. Stopping, I found it hard to swallow, thinking of neighbors' heads as landings for thrushes or lights for my path.

Shivering, I forced out the bad thoughts and absorbed the perfect symmetry of the streets. The past kings, as well as Tegbesu, had used the stars above to design Calmina. It was beautiful, more orderly than Gbowélé.

Finally, I arrived at the palace. Its front court was populated with the king's lise trees. They shaded the hounwa, the great porch where Tegbesu sometimes slept.

A lamp burned beside a hammock that stretched between two trunks. Like the barracks, the palace walls were mudded, smoothed, and oiled until the shine became like the reflective surface of the calmed Denham Lake.

"Gaou Adbaraya Toya, is that you?" Tegbesu. His voice sounded calming and powerful.

I fell to my knees. "Yes, my king, it is I."

He'd come out to the hounwa. After dismissing a servant, he sat on the hammock. "Arise, Gaou."

He wore a sleeveless tunic that was pure white. It was stark against his onyx skin. "You're dressed for battle, Gaou, or have you come to surrender?"

"I'm here for an audience with my king. Will you hear my voice?"

Highlighted by the burning lamp, his midnight eyes seemed vivid like a panther's. His beard was trimmed, and the berry-purple turban covering his head seemed regal, regal enough to rule the earth and sky. "I do hear you, Adbaraya. We are talking. But if you need permission to come closer, you have it."

I moved to within a foot of his lise trees. On one knee I bowed again. Laying my spear down, I balanced and clasped my arms across my chest. "Yes, my king. Nin axɔsu ɔ dé gbon? My words get jumbled when my thoughts are heavy. I do not mean to speak in riddles."

"Well, come nearer." He tugged on his robe, of burgundy with appliqués of buffalos to cover one arm in the royal tradition. His exposed shoulder showed the edges of the scarification on his chest. "Closer, that I might look at you."

My heart pounded.

My mind shifted, then settled on three wet seasons ago when I saved the king from Oyo soldiers. I killed the infidels, and Tegbesu offered me the choice of becoming a first wife or Gaou. Though my heart had feelings for this man whom I admired, who set me on this path, I declined his love. I'd not separate from the women, the sisters who needed me.

"Adbaraya," he said in low sultry tones. "Take a walk with me."

With grace and ease, he arose from the hammock. I followed him, then joined him midway on the sacred porch that stretched from end to end of the palace. He guided me to the stage where his royal stool sat and where he offered judgments.

Tegbesu paced in a tight circle about the stool. The curved seat of polished wood had a dark patina along its fretwork. This reflected the age of it, a piece that had been handed down from king to king.

Then he waved me to his side and sat, his robes obscuring the beauty of the stool. "What draws you to me, Adbaraya?"

"I heard you're restless. I am, too."

"Restless? It's never good for my Gaou to be that."

When I nodded, the beading from my headdress smacked my dampening brow. Eghosa was right. I had wondered about the path I hadn't chosen. Wise Tegbesu knew me, knew the questions I'd always have about him and life. He was my bridegroom, the man who knew the gods' will for me. Couldn't he tell me the answer, that choosing my sisters was right?

"What is in your heart, Adbaraya? As friend to friend, or savior to savior."

No one said my name like him, like it melted in his mouth.

Finding it impossible to swallow, or even think, I turned away from what I read as an open invitation. "My responsibilities to you, the Minos, the Dahomey . . . I do not want to disappoint you."

"Look at me, Adbaraya."

I did. In the glow of the hanging lamps, his noble nose, wide and flat with a little peak in the center, seemed perfectly sculpted. His pupils were obsidian stones shining like stars.

"You've disappointed me once, but it was for the best." He shifted. The opening of his tunic again showed a glimmer of his royal scars. "My heart is prideful of the Gaou you've become. Gaou Adbaraya Toya will rival the memory of Gaou Hangbé."

Like the roar of a sated lion, my name and title echoed from his lips, but I fell at his feet. "I have questions about choices and forgiveness."

His hands crossed his lap. Then his fingers splayed upon his knees. "Are they the same question or different?"

"They are both. I want to know how you decide who lives, who dies, and who is sold."

His hand touched my brow. His thumb flipped the drooping beads. "Xevioso, the god of thunder, shows me truth. The twin creators Mawu and Lisa give me dreams. Why do you ask?"

"I have dreams of before. I think of those sent down the red clay road."

His gaze warmed me. I hoped he'd say those choices had nothing to do with money. Our deities couldn't want foreign coins to sway the king.

"You believe I am directed to do what is best for the kingdom?"

"Yes. Axɔsu Tegbesu wɛ ɖÓ acɛ daxÓ é è nan ɖɔ lé é mì nan nɔn gbon é nu mì."

"Then know I'm making decisions to keep us strong, to thwart evil, and to kill those who must be punished."

I leaned into his knee. The foolish thing Eghosa had said about money must be jealous words. "Thank you, my king."

He caressed my cheek. "Is that all of your cares?"

With a shake of my head, I said the rest. "I suspect one of my guards may have compromised her integrity. If they have not sinned, can they appeal to you for marriage? Will you let her go?"

"I have let go of bigger treasures." His pinkie plucked the shells of my helmet. "Hearts are fickle things. They love things done in secret.

How will you know if your Minos has been faithful? Will she continue to be a faithful guard if the lover does not want her?"

Those thoughts hadn't crossed my mind. Why would those in love not want to be together? "I wouldn't come to you and ask if I couldn't attest to her desire to serve you."

His hand went to my face again, right to my chin.

His touch. I needed it for strength, to know what to do, to fight the darkness drawing Eghosa and the niggling fears that Dahomey's participation in enslavement was merely about money.

"We need to stay in Calmina until our Minos are at full strength. I don't want to risk you. I don't want there to be any opportunity to put my king in danger."

"Is there something you have found to make you think I'm at risk?"

"A feeling. I just know you are safer here, not on the road to anywhere." I wouldn't say names until I found proof. I'd not condemn an innocent man. My dislike of Nosakhere wasn't proof.

Tegbesu's fingers didn't move. I felt his thumb curl over my jaw. "You've always done what is right. Your decision to lead was right."

The way my king looked at me now with such warmth—it didn't seem like he agreed, but that he was settling for what was best.

The Minos needed a leader, and I couldn't part from them even to reward my imprisoned heart.

"Take comfort, Adbaraya," he said. "I'll not move until you say so. My faith in you is complete. And I give you the power of life and death in this situation with your servant."

He stayed in place, his palms now resting on his knees again. Yet in his eyes, I saw the future I couldn't have. I backed away. "Thank you, my king."

Gathering his robe about him, he stood. The smell of cedar and comfort ushered from his garments.

Inches apart, touchable inches, I leaned a little and stilled. A mere half breath of him filled me.

"Do what you must, Adbaraya. Then find me. Inform me. Come into my presence when you're ready. I give you permission."

I listened to his footfalls as his sandals of perfect woven disks clapped away. Motionless until his shadow disappeared, I chanted softly to myself. The decision to be Gaou, not Beloved, was the path I chose. I'd not make the fire's prophecy true or be one among ten wives. The only competition I wanted with other women was throwing spears.

Turning, I saw Tegbesu's grand parasol of bright colors, red and blue, stitched with gold braiding about the circumference, under which the king would sit and administer justice.

He'd given me power to judge Eghosa and time to uncover a conspiracy. I prayed for the wisdom to do both and the power to destroy whatever came against my king.

5

Adbaraya

1758

Calmina, Dahomey Kingdom

I stood at the threshold of the barracks feeling prideful. "Rest well, Minos. Thank you for bringing the news." Twenty new recruits would join us by morning and add to our dwindled numbers. The gods had granted such favor.

Raising my hand to my chest to give honor, I left them to sleep, two of the fleetest women of my group who'd made the trek in advance of the Minos coming from Lama Forest.

For such a feat, I must personally reward my lead trainer. She was my second in command.

I walked to the edge of Calmina to spread the news and inspected my guards, but the realization that I'd taken Gaou Hangbé's system of leadership as my own must have hurt Eghosa. I hadn't elevated her. Perhaps that had led to her feelings of rebellion.

This was the past.

Eghosa and I were better. We'd even roasted an ogbono seed two moons ago. I was no longer sure she'd sinned. Perhaps the rogue attitude was a test, one I must've passed.

Nothing more progressed with my theory of conspiracy and assassination. When the king indicated to the council he'd remain in Calmina until I advised it was safe to leave, no one questioned moving anymore. The great counselor, Nosakhere, even complimented my forces.

All my worries disappeared. I floated to gate after gate, sharing the news.

When I neared the western gate, I must've levitated. Everything was going to be well.

As I walked out of Calmina's walls, readying to surprise my Eghosa with the news, she stole my breath.

My chest hurt.

She wasn't at her post.

The western gate stood unguarded. Her spear lay against the shimmering wall.

The moaning of the thrush sounded, but it wasn't a bird at all.

Naked, glistening in the moonlight, was Eghosa. Her arms and legs were wrapped about a man as he pinned her to a tree.

Rage caved in my lungs. I couldn't speak. I ran toward them with my spear raised.

Halfway to them, one or the other saw me. They parted.

"Let me explain!" Eghosa crossed her arms about her naked bosom.

"Adulterers to the king, to our ways, to me." My voice started low. Then it returned with power. "Death to you both!"

The stars exposed her lover's shiny braids. Nosakhere?

He defiled a bride of the king. He took Eghosa for himself.

Blood pumped and I felt as if it spurted from my eyes. "Death to you both, so says Tegbesu."

She leapt behind the tree and pulled on her breastplate. "Adbaraya? No."

Eghosa came forward and grasped the tip of sword. "Let me have my say."

Brave and foolish . . . this was my friend. "How could you break the heart of the king and me? You pledged fidelity. This means death."

Eghosa tugged her lover behind her and then drew her cutlass, the sword that I gave her, that I'd had the blacksmith forge with her mark.

"It's not what you think, Adbaraya. We are no longer hiding after tonight. Tell her. Tell her."

The counselor to the king said nothing. He stood like an exalted one, naked and sweaty, grimacing as if I'd done something wrong.

This was sin.

She'd broken her vows. He'd compromised a Royal Bride.

They knew the penalty.

Thick-limbed Nosakhere lumbered forward, snatching on his robe. "Stop, Gaou Toya. This is a mistake."

I wanted to swing at him. "How is it a mistake to touch one of the king's wives? To plant seed in her against a tree?"

The air smelled of them, what they'd done. Guilty. "You're of the king's bloodline. You are marked by his hand. Nosakhere, do you want death now or in front of Tegbesu?"

As if his throat had closed, he made a sound like a drunken owl.

"Eghosa, tell me how this man has bewitched you? But do not beg for your life. Die with honor."

"I'm not defiled. I've been loved. Touched by a man. Fulfilled. You can survive on fleeting glances or even a friend's embrace. Not me. I've found love, the love we all should have."

Defiance, not shame, painted her eyes. "This is the life we should've had before war took it away. Nosakhere and I did the water ceremony. We've wed. Let my husband and I run away. Let us be free. Tell her, Nosakhere."

"No." He bent and found his rattling beads. "Gaou Toya, this was a test. Your Minos has failed. You have failed."

Eghosa stumbled and turned to him. "No. Tell her how we will be together. We are in love."

I put my spear to his Adam's apple. "You'll die in front of the king." Biting my lip, holding in my sorrow for my friend, I pronounced her judgment, too. "You, Eghosa. You will also die for adultery."

"Adbaraya, please." Eghosa started to cry. "Tell the truth, Nosakhere. We have loved for many moons, but tonight we were to run away before the new Minos arrived. Let us go. I won't be missed."

"Why didn't you tell the king, seek his blessing? He's let others marry his advisers. You'd no longer be a Minos . . . that is what you want?"

"Adbaraya . . . Adbara, remember the old. *Adbara*, the dreams poured into us by our mothers. Those ways were holy and good. They didn't require us to be killers, to feel nothing as we shed blood. They never wanted us to be in allegiance with a king who can have anything he wants and yet commits us to live alone."

The bitterness in her voice—I'd never heard this.

Or maybe I hadn't listened enough.

Looking away from her teary face, I lowered my spear from Nosakhere. "Tell the truth."

The grimace on her lover's face—as I had missed her heart, she'd missed his ambition.

"Tell her, Nosakhere." My tone was firm, then I poked his throat with the jagged metal point of my spear. "Tell her the truth or I'll ram you through."

Nosakhere made the birdlike call again.

"The fear of dying has driven you mad. Stop embarrassing yourself, pitiful counselor."

Eghosa swaddled her tunic around her hips, then clasped his arm. "The king might be merciful to his blood if he was convinced of our union. He knows of love."

Freeing his shoulder from her, he tried to take my spear. Then his hands dropped to his sides. "There's no need for mercy. I've done nothing. You saw nothing, Adbaraya. You need to go. I'll handle this."

He made the bird call again.

The noise of something or someone coming from the trees caught my ear.

Waving me away, Nosakhere pointed to the gate. "Return to the city, Adbaraya Toya, now."

Ten shadows appeared in the grove. They moved forward.

It hit me like thunder. "Eghosa, how stupid can you be? He's not running away with you. He's ensuring he's not caught by selling you to slavers. With you gone, there can be no seed to prove his infidelity."

Her brown eyes grew big as the sun. Eghosa touched her stomach, then spun and took my spear. She jabbed her lover's chest. "That cannot be true. You said you love me. We wedded. You promised—"

The man's face blanked then frowned. He shrugged. "Your Gaou speaks the truth. My friends have paid a fair price for a Dahomey warrior. I suppose they'll have to take two."

A gang of white-skinned men bore down on us with lanterns and guns.

WITH MY CUTLASS, I CHARGED THE FIRST SLAVER, RIPPED THE MUSket from his hand and used the butt to knock him flat. In rapid succession, before they could stop and load their muskets, I'd sliced the throats of three.

Then bullets came. Balls misfired and rained about me.

Muskets were unreliable weapons. The hot iron shot went everywhere. But the notch of a bayonet was deadly. With the gun in my hands, I stabbed another and didn't look again to see which way he fell.

The ferrous smell of battle filled the air, more than gunpowder. This scent meant I was winning.

Then Nosakhere headed to the western gate.

Eghosa screamed.

Couldn't look at her, couldn't let the schemer walk back into Calmina.

"Stop right there, Nosakhere! Not another step."

He turned to me, his face holding a menacing grin. "Ready to see the rest of the Minos die? Unless you surrender, these men will charge into Calmina and kill them all. There's not enough warriors here to stop the slavers. Will you, Toya, be the cause of another African leader being captured and enslaved?"

"What?"

"If Calmina is overrun, Tegbesu will join hands with Gaou Guinon and be enslaved in Saint-Domingue. That's where the French take them."

Our oral traditions taught of Dahomey King Agaja and his overthrow of Guinon's Allada. The military leader Gaou Guinon was sent away.

"The humiliation of being sold to enslavement," Nosakhere said, "is great but not worse than execution. Alive there's the possibility of a new life."

The fool tried to explain his treachery even as men tied his lover's wrists and began dragging her over the hill.

Sweaty, smelling of Eghosa, Nosakhere planted himself in front of me. "There are more whites nearby. They'll destroy or enslave all the Minos and overrun the first wives, too."

He'd done this, made a warrior vulnerable, made my Eghosa sin. She'd walk the red clay to be sold at Ouidah. Now this snake who'd return to Calmina and stand near Tegbesu threatened to destroy the Minos—the ones left. The new recruits would arrive too late.

My heart sickened, and I wanted to explode. My Minos. I had to put them first.

I was about to drop the musket when the shadow of a cutlass swung near.

Wrists still bound, swinging her cutlass, Eghosa had freed herself. The men who weren't run through with her blade were fleeing to the trees.

It was just us, the serpent Nosakhere, and the dead.

Eghosa's foot fell on an unfired musket. "Was this always your plan, Nosakhere? To have me, then leave me to these slavers?"

"We will die," he said, "if the king knows what we've done. I can't risk my position, and now these whites will come back with vengeance for the ones you've slain. I'll tell them it was an ambush in the dark. Their minds won't let them think two women did this."

Eyes burning, Eghosa struck him with the back of her cutlass, blackening an eye. The woman didn't kill him. She had the chance. She'd been trained to do it, conditioned to choose Minos over everything, but she fell to her knees. "I've doomed us all."

More whites arrived.

"Go with them, Adbaraya Toya." Nosakhere's voice sounded calm, assured. "I'll make sure none enter the city. The king and all in Calmina will be spared with your sacrifice."

"Let's fight these men." I held up my bracelet and the hat signifying me as Gaou. "Be a Dahomey man of honor. Help defeat this threat."

With a shrug Nosakhere walked past me, shook his head to Eghosa, and went to the white-skinned men. They chattered. I heard our word for ambush, then more of the whites' broken-sounding language.

The foreigners, these men who bound their flesh in tight clothes, put silver pieces in our betrayer's hand. Then he returned to me.

"What did you tell them, Nosakhere? How to stab our king?"

He wouldn't say until I blocked his path.

This man glanced at me like he was unashamed, like there weren't coins in his hand. "I told them two slaves for the price of one." He swallowed, his frown growing. "Eghosa, with you gone, both of us can live. It's easier for women to begin anew."

She spat at him before one of the slavers took her cutlass.

"Gaou Toya, I didn't mean for you to be caught in my trap. At least you've trained successors. The new Minos, when do they arrive?"

"Tomorrow," I said, thankful they weren't here to be endangered. "Keep the king protected from these whites."

"The new Minos will serve the king, whoever he is when he claims his seat in Abomey." A smirk appeared, then he turned his wide back to us and again headed to the western gate.

The world slowed to a grubworm's crawl.

Eghosa flipped the musket into the air. It whirled, bayonet tip to butt, end over end, until it landed in my hands.

She lifted her wrists for me to slice through her ropes. "We die fighting together. We are not separated in this."

No.

I would choose how I separated from the Minos, from my world. I flung the gun at her. "You fight. I'm saving my king."

Leaping faster than a lion, I attacked Nosakhere from behind, bringing him down like an elephant.

He bounced and I used the ground to steal air from his lungs.

Pinned, he tried to roll me off, but I pounded him. He landed a blow but only tore shells from my breastplate.

My shiny gold cowrie sprinkled and hid in the grass, never to be seen again.

When he lifted his head and started to talk the slavers' words, I grabbed his throat and choked him.

Nosakhere gasped and kicked, but nothing could break my hold, the crook of my arm wrapping and squeezing life from him. "No adulterer, no usurper who violated the king's law, will ever set foot in my city."

Eghosa groaned. It was distant, barely audible.

From the corner of my eye, I saw her carried away like a hunk of elephant meat.

My heart didn't have time for regret. I had to restore my honor, our honor, by saving the king from this deceiver.

Clawing at my grip, Nosakhere tried to roll me off. "Stop, I don't want to—"

"Die? Shouldn't I kill you now for stealing the king's bride?"

"No. No theft. Pleasure given freely. The water ceremony was *our* lie to escape death, but I couldn't trust that she'd not tell." He struck me with his elbow. "I didn't mean for you to discover us. I don't want to kill you, but if I get my arms about you—"

"Never, deceiver. You can't hold me."

He struggled but stopped when a gun pointed to my bosom. The smell of its powder burned my flared, bleeding nostrils. This close, it wouldn't miss its target.

"Tell him, Nosakhere, it's three for the price of one, or I'll snap your neck before a shot is fired."

He jerked, but he surely knew he'd die. "Your death is under a woman." My voice dropped to a whisper. "Nosakhere. A Minos has saddled you like a beast and ridden you to the land of death, Orun Apaadi."

With a weak gasp, he said something to the white man.

The fellow lowered his gun, grabbed one of Nosakhere's ebony wrists, then the other, and tied them.

When the fool was secure, I released his throat.

He tried to tell them something different, but I mocked his words, the ones getting the fool bound. Over and over, in their odd dialect, I said, "Th-ree-for-one."

These men in tight clothes led us up the hill where they'd taken Eghosa.

Nosakhere coughed. "You've given us all to bondage, Adbaraya. For you the holiest of Minos—what is your crime?"

Didn't answer him, just prayed aloud. "Axɔsu Tegbesu wɛ ɖÓ acɛ daxÓ é è nan ɖɔ lé é mì nan nɔn gbon é nu mì."

Calling out the king's divinity silenced Nosakhere. It gave my heart renewed courage. I'd delivered safety to Tegbesu. He would live in peace even if I never saw him again.

Axɔsu Tegbesu wɛ ɖÓ acɛ daxÓ é è nan ɖɔ lé é mì nan nɔn gbon é nu mì.

We walked for miles over grasses and sandy patches. Then my feet touched the hard, sunbaked ground. The torch of the lead man showed the red clay. I was young again, on the path where I breathed Gbowélé's ashes.

This route frightened my mother. That was why she gave herself over to the flames. I knew this now. I felt her sacrifice in dreams. Never would I have left my iya's side. She died trying to give me a life with the Dahomey.

Was she with the ancestors cursing me for my choice?

Sticky mud seeped between my toes. Eghosa marched far ahead, almost out of sight. Nosakhere poked behind four paces. Red dust, Ouidah's dust, would soon cover us.

Gaou Hangbé's flame prophecy—I fulfilled it, my way. I'd separated my flesh from the Minos, but I'd given my body, all of me, to enslavement.

The Prophecy

One day gods from heaven came down.

The earth shook, dancing from the sound.

Zinsu, Zinsi will loose the bound,

And this hope made the world feel new.

Poisons and flames, evil whirled

Lightning and venom, arms hurled

But twins set out to save the world.

Alone, apart, their missions grew.

—ANONYMOUS, STYLED IN THE FORM OF UTENZI

6

Marie-Claire

1764

Cap-Français, Saint-Domingue

My parents are an affectionate lot. Maman clings to Père's coarse shirt as if he'll disappear from the center of Place Royale. Bored, I stand in the distance leaning against his dray, watching her kiss on him.

The morning light is strong, and I've just crawled from the blankets in the back of the dray. Head covered in a bright yellow scarf with my arms bunched in a cream shawl, I stare at them. Maman seems determined to prove to strangers in Le Cap how strong their love is.

"Renmen ou!" His Kreyòl "love you" is thick. The tall man's smile lights his face like stars in the night. I think he's handsome, with dark skin and matching black eyes of jet ametiste stones.

"J'adore," she says, holding him tightly. "J'adore. J'adore."

He pulls back and offers a wink. "Sainte, if you were always this free, Marie-Claire wouldn't be an only child."

Skin flushing to bright pink, Maman clutches at the ruffles of the fanciful dress she's spent hours pressing. "Guillaume, are you saying this is an act?"

His big arms pull her closer. "Oui, but it does not mean I don't like it." Then his lips disappear, and his countenance gains a faraway look, thoughtful and even shy.

When she tries for another kiss, he releases her fast, as if he's touched or taken something that wasn't his. Then I see my mamie, Grand-mère Lobelot, coming.

With arms folded at his back, he leans down. "Sainte, you have nothing to prove. Be easy and enjoy this visit. And I'll think of you ever' day at sea."

He bows to my grand-mère and then turns to leave. Spinning me around until I'm a dizzy top, he whispers good things like have fun, mind your maman and mamie. When he climbs aboard his dray, he gazes at them, then me. "Remember, you're loved and special and beautiful. Your father knows a little more than those women."

"Père? You are leaving us here?"

"Le Cap is nice. It'll be good for you, but it's just a city. Renmen ou, Marie-Claire."

Watching him go with the odd blessing is strange until I see Mamie and Maman arguing about the *slave* scarf on my hair.

HAMMERS POUND, CREATING A DANCEABLE RHYTHM, LOUD ENOUGH to cover the loud argument happening above me. Not very tall for my six years of living, I squirm, count the windows on the stone buildings, and wait for my mother, hot-tempered Maman, or my grand-mère, stoic Mamie, to give up and walk away.

One of them usually does.

Two days in Le Cap and the gentleness is gone. It's a pattern, their arguing, like the repetition of stitches in sumptuous bobbin lace. The trimmings are a treat Maman says her father used to buy her. I wish I'd met him. Maybe if he had lived, Maman and Mamie would be better friends.

"She'll not go back with you," Mamie says and tweaks the pale peach bonnet on her head. It's well styled on her rich black hair, which has bits of silver at her temples. "Elise has her calling. She'll stay and pursue what she wants. You should understand doing what one wants."

"My sister is not suited for this. She should come back to Léogâne and live with Guillaume and me again. You're trying to get her to take to city life, to city expectations. Are you still after one of the Lobelot daughters to attract a Grand Blanc?"

"No, I want my girls to struggle in life with the poverty only a newly freed Black fisherman can bring."

Maman stands there silent, wordless.

We are poor in Léogâne, but we have food and a house. Often, we help others, especially the other mothers at the cistern.

More sharp-tongued words are exchanged. I should interrupt and try to make them be easy like Père wants.

But I cannot.

The place of a child is to be voiceless. That's how it's been explained to me. I was born in 1758, under circumstances my aunt Elise tells me were romantic and scandalous, and I suppose my little thoughts don't matter.

"Sainte," my grand-mère says, "go see Elise's rehearsal, but do not try to change her mind. The theater is the North Star of her dreams. You of all people should encourage your sister to take what she wants."

Mamie snaps her bonnet, flicks a drooping curl, and heads to the hospital.

Staring and taking long breaths, my mother calms. The red in her light face pales. "So, Marie-Claire Bonheur, daughter of Guillaume Bonheur, the best fisherman in the world, you and I will brave the walk alone."

Taking my hand, she leads me away from the U-shaped cluster of buildings down the dusty, well-traveled road, Rue Espagnole.

She's silent until she tells me again a story of how great her father, François Lobelot, was, and then adds one about my père. And I wonder how I'm so lucky to know these great men of Saint-Domingue.

But, Père is good. He listens to me, likes my squeaky voice.

"More stone, Marie-Claire, more stone and daub treatments in Le Cap like your father has done to our house in Léogâne.

"Marie-Claire?"

"Oh, I didn't know it was time to talk."

She put her hand on her hip, making the fall of the ruffles of her marigold sacque gown wrinkle. "I do tend to run on in Le Cap. We used to live here with Père and Maman."

A man starts to pass, but the Blanc stops and takes a long leering glance at my mother and tips his three-cornered hat. "Mulatto women are the prettiest in Saint-Domingue, maybe the world. You're the fashionable set of society here."

We nod and go around him.

With her soft ebony hair braided and curled under the wide brim of her straw bonnet, one she's decorated with dried burgundy and gold lepanthes orchids, my mother looks pretty. Maman has worked hard on her outfit, taking in extra sewing and washing to afford the cloth and all the embellishments of tacked ribbons. We don't look mouse poor, as Mamie would say.

Several blocks later, I deem it safe to talk. "Were the streets as busy as they are now when you lived in Le Cap?"

Before she can answer my question, I scamper out of the way of a fast-moving handcart. A vendor dashes past, heading toward the markets of Place d'Armes.

Maman takes my olive hand in hers. "Careful, Marie-Claire. They won't notice you here."

Her words sting my chest. I see the treatment she receives is different. Even different from Mamie's.

"Come on. We can't be late." She tugs me a little.

"May we look for lilac ribbons after Aunt sings? We couldn't find any in Léogâne."

"Not now, Marie-Claire. What is the cross street?"

Quicker than a spark flitting on the tip of a wick, I release Maman's hand and dance a little farther from her side, more into the wide street. I must see if ribbons are on any stands.

"Marie-Claire, get out of the middle of the rue. A dray or carriage could run over you."

I twirl. "Don't you feel the draw? It's too exciting, different than where we live, ole sleepy Léogâne."

Maman glares at me. "Our home is fine. It's better than a noisy, showy place filled with construction."

Horse hooves from a passing dray kick up dust. The scent is ashy, chalky, like the streets. "Why aren't there cobbles here, like at the docks?"

"I don't know, Marie-Claire. I didn't marry an architect."

The edge in her voice is rising. Why does she need to defend everything? "It was a question," I say with a pout. "You used to live here. Mamie is proud of having a home here."

"She lets me know it every moment I'm here. I'm a disappointment to her, and I fear she's pressuring my sister—"

"To marry a Blanc, not a Black, no one like Père?"

It's an open, naked statement I make. There are colors of people all over, but those my maman and grand-mère always bicker about are Black and white.

Her face changes from a frown to something distant, even grand. "Happiness matters. When you find your heart, you leap for it. True freedom is love, Marie-Claire."

This voice is low and thoughtful. I like it. She usually hides her thoughts.

Seizing her hand, my own brown one against her light cream, I offer the biggest smile. In the noon sun, the warmth makes everything moist and sticky, but I'm happy to have her fingers linked with mine.

We walk together until a vendor with ribbons stops ahead of us.

When I see lilac, I risk a full scold and tug Maman to the bright wares.

The way the sunlight streaks across the satin makes it shimmer. Drawing my hand close, I want to touch one and see if it's silky like wax.

"Marie-Claire. No. Come back."

The vendor adjusts her yellow turban and grins like I'm naughty. "Too good for you. Listen to your massa."

Maman scowls, and I don't understand the taunt.

"Daughter, come away now."

The old woman puts her back to us and haggles with a soldier. The man in his French blue uniform glances at my mother, even doffs his hat.

Maman drags me halfway down the rue before stopping and fanning herself. Her eau de cologne of lilies has faded to perspiration. "We are looking for Vaudreuil and Saint Pierre. Let us turn down Rue Sainte Marie."

A distant toll of bells hastens our pace. "I don't want to be late for Elise. This is important to her, Marie-Claire. When she lived with us, singing was all she ever wanted to do."

My aunt is only five years older than me, but her voice is powerful. Elise singing is all I can ever picture of her—singing at the river on wash day, at church, everywhere. Until last year, she was with us in Léogâne. I miss her terribly. Sometimes I wish I could live with her and Grand-mère at the Hôpital de la Charité. The city of Le Cap is much more than the dreams Maman wishes for me.

"Elise is like my big sister. I want her happy, but I want her near, too."

With tears in her eyes, Maman looks down at me. "I haven't been a good sister to her. I want her to have her heart, but there is too much hurt in the city for the Affranchi. The country is better."

Affranchi, the free Coloreds. That's what we are, but she only uses words about class when she's in Le Cap.

Suddenly Maman's brows knit together and her face changes to one of deep sorrow. Her golden-brown eyes are shiny and wet. "Our old house."

In an instant, I know what she means. At Rue Sainte Marie is the place where she and Elise were born, where they lost their father. I suspect, though no one says, that's the day the love between Maman and Mamie disappeared. Grief is strange.

"Grand-père Lobelot was wealthy, Maman, to have a home near Place d'Armes?"

She doesn't answer. It's like she's trapped in thoughts.

"Maman," I say and tug her arm. "Maman?"

"He . . . It was a fine house with a veranda and stone balcony. From there, I could see the mountains or even the square with the fountain, Place d'Armes."

The walls of the house are gloriously ivory. The foundations are tarred, jet black. The wide windows have hints of yellow.

Yellow in the middle, caught between everything. And Black is at the bottom. This is sad.

Maman has us moving again. We cross onto the Rue Vaudreuil.

She peers down with flustered pale cheeks. "They may not let you . . . especially if we are late."

"Because I'm Black?"

The look on her countenance, with her light hand again fastening to my darker one, tells her silent truth, her fears that Le Cap and this world of colors will always exclude people like me.

"You're smart, Marie-Claire, but there are things that can't be put into words. Others that shouldn't be said."

"Then when am I to use my voice?"

Maman looks away and pulls me down another rue. Saint Laurent, I think.

Yet my insides are roiling. Color has defined almost everything in my life. Why is light or white better? My père works just as hard as any. Why are he and I looked down upon because our skin is not like Maman's or Elise's or even Mamie's?

"Marie-Claire, look for Saint Pierre. It has to be here somewhere."

Craning my neck from side to side, I pretend to hunt for it, but all I see are the hues of people walking past, smiling at my mother and ignoring me. I disappear inside myself. My mother and I are different, opposites.

The smell of cassava and something nutty makes my stomach growl. We turn a corner and a young woman and her mother have a stack of flatbreads, freshly made in her skillet.

"Kasav, hot and fresh." The older lady flips a cake.

Her way of saying cassava is like Père's. Her Kreyòl dialect is thick.

My gut makes another loud rumble, but it doesn't drown out the sound of a beggar shaking his cup. He's half propped in an alley. His tattered blue uniform offers a tart smell.

Everything in me sours. I had been feeling bad about my life, but I have a good dress and will eat as soon as we walk back to Place Royale. I even wanted ribbons, but this man who's fought in one of France's wars has nothing. "I wish I had something for him."

Maman stops, rushes back to the ladies selling the breads, and buys one. She offers it to the old man, who repays her with a gummy smile.

This Blanc soldier doesn't care who we are or what we look like. He takes our offering with cheer.

"Sir," Maman asks in her easiest tones, perfect French in pitch and pronunciation, "quel chemin pour Saint Pierre?"

He gobbles the cassava. "Straight ahead, then left, madame, mademoiselle."

"Merci bien," she thanks him and takes off running.

We arrive at the theater. Maman stops and straightens the yoke of my bodice, then fans my arms dry of the sweat darkening the yellow sleeves.

"Do I still look respectable, Maman?"

Her twitching smile doesn't offer much confidence. I suppose she hates being late more than me perspiring.

Chin up, barely breathing, she heads inside.

A man is behind the door. "What are you doing? We're in the middle of rehearsal."

Maman sighs loudly. "I have been lost, monsieur. Help us to our seats. We are guests of Mademoiselle Lobelot."

His bushy brow rises as his rosy cheeks darken. "Yes. Her."

Each simple word sounds angry.

My mother seems unbothered and smooths her sleeves. "Mademoiselle assured us we can watch. We will be no trouble."

The man's thick black mustache twitches as his nose pinches.

Does he smell something foul?

We are far from the docks brimming with fish. I'm sure we do not smell of the streets—neither the food, nor the sour old man. This is pure annoyance at our being late or being like *her*, the Affranchi, or me being Black.

"I'm not sure I can seat you without causing a disturbance."

Before my mother responds, a gentleman with graying hair and wrinkly brown skin, Mamie's complexion, comes toward us.

"Sainte Lobelot Bonheur?"

Maman turns and hugs this big man.

The fellow behind the door looks as if he wants to shoo us all out of the theater. With a long, extended sigh and a cough, he says, "Monsieur Joseph, you're Mademoiselle's manservant, can you show these two where to sit and keep them quiet?"

"We understand." Maman's voice is still sweet.

Monsieur Joseph offers a nod and extends his arm. Maman latches on to him like he's a lost uncle or brother.

I follow, trying to model her poise, even the slow motion of her hips. Then I become bored and study this theater with its wide stage. Blue and gold paint decorates the walls. The seating is finely polished pine.

"I watch over Mademoiselle Elise when she has rehearsals. I've come with Madame Lobelot in the expensive private boxes for the free Coloreds. Pity when this run of shows ends, it may be Mademoiselle Lobelot's last."

Part of me wants to clap. That means Elise can return with us, but Maman looks heartbroken.

"Non, Joseph. Singing onstage is my sister's whole life."

"Well, it's good she's young. Like your mother, she'll find a way to reinvent herself. It can't be helped. The Blancs want this taken from the Affranchi. The Coloreds lose again."

Maman shakes her head, then she and Monsieur Joseph exchange whispers. Something about my mother still having *those dreams.*

Music starts below. Soon sweet lyrics flow. Figures are on the stage, but not my aunt.

Maman leans close to my ear. "They are performing *Le Devin du Village*, which means The Village Soothsayer. Your aunt plays the soothsayer who gives advice to Colette on how to return the affections of her wayward man, Monsieur Collin."

What an odd story. What does it mean, chasing a wayward man?

My heart drums as Aunt Elise takes the stage. She raises her hands and sings. Her pretty voice echoes. It's sweet like a thrush, a red-legged thrush tweeting in the morning, dancing with her feathers, bright garnet whirling.

"Maman, why is Elise covered up with a turban? Her flowery robes look heavy."

"She must wear what the play demands."

But with so much tulle, Aunt looks like a monster bird. "One can barely see the thin young woman she is."

That twitchy smile of Maman's returns. She puts a finger to her lips. I go silent.

There are no other questions to ask, for I realize they, the *theys*, don't want her seen. The people putting on this opera want Elise Lobelot's voice but not the beautiful golden skin she and my mother share. Though light, with the barest hint of roasted coffee, they aren't white. White is meant to take the stage and be the center of the opera.

At six, I shouldn't notice or dwell on these things. I should be thinking of cooking and reading.

Tears leak, and I wish I could remain ignorant of how everything is made hard by skin.

Maman wipes at the wetness on my face and smiles. It's a true one, the one she saves for Père when he brings her a perfect rose. "You're mature. I knew you'd understand the beauty of these songs. I'm proud of my sister. Your voice is pretty. You'll be good at hymns."

"Aunt Elise says when I'm bigger, I can return to Le Cap for my education. I can show them how well I can do."

"Non. This place isn't for you. You won't do well here."

The swallow in my throat sticks and lodges at the beaded necklace Mamie has given me. Do she and my mother believe my future is sad because I'm not a mulatto like them?

"The song is beautiful." Maman clasps my hand, the hand I want away from hers. I don't want her touch, not until I can grab the whole world with my dark fingers.

7

Toya

1765

Cormier Habitation

The dray dragged up the dirt road to a flat land called Grande Rivière du Nord. My backside must be rocks. I banged against the hard wood on every bump. To steady myself, I clasped a rough knot on the rail.

"They aren't singing, Garnier." A mouthy man with a clipped tone kept looking back at me and the two women and lone man sitting near. "Thought they were musical. Oy. Oy. Oy."

He mocked the song they made us sing when granted a moment to go on deck out of the slave ship's hull. I'd have sung or said anything merely to stand up straight and breathe clean air.

The enslaved man looked amused, but his breath smelled of the tafia wine many drank. We'd been purchased from habitations near Port de Paix. I'd been bought and sold three times since coming to these shores, but each time the price was higher than the last. It wasn't for my strength or some animalistic way to breed chattel but for my iya's knowledge. The skill of medicine was in demand because many enslaved died from chest fevers, plagues, and Massa's abuse.

Though I'd made Gaou Hangbé's prophecy come true, separated from the Minos to protect my king, how would I get back to Calmina? Would I die on foreign soil?

I wondered about Eghosa and Nosakhere. We boarded the same boat at Ouidah, but after a prayer by a priest holding a Bible, we were sold at the docks of Le Cap to different massas.

The enslaved I met on these shores called being here a slow death. After seven years I understood what they meant. Had I known, I wouldn't wish this fate—constant punishment, pain, and pacification of the commandeurs and owners—upon my enemy, not even the Oyo.

Didn't take long to figure out it was better for these white-skins, Blancs, to think of us as servile and stupid, incapable of plotting rebellions and conspiracies.

Those that came before had used poisons and revolts to strike back, but this made the massas wary. They tightened their harsh fists. I couldn't organize resistance. Those born on this soil thought of women like Massa did, good for nothing but fleshly pursuits. They wouldn't follow a female to lead a battle even if she was a Gaou and a great warrior.

"Not much farther, right?" the mouthy Blanc said to the red-haired man driving the dray.

"Non," the fellow grunted and pointed to a road lined with palm trees. "This is the turn."

The dray followed a graveled path, long and winding with familiar sights: sugar vats, drying sheds, nice houses for the commandeurs and other white servants, huts for the enslaved, brick- and pottery works. Somewhere out there, there had to be a mill and a storehouse and a building for the hospital.

The mouthy one elbowed redheaded Garnier. "Are they new off the boat? I thought one or two would say somethin', maybe chant or dance."

He grinned, probably thinking we didn't understand. But I'd learned the Blancs' choppy language and would speak it, too, when necessary.

The talkative one leaned back. "Welcome to Cormier Plantation."

"It's *habitation*, you Brit." The driver flipped back his black triangular hat and punched the talker in the arm. "We say *habitation*."

The Brit rubbed his shoulder. "Excusez-moi, Monsieur Garnier."

With a shake of his head and a grimace, the quiet one pointed left. "There's the hospital. The tall woman will work there. To the right are the cane fields and gardens. That's where everyone else will be."

Sugar was in high demand. This colony was rich because of it and coffee beans. White and brown gold, the slavers loved each of them, but truly they were twin deaths.

Both plants, cane and coffee, worked men and women into early graves. Thirty wet seasons was an average life for Blacks on this island. At twenty-seven, I already felt like my time was up. Yet in the distance, beyond the hundreds of Black dots sowing in the sun, and the green stalks, and brown coffee plants, loomed beautiful mountains.

Dèyè mòn gen mon. That was what the enslaved said about this place, "beyond mountains there are mountains." They meant behind every problem was another.

I wasn't looking for those, just the peaks. I'd persist and figure out how to escape into those heights and find freedom. Maybe I'd leap and touch the face of the god I'd angered. If he or she could be appeased, I might find my way home to Dahomey.

The dray stopped in front of a large, whitewashed house with a hounwa porch that spread from end to end. "This is the grand-casa of Monsieur Duclos," the Brit said. "Get out and greet him. Bow down to him. He'd like that."

The men laughed, but I memorized the size of their heads and pictured how their skulls would look skinned and used as lanterns.

There weren't enough lamps for these dark days, and I wouldn't mind making these mocking fools lights for my world.

"You're hard of hearing?" The Brit made signals with his hands, as if I and the other two enslaved were deaf. "Get out."

"The body takes time to move after a drive like this," I said, then told the women in their language of Twi to leave the dray. The poor fellow lumbered and followed.

The Garnier one, his brown eyes popped wide. "You do speak?"

Stepping onto this dirt felt the same as it had at the other places I was sold. "When I need to, I do."

The Brit pointed to where others cooked at the huts.

"Suppose you want us to go there?" I leaned a little over him; my height, almost six feet, made the small man back up.

"Yes," said the Brit. "Duclos wants the women in those huts. Tomorrow, talkative one, you'll go to the hospital building and become acquainted."

"Is it ruined inside?" I straightened my shoulders and pulled my onyx shawl about my arms. "Hate working from filth or ashes."

"No. It's not," Garnier said. "You're a hospitalière, a medicine woman. You cut the death rate at Tulle Plantation in half. We need you to do that here."

"That requires a lot of listening. Hard for Blancs."

With reddish-brown hair like a baboon's, but tall and thin, Garnier took a step closer, glancing at me eye to eye. "You have to do it or more children will die. We lost twenty from mal d'estomach during the wet season. Horrible, their guts extended. The adults dying from maladies vermineuses is just as bad. Those worms . . . evil."

He shuddered. "Anyway, tomorrow, I'll show it to you. "Gwo parèy," he said in the Kreyòl, the language formed by the captive of the island, and pointed to the enslaved man. "Big fellow, follow us. You women go that way."

They did, shadowing me until I explained we had to go to the provision grounds. Halfway across the graveled main road, a woman ran at me. My reactions were slow, but I moved into a defensive posture, blocking with my arm, crouching, but this bag of skin and bones leaped at me, bloated belly and all, and hugged my neck.

"Nanwé ce dagbé," she said, which was "sweet woman" in the Dahomey's Fon language.

"Nanwé ce dagbé." She said it again and she wouldn't let go. "Adbara." Her whisper stopped me from prying free. It pierced my callused skin and lodged like a burr into my chest.

That voice . . . I traced her nose, the point of her lips. "Eghosa?"

"Yes . . . Oui." The latter word she said in the slaver's tongue, and she wept in my arms.

My chin felt wet, then it became a rivulet, deep with raging waters. I grabbed her up as much as I could, this woman I hadn't laid eyes on in seven years, this woman I'd loved and betrayed.

All the words I had in my head, that I wanted to say at Ouidah . . .

Or the whispers during the cramped passage in the stinking slave boat.

Or the wishes at the docks of Le Cap when she boarded her new massa's dray.

Or in every whimsical dream I'd had of us at home, hugging, loving . . . disappeared in my sobs.

My arms wrapped around all of her again. Everything but my regrets melted away. "Nanwé ce dagbé," I finally said. "Sorry, and I love you."

The press of her bony ribs against my bosom hurt. I'd sentenced her to this place of slow death by not rescuing her. I condemned her instead of acknowledging that she could be human, that a warrior could be weak and make mistakes. "I was self-righteous. I'm sorry, Eghosa."

"No. Adbara, I am. I betrayed you and my vows, our king—"

I put a finger to her lips, lips that despite her tears were dry and cracked. "No more. You've died to any sin already. This is my fault. You didn't deserve this. No one deserves this." Placing my palm on her pregnant middle, I said, "All debts are paid."

"Even to our king, Adbara?"

With a kiss from my soul, I touched her wrinkled brow. "He's not here to complain, is he?"

I said a blessing over her womb. "We're together at the right time. This time I can be strong for you. You have all of me, all of my attention."

She clasped my hand to her fast-beating heart. "Let me introduce you to my son." Calling over her shoulder to a group of little ones, she said, "Janjak! Come!"

Two of the boys wearing no shirt, just short pants, stopped rolling a barrel hoop and stared at me. Standing near a lone girl in rags, another one, the littlest fella, wore a ripped sleeveless tunic. Thick lips frowning, he lifted his head.

These innocents were dressed in castoffs. They wore no beads or bracelets. No need to ask about their purification ceremonies or inheritances or scarification. Anything to show pride of family or the nations of their ancestors had been erased.

Seven years in Saint-Domingue, I'd seen plenty, but nothing hurt me worse than this, a loss of heritage for the young.

My nervous guilty finger pulled at my silky scarf and cotton tunic beneath. My full gray skirt was of linen, not osnaburg, the fabric of the enslaved. These clothes were gifts from my last massa's wife. She thanked me for saving her son from the bad fever that made his eyes turn yellow. My devil's bargain, working as a hospitalière, was to save both the enslavers and the enslaved.

"Janjak! Leave Da'mon, Agwé, and Fleur. Come. You must meet your aunt."

The smallest boy came to her leg dragging a hoe. Rubbing his elbow, he squinted. "Manman hurt?"

"No." Wiping her face, Eghosa stooped to him. "Janjak, this is Adbaraya Toya."

"The priest with the stick forced me to go by Victoria. The infidels couldn't say my name, and I refused to teach them. Victoria Montou is what I'm called, after my first father here."

I rambled, but this was the friend who had helped me survive Lama Forest, and her vibrance was wasting away. I'd defeat the slow death and make her strong again, then we'd sneak away to the mountains and await liberation. Our king would liberate us. Seven years forsaken was too long.

Eghosa hadn't stopped crying. "Seeing you is the miracle." Her words were thick and choppy like the sounds the Blancs uttered. "They call me Elisabeth. They failed at Eghosa, too. I don't remember anymore my first name, my Igbo one."

She rubbed her belly. "The father here, Duclos, likes me a lot."

Eghosa didn't have to explain. I knew what the wretches did to our beautiful Black bodies. They talked of ugliness, but they craved the ebony silk of our skin. They longed to touch us. We were forbidden fruit.

Now, I understood why the gods put us together again. "I'm to help you with this birth."

Biting down on her lip hard enough to draw blood, she took my hand and put it on the boy's head of thick curls. "At least Janjak is Dahomey."

"How? How old is this one?"

"Seven, born in 1758."

Nosakhere's son?

Fanning my shawl as if it were priestly robes, I bent almost in a bow and stared with such longing into the boy's small face. I was searching not for the infidel who started us on this course, but for Tegbesu. It was his royal bloodline flowing through Nosakhere. It should belong to this one.

Janjak came closer and touched the necklace I'd made of shells, beads, and twine.

Eghosa said, "This is my friend, son, the one who could fight, fight better than any. Perhaps she'll teach you."

I took his small hand and stood. "That and more. The sky and stars, everything for the king in you."

He smiled. The apple dimples of his cheeks exploded, but he said nothing.

"Toya, he doesn't talk much. The Blancs have him fearful."

That would never do.

Never ever.

A conch blew.

"That's the call of the commandeurs. They drive the enslaved to work the field. The meeting at the grand-casa, it will acquaint you to Cormier."

The commandeur trumpeted again. A second one joined in. Looked like a holy man was at the house.

Nothing in me wanted to listen to the man in robes sermonize about their god. Seven sacraments, seven duties, seven days to form their ruined world. Seven for them was completion.

Like before, like always, Eghosa touched my arm and stared into my eyes. "We sent people to this, those we conquered, those who failed training. I didn't know it was like this."

That was why I'd complied to this point and even tried to be useful. I had to pay for my sin, for the guilt that weighed down my gut like a stone. Thousands I'd made walk the red clay road. I sent them to this slow death. "Not knowing doesn't absolve us, Eghosa. This is divine punish—"

"Go on, Toya. Duclos can be very mean when he's angry. Return here when you're done. Stay with me and my son."

Through watery eyes, I nodded and then went to the large house, the grand-casa.

I swiped at salt tears and listened to the Grand Blanc Duclos strut and cuss and parade from side to side on the hounwa, the veranda, as he called it, shouting at us his rules.

The priest reddened at the foul man's words, but did nothing, not even offering a prayer. Then I knew the Catholic god couldn't count. Seven years in Saint-Domingue was not the end of my penance. Yet with Eghosa and I together again, my sister and I united had to mean we were closer to freedom.

8

1766

Cormier Habitation

Leaning against the trunk of an old tree near the coffee fields, I enjoyed the thick emerald canopy of the leaves. It provided good shade and time to think and eat a mango. Here they called the ogbono that.

It was as close as I could get to the fruit I missed. Yet it was different. The seed was inedible in a ripened mango. One either picked it early when the meat wasn't sweet and roasted the seed or ate around the fibrous middle. Having to pick the right time was as complex as trying to plan when to escape Cormier with my new family, Eghosa and her sons.

I saved her new baby boy by rubbing him with the oil of Palma Christi on his forehead and gums. This staved off mal de machoire of the jaws. That illness was common here and could lock a mouth so that a child couldn't suckle.

Before Eghosa could properly heal, Duclos had her impregnated again. She was too fragile to take into the mountains. The sick here were very sick. Fatigue in the fields killed many, as bad as yellow fever. I would never get used to death when it came to the young, the children under twelve. Life should be beginning for them.

"Egberun, my god of protection, am I supposed to be here to help the young at Cormier?"

No answer. Just a small breeze that did nothing to relieve the sticky heat on my arms.

Halfway into my climb to get another mango, with my arms stretching to the branch, the conch blew. Squinting, I saw the father of this land, Henry Duclos, come out of his big house. He stood at the rear near the gardens peering in my direction.

The small man was impressed with the number of babes I'd saved this year. He'd given me full responsibility for the hospital. More power and leeway to do something, but what?

Nimble, gangly Garnier left Duclos and came up to me. "Massa wants you to go to him," the lead commandeur said. The fellow looked scared or guilty.

"What is this about?"

"Uh. He wants to talk with you in private."

Talk, like he did to Eghosa and half the women here? I climbed down and Garnier stepped out of the way. Too committed to his king, his employer, the commandeur was no help.

When I approached the grand-casa, two women grabbed my wrists. "No, Victoria. You must be prepared before you go to Duclos."

I cut my eyes to the women. "Call me Toya. And I am prepared as I am."

They backed up, but Garnier chased like a pup. The man, sweating in an open white shirt, brown breeches, fanned a dumb black tricorn as he came to my side. "Victoria . . . Toya, he'll hurt you and more if you don't—"

Eight years, I'd avoided defilement by frightening or killing those who tried. I'd not be lowered now.

Forcing my way through these people, I went to Massa. He sat on a chair on his veranda. His legs were up on the rail. Women waved palm-frond fans at him, this cheap imitation of a ruler.

I stepped onto the raw decking. "Garnier said you asked for me?" I walked to Massa with a face of stone. "You want to talk about the hospital?"

"No." He looked at me with his face twisting. "You need to wash before you come inside."

"No need to go inside. That's your house. Where I stay is the provision grounds."

His jaw hardened, locking down like he had mal de machoire. When he stood, his bald head reached as high as my bosom.

"You've been here for a year, Victoria. 'Bout time you complied with everything." He raised his hands as if to touch my face.

"It's Toya." Staring at the shine on his bald spot, I grimaced. "I work the fields and the hospital. That's all."

"Everything I require is work."

No. Rape and cruelty weren't. It was evil, part of the slow death. Folding my arms, I shifted a little and frowned more. "Don't change my opinion of you."

"What?"

Counting the ways I could angle his head on a post kept my voice from rising. "I spoke. You heard."

The man sneered. His breath smelled like tobacco or snuff. "Toya, I'll have you lashed for defying me."

"For speaking? You want me never to speak? Tell your enslaved I will stop caring for them. They can get sick again."

His eyes flashed, the white part surrounding the beady blue stretching. "What do you mean sick again? Poisons?" His hand fisted at his side as if I'd struck his money purse.

He paced a little, his black breeches wrinkling, his embroidered waistcoat flapping. "They said no poisoning occurred at your old habitation. I was clear about that."

"I kept my celibate vows there. If my faith is violated, I'll no longer have favor. I won't be able to help when the air becomes deadly. The soil, too."

Picking up Madame Duclos's lacy fan, one she'd left when she went to visit a sister in Le Cap, he whipped the hot air about his reddening face. He hesitated, rubbing his chin. Money for the Blanc was worth more than rape.

"Victoria Montou. Why are you different?"

"Say it as 'Toya.' And it's my vows. The priest at the last habitation said I'm like your nuns. My faith has promised me to my king. You're not my king."

The bleating noise of the fan stopped—the poor serving women stood completely still.

Duclos backed up. "Can't be much of a king to allow the French or Portuguese to take you from his land. Or maybe you're not much to him. He did allow you to be sold."

It took too much to explain how I captured myself to protect Tegbesu and to defend principles I no longer saw as good. I wrapped my palm about one of the fancy carved posts supporting the roof. "This should have faces to honor your dead."

"What? Vic . . . Toya, no." Duclos looked bothered and heated even in this shade.

"Massa, just know if I break my vows and am touched by any man, you or those close to you will die within the week. My power to improve health for your heirs goes away."

Duclos swallowed. "That's Vodun magic. Don't believe in it."

"You don't have to, Massa Duclos, but I do. My vow is powerful. It will be made true." I'd make it true. Everything my mother taught me, all the wisdom I hadn't understood, was mine now. I no longer suppressed any memory. I was Dahomey and Gbowélé and my mother's daughter.

"The poisonings that happened on the plantations near Le Cap, was it your magic? Have I brought a killer here?"

His upper lip had a sheen. I didn't think sitting in the shade of the grand-casa did that. Maybe he had a fever. I towered over Duclos, letting my height and muscles smother him in dark shadows. "May I go? I must work in the hospital."

With hands to his sides, he nodded. "Yes. Go back to your duties."

I bowed my head as if I had given him honor, but I'd bought time. The Catholic god and mine needed to awaken and fix the cruelty of Saint-Domingue before I figured out how to do it in my power.

. . .

WITH JANJAK CARRYING A LIT TORCH, FOLLOWING ME INTO THE mountains beyond Cormier Habitation, I carried Eghosa in my arms. My dearest friend was weak and light as dust. Bearing children, one after the other, when a woman was low, was hard. In the wet season plagued with the fevers, childbirth was deadly.

"Janjak, keep going."

"My friends tried to prepare me, Aunt Toya. Da'mon and Agwé said not to cry. To look at the mountain behind all the mountains."

Could see nothing but the back of the boy's head, his thick hair. Heard his sniffles. Knew he was trying to be brave.

His tears drew mine.

A year and a few months with Eghosa wasn't enough. We hadn't roasted enough mango seeds, nor hunted enough elephants or whatever game they had on this island.

By morning, there would be no more time for anything.

Eghosa stirred and whimpered. "Adbaraya Toya, you will look out for my boys?"

"Yes, but I have made arrangements for the two young ones to be nurtured by mothers with milk in their breasts."

"Claim Janjak, according to our ways . . . Claim him for your line, your seed."

My friend, my sister, mentioned the old practices of inheritance for the female line, of other women bearing children for another's household. "I gladly claim him—our seed forever."

"Good, Adbaraya."

Holding her hand, I gazed into those golden-brown eyes. "I'll carry the best of you with me."

Her arm lifted and she flicked a bony finger along my cheek. "The scarification ceremony, hurry."

Janjak stopped in the shadows of a tree at the hole I'd found where a stump had been uprooted. It would make a perfect chamber in the tradition of the Dahomey to receive the earthly body.

Dropping my sack, I kicked it toward the boy. "Janjak, take the sheet out of it and lay it out for your mother."

When he did so, I eased Eghosa to the linen and made her comfortable on her side. When she left this life, it wouldn't be hard to wrap her for burial. "Duclos is pleased with the recovery rates of the sick. He gives me what I request. I wanted sheets, his best. The cook in his kitchen gave me knives and looked the other way for a brewed calabash of tafia."

"Bending rules for some bad rum? She must not know the joy of climbing trees with you or roasting ogbono."

"Fun is whatever can be claimed."

Sitting beside her, I motioned Janjak to come.

"Wi, Aunt Toya," he said.

"She's Tante Toya from today forward. Understand, Janjak?"

He nodded and tried to look strong as Eghosa struggled to breathe. "And tell the other children to call her Gran Toya, for the honor she's due."

"You are due honor, too." From my sack, I drew out the green mango. "Not the sweetest, but the seed is good."

"You stole it, too?"

"Eghosa, why should I be picky about things now?"

She laughed and coughed. With the knife I'd sharpened, I sliced the fruit. The three of us shared it, but I held up the seed. "You can eat these like ogbono."

"The young seed is good. It's the one to mold. Mold Janjak."

"I will. He's the seed between us. I'll nurture him. You will bless him from the stars. He'll prosper. Our seed will prosper."

The boy finished his pieces of mango and smacked his lips. "Do I clean the knife for you, Tante Toya?"

I shook my head. "I have a mate to this one, which has been purified. Eghosa and I will mark you with the signs of our people. It will hurt, but you're old enough to decide if you want to proceed."

"I'm almost to my ninth year," he said, his little voice booming. "Mwen vle istwa ou rakonte yo, Tante Toya . . . I want the stories you tell of my proud people. I want to be like your king."

It was the most he'd said ever, and it was a noble dream.

Or prophecy.

Lifting his chin, I said, "Then we do this, son of Eghosa."

My poor friend nodded; a piece of the pale orange flesh of the mango was on her mouth. "He's our son. You'll be a manman to him."

I wiped her lips. My mother's creams had made them soft again. "Yes. Sins are forgiven. É non ɖu hwɛsɔkɛmɛ wɛ. You go from this life with peace."

"I have none, Adbara. If I'd been stronger . . ."

"Eghosa, you got to be a mother. That was a dream. No one will forget you. And this boy of royal blood has to be the reason for it all. No sin. Man sɔ non lɛ kɔ kpon nu é ko wayi lɛ é o. Do not look to the past."

"Un nyi wan nu wé. I do love you, Toya."

Claiming her hand while it still had warmth, I said to her what I should've said to my iya. "I don't understand or agree with everything done, but know I love. I see no more betrayal between us. I only see love. Un nyi wan nu wé."

A weak palm returned my squeeze. "Hurry. I will hold on to this life and be a comfort to Janjak one last time."

The boy and I set a fire. Then I cut down leaves of palm trees and made a bed for him. In the sick house, I had created an ointment close to the mixture I knew. "The medicine in this jar will keep the scars clean. It will set the pigment to decorate the wounds. Are you ready . . . son?"

He nodded and lay on the leaves.

Then, from my memory of Nosakhere and Tegbesu, I mapped the pattern of the royal scars to Janjak's middle. The skin was tender and pliant. My sharp, sharp knife made small incisions. I kept going, one cut after the other.

The boy didn't whimper but clasped tightly to Eghosa's hand.

As fast and as cleanly as I could, I made all the marks, then I washed the scars and slathered on the salve.

Eghosa smiled at him. "Un nyi wan nu wé."

Then her eyes stilled.

As softly as I could, I touched her face a final time and closed her eyes. The Catholics spoke of a prince and a warrior, the holy love of friends. I understood this better. This love for Eghosa touched as deeply as the love I once had for a king.

"Tante Toya? Is Mama gone?"

"Yes, Janjak. Your mother, my sister, a warrior of King Tegbesu— her soul is free. She's no longer enslaved to Duclos."

The brave boy stretched to her and kissed her hands. "I will come back to these hills to pray. To look at the world and hope to feel her."

I clasped his hand and nodded. "Now we must finish, Janjak."

Praying, I crossed my friend's arms and put her in the curled position. Then I sat still waiting for her limbs to stiffen.

In an hour, the warmth had left Eghosa. I wrapped the sheets about her curled form. Then I buried her in the tomb with my necklace, the plate from which she ate her last meal, and the knife that cut Janjak.

That was how royalty was buried, with treasures.

When Janjak and I finished, it was almost sunrise. We had to be back to our duty at Cormier. There I'd redeem these years by training up our seed. Then this babe, born in 1758, would be the son of promise. Without giving up the ghost, Janjak would see what true liberty was, here in Saint-Domingue. I'd make sure of it, or I'd be separated again, from him, from all, by death.

The Prophecy

One day gods from heaven came down.

The earth shook, dancing from the sound.

Zinsu, Zinsi will loose the bound,

And this hope made the world feel new.

The chosen ones had to obey.

Unequal yokes thrust them away.

Darkness, light, they battled always.

Yet how were sins paid by just two?

—ANONYMOUS, STYLED IN THE FORM OF UTENZI

9

Marie-Claire

1771

Cap-Français

The second floor of the Hôpital de la Charité in Place Royale is quiet, but I'm moved to tears. While I've helped with cleaning and sweeping, then made a pile of bandages, the patient Mamie read to has died.

I knew death.

The big earthquake last year in Léogâne killed many, hundreds. Maman and I saw the mangled bodies as we pulled a wagon about the city delivering food to the hurt and homeless.

Surely, working in a hospital, Mamie has seen many passings. Yet her reaction, the brokenness and tears, surprises me. Did she not meet this man only yesterday, when he came to the hospital? She's always strong. I've never known her to be weak.

Mamie sobs as if she's known the man all his life.

When she comes to the supply room, I touch her hand, then embrace her with all the strength my lanky thirteen-year-old arms can manage. "Mamie, you did what you could. He looked pleased with the letter."

She pushes at her lacy cap. "It wasn't enough. Sometimes, despite your efforts, it's not." She sniffles and clasps her arms. "Marie-Claire, you're done today. Go for a walk in the sunshine. Spend the afternoon in the garden you love. Be away from here. Enjoy life."

That is easy in Le Cap and Place Royale. Every inch is exciting and new. But I love the garden the most. The hidden space with exotic flowers and plantings has become special. It's where I go to think. "Are you sure, Mamie?"

"Oui, then pick up the bread for dinner." She pushes me out the door before I can tell her of the trouble the baker has given me. Yet with her eyes reddening, I say no more and strip off my apron. Mamie's private. I'll give her time to grieve while I explore Place Royale.

My aunt catches up to me near the gardens. Her wide woven bonnet frames her slim stature and adds shadows to her light face, one buried in a copy of the popular newspaper *Affiches Américaines*.

"Elise, I have the afternoon free. Would you like to walk to Morne Lory? It's high, you think there's time to reach the peak before evening prayer?"

She shrugs, then offers a tight-lipped frown. "The roi, stupid King Louis XV."

Upset with a French king, one far away? "What is the matter?"

She balls the paper. "The king has offered clarifications to the Code Noir. He and every Blanc want to define whiteness, but it's only to exclude gens de couleur from everything."

"Why do you care what a man on the other side of the world says? It's not singing or even a play."

Her glance tells me I've said something stupid or I'm too immature to understand. I smooth her paper, looking for the words that wronged her. "Talk to me. I want your voice."

"They are trying to say any speck of Black blood is contamination and the mulattoes are no better than slaves. They will use this to take away everything. This is why the stages are running out of parts for me."

My aunt, who's only five years older than me, has a much, much bigger temper. I think she's used to getting her way and is heartbroken when she doesn't.

Yet, no more plays for her is a sacrifice. But what of me? If she loses a little, I lose all. My Black self will be excluded from everything. I'm motionless, stunned at how she hates to be reminded she comes from enslaved blood. My skin tells my story when I walk into a room or a bakery.

"Marie-Claire? Your big frown, are you well?"

"Well and Black. I think I'll head to the gardens instead of the mountains."

Her soft eyes blink, and she puts a hand to her mouth. "I'm sorry. I know it sounds terrible."

In Léogâne, we seemed like sisters, but we were much younger and the world was smaller, untouched by a French king's decree.

"Let's go up to the mountains and see boats pass Saint-Domingue." She scrunches her sleeves, which have long bothersome lace ruffles, the same style as the year of her triumph onstage. The flowery print of her gown is layered with a sheer shawl. She's timeless and pretty, even with her eyes growing sad. Elise knows she's letting color separate us like Maman and Mamie.

She grabs my arm. "I'll do my scales. You can help me practice for auditions next week."

Staring at her golden face, I examine her expression—part sorrow, part rejection. I've seen it more and more as she turned away from the theater.

Offering her a hug and forgiveness, I wish to encourage her. "The next role is yours." I want to rally her spirits, even if mine must diminish. She didn't make the world or its rules for color. "It shall be yours, Elise."

"Maybe not. The Grand Blancs have pushed the king for these laws. It's all for show, all for their public wives. They'd rather I sing in private as a mistress."

"What?"

"I've had offers. Some violently ask." She fusses with her sleeves again. "I would be a nun if they allowed dames de couleur to take vows. Nothing I want is allowed."

"St. Louise fought for things not allowed. She didn't stop doing for the sick and the poor until change was made."

"I'm not her, Marie-Claire."

"Perhaps you should change your dream, since the world is telling you no."

Elise's stare, cold and cutting, slices my tongue. It's these moments when I know my aunt refuses to settle. She likes extra ribbons, extra privileges, the things others have to beg to hold, for things I know better than to ask.

Anger creeps into her creamy, ivory cheeks, and I realize as sweet as Elise is, she needs Le Cap and the world to work for her. And her alone.

"Sorry." It's all I can say then.

I clasp her fingers gently, like I'm holding a hissing kitten. "The flowers in the garden have started to bloom. It smells of honey. Come walk there with me. It will give us peace."

She inhales deeply. "My prospects are not hopeless. The Brothers of Saint-Jean de Dieu will allow me to continue as a governess and now as a music teacher. That might be something they'll let you do. I hear they're happy with your work at the hospital."

This news makes me want to dance. I love Le Cap more than small Léogâne, but my aunt's expression is bitter. She's jealous my hopes are expanding. I stand still. My face is hot, and I can't help but frown again.

As if she's finally seen the hurt she's caused, she starts to run.

"Elise?" I try to catch her. "Wait."

Her feet slow, then her low-heeled slippers dig into the road. A cloud of dirt floats everywhere, dusting my hands in gray powder. A small part of me wonders if Elise wants to be colored like ash to be accepted in the Blancs' world.

"I'm sorry. I want things fixed now. I don't think about how callous it sounds. I don't mean to hurt you."

Before I can respond, Elise puts a dramatic hand to her temple. "Marie-Claire, I just remembered. I've to do something. I'll see you at dinner."

"Yes, I'm to get the bread. I hope the baker will be easier with me."

My aunt is paces away and probably hasn't heard my complaint. I pray something good happens for her. My steps lead me slowly to the center of the U-shaped ring of buildings. They all look identical. Not sure which leads to the baker's ovens.

And I'm not ready to face him, a Petit Blanc, as they call those white men who aren't rich, and explain again that I'm allowed to help Mamie . . . and I'm not her slave. Instead, I wander into the garden, my favorite place.

I'll bring my aunt a flower, and maybe my grand-mère, too. The scent of mango, sweet and spicy, blends with other heady fragrances, a lime tree and plenty of flowering cacti. The garden grows unusual plants and trees. Even palms from the Cape of Good Hope are here. I guess it was sort of nice to think of the big ships bringing things other than people.

Adjusting the skirt of my gown, a striped, pink taffeta with gathers at my waist, I sit on a mahogany bench. I'm swimming in silk and pleats. Mamie insists I dress with care, then my station is always known. Never, ever can I wear a scarf outdoors, only hats like all the other free women or nothing at all. It's the way of the Affranchi. And unlike Elise, my skin says I'm Black and descended from survivors.

A small breeze kisses my face with those glorious, sweet smells, but I hear movement. I brace like the world is about to shake and crumble.

More noise.

Dark eyes in the bush have spotted me.

Topaz, with smoked circles rimmed in yellow, spying on me. "A goat or calf. That's what you are. Nothing to fear. Avoid the butcher," I yell. "He's down the road, the chemin to the hills."

A low growl answers.

My courage flees and so do I.

But something grabs my dress. I've backed into a prickly pear cactus. Its spiny branches have caught my hem, biting into the lace.

I try to jerk free, and the sound of fabric tearing makes me still. This is one of my best skirts. Mamie will be disappointed. I—

A hand, dark and thin, stretches from under the bench and frees me.

The fingers disappear.

I'm grateful but too scared to move.

CAN'T HEAR ANYTHING EXCEPT MY POUNDING HEART. FREED FROM the cactus, I back away from my bench in the middle of Place Royale's garden.

Still, I don't run. When nothing jumps out, I get braver. "Hello. Are you there? Who are you?"

"Non."

It's a squeaky boy's voice. Nothing to fear from frightened, big, wild eyes. Pretending I'm Mamie, I put a hand to my hip. "You're there. Come out."

The clip-clop of horses sounds. Then the pounding of boots passes the garden. "Soldiers at the entrance," I murmur.

"Sòlda? Definitivman pa gen moun."

His words are distant, and more French Créole than French. Papa speaks this. Yes, Kreyòl when Maman is not around. "You definitely are here," I say to the voice. "I'm not alone, but I won't draw the sòlda or anyone here, Wide Eyes. I'll lead them away."

Moving to the garden's entrance, I see the military parade, a line of men in uniforms leading a cannon on a cart. Black men are actually pulling it. The way they're dressed, in rags or shirtless, these fellows are probably enslaved. Soldiers in fine blue uniforms are prancing all around the long barrel acting as if they are helping.

Why is a weapon of war near a hospital?

This exhibiting is too slow. They need to pass before I can return and learn everything about the boy hiding beneath a bench. Who is he? Where does he come from?

The lead man with medals pinned to his frock coat rides over to me. The officer, tall and ferocious in his saddle, points his finger. "Girl!"

"Oui?" My voice is pitifully low. Remembering how the men in uniforms harass my mother, I clasp my shaking elbows. My thin sleeves stop there without volume of lace at the cuff, like Elise's dress. My shivering hands are exposed.

"Girl?"

I want to answer but his horse brays at me. Its mouth leans closer, sniffing and hovering as if my uncovered braids are straw.

In a blink, I'm hiding with Maman at the docks of Léogâne, fearing the men in blue who chased us. They called her whore and wanted—

"Girl! Are you mute!"

My head whips from side to side. Mamie taught me how to stay safe. *Stand your ground. Stay.*

Don't let the Blancs know you're scared.

My lungs fill with the deepest breath, and the words Père taught me to keep from being punished in the stocks come out. "Sir, I didn't mean to ignore . . . you. I was silenced by the commotion."

With a spur to the side of his beast, he makes it retreat. "You're not in trouble. I need assistance. Do you know the way to the quarters, Bazac pour la Vente des Negres?"

Directions to the slave quarters? That was all?

Not able to stop the trembling of my lips, I point. "Down . . . down the way heading to Chemin du Port-au-Prince. Keep straight, then go left. Toward the pigsties. It's there, right—"

"Marie-Claire! There you are."

My grand-mère heads toward me. The satin bonnet she wears has a sharp wide ebony ribbon. She has changed from hospital aprons and shapeless tunics to a yellowish gown. A cream-colored muslin kerchief shrouds her shoulders and tucks beneath a gray sash at her waist. The ebony fleur-de-lis printed on the silk looks very fine, expensive. One would never know how frugal my mamie is.

The soldier tips his hat to her. "Your girl, mistress, is here. Causing no trouble."

Mamie grins up to him as if his words are helpful or praiseworthy. They are neither. This soldier has politely called me enslaved.

She takes my arm as the officer continues with his men and cargo down the road.

Waiting until they pass, she releases me. "Elise said you've been having trouble with the baker?"

"Oui." My aunt did hear me.

Mamie makes the distance between us evaporate. She sweeps me into her arms. "I should keep closer watch over you. With more soldiers coming, I'm nervous."

More sòlda? And I've never seen this bold woman actually scared. What is truly making her fret? If I ask, I know she won't answer. "It's safe in this garden. I feel normal here."

"You're welcome to come here whenever your work is done. I've special permission for you to be at Hôpital de la Charité. Do not be fearful."

"Fearful and respectful and not moving. Oh, and not saying the wrong things. My aunt is right about the world trying to make things harder for Blacks."

She leads me deeper into the garden. "What happened? Did they touch you?"

To protect my wild-eye friend, I steer her away from the bench. "Non. Look at the cacti, prickly and aloof. I got all tangled. Then the soldiers—"

Mamie hugs me again. "The botanist and learned men bring these cacti here to cultivate the cochineal."

She points to a cactus flower that's yellow with an orange middle. Tiny garnet creatures are inside.

"Those little red insects love to eat these prickly things. When the bugs are good and fat, they are harvested and dried out to make a powdered red dye."

It seems a shame to breed something only for it to be consumed. But isn't this the way here? "That seems French, very Saint-Domingue, to cultivate things for their color."

Something shifts behind us. The bushes near the bench sway. My friend must've waited to say goodbye. I didn't thank him enough for saving my lace. I didn't get to ask where he sleeps or if he's hungry. His fingers looked thin.

"Marie-Claire, once they know you at Place Royale, it will be better."

"I'm not changing color, Mamie. How do things change?"

"Time," she says. "Time is the only thing that fixes the world. The more it passes, the easier things become."

I shake my head. "But your patient ran out of time. We aren't promised anything."

"Time," she says again. "That softens most people."

"Even between you and Maman? What happened to make you both bitter?"

She sighs and turns like she's spied something.

My heart forgets to beat, and I wait for the accusations that I'm being naughty like my mother, or childish, like they say of the enslaved.

"Sainte is not easy. We've made progress. She allowed you to come." Mamie rubs both my arms as if to make my blood pump more fiercely. "Let me take you to the baker and explain again that you are my helper."

"How many times, Mamie?"

"Till it sticks." She grabs my fingers. "We go now to the baker. I'll fix this."

I stand up straight, but my feet are planted in the dark dirt.

"Ready to quit, Marie-Claire? Ready to run because one man made things difficult? Can you bear telling your parents you can't handle the big city?"

"Non. I'm just disappointed. Léogâne is small. The townsfolk know me as Guillaume Bonheur's daughter. He's the noble fisherman with his faithful wife, Marie-Sainte Lobelot. They see Maman as special, feeding the hungry. I hoped the big city would be different, more willing to see me as me."

"There's judgment everywhere, but also hope. Things have improved. We're not enslaved. My child's daughter is not enslaved."

The thing about time and patience seems so slow. I know I'm not like Maman, but not sure I could be like Mamie, either.

"Come." My grand-mère tugs me. "We go for the bread. You'll give Le Cap more time. Then you'll make friends. People will know you. It will become easier."

I've made a friend, just not someone Mamie or Maman or Elise might approve of. I hope Wide Eyes returns.

Walking hand in hand, Mamie and I head up the street. The soldiers are in the distance, approaching the enslaved quarters. More than ever, I want to stay and help.

BAZAC POUR LA VENTE DES NEGRES SOUNDS FANCY BUT IT'S JUST huts where the priests house their enslaved. You'd think holy men wouldn't participate in such unholy acts, but they do.

These provision grounds as they are called lack provisions. There's not enough food. The people are miserable. This place is situated alongside the road that leads to Port-au-Prince and Léogâne. How many times had I passed by and not stopped? Today, I stand in my good dress, handing out kasav bread to women in rags, to babies that look so thin I wonder if they will survive the coming wet season.

"Mèsi." One mother about my maman's age thanks me.

Glancing at this face that glows for a little bread, I find her countenance is haggard but with no lines upon her brow. I realize she's younger, much younger, than my mother. These cruel conditions have made the hungry woman age.

I nod, I think, then walk back to the hospital, the place where the hurting—the hurting Blancs and free Coloreds—are supposed to be healed. I came looking for Wide Eyes, to offer him food. I leave ashamed. I'd been in Le Cap for months and didn't know suffering was so close. My family frets over losing rights. We should care more for those who have none.

WITH SOLDIERS IN THE BAZAC, I CANNOT RISK BRINGING THE PEOPLE food. I have kasav and a calabash of water stuck under my arms, hidden beneath my madras scarf. I snuck into the convent's kitchen to make the bread and now I have no one to give these to without being caught. As carefully as I can, I back away from the chemin and head toward the garden.

Perhaps I can find Elise and offer her some, but she's probably wanting solitude practicing a part or reading her *Affiches Américaines*. Mamie calls it the renegade paper.

Soldiers march toward me as I make into the garden. It's like an escape to be hidden in the trees. When I stop and the ornamental grasses have stilled, I hear boots echo. Even though it's fading, my pulse pounds as if they see me and know I've done something wrong. "Oh, St. Louise, did you have such troubles ministering to the people?"

Settling onto my bench, I wait for everything to be safe and calm.

In an hour, my nervous stomach settles and finds hunger. I unwrap the kasav, and nibble on one.

"That smell. Ki kalite manje? What kind of food?"

The words sound heavy and familiar. Wide Eyes?

"Ki kalite manje?" he says again, and I try to find him in the bushes. I can't. He's well hidden. "Slow down with your words. You understand my French better than I do your Kreyòl."

"Ou pale anpil. *You talk a lot, a lot.*"

Either he has a good sense of humor or he's visited my garden and listened to me praying to the saints. Concentrating on how my père speaks to his friends, I say, "Li bon. Se pen kasav. It's good. It is kasav bread."

The sprite under the bench pushes his hand out and I put it into the pink palm of his jet hand. The smacking of his gums is loud. I wonder when he ate last.

He crawls out from under the bench and asks for another. His face is round, with the most attentive dark eyes with yellow rings. Through his rag shirt, his chest shows scars, lots of them.

He takes another bread and curls back under.

"You shouldn't be out here." The voice is low, almost guttural, but his French is perfect. "Too many soldiers."

"There are always too many soldiers. If I follow your advice, I'd never leave the monastery."

"You training to fè yon prèt? Didn't think they let girls do that."

A priest? Non. But at least he didn't say Black girls, like the apologetic baker. "Sir, are you here for sanctuary?"

"Sekirite pou mwàn yo? Non. They own slaves, too. I come from the hills. I visit with manman m'nan mòn yo."

"Your mother lives in the mountains?" I'd heard of the runaways who become maroons. Was she one of them? Was Wide Eyes?

His smile fades. His eyes become serious, maybe haunted. "Manman mwen mouri. Dead."

I'm full of sorrow for him. And admiration. He journeys up high to talk to her in the sky.

"Then I saw you and your sister singing."

Oh. He's probably here for Elise. Many men see her and profess instant love. "My aunt's singing draws crowds."

"Your singing, mezanmi mwen. Your face, it drew me. It draws me back."

He called me dear. Was I dear to him, after one meeting? My cheeks flush. Guess with his head poking out from under the bench smiling at me, he knew I was flattered. His hand pops up and I put two kasavs into it.

More smacking and pleasurable sighs utter below. I'm glad I've fed someone after all.

"This garden has the nicest mangoes. My Tante Toya loves them. My mother did, too."

That sentiment, something with yearning and sorrow, vibrates in his voice. Maybe he's like my father, who's open about what pains him, his plans, and his purpose. "Mangoes and dates in the garden are big and lush, but I never think to partake. I would say take one with you, but I should ask. The botany men do experiments in here."

A laugh rumbles out. "If I asked, I wouldn't know what it tastes like. Then of course I wouldn't be here with you, mezanmi."

"I know you're not from the Bazac. Where . . . Do you have to ask permission to come over the hills?"

"Ou pa bezwen mande?" He laughs again. "Don't you?"

Have to ask? "Non. Not once my chores and lessons are done." We talk like old friends, but friends have names. I haven't been brave enough to ask.

Finishing up the kasav, letting a big chunk melt on my tongue, I'm silent.

"You still there?"

"Oui," I say when my mouth clears.

"Are you angry I took a mango? I'm a thief, but it's a shame to let it waste. I'm a fool for taking such risks, stealing the mango and coming to see you. But here I am."

My shoulders shrug on their own. "I'd never call anyone braver than me a fool."

His hand curls on the bench, fingers splayed, searching.

I push another kasav into his palm.

It disappears, and the sound of contentment ushers forth. "Very good. Trè byen."

"How far is it from here to your home?"

"To the stars and back. To the other side of the sea, that's where my true home is."

When he speaks slowly, it doesn't matter what language he uses. I hear him. And I love what he says. "That sounds far, to travel to the stars."

"Yes. Tante Toya, she's like my manman now, she makes our home in Calmina sound wonderful." He sighs. "Too far to go but for dreams."

"But where do you stay, sir?"

"No, not here." He shifts and his head pops out. That pleasant face, darker than that of any visitor to Place Royale except by way of the enslaved provision grounds, has a regal wide nose. His eyes, which have to be my favorite, are as fine as the dusky part of the day—large yellow-white rings with topaz brown centers.

The markings on his chest are too regular, like bobbin lace patterns.

I tumble the words in my head out and ask his status. "Did your owner do all that? Does it hurt?"

"Non." His thin fingers rub at his scars. "These honor my king across the sea. Everyone is free there. I want everyone free here and to have their own mango tree."

"So, you are enslaved, just not here."

Shame crosses into his eyes. "Go. Before your mother finds you and fusses."

"Don't leave. And you must mean my grand-mère. Mamie does fuss, but it's a sacrifice for her to get me schooling here. At thirteen, it's good for me."

"Born in 1758 or 1757?"

"Fifty-eight."

"Me, too. It's good one of the children of '58 gets school."

"Oh, goodness. We're the same age." But look how different our paths are—him enslaved, me free.

I bite my lip. Guilt covers my soul. Like the women in the Bazac, in this boy's wonderful wide eyes, I must have a lot. My family is poor in Léogâne, but we never hungered. Here I am blessed, blessed with chores and schooling, blessed with freedom. I must remember this around bakers and soldiers, or anyone who wants to say I'm not special. "Before you go, I want your name. I'm—"

"Janjak. That's what I'm called."

"Jean-Jacques." My syllables are long and drawn out, as if I were singing a church hymn. "That's how I'll say your name. Mine is—"

"Non. It will be a treat for you to tell me next time."

"Wait, do you want something to drink?" I shake the calabash. "Water."

"Non, not until we know each other better and you're sure you want to share."

My hand lowers. He sounds cautious about water, but the wave of well poisonings on the habitations close to Le Cap have everyone terrified. This boy doesn't know me well enough to trust my water. I suppose my food is different.

"Next Sunday. You will talk more."

I hope he meant we'd talk more, not me prattling on. "You'll come back? There will be more soldiers. That's dangerous. Maybe it is best to learn my name while you have the chance."

"Non, mademoiselle. I'll take the risk. It will be my reward."

"I, Marie-Claire, will be here."

He shakes his head, laughs, then goes deeper into the trees.

The bushes rustle. Then the sounds of the garden cover Jean-Jacques's footfalls.

My new friend left to return to some provision ground somewhere.

In my prayers for the world to change, I'll ask St. Louise and St. Michael to look after Jean-Jacques's safety, and make sure he avoids the sòldas and returns soon.

10

Toya

1773

Cormier Habitation

The morning sun already scorched the ground below my feet. I stood near the mango tree, but not underneath its shade. I craved the light too much.

The hot sand might burn the bottoms of others' bare feet. To me and those born of Africa, who remembered home, it was perfect.

The Blancs were too soft. They needed shoes to go anywhere. Then there were the enslaved, who'd become domesticated by these horrid conditions. This had to change.

"Stretch, my children." All twenty did so. My Janjak, in the first row, reached higher than the rest.

My plans to escape changed when I started mothering him and then the others. Priceless smiles bloomed when I taught these precious ones about the world. Even if I had planned to flee with Janjak, I couldn't leave the others, not now.

Watching over them as they grew, caring for them through chest fevers and other maladies made me understand why Eghosa had wanted a life with young ones. At thirty-five, I didn't feel I'd missed anything. I was proud of my celibate vows, but I understood why the gods had kept me, preserved me. I was to teach these and make them warriors.

Not suspecting I'd make them to rebel, Monsieur Garnier allowed me to exercise the children.

The gods redeemed the time. This generation would be ready to fight. Resistance from the boys disappeared when I flipped a few of them off their feet. My spear work was not as sharp as it had been, but with my staff taking down the biggest brutes, I showed those who thought a female nothing, the power of a woman.

Some feared me.

Others craved to know more.

Janjak wanted everything I could teach.

"Now relax." I motioned my hands to my sides. "Now stretch again."

They did, reaching for everything the sky could give.

My boy and his friends had grown. He still wasn't as tall as fifteen-year-old Da'mon and Agwé, but he worked harder. His muscles were stronger.

Da'mon, who I thought was of Bassari descent, from the foothills of Senegal, wore his long hair parted in rows of braids. Agwé cut his hair low about his dark brown face. He yelled and danced like the Taneka. This island gathered many tribes. It had to be the place the gods designed for unity.

These three boys used their Saturdays and Sundays off to find adventures. Janjak tried to be secretive, but I knew he trekked to the mountains to visit Eghosa. And I was pretty sure all traveled as far as Le Cap. So far, they'd been lucky returning on time, eluding Duclos and the other commandeurs. Young people coming of age needed to stretch their wings, wings I had to ensure remained strong so they could fly.

In Africa, each would have been ready for manhood initiations years ago. The way they all made stray glances at Fleur; it was more than time. Her perfectly round countenance bloomed. She was beautiful. Her dark brown skin held a rich glow, and her mother wove her braids, thin and long ones, into a cylinder-like crown about her skull.

Very pretty, but all Krobo women were. I wished she had the ritual yellow beads to wear about her neck and waist. Then everyone would understand the true beauty of Africa and what we'd lost by our feet being on this sand, the powdery brown sand of Saint-Domingue.

"Stretch!" I hit the ground with my staff, a solid limb of kajou, the West Indian mahogany. "Once more."

Poor Fleur couldn't reach far enough. Her slender arms didn't go up straight. Many of the boys had the same crooked posture.

The burden of carrying heavy baskets to gather the crops—cotton, coffee, and cane—had taken a toll.

"Tante Toya?" Braids flinging back, Da'mon craned his slender neck up. "Can we stop now?"

"Non. Continue." Janjak's voice sounded firm. It sometimes cracked then would deepen. "She's giving us training." He reached higher than the rest. I knew he'd touch the clouds one day. I could see him racing for the royal stool. Eghosa's smile would burst and I'd bow to our king. Axɔsu Janjak!

"Can we stop?" That whine was Da'mon's.

"Tired, children?" I asked. "Well, you must go beyond tired. You must prepare." Like Janjak, none of these spoke the mother tongue, so I used what French had given them, bits and pieces of words that sounded nothing like Africa. "Again," I said and angled Fleur from her hunched position to erect. "Now, stretch as far as you can."

With my staff, I hammered the dirt three times. "Again."

"Èske nou ka sispann kounye a? Please. Please! Stop now!" Agwé, with tight curls of ebony and skin of warm bronze, looked as if he'd fall over. "Please."

Janjak stepped to him and whispered to the fellow. My boy's laugh was easy. I overheard something about how the exercise helped to dance with girls.

Agwé's eyes fixed on Fleur, and he moved as if he'd become possessed.

Stepping out of line again, Janjak stood beside me. "Tante Toya is getting to the good part. She's going to make us warriors." His voice growled lower, and he shook his fists like he held a spear. The ancestors would be proud of his eagerness. Tegbesu, too.

We were able to do twenty more stretches. "Now I will teach you something new."

They giggled, and I was almost offended until I saw the glow on their cheeks. Newness, for children used to worn clothes and brokenness, was magic.

I remembered the good things I'd possessed—my breastplate of gold cowrie beads, my bracelets of brass. The headdress that identified my status as Gaou. I had only to close my eyes and I'd be before my king. The way he gazed at me when we went to battle, the tenderness in his voice as we spoke the last time in Calmina, I'll always treasure.

"Show us fast, Tante Toya. Then dinner." Agwé's begging made me smile. I was glad they looked forward to dinner. I'd helped improve their diets. Their provision grounds produced more manioc and potatoes to fill their bellies.

Yet I remembered dining on the fat of bush beast roasted with nuts, layered with grilled pineapples. In Calmina, we had had so much food I thought my gut would burst.

I felt that way when I lived in Gbowélé, too.

Ignoring the grumbling in my stomach . . . my heart, I strode through my column of children like they were my Minos preparing for attack. "Ready."

Lifting my arm as if I had a cutlass, I charged three steps.

They did the same in perfect unison.

Excellent.

We did this move over and over until each one wobbled as if they'd fall over. I was proud. I thought they'd even survive the Minos wilderness test.

The noise of horses' hooves made me turn. Duclos rode toward us. He and his lead driver, the commandeur Garnier, bounced in their saddles, clopping across the plateau.

"Done for today, but hold still for Massa Duclos's review. Then return to your huts."

The Grand Blanc and his Petit henchman stopped their horses in front of me.

The king of this place jumped down. Duclos's new-looking boots held a polish.

"What's going on here, Victoria? I mean Toya."

I tapped my staff, wishing it were a spear. "Your commandeur gave permission to work the children."

"Work? There's no cane up here." He turned to Garnier. "What is this?"

His man waved his arms. "Not work, exercise. She's says it can make them stronger."

"Stronger? They look like they are planning an attack."

Garnier laughed. "You afraid of a woman and some youths? Monsieur Duclos, you know how few we lost during the last wet season. Her crazy methods work. They've cut the toll to half this year. She's saved you money."

"Half. Hmm." Massa nodded, but his face twisted as though he hated I'd saved the enslaved. "Was children's ministry part of your nun duties, Toya?"

"Preparing new members was." I took my hands and held them the width of his neck. "Soon I'll show them how to make lamps."

"My, you are talented." Duclos climbed back on his horse and spirited the animal around me and the children like he was about to snatch one of them up.

He made another circle, then he stopped again in front of me. His mount was so close, I could smell the tart lather of its flesh. The fool worked horses to death, too. "You're stoking rebellion, Toya? I've had bad dreams. I think the poisonings will start up again. Good men, friends died."

No sadness for the women forced to kill to stop abuse. I shook my head. "Dreams, hmm. Interesting. Like prophecy. Are my gods trying to tell you something?"

Duclos's horse bucked at the flexing of my staff and my muttered truth, but it was easy to spook both beasts—Massa and his jittery Paso Fino.

Garnier laughed and slipped a little in his seat. "She's a funny one." That wasn't humor.

It was truth. "May I send the children back to their huts? They need dinner."

The fool Duclos nodded and whipped his hand forward. "Go on

now. I expect you all to cut cane faster when you help in the fields bright and early."

Doing lunges and holding their pretend cutlasses, everyone but Janjak left. "Come on, Tante Toya."

"Go on, Janjak. Massa looks like he wants to talk about his dreams."

Looking panicked, with his eyes wide, my boy leaped between us. Duclos's horse reared and dropped the fool.

Dusting off his soiled white pantaloons, he cursed and charged at Janjak. "What the devil, boy? You did that on purpose."

"Massa. Don't touch Tante Toya." The seed of Eghosa and me wrapped his arms about my hips. He understood that Duclos's *talks* were Blanc dribble to hide their continued raping of enslaved women. Duclos killed Eghosa as much as the birthin' fever.

Patting his shoulders, I shook my head. "Not that type of talking, not like your mother. I'll be fine. Go."

"Hold it right there." Duclos yanked him by the shirt. "You'll be whipped."

"You did it yourself, Massa." I pulled Janjak behind me. "Not his fault you can't hold your saddle."

Massa sneered, showing off his tobacco-stained teeth. "Then you shall be whipped."

Garnier stepped forward. "Sir, you did rather fall. You—"

Duclos growled. "Hand me your whip."

Unlike the thick older massa of Cormier, who looked like he ate good bush beast each night, Garnier was thinner, younger, possessing greasy red hair with no curl and seemed to have a fear of losing his position. "Sir," he said, "the boy's just protective of Toya. Don't do this. And I need Toya to keep them calm. She's difficult but effective."

"Your whip or go find a new employment." Duclos sneered.

Garnier looked at me, then unhitched the braided leather and handed it to his massa.

Any hope I had of the commandeur being different dissolved. No Blanc apologized to Black for his wrongs. No Blanc risked his money for Black.

Janjak jumped again between us. "Non! Kite Tante Toya pou kont li. Beat me."

"Tante or maman?" Duclos said. "He's acting like you're his mother. Been cheating on your king?"

"It shows respect, Duclos. You do know what that is?"

He gritted his teeth and hauled Janjak to the trunk of a tree. "You'll take lashes for knocking me down and ones for your Tante Toya."

Garnier lifted his hands. "Sir, he didn't mean . . . he was just—"

The cracking of the whip deafened. It snapped twice against Janjak's back, then Duclos struck his legs with the whip.

With my staff, I readied to kill Duclos . . . for what he'd done to Eghosa and now her son.

Garnier stepped into my path, blocking me. "You're too valuable. Let it be."

"The boy is valuable, commandeur."

His look at me said otherwise. Black bodies meant nothing, even to nice Blancs.

Duclos tossed Janjak to the ground.

The man-child I loved had no water pouring from his face but winced with each strike of the leather. The torn, miserable osnaburg cloth of his shirt exposed whip welts and blood.

"Wait, what?" Duclos lifted a section of the rag shirt. "Good God," he said. "My whip didn't do all that. There are scars all over him. How?"

The scarification on his chest was beautiful on Janjak's skin.

With a shrug, Garnier got close and took the whip. "He's had enough."

Duclos released the weapon. "Well, Toya, I've got you now. When you step out of line, I know how to make you suffer without risking your valuable services."

Grinning like the fool he was, he smoothed his wrinkled sleeves. "You're increasing my profits keeping them alive. But I have your weakness. This is a good day."

With his commandeur's help, Duclos climbed onto his horse.

"Garnier, I think I'll sleep well tonight, better than I have since Toya came to Cormier."

Laughing, he rode off.

The commandeur rolled up his braided whip. "He could have killed the boy for being disrespectful, Toya. Consider this a warning. Janjak, be smarter. You work harder than any. Don't make your burden heavier."

Garnier left. His horse kicked up dirt.

Stooping, I put my palm to Janjak's shoulder. "That was brave but unwise. We must save you, all your strength, for the right time."

"When is it right? When he kills you like my mother? I should run away for good. Then he can't hurt me. You should run, too."

Dragging my arms about him, I summoned all the love I had for him, that his mother had, then I became the softness he needed and held him until he stopped shaking, till the fury settled in his chest.

"You're meant for more than this, Janjak. You have royal blood in you. Don't shed it for a fool. It's not your time to rise. It's not."

The gods would send him helpers. Minos and men would come and bring liberation. I felt it deep in my bones.

Releasing him, I pointed to the hills. "Tonight, we go up and I teach you more about the sky. I'll show you how to use the stars to guide troops."

"The brightest ones are meant for us. That's what Manman said." He looked up with Eghosa's nose and Nosakhere's wide eyes. "Someday, I'll fight Duclos. I'll be free. I'll bleed for it. I'll die for you."

Again hugging him tightly, I whispered to him prophecy. I even made up some to encourage him. But Massa should pay for these lashes, and I wouldn't mind spilling Duclos's blood at all.

11

Toya

1775

Cormier Habitation

After scraping up the weeds between plantings, I leaned on my hoe. The coffee bushes were much easier to work than cane, except some of them had been allowed to grow into trees.

Shameful neglect.

I'd have to climb the trunk to reach the coffee cherries that were high in the canopy.

The clouds rolled and clumped together like dirty cotton balls in the sky. The air felt damp, pregnant with bitter rain.

"We must hurry. The weather is coming," I shouted to the women gathering in the field closest to the hospital building.

I pointed to Fleur. She'd been at my side learning the ways of medicine. "Gather the low beans, the easy ones. I'll talk to Duclos again about trimming the coffee trees. It will help improve the quality of the yield."

Fleur nodded and laughed. "Si yon pyebwa kafe toujou bay yon sèl cherry, Duclos pap manyen li, pou li pa pèdi lajan cherry la pote."

This tongue sounded better than Duclos's. I understood and agreed with Fleur. Duclos was cheap. Cheap and superstitious. If this tree still gave him a single cherry, he wouldn't touch it, lest he lose the money for that single bean.

Sort of why he didn't touch me; I healed up folks for him. Folks he'd abuse again to make more money.

As he headed toward our hut, Janjak waved to his friends. Agwé and Da'mon would have him sneaking to Le Cap this weekend again. The boy I'd raised was now seventeen, and whether running to town to sell yams . . . or to sow seeds, he took risks. Yet, the way he came back smiling, smiling like I hadn't seen, the risk or the love must be good to him.

That boy.

Medium height and stocky, he was brilliant and quick, with a great laugh. Janjak could be much more if he were in Calmina or Abomey. He'd be a proud Dahomey.

And Fleur would make a good bride. Soon Duclos or one of his commandeurs would notice her. They'd not miss a pretty girl.

A droplet hit my hand. Then a downpour came soaking the ground beneath my bare feet. I was wet and guilty.

Waiting for the right time to rebel made me complicit in the doings here. Working for Duclos as if he were my king was horrible. Where was my resistance?

At several habitations close to Le Cap, the women had revolted. They started poisoning their massas and massas' families. It was an ugly way to die, painful, but faster than the slow death of enslavement.

In some ways, poison was cowardly. Death should be faced head-on, but what other way did women have to fight back? This world thought us less than human. This meant we should resist in any manner.

The rain kept falling.

My linen tunic with no beading or adornment became soaked against my breasts.

My indigo-dyed skirt, drenched, slapped against my legs. Fleur's cheap osnaburg showed her shapely thighs. She was definitely a target for any male on the habitation. Though I had scared away a few, I wasn't everywhere. Maybe I'd teach her which medicines killed.

"Fleur, run to your provision grounds. Let no one see you."

She nodded and dashed away.

The young were getting older. I'd helped them be strong but not free. Arms raised to the heavens, I stood still. I wanted judgment now, a lightning bolt, a quake of the earth like in '70. Something to show I wasn't forsaken.

Let this old, rugged coffee tree fall upon me. I named the sins for which I had to be forgiven—pride, omission, hate, vengeance, anything. Seventeen years enslaved, wasn't this enough?

Rain pattered on my face. I tasted salty tears across my lips. Then I thought of the years I was a proud Dahomey and sentenced people to this.

I had no right to ask for expedience or fast judgment when I was guilty.

Thunder drummed in the mountains. My deserved lightning strike never came.

My iya would say my work was unfinished. But I didn't think hers was, either. She willingly submitted to the fire. And I grabbed the chance she gave me to be among the chosen. Then I worked harder than any to become a warrior, an instrument of evil.

Guilty.

Still, I begged for mercy. "Gen pitye pou mwen!"

Garnier blew the conch and waved to everyone working to stop. It sounded again. Then he rode toward me. "Come on, Toya. Get out of this rain. You know how it brings sickness."

My braids had come down from my scarf. Everything dripped and lay soggy at my neck.

"Toya. You well?"

I wasn't. I was sick, not from the rain, but from my shame of thinking Ouidah was a better punishment than execution.

Axɔsu Tegbesu wɛ ɖÓ acɛ daxÓ é è nan ɖɔ lé é mì nan nɔn gbon é nu mì. These words, which had once brought me comfort, haunted my dreams. King Tegbesu's divine right—did he truly know what it meant to sell someone into slavery? In my heart, I wanted to believe he didn't understand it was a death sentence.

But how could the all-knowing man not? Unlike beheading, enslavement enriched the kingdom. Like the devils in my midst, would Tegbesu sell Africa into slavery for silver?

Garnier held his tricorn hat over me. "Toya, snap out of this.

Monsieur Duclos has bought more slaves. If there are any young ones, you'll need to teach them and get 'em prepared. You've made all the little ones healthier and more resilient. Everyone is happy."

Happy? Happy being owned?

These words punched me in the chest.

The rain continued, drumming along my cheeks. It wasn't enough to wash me clean. I was complicit. I deserved my fate. "Not resilient. Persistent. We persist against the perils. There's a difference."

"Are you well, Toya? We can't afford you getting sick." Garnier wiped at water pooling on the brim of his black tricorn. "Someone has to protect the young."

If they were Dahomey youth, they'd be given protection and educated in the pride of our people. Blancs didn't care for us any more than they cared for a tall coffee tree.

Starting to walk away, wanting to run away, I headed to Duclos's grand-casa, outside his big porch where he'd parade his new purchases.

The closer I came to the cart, the clearer it became Duclos had bought more young ones, ones half Janjak's age, maybe less.

Stopping in front of the dray, I said in Fon and Twi and Yoruba, "Go to the provision grounds."

A second dray held one man. He answered me in Fon. "Étɛ Mì sixÚ blÓ axɔsu ɔ mɛvo?"

What do we do without a king?

This man arose and jumped off the dray.

Six feet away, the sight of him . . . I hadn't glanced upon him in years, not since the docks of Le Cap.

With his shorn head devoid of rich onyx locks, he glared at me.

His skin of ebony polished to a shine dripped with rain.

"Toya, you're staring. You know him?" Garnier waved his hand in front of me. "Toya?"

Of course I knew the great adviser to the king, Nosakhere.

His posture hadn't diminished.

His half-naked form, clothed only in an apron about his waist, exposed the scarification of his chest as well as damage from Massa's lashes.

He'd never be compliant.

He'd never let himself be a tool of the Ducloses of this world.

Of all the places, all the colonies an enslaved Dahomey would come, Nosakhere would show up here. Didn't know if I should greet my kinsman, tell him of his son, or avenge Eghosa in combat.

"You do know him, Toya." Garnier's shout broke through my memories—the battles, the betrayals, the second thoughts.

"Wi." It was all I could say as Tegbesu's usurping counselor approached.

His eyes, deep brown smoked with a yellow ring, narrowed. As if we were within the walls of Calmina standing safe, secure in front of our king, he bowed with a simple nod.

My blood chilled.

Nosakhere had marked me for death.

SITTING ON THE FLOOR OF MY HUT, I REMEMBERED THE BARRACKS in Abomey and the ones in Calmina. The shiny walls remained part of my dreams. They were much more comforting than the mud-daub walls of this dwelling. The roof of palm thatch was the same, but without the decoration of skulls. That was best, for here they wouldn't be the enemy's. They'd be fellow slaves'. Life spans here were short. I was old at thirty-seven.

I prayed again for answers. Yet I opened my eyes to dread.

Nosakhere stood at my threshold.

"Come . . ." My breath and words hitched. "Come in."

When he entered, fire was in his countenance. "You chose wrong, Gaou Adbaraya Toya."

I didn't move. I let him circle like a lion stalking an elephant. When he stopped in front of my firepit, he glared at me. "That's all you have to say? It's been seventeen years."

His eyes moved about the room. Was he searching for weapons or calculating if anyone would hear him killing me? He stroked his chin as if he had misplaced a beard. "Where's your slew of Massa's children? Has he not raped you and stripped you of your Minos vows?"

"My honor is intact. I've never been led astray. No children of my own, but I have raised ones for murdered parents."

His nose was in the air as if he were still part of the high council. "Do you hold to Dahomey culture?"

"As much as I can, Nosakhere. I try to teach the young. They know nothing of it. They need it to have pride."

He stopped and poked at my walking stick that leaned against the wall. He fingered the wood grain. "Why have you not taught them how to throw off Massa's chains? The great Gaou has instructed many warriors. You should have them all subdued."

"You've been enslaved the same as I. I could ask the great counselor the same."

"The Blancs are too fearful to allow me to linger with the enslaved. I'm sold often."

"Or they find no use for you. That's not a bad thing, just truthful, Nosakhere."

"Gaou, I ask again, why stay a captive?"

"There's not been an opportunity to overtake the Blancs. They have more weapons, more training in warfare. They also have no honor. They torture those that fail, unlike the Dahomey way." I stirred my coals. "We preferred a prisoner's fast execution than a lingering death."

I'd just told him how I wanted to die, but he looked away. "Have your jokes, Adbaraya." Nosakhere turned as if to leave but instead picked up my stick and tossed it at me.

I caught it with one hand and spun it before easing it to the ground.

Laughter poured from his broad lips. "You haven't grown soft. I ask again, why haven't you rebelled?"

Waiting for the right time? An answer from the gods? Gu, the god of war, hadn't sent me a plan. Zinsu and Zinsi, the divine twins, hadn't offered me their mercy.

"What say you, Adbaraya Toya?"

The tiny hairs on the back of my neck tingled. His attack was imminent. I drew my walking stick closer to my hip. "My words are nothing to you, as your oath of loyalty to our king was nothing."

He stopped and clawed at the necklace about his throat, a thin strip of leather with round beads, white ones, like mine of carnelian for the purity ceremony.

The marks on his shoulders and his bared chest were similar to the ones I'd given Janjak. I was glad his son was away. Nosakhere wasn't worth his spittle.

"I've sought repentance, Adbaraya. But seeing you still breathing . . . I'm here seeking revenge. You're responsible for my enslavement, for my pain."

One hand balled in a fist; my other curled around the stick I'd break about his neck. "That's not how I remember it. You betrayed Eghosa. You planned to usurp Tegbesu. That treachery sent us here."

"A young man talks a lot of nonsense and even does foolish things. You could've looked the other way. I wouldn't have turned on Tegbesu. He'd given me my position."

Now I gawked at him. "Your word is meaningless. You used my friend. Eghosa believed you loved her. She married you with the water ceremony. It was to make her break her vows—all for lust."

"I regret what I did, but our mutual attraction led us astray. She wanted me, and I couldn't deny myself. The water ceremony was a convenient falsehood, but our mutually agreed upon falsehood if we were caught."

I'd never asked Eghosa another thing about Calmina and what led to it. It didn't matter now. "A lie is a lie, whether it's agreed upon or one you invented."

"It does matter, Gaou." Clenching his wrist, he stood before me breathing, taking no blame for our predicament.

Right. I hadn't killed him . . . yet. "You think your lying tongue is enough to make me walk away from the serpent who bit my friend, the asp who wanted to be near my king? Never."

"You traded with the devils and sold yourself, too."

"Just improved your deal. Remember. Three for one. And yes, I sentenced myself to torment in order to send you to hell. You should've had enough honor to go to the king and submit to his mercy. You were a royal counselor. You had high responsibilities. You should've had more honor. Instead you tried to send Eghosa here alone."

The muscles in his jaw tightened. "Women, I'd heard, had easier treatment. I was wrong, very wrong about the suffering."

He sounded regretful but he was a liar. "Have you paid enough, No-sakhere? Is that what you've come to say? You're alive. Tegbesu might not have had you slain, but he wouldn't have kept you as an adviser. Maybe he'd have sent you away to be a blacksmith. Was no longer being a royal adviser worth destroying my friend?"

He groused over my firepot. The glow of my coals cast orange light on his powerful legs. The apron did little to hide his thick thighs. "Tonight is about you. I'd hoped for your death on the boat to the West Indies, from the filth and disease. Or here by some massa's hand. But you're alive, unharmed. Perhaps the gods have truly given me the chance for final vengeance."

"Your head should've become a decorative lamp along a street in Calmina."

His hand fisted. "A lamp to light the way. Something for you to see and think of me." His gaze whipped about my hut. "Perhaps I should bring you a barrel to use as a surface to cut off my skull."

"A barrel?"

"Yes, it seems I'm quite good at being a cooper. I learned in the Bahamas how to make use of my metal skills. Duclos bought me, bought me for top dollar. I hear you're his witch doctor."

Something was off in his stance. The way he favored his right side.

He stretched and leaned against the wall. "Why do you stare, Adbaraya Toya?"

"I'm imagining where to hang my new lamp. My hut will finally have good lighting."

Nosakhere laughed loudly, like a hyena, as if he'd lost his mind. "Eghosa said you had wit. Didn't believe her."

"Didn't deserve her. May she rest in peace thinking you dead."

Something whipped across his face, and for a moment, an instance, I saw the deepest sorrow. Then his countenance blanked, hiding the soft look as if it were weak to have regrets. We all die with them, why should he be different?

Nosakhere looked up to the leaky roof. "She didn't deserve to be here." His voice fell to a whisper. "I sold prisoners, hundreds upon thousands, on Tegbesu's behalf. I counted the tribute and stashed it in the king's coffers. I thought enslavement was better than decapitation."

"It's a slow death, Nosakhere, and I wrestle with my sins daily. I sent people to walk the red clay to Ouidah. Every territory we conquered, those who failed my training . . . I sent them to this fate. We are all guilty of enslaving Blacks."

My leg had become numb. I shifted and made the blood work. "We should pray the king becomes enlightened."

"Is that your crime, Adbaraya Toya, blindly submitting to the king?"

A prophecy given by Gaou Hangbé had sealed my fate, to separate me from the Minos. That hurt as much as death taking my mother. But why should I say this to the man who'd come to kill me? "My sins are mine. Have you repented? The false ceremony with Eghosa to have her flesh . . . what did you give her for the lobola, the bride price? Weeks of hope, to be told the sour truth, she meant nothing to you."

"You know nothing of what I did, felt, or said." He flexed his arm. The taut muscles looked as if they'd rip from his shoulders. "I was rightly judged for my boasts, the ravings of a fool who'd been caught."

Nosakhere moved fast, took my staff, and jabbed it into my chest. "But Tegbesu knew. He had to know what Ouidah meant."

As in the old days, the way I taught the Minos and now the children, I slipped away, yanked, and spun his foot, making him fall flat. Down he went with a thud. Before he could get off his back, I cut my forearm across his throat. "Why are you trying to lower the king?"

"Tegbesu, his divinity, had to know, but he kept selling people for money. We are complicit because of Tegbesu."

"Blasphemy." I pressed down, crushing his throat. "He's our king."

His flailing knocked the firepot. A coal flung to my leg. It burned. Hopping back, I ripped at his apron.

Gasping, Nosakhere sat up, wrenching his neck. "You haven't lost your skills."

But I couldn't understand what he said. With his covering in my hands, my gaze pinned to his flesh, what he'd lost or what was missing from his loins.

He lay there a moment fully naked, showing me the extent of the horrors done to him.

"Castrated?"

He pulled the cloth from my fingers, stood, and wrapped himself. "I refused to breed with unwilling women. My second master decided I'd breed with no one."

Nosakhere came toward me, backing stunned me into the wall. "Am I less of a man to you? Is this not enough pain to make amends for my treachery to Eghosa?"

His large hands went to my shoulders. "I've seen how lax Duclos's men are. He allows his chattel to go to town."

"Yes, he observes the Code Noir. The law gives time for rest."

"Gaou Toya, we can use their lowered defenses and seize control of the habitation. We can rule."

I shook my head. "The people aren't ready. They don't have weapons."

"We can make them, and then strike. You the commander of the guard, me the tactical planner. We can do this."

"Why would I help you? This is Massa's land. He's the father of this place." These words came despite my disgust for Duclos. Nosakhere needed to prove his convictions. Great suffering didn't mean his heart had changed. And I'd never put my faith in the man who betrayed Eghosa. "Leave. Go to your provision ground. Convince another fool you'll be at their side when things are difficult."

"Duclos is king of Cormier by rape and money. This is not Abomey or Calmina, but as Dahomey we have a divine right to power. I have the blood of kings and you're the leader of the king's Minos."

It was true.

Saint-Domingue was territory to conquer, just like our battles with the Oyo. If thousands of enslaved were organized and had weapons, we could defeat the superstitious Grand Blancs. The Petit ones, too.

I'd hesitated too long. Nosakhere put his hands on my skull. I couldn't shake free as he applied pressure, enough to split my head open like a melon. "You'd make a good lamp or trophy for my wall."

"Do it. Stop talking about it. Do your worst."

He released me and moved to the other side of my hut. "I need you alive. A rebellion can't be done by one. You must convince the enslaved to follow us."

"You mean follow you? You think you are the only one of royal blood who can be king because Tegbesu is not here."

Those wide imposing eyes stopped me from exposing the one blessing out of all the misery, Janjak. Nosakhere nodded. "Tegbesu can no longer rule. He's with the ancestors."

"Dead?" My knees gave way first. I hit the ground hard. "You lie!"

A low, almost sympathetic voice grazed my ear. "Slaves still come from Africa, sent by the Dahomey. They talk of his son, Kpengla, taking the throne and increasing the slave trade."

I remembered the prince. At twenty-three, he'd been sent away to a place of his own a year or two before I became Gaou. It was to protect him and prepare the young man to take his father's position. Did Kpengla now rule?

Was Tegbesu dead? Was I a widow?

Nosakhere stooped and lifted my chin with a finger. "We can honor Tegbesu here. If you believe him misguided about enslavement, I will, too. And we'll build a new Dahomey state in his honor. This one will be fair and safe. As in Abomey and Calmina, no one will go to bed hungry. Everyone will be protected. No man or woman will be raped."

His raw jagged thumbnail pierced my chin. He had the strength to push through my skull. "Kill me now or after I help slay a nation. How am I to trust you?"

Tossing me away, he started to laugh. "You mean how to trust a eunuch?" His face, his voice, everything was pained. "Adbaraya, I need you. I can't do this on my own. Freeing people here is my calling. It's my . . . our redemption. You and I together can do it."

"Leading them is what you are after. To be made king here."

He strolled to my door, as if the treachery he'd done had vanished and trusting him was simple.

"Think on it, Adbaraya Toya."

In a blink, he was gone.

If not for the pain in my thigh, I'd think his visitation a dream. For now he'd left me alive, but there was no way to trust Nosakhere. A wounded man with ambition was more dangerous than a hundred Blancs.

Good intentions would fade. The raw blame for his circumstances would rage anew. Then the two of us, darkness and light, would battle to the death.

12

Marie-Claire

1777

Cap-Français

The newly paved Rue Espagnole feels different, but everything is different to me. Visits from my wide-eyed friend are regular. Our talks about dreams are something I enjoy, that I crave. I think I can float when we whisper dreams.

"Marie-Claire," Elise says. "Hurry."

My leather slippers kick up pebbled gravel as I catch up. "Elise, is this supposed to make travel easier for drays and carriages?"

"Oui. Pierre Lunic, the new master cartwright for the Brothers at Place Royale, says this will save wheels."

This is the second time she has mentioned the Frenchman. I wonder what she's thinking. Sometimes it's hard to know. "Wooden wheels without wear? That will put Mr. Lunic out of business, non?"

She shrugs. "He's not fretting. The man has other amazing skills. The crucifix he sculpted for the chapel was wondrous. The Jesuit priests took it with them. The transfer of our order to the Capuchins is complete."

One feuding Catholic group replacing another seems comedic, but Elise is hurt by it. She wears a fake smile while talking of the changes, but the Capuchins limit more things, even what the Affranchi and enslaved can do for church service. Yet, through her good work, she's able to maintain her position. No priest ever voiced replacing Mamie at the hospital.

Perhaps this Lunic can sway my aunt from a life of solitude, give her some lasting joy.

"Marie-Claire, I asked you to come so that we can talk about the Bazac and visiting the enslaved."

She knows?

In silence, we walk farther down the rue. New houses and buildings of all kinds are appearing, but I want to learn what Elise knows or suspects. My voice dies inside.

We pass the women in bright colors selling all kinds of goods. The chatter is happy. Money exchanges hands. Their world is still moving.

The bells of the new cathedral, Notre-Dame de l'Assomption, ring. Its two bell towers can be heard across Le Cap. The sound is bold. It's a beacon for rich and poor, for all colors, but I'm beset with worries. My helping in secret has been found out.

"Keep up, Marie-Claire. Or perhaps you need to be where it is slower. My sister writes that you should return to Léogâne. There's plenty of unfortunates to help there." Elise's voice is sharp. She does not approve of what I've done, but will she tell?

"Maman and Père visited to hear you sing for Monsieur Gervaise. They didn't mention anything about Léogâne. Perhaps they were too taken with your old theater music master's performance."

"My sister and Guillaume are always so in love—holding hands, exchanging longing looks. You should consider marriage, to be settled before you give the new priests reasons to dismiss us all. Stealing food—"

"I steal nothing. I buy cassava root. I make everything and choose to share my bread with those who have less."

Elise looks through me or past me, then keeps walking. "My père's old street is coming up. It would be such a short walk to the cathedral if we still lived there."

In a blink, she's changed the subject, and I'm supposed to not notice she thought me a thief. My aunt looks wistful and tugs her short sleeves. Her dresses are old-fashioned with long ruffly lace that starts below her elbow and falls to her wrist. This is what she chooses, and Elise gets what she wants, except singing onstage. Even helping with the scenery is getting hard.

Mamie keeps me in fashion with long narrow sleeves of yellow flowers and ivy green stripes. I look well-to-do, put together—no one to cause trouble. "Elise, I'm sorry, but I'm careful, or I try to be."

She shrugs, then stops to buy a copy of *Affiches Américaines*.

Two beautiful women, one Brown, the other Black, have orange and red glazed pots on their heads. They've come from filling these vessels at the fountain in Place d'Armes. They're chatting and are deeply in each other's confidence. I want that with Elise.

Yet to do that I must be transparent. She must see into my heart, and I must tell her my other secret, my friendship with Jean-Jacques. I want to share with her that every other Sunday these past six years in my garden, he and I have been together, side by side on our bench talking about silly things or nothing at all.

I encourage him and have taught him more French. His speech is better. His dreams are sharper. "Elise."

She's flipping through her paper when her face twists. "Well, it's official. The Treaty of Aranjuez is signed. This half of Hispaniola is formally French Saint-Domingue. Spain has let go."

"We were already under French control. Why is this newsworthy?"

"Marie-Claire, it means we might have more soldiers coming. They'll come to maintain the peace."

"But there's more unrest outside of Le Cap. More cases of poisonings have been coming to the hospital. Why patrol here when the habitations need help?"

Her cheeks become white as a ghost or like a bleached linen shirt of the wealthy Grand Blancs.

"Elise?" I grip her hands. The paper crumples between her palms. "What's wrong?"

"More poisonings?" She collapses against me. "They have to stop. Poisoning and burning are the worst ways to die."

This distant look is the same as Maman's when she reminisces. I wrap my arms around Elise and draw her close. "I'm sorry. You haven't been working at the hospital lately, but the signs of trouble are everywhere."

She recovers and fans her face. "Turmoil will lead to more restricting of Affranchi rights, like we'd helped the enslaved poison people."

"The Blacks and Browns in chains want to be free just like us, like the Americans. A whole colony is battling Britain's king now."

"That's why you have to stop your doings at the Bazac. Anything that will make us look guilty shouldn't be done."

I squint at her. "You're afraid of doing what's right but you're fine with the killing wars? That's what your papers want."

"Quiet, Marie-Claire, someone may hear."

We step farther from the vendors and Elise whispers, "War may help everyone to come together. I support anything that will take all the barriers that steal rights."

"Rights for all, Elise?"

She nods, and we keep going, but I look at her with her golden chin exalted. She wants war even if it's merely to clear away the restrictions on the theater or church. She wants what she wants and if others benefit, that's fine, too.

"I hope your war goes as you want it."

"Marie-Claire, women don't declare war."

"But we are left to patch up the wounded."

My aunt does not respond and does not stop at Rue Notre-Dame or the markets at Place d'Armes. I know she's going to torture herself. She marches us to the new theater, Comédie du Cap.

Handbills are nailed to the door. She fingers one. *Le Sourd Dupé* by Bisset is performing next week. That wasn't in the *Affiches Américaines*.

"We can't believe everything we read," I say.

She offers me a frown like I've blasphemed. "Bisset's a local composer. I wonder if it will involve songs of our weather. He loves rain."

"Well, if there's war, there will be more soldiers. They'll be patrons, patrons who want mulattoes to sing. Then you could try again."

"The day is coming when I won't be hidden behind painted scenery. I'll sing lead. I won't be used to bolster others' voices. I'm worth more. I refuse to be used."

Despite our differences, my love for Elise grows in times like this. I want to be as confident in my decisions.

"Let us turn back to Place d'Armes," she says. "Then head to the church."

She doesn't mean our convent chapel but the big palace near Place d'Armes which has been made for God. It does not take long to wander to the elm-lined square filled with vendors. The cucumbers look good. Ribbons, even lilac ones, are on tables. Warm kasav scents the air. My stomach churns.

I'm about to steer Elise to food when I see Wide Eyes.

My pulse races and pushes hard against my chest. I feel like I might die. If Jean-Jacques notices me, I will.

And if he doesn't, I will.

He's in trim black breeches and a nice shirt that's untied and open. Hints of his scars, these tracks to his heart, are exposed.

Standing with a group of young men, he's not as tall as he seems in the garden.

My aunt is talking vegetables, but I can't concentrate. I'm staring too hard. A pretty woman selling yams calls him over. His friends hoot, and he goes.

She touches his hand. He dances her from her table, his hips swaying with hers.

"Marie-Claire, come on."

It takes everything in me to keep walking and pretend my world is normal, that the young man who makes my heart skip isn't on the other side of Place d'Armes . . . entertaining someone else.

I follow the swish of my aunt's big skirt to the front entrance of the cathedral.

Notre-Dame de l'Assomption has the largest entrance I've ever seen. Solid double doors frame this place of worship. The limestone is brilliant white and contrasts with the pinkish-colored columns. Everything works together supporting swirled glass. The sun sprinkles light on my skin.

It's magnificent to be exposed, not hidden in the shadows. "I understand, Elise."

"What?" Her brows furrow, then ease. She's taken with the church, too. The vaulted wood ceiling must touch the sky. I change my mind. This is more impressive than the doors. Things hanging over your head should have more weight than something you walk through.

"Impressed?"

"Oui, Elise. Who wouldn't be?"

"When I sing by the altar, I think the echo reaches God's ear. Do you wish to dedicate your life to His service? I intend to never marry, and if you are the same, I'll make sure you stay and not go back to Léogâne."

"I thought you liked Monsieur Lunic, the new carpenter for the Brothers."

"Non. He's a nice man, but I don't want a husband." She takes my hand in hers. "I'll not find a love like my sister. And I don't want a man who only wants me because I'm Colored, or a daughter of a Grand Blanc, which will make me acceptable to his mother. I'll never be a mistress. As I wait for the world to war and change, I'll sing to God."

"You sound like a nun, Elise, but there are no orders for free Blacks or Coloreds, just helper roles. Shall you be a nun in secret but not a singer hidden onstage? I don't understand."

"Oui. God sees me everywhere, but man only sees what's centered in the light." She leads me into the nave. "You're coming of age, Marie-Claire. You must decide what's right for you, but if you are not like me then you need to be someone's wife. Your mother agrees."

"No. None of her meddling or matchmaking. Epi? Epi anyen." I cover my mouth. Jean-Jacques's Kreyòl had come out. I guess I learned from him, too.

"What did you say, Marie-Claire?"

"Something I heard about waiting. She wants this and that. And then, nothing. Nothing for me. I'll have none of what I want."

Her hazel eyes grow wide and misty. "Maybe I have misled you by the freedom I have. I live at the convent teaching music. I lead the small choir there. I'm an exception, but all those things are all going away. Free Blacks and Coloreds will no longer be church wardens. They won't let the enslaved be choir leaders or beadles anymore. The church is slowly ridding itself of color except in the yellow tint of the windows."

She walks toward the pulpit. The sun reflecting through the panes casts golden rays upon her. She looks angelic.

But I know her as if she is my sister.

There's pain underneath everything. The rules are silencing her, keeping her from living in the light. She's running to God as a last resort, but that's not my path.

"Why not fight? Rebel, Elise. You want war. Let's go back down to the theater and demand a role. Let's make paper bills for all the men who leer at you to entice them to come."

"You're being ridiculous."

"I'm being a fighter. Mamie and Maman, in their own ways, are fighters. We should be fighters, too."

She sighs and all her encouragement steams out of her flared nostrils. "Le Cap is growing and changing while the rights of the free, whether Black or Colored, are shrinking. The Paris of the West Indies is for the French Blancs, the Grand ones. You and I have to hang on to what we have and hope for more exceptions or a revolution like the Americans'. They are throwing off the old. Why can't Saint-Domingue?"

The need for war in her voice wraps about me. The hold is tight, and I want it, too. Then Elise, golden, quiet Elise, sings.

> Let all that dwell above the sky,
> And air and earth and seas,
> Conspire to lift Thy glories high.

The echo goes to the heavens and with it I see her heart rallying. God may hear. Maybe he'll be moved.

A man enters from the side. He wears a cassock similar to the dark brown robes of the Brothers, but his has a red stole. "Mademoiselle Lobelot, you've arrived on time. Come, let me show you the new hymnbooks."

"Marie-Claire Bonheur, this is Father Philémon. Please stay here. This won't take but a moment. Then we'll take another walk and I'll share what Sainte writes."

"Maman—"

"Marriage, and the eligible candidates she's found for you in Léogâne. It's for the best." Elise says this in front of the priest and I cannot react with fury.

Thick blond hair bobbing on his head, Père Philémon stares at me as if he knows something is wrong, but the two go.

My mother writes none of this to me. She's trying to control my life through her sister. I don't know what I want, but I'm sure my calling isn't to be in a small town, waiting for a fisherman to come home.

Then I realize, I'm lying.

I've waited for one young man for years, to make plans and include me. I keep wishing for him to tell me he's free and that we can wed.

A moment is all it takes to decide I'm done waiting. And another for Jean-Jacques to step through those large doors looking as if he wishes to speak.

MY FRIEND, WIDE EYES, STARES AT ME BUT DOES NOT COME DOWN the aisle. Instead, he slips into a pew midway. He says nothing, but his gaze is touching me. I feel the brush of his hand, the scent of his skin and mangoes, and he hasn't moved, but that's how it feels when we're alone in the garden.

"Will there be a service today?" he asks, with his hands waving me to him.

My tongue grows heavy. I shrug and stay in place. "There's a service for the freeborn and Affranchi . . ." But none for the enslaved, though their labor built this church and all the things I've admired.

That distinction, free or enslaved, is like another color, and I feel

Elise's frustration. The colonial government keeps highlighting this difference and adding more restrictions. One would think God should draw all people nigh, not push us apart.

I shift my stance but don't go to him or fall for the draw of his eyes. "I didn't know you'd be in town today."

"It is Saturday, and there's no harvest. Duclos had no reason to deny a day of leisure." Jean-Jacques cups a hand to his ear. "It's hard to hear you. Please come closer."

His dialect is becoming easier for me, or I've grown used to his way of speaking. A thousand thoughts run through my head—why is he here and not at Place Royale? Is he always in town every weekend, visiting other girls?

Rubbing my temples, trying to press out these jealous thoughts, I step forward. I come almost to him but sit in a pew ahead. "You look well."

He laughs. "Thank you, my shy . . . what is the word. Chatterbox."

His voice sends a shiver of pleasure down my spine. The thrill of the two of us together out in the open courses through me.

"Are you mad, Marie-Claire? You usually say more."

"Jean-Jacques Duclos, I'm surprised to see you."

"You sound mad, but I know you to be sweet like a honeyed pear."

"I'm a fruit? What are you talking about?"

"You're not like other girls."

"There are other girls, Jean-Jacques?"

"I feel different when I'm with you. I want to tell you more, but I have tasks to do before I can."

"Tell me now. Then I'll decide if I'll wait. I think I have waited long enough."

The bench behind me creaks.

Before I can turn, he plants his hands on either side of me, a thumb's width from my shoulders. "No need, mademoiselle. I think I know you, what you want. You made a decision long ago."

I'm not sure what he means, but it's hard to think with his breath on my neck. "I'm going away to fight for my freedom. There's talk among the gens de couleur to fight with France to aid the Americans. Free or enslaved can serve, and if I do, I'll be a free man. Liberty, Marie-Claire. I want it most of all."

"Free or enslaved can both die. War requires no distinction to kill. Horrible plan, Jean-Jacques. And you'll have to hurt people."

"I will do what I must." His sigh is harsh. His voice rises. "I'll raise my gun and imagine every Grand Blanc who's caused suffering, who's humbled my mother, who hurt my friends. Every soul who has bled for their profits, I'll kill them all. I—"

Rearing forward, I shake my head. "I've never heard you speak this way. Jean-Jacques?"

A minute surely spins past. Then I hear his big chortle. It sounds gentle, like the boy I know. "I'm sorry to bring such violence to you. But I will take pleasure in bringing liberty to others."

Easing back, I try to understand. "You're a good man. Don't forget that."

"Fighting is in my blood. It's my legacy."

"The legends your Tante Toya tells you are fantastic, but all your family is dead. Only this aunt lives. Fighting cannot be the way."

"Holding weapons, spears and knives, feels right. But I have not held you yet."

My pulse awakens and readies me to run to him, but I must stay calm and dissuade him from going to war. Yet hadn't I just encouraged Elise to fight? "America is too far away. No one can visit."

"It's war, Marie-Claire, there's little time to be social."

"Then how can we continue?" I feel like a weakened vessel ready to shatter. I didn't know, not until this moment, how much I love Jean-Jacques.

I fold my arms about me to catch myself from falling deeper. The pew is the only thing keeping me upright. "If you go, how will I know you're well? And if you cannot come back, how will I know? You'll just stop showing up. That's the way I'll know you're dead."

His finger is on my face, flicking away tears. His skin is rough from toiling on a habitation, but it brings the comfort of his warmth and the knowledge that he's here and safe. "You'll know. Like you felt me in a garden or in a market square. That's how I sensed you in Place d'Armes."

"Didn't stop you from dancing with that girl."

"I like to dance. Always have. It's a shame to waste a song or a dare."

His thumb traces my neck. In the pew, I'm leaning back as far as I can to feel more of his hands. Just a little longer, longer than a moment—it's all I may ever have of him.

"You'll know. I'm always with you, as you're with me."

We've never done this, never touched deliberately. The brush of his fingers along the fabric of my dress, my elbow, the edge of my bosom—this is new. I hunger for more.

"I see no other way to gain my freedom. It will take a long time to earn enough selling fruit in the markets. The military seems right. Les Chasseurs will use the knowledge in my blood to win battles. Maybe someday I can fight to free everyone here, as my people are free in Calmina."

Fighting? Non. He could be killed. Yet if this is his dream, I can't discourage him. "You'll be a fine soldier. I can see you in French blue. But what if Monsieur Duclos refuses to let you join?"

"I'll work hard to persuade him, just as I have persuaded you we should be together."

What? "Persuaded me how?"

"You know I have, and when I return from battle, we'll stand in a church like this and I will say to you, 'Mwen, Janjak, pran ou, Marie-Claire, yo dwe madanm mwen.'"

He quoted the priest's marriage vows, but in his sweet Kreyòl. He begins anew. "Gen epi kenbe jou sa a pi devan, which is to have and to hold from this day forward."

My head falls back. I'm looking at him upside down as he makes promises for us.

"For better or for worse," he says, "for richer, for poorer, till death separates us."

"Those are serious words, Jean-Jacques. It would preclude you from dancing with other women."

"Then make sure you're always available. I do like to dance."

His lips are close. His breath burns my cheek. His fingers stroke my jaw. This is scandalous and thrilling, and I want his hands and his lips on me.

Then I remember myself and pop my head upright. Elise and Maman are right. I want to be a wife, Jean-Jacques's.

"You need another plan, sir. You have to be free, then we—"

Noises pound down the hall.

Then they become clearer, footsteps.

Three distinct pairs. Two coming, one going away.

When I see my aunt and the priest enter the sanctuary, I know my love has fled. No need to look when his absence draws heat from my soul. I cross my arms again hoping some stays inside to keep me warm, but that's when I discover it's always been there, my longing for him, my birth-year twin, the young man who's won my heart.

But fighting in a war a sea away? He could die alone.

"Marie-Claire, I have the music." Elise hovers near my pew. "Marie-Claire, are you all right? You're flushed."

"Fine. Caught a chill."

"In this heat?"

I nod and keep trying to hold in my fears. Oh, the saints must forgive me for fibbing in church. I'm disturbed, even a little lost. Jean-Jacques craves to fight as much as he lusts for dance. Until he has won his desires, I'm not enough.

13

Toya

1777

Cormier Habitation

The sweltering sun dampened my tunic. The rough osnaburg scratched my wet, sweaty shoulder. I had stopped wearing the fancy linen. It was time to resist in every way until I found the path forward.

My Janjak was miserable. He had a plan to join Les Chasseurs and fight in the Americas. Duclos said no and humiliated him, making him wait on Massa's nephew—carrying his portmanteaus, plates, cleaning after him—anything the Blanc had deemed women's work, as if that were the highest insult.

It wasn't.

Women always did the things that needed to be done, from protecting kings to creating them.

The conch sounded. Three short blasts and then a long one meant we were to gather at the grassy hill in front of Massa's grand-casa. I called it the kpodoji, as Tegbesu would.

My king couldn't be dead. That was just another way for Nosakhere to corrupt me and use my skills for his evil.

When I arrived to the kpodoji, I saw Massa at the top sporting his Sunday indigo waistcoat with shiny silver buttons. That meant he'd act the fool showing us his wealth or power.

Garnier spied me and shook his head as if to offer me a warning. It was unnecessary. I saw Massa strutting and steeled myself for this performance.

Duclos stretched his arms wide. "Samuel, my boy," he said to his nephew, "when you run a habitation as big as this, you must maintain discipline. Show no mercy." Massa's voice and laugh were loud.

Three women in jewel-toned madras skirts woven from banana fibers fanned Duclos and his nephew. One was Fleur, and my heart broke.

They stood around waving palm fronds, sweeping them through the humid, sticky air. The jade-colored scarves on the women's heads should have been used to cover their breasts. Duclos had these poor souls exposed, their brown skin polished in oils to look exotic for the Blancs' lust.

The nephew, a tall skinny man, leered at the women, as did all the commandeurs, including Garnier. They'd snicker at our blackness but took every opportunity to behold our skin. Deep down, they coveted us as treasures.

Tegbesu, who'd be arrayed in rich robes and sitting beneath an umbrella in his kpodoji, hid his first wives with veils. They were revered. My king valued women. That meant something.

"Some of you are new to Cormier," Duclos said as he motioned for the women to stop. "Let this be an example of how I deal with treachery."

With a snapped finger, he had the commandeurs bring forward two young men, Da'mon and Agwé. They'd been beaten, stripped, and bound at the wrists.

"Non. Not them." My voice barely came out. Knowing what came next, my gut felt kicked in, trampled by elephants.

If the king of Cormier heard me, he ignored me and shouted commands. Three other enslaved men dug holes.

Da'mon, the proud boy with his long braids, wept and begged for his life. Agwé stayed silent and stared at the ditch that would become his grave.

"That looks deep enough." Massa peered over his gut, which had grown bigger from eating the fat of the land. "Yes, good and deep."

The nephew, the next in line to be king, laughed. "You're really going to kill them for returning late from their leisure time, Oncle? That's not theft or rebellion."

"That's stealing from my table," Duclos said. "The new clarifications from the colonial assembly say I can do anything to the enslaved. And I shall. These men are condemned to die."

The way he said *men* was as if Da'mon and Agwé were old. They were young, barely nineteen. I'd watched these boys grow from children. They were precious and curious and eager to explore the world.

I couldn't look up, couldn't bear to see the sobbing faces of their mothers. As a warrior, as giver of care to these boys, I had to. When I lifted my chin, I watched Duclos close his fist to the pleas of mercy. It transported me to those times when Tegbesu did the same. A parade of faces danced before me, the men I executed because my king chose death. He picked the ones to be sold, too. He was guilty and so was I.

"Bury them up to their necks!" Duclos clapped as each man-child was dropped into holes.

Da'mon pleaded, "Massa, tanpri, pitye; Massa, please, mercy. Massa, tanpri. Massa, tanpri, pitye."

Duclos sneered. "Should've respected my time."

Nosakhere strode to me. He was draped in a tunic with striped short pants covering his legs, but I thought of his mutilation and wondered if he'd begged when sentenced like Da'mon or had he remained stoic like Agwé?

"What's happening, Gaou Toya?"

Hated that he gave me honor using my title, the title that handed me the authority to execute people for my king. The remaining rocks in my chest became dust. I coughed and ached inside. "The syrup death. Massa pours boiling cane on slaves buried up to their heads. The hot sugar burns like fire. The sweet honey scent makes them like immature elephants. The aroma invites the ants to come and feast on their flesh."

Nosakhere's face wrinkled. He stopped looking at me. That was good. Because my eyes began to leak.

"Treason? Spying? Touching Massa's wives or concubines?"

"Non." I shook my head, dried my faces. "Late returning from town."

Janjak came from a far field, his mouth dropping open. He was closer to Da'mon and Agwé than his half brothers. When he wiped at his eyes, I prayed to Ga, to Zinzi, to Zinsu to make my boy stay back and not give Duclos a reason to claim another life.

The Minos training, the rote way we practiced, made me feel no sorrow over the dead. I felt nothing for those I executed or sent to Ouidah. I took pride in doing my best for the king. Being here in Saint-Domingue with Eghosa and the young and all the suffering . . . a dam, the wall holding in the sadness, crumbled. I felt now what I should've felt then—pity and regret and the greatest sorrow. *Gaou Hangbé, was this why I had to separate? To see evil for evil? To remember pain? To repent?*

Garnier took the shovel from one of the diggers. "They're done. But, Monsieur Duclos, I thought we agreed not to do these punishments anymore. We can stop here with just giving the boys a good scare."

Cheeks reddening like he'd been slapped, Duclos shook his head. "Nothing teaches a slave better than harsh consequences. My nephew's starting a habitation down the road." He patted the fellow on the back. "He's learning how to handle chattel. Garnier, the buckets."

Da'mon and Agwé struggled but the gray dirt covered them, leaving only their faces visible.

Two women carried steaming vessels filled with boiling cane straight from the presser's cooking pot.

They put them at Duclos's feet and ran.

"All of you are cowards," Massa said. "Toya's afraid of nothing. Come pour these out. Exact my punishment."

He wasn't my king. I didn't have one anymore. I glared at him. "Don't do this. You'll call down death on your household."

Hands on his fine waistcoat, Duclos looked up to the sky. "I let my superstitions constrain me too long. I'm not beholden to your gods or you."

I boldly stepped forward. "Don't do this. Show mercy. Pitye, pitye. Bless your house, don't curse your family."

"Toya, I tolerate you. But don't say another word unless I have a third hole dug." His glance wasn't at me. It was toward Janjak, who'd only been saved because of the menial tasks Massa set him to.

I should be grateful that what I treasured most—mine and Eghosa's seed—had been spared.

I wasn't Gaou or Dahomey anymore. I was Adbara or maybe I'd become brave Iya. "Burn me in the sugar fire instead. Massa, let these two have a chance to see tomorrow."

Hat in hand, Garnier came to Duclos. "The poisonings still happen elsewhere but not here. They've stopped since she arrived. Let's not tempt fate."

The soft rebuke made Massa's face redden more. He stared at the crowd. "You're not condemned today, *Victoria*. Those slaves are. Garnier, pour the sugar."

"But sir?"

"Do it, Garnier!"

The commandeur's pale face turned bright garnet, as if he'd been burned by the syrup. He grabbed the buckets, made a mark of the cross on his chest, then dumped them.

The boys screamed.

The burning ooze dripped.

Hot sugar tore into their scalps.

It melted and pooled at their chins.

The scent of death and sugar called to the ants.

"Done, Duclos. No more." Garnier's voice was grumbly and low. Yet he'd do his king's bidding again if asked. He was weak, weak the way I had been to Tegbesu.

"The lesson is over." Garnier waved and blew his conch. "Go back to your work or provision grounds."

Nosakhere forced my feet to move. He stayed at my side. "If the two enslaved are not dead by midnight, I'll finish their execution. It will be painless. I've made knives."

Grabbing his arm, I looked at him. "You can't do Duclos's bidding. He's not our king."

"These men have been sentenced to die. Death should have honor and be humane and quick, not this. That's what a good king would do."

Was he right? I wasn't sure anymore.

I let go of him, only to see Fleur wailing as she was scrubbed and draped in white sheets to entertain Duclos's nephew.

This wasn't the way.

It was only a matter of time before it was Janjak dying like his friends, or his soul rotting away like Eghosa's, like Fleur's would soon do.

Watching Nosakhere's proud march to the provision grounds spoke to another way.

Partnering with the devil had to be better than living in hell.

WITHOUT ASKING, NOSAKHERE STRUTTED INTO MY HUT AND SAT near my fire kettle. He tossed his knife to the ground. It was jagged but sharp like a spear . . . and stained with fresh blood.

"It is done. This place is as bad as the other places I was sold."

If he wanted me to ask his story, I wouldn't. There was no space in my head for more sorrows. Instead I wetted a cloth and tossed it to him. "Clean it. Nothing needs to incriminate you."

Scooping up the knife, he wiped the blade, then dropped the bloody rag into my firepot. He sat crossing his legs and leaning forward. "Adbaraya Toya, despite the show today, the habitation is poorly protected. The commandeurs have few weapons. Most are drinking. We can take them."

"What do you mean 'we'?"

He picked up his knife. An image of flames reflected along the blade. "I've seen how the people look at you. Even Duclos's headman depends on you. You could have them follow us."

"No Petit Blanc is going to follow a Black. And no woman should help you."

"There's no convincing the great Gaou." He stood. "I'm leaving Cormier."

"To go where?"

"The hills. I've heard men are seeking refuge there. The Blancs don't chase. They fear Vodun spirits. The Arawak and Taíno tribes help the enslaved. They've hated the Blancs since the Spanish army conquered them. You can imagine the indignities they've suffered. Spanish massas are as bad as French ones."

I stoked the flames until every bit of the cloth had burned. "Something poetic about white cloth being burned tar black."

"One last time, Gaou Toya, you lead us. I'll follow you. After the cruelty we've witnessed today, who wouldn't join us?"

Maybe it was fear of what he asked masked in madness, but my laughter came quick. "There is no us. If I put my back to you, one of your self-made knives will wind up in my spine."

"That would never happen."

"Nothing is stopping you from leading a rebellion here or leading one from the mountains. Perhaps the Taíno will crown you king. It's what you want."

"I'm no king. And the Taíno, who are the most trusting of people, won't put faith in someone whose own people have none. After today's cruelties, the enslaved have to believe in someone to protect them. That's not me."

Was he saying he had faith in me? The feeling wasn't mutual. "Perhaps the people of Cormier sense your treachery."

"I'm a viper, very much an asp. But you miss the battle. The chase, the hunt, the strategies. You want revenge. I saw it on your face. Massa and his men must see their end soon."

"Have to put what's best first. A true leader will come, one for the whole island, not just here. The gods will give us a plan to win. I've seen it in my prayers. He'll make the people believe, and he'll bring true liberty, true peace."

"You want me to wait for this miracle, Toya? How long? Until I'm old and useless? No. I head to the hills tonight."

"Do it. Stop talking about it. Don't have a woman take a risk for you. Or take the blame when things fail. The first instance of trouble, you'll quit, and blame me like you did Eghosa. If I'd been weak, you'd have gotten away with everything."

"I was weak. And I failed her and myself, but you're strong. You sold yourself into hell." He put his large hands to the base of his neck. The curse he made was guttural and deep. "You'll never forgive me. I must die for you to think I've changed. You'd make a good king, like Duclos and Tegbesu. Both are unforgiving. Both demand living sacrifices."

He strode to the door. "One day you'll beg to be on my side, because you know I'm right."

When he turned, he bumped into Janjak and knocked him over.

He grimaced, then looked at me.

"Janjak is Eghosa's son. The first of her three. He's the only one of pure African blood, royal blood."

Nosakhere's face became unreadable, but he must know what I meant. If there was anything good in him, he'd stay for his son.

This supposedly reformed counselor looked at his own flesh, then went out into the black night.

The selfish man hadn't changed.

This boy, my son, was better without the father who'd rejected him. Janjak was my seed, now and forever.

"Why is your face like that, Tante Toya?" He got off the ground, dusted his pants. "You look like I feel, ready to fight."

"I'm ready to slay, son. And you need to be ready, too. You go after what you want. No blaming Duclos. No waiting on others. Do what you have to do."

"Even if I must risk my life going against Duclos?"

I took him into my arms and gave him the embrace Eghosa would give. "Everything is a risk. The whims of a bad king mean nothing is promised. I'll let you become the man you're called to be."

"Good. For there is a woman in Le Cap at Place Royale. Marie-Claire Lobelot. If I die, she must know it was with honor. I promised to let her know."

Nodding, I couldn't have been prouder or more fearful. Janjak was ready to rebel, to take control of his life, and it stretched beyond the Cormier Habitation.

Staring at the knife, I imagined throwing it and carving up elephants. The leaders promised by the gods would come. My son was ready to serve. I would be a faithful Gaou, willing to be used by the gods to overthrow all the massas of Saint-Domingue.

The Prophecy

One day gods from heaven came down.

The earth shook, dancing from the sound.

Zinsu, Zinsi will loose the bound,

And this hope made the world feel new.

Poisons and flames, evil whirled.

Lightning and venom, arms hurled.

But twins set out to save the world.

Alone, apart, their missions grew.

Plague and black death were on each head.

The blood of kin paints the land red.

Violation claimed every bed.

Judgment only escaped a few.

—ANONYMOUS, STYLED IN THE FORM OF UTENZI

14

Marie-Claire

1786
Cap-Français

As a favor to my grand-mère, I show the dashing cartwright from Port-au-Prince around the grounds. She's partial to him. Many are, with his kind silver blue eyes, easy smile, and dimples.

"Monsieur Lunic," I say, "Place Royale is special. Now that you have a larger position, supplying not only the carts for the church and hospital but carpentry, too, everyone will love your artistry. The chair you made Mamie is wonderful."

It is grand, with beautiful turned spindles. It rivals Grand-père's rocking chair.

"Thank you for the compliment, Mademoiselle Bonheur. Your grand-mère was instrumental in the priest seeing my talent. The chair is a small token." He takes a deep breath as if he's willing the sea breeze to reach us. "With the growth of Hôpital de la Charité, I'll have to examine everything anew. I loved it before. It can only get better."

His tone is merry. His conversation has vigor. I like talking with him.

He leads me away from the hospital. "Madame Lobelot says you're particularly fond of gardens. I'd love for you to show them to me."

Non. Not my special place with Jean-Jacques. "I do love the gardens, but you'll have a better tour with the botanists. They can name all the plants and where they originate from around the world."

We keep moving down Chemin du Port-au-Prince. The entry to the garden is on my left, and I force myself not to look or hope for Jean-Jacques. He's working hard to earn his manumission. He only visits once a month.

We pass the Bazac. When I sneak food here, there are fewer enslaved to feed. Not sure if it is the Capuchin way or if the bulk have been sold to appease the Grand Blancs. They want the order to be dependent on tithes, not the money generated from slave labor.

"Mademoiselle? Mademoiselle?"

"Oui. Oh, pardon."

He offers an understanding smile. "I said this is the route I take to my house in Port-au-Prince. You, your lovely aunt, and your grand-mère should come. It's beautiful. Only in need of a woman's care."

"I suppose one has to hire a maid."

He shrugs and laughs. His face is pleasant, ruddy and lean. When he's happy his eyes seem to brighten beneath his long eyelashes. He turns back toward the hospital. "This city can be more grand. There should be an arch here to welcome visitors to Le Cap."

"That sounds expensive." I lift my hands and frame the hospital between my thumbs. "I suppose it should be made of wood and built by an ambitious carpenter."

"Non. Not wood but marble, or the best limestone." He tugs my arm onto his. "But the ambition part is right. There's lots of things I want."

I don't think he's talking about stone anymore. And those kind eyes have sharpened, with the same intensity I see in my love's.

I pull away. "Do tell me of the latest with the colonies; you said your shippers brought news."

"Nothing but instability. Many of the supply contracts I had in America are null and void. The British contracts. I suppose I should celebrate the Americans' independence and renegotiate."

"Well, according to the priests"—and my aunt's papers—"the peace treaty allows you to do so." The Treaty of Paris was signed in '83, and he's still grousing?

"Une jeune femme intelligente. Very smart woman."

"The priests are, Monsieur Lunic. I merely listen."

"You're a good listener." His smile broadens, and he moves and gives me a chance to smell the cedar of his latest project. It's in his coat. "You think it is wrong for people to want their liberty?"

He looks at me and then to the brown dirt road beneath my slippers. The man must know I'm not many generations from enslaved blood.

"I suppose my thinking must sound old to a young woman like you."

I'm unsure of his age, probably thirty-five or forty. And I'm not young at twenty-eight. "Well, a tad stodgy sometimes, but I still like our conversations. You must understand liberty is the most important thing."

Tall, well built, carrying himself with an elevated grace in a loose cravat and waistcoat, he slows his gait and I stumble on the fringed hem of the new pale-rose gown Mamie has given me.

He steadies me, his arm wrapping about mine. "I'm glad I'm not too old to have my thinking challenged. Dans une grande âme tout est grand."

The saying from Blaise Pascal about great minds thinking great things shows Lunic is enlightened. His voice is pleasant, his French divine, better than I would assume for a man who makes a living with his hands.

No wonder Mamie likes him; a learned man with ambition won't long be relegated to the Petite Blanc station. Lunic will build a fortune and be elevated to my grand-père's status, one of the next generations of Grand Blancs.

As nice as he is, Lunic is not what I want. Though our chats are lovely, I'll not lead him astray. "It's time to head back. I must pick up the bread from the baker's. Thank you for this walk."

"Mademoiselle, wait. I will help you. I insist. S'il te plaît, laisse moi t'aider."

It would be rude to dash off. I nod and allow him to follow. The loaves typically load my arms and I could tip over in this gown. "Merci beaucoup. If the baker has the ones for the hospital prepared, it can be quite a lot."

He places a finger to his chin and taps. "You do not like the gathering of bread."

"It's one of my favorite chores. I don't want a single person to go hungry."

"The world needs to hear from more people like you, mademoiselle."

His words send warmth to my cheeks. I hope he does not notice how I crave to be listened to, not pacified or disregarded.

"My brother was in Pondichéry with the French India Company. When it dissolved, he moved to Delhi. He's still there working with the British East India Company to aid with the famine. The Chalisa famine is widespread. The suffering is horrible. He says hunger is a horrid way to die."

Images of Léogâne, the suffering of many, fill my head. Maman and I fed a lot of people. I turn back to the Bazac and think I helped when I could. But it is not enough.

"Are you well, Mademoiselle Bonheur?" He put his hand on my shoulder. "How can you let me talk while you're being overwhelmed by the heat?"

"I'm fine, Monsieur Lunic. And it's good to have a sibling to be proud of. I'm an only child."

"I love my brother. He and his family will soon sail to Saint-Domingue."

Peering up at him, I notice the gentleness and care in his face. Locks of sandy brown hair with streaks of gray are tied back to keep from falling to his high cheekbones.

"Monsieur, I truly am well. I'm isolated here. I wonder about feeding people outside these grounds."

"Mademoiselle Bonheur, hunger is everywhere." He strokes his chin. "The building with the bakery is far from the hospital. I shall make you a cart. That will ease your burdens."

"Non. You don't have to."

At the baker's shop, Lunic traps my hand. "Tomorrow, a picnic lunch in your garden. You can tell more of feeding people and convince me not to make a present for you."

"Non, monsieur. Mamie will need me in the hospital."

He doesn't move. He stares, then I realize he still has my hand. "You need to go through the door, mademoiselle. I'm to help you with the bread."

I do as he says and enter the baker's shop. Later, when I'm alone, I'll come up with the words to tell Jean-Jacques I need change. I need to see if I can help outside of Place Royal. And I cannot keep fighting my mother or Mamie when they may be right. To be still in my grand-mère's care, with no family of my own or even a husband to help, feels lonely, sad and lonely.

I'm not Elise, and I'm not called to be celibate, not when I dream of the man I can't have.

It's ridiculous to keep hoping for a future with Jean-Jacques if he's never to be free.

15

Marie-Claire

1787
Cap-Français

The gardens of Charity Hospital are loveliest in spring. Yet it is when I'm the loneliest. Another year has passed and I'm still sitting on the bench, still waiting for my friend to show.

I feel the warmth leave the basket of fresh kasav. I brought it for Jean-Jacques, along with a calabash of water and a bowl of soup.

I've been experimenting with what will make people healthy, especially if they haven't eaten in a while. The botanists say pumpkins have the most nutrition. The sound of my chopping can't be hidden, but the brothers don't mind my cooking when I tell them it is to help the poor. They assume poor Blancs. I intend all.

A breeze stirs. I look around but I don't see Jean-Jacques. He works on his leisure day, even on the day for church. He's selling fruit, vegetables, and even pots in the markets, doing everything to earn enough to be free. This means more meals and walks end up going to Monsieur Lunic.

The handy cartwright is appreciative, and I'll waste nothing.

Yet my heart is low. I miss the one I miss. Saying goodbye to the love I built in my heart for Wide Eyes hurts as bad as my worries, my wondering where he is.

I sit and wait until the sun begins to fall, then a whisper cascades down my neck.

"Marie-Claire," Jean-Jacques says, "I've missed you. I hoped you'd be here."

Hands, his rough hands, caress my throat, then trace a path to my ear.

The warm feel of him.

Mangoes. The scent of them and limes clings to his shirt. "Hunting for fruit again?"

His eyes slant to the left. His sheepish grin shows. "Must take what I need to survive."

I wave a finger at him. "Monsieur Jean-Jacques, are you surviving without me? I'm convinced you are."

"Never. I'm working for my ransom. Once I have it, I'll pay Duclos and be free."

"How much longer? We've known each over fifteen years."

He walks around the bench. "Fifteen beautiful years." Jean-Jacques sits beside me. At first there is distance between us, then I scoot, and he does, too, until only my basket separates us. "A snack for us?"

"Yes. For you. Along with water for your thirst and soup for your bones." I uncover the handkerchief and unveil the cold kasav. "How much more must you work? How much must you pay?"

"Long enough. De mèg pa fri; two lean things don't fry. Two poor people shouldn't get married."

"Married?" I fold my arms. "You want to marry someone."

He laughs and shoves a kasav into his mouth. His cheeks fatten for a moment and he says, "If you don't know who, then I'm in the wrong garden."

Pointing to myself, I scoff. "Oh, me? That's who? Why is this the first I'm hearing of this?"

Jean-Jacques takes the napkin and slowly wipes his fingers. I look at him. Perspiration stains his wide sleeves. His posture droops from exhaustion. "I should've returned to Cormier by now, but I couldn't go another moment without looking at you."

"You say such pretty things, but it is not enough."

Picking up the calabash, he swings it between his index finger and thumb. "I see you're trying to marry me again."

My brows scrunch. "What?"

"The marriage ceremony of the Dahomey. You and I drink the same water without spilling a drop."

"My parents? Just like them?"

"What?" he says, almost mocking my surprised tone.

"Like Père and Maman's first wedding. Then they went to the priest at the Church of St. Rose de Lima." I jump off the bench. "Oh! Every time I offered you water . . ."

"Yes, Marie-Claire, you begged me to declare our love."

To accuse him of joking would be wrong. He's serious about his heritage. "Why didn't you say something?"

With a stretch, he moves away. "I couldn't drink your water and bind you to me when I've not secured my liberty. And since you didn't know my intentions after all these years, I'm glad we are merely friends."

"Jean-Jacques—"

He turns to me, his eyes big and shimmering with questions. "You do look like the girl I visit every waking moment. My girl, ma fille," he says with the perfect French I've taught him. "Ma fille should know she's not out of my mind, never."

Striped blue skirts flailing, I run to him and embrace his back. "Don't go."

"I'm not free of you or Duclos. I have to earn his money, then ours." He spins fast and I'm in his arms. "That is, if you're mine?"

"I want . . . I want this, too, Jean-Jacques."

Those hands of his are on my neck again. Then thumbs trail to my chin. Everything in me is tight. I can't breathe waiting for what comes next.

He dips his head and kisses my cheek. His teeth nip the fat of my jaw, but his mouth doesn't touch mine.

"Must you tease after calling me your girl, after saying I'm yours?"

"Want you to be sure. I've been sure since we met."

I squint at him. "But you didn't drink the water."

"You weren't sure. I'm not sure you are now. Marie-Claire, are we betrothed?"

"Let me take you to meet my aunt. She must see you. Elise—"

His hold grows stronger, as if nothing can separate us. "Will she give me your answer?" His hands fall away. "For a woman of such grand ideas . . . maybe you're not grown."

"We're the same age, both born in '58."

"Same year? Perhaps we are related. My sister? That is it, why this is wrong."

"Any man who untangles a woman from a prickly pear cactus without insult must be a brother." I lean up and kiss his nose. "There. Sisterly affection."

When I try playfully to leave, he presses forward and holds me about the waist. "We are at an impasse, but I believe you're the twin to my heart. The piece of my soul that's been missing forever. With your love I can soar to the stars. Do I have your love? Èske mwen gen lanmou ou?"

He asks in his Kreyòl. It sounds silky and pure on his tongue.

"We are twins, like the celestial Gemini," I say. "If you stay until it's dark, I can show you them, our stars. Then you can tell me your dreams again."

"Staying for my woman? You've not answered."

I can't, because the next question will be how long before we can be together. "You'll have to decide if you're Romulus or Remus."

"I think I like the name Romulus. It sounds strong."

"He was the stronger twin. He slew Remus, though."

Jean-Jacques makes a tsk sound in my ear. "Romulus is a nice name, but I'll never hurt you. It's powerful—"

I kiss him, forcing my lips to his, stopping the foolish babble keeping us apart. He's said enough, the not-hurting-me part.

His strong arms scoop me up. My heart slams against his hard chest. Everything becomes wet and warm as he searches my mouth. Dangling like a puppet on strings, I mold to him, clinging to his arms, his shoulders.

All my doubts disappear until he releases me.

"Non." My whimper probably can't be understood. I try to kiss him, but his lips only trail my cheek.

"You're a lady. And we must wait."

I stretch to the bench and pick up the calabash. "Then marry us now. Non, pa gen plis ap tann, pa gen plis dout, pa gen plis reta." I say the words in Kreyòl like Père does to my mother, then murmur them again. Jean-Jacques must know I love him and have no doubts.

He puts my palms to his face, covering those big lips I hunger to taste.

"Non. Not yet. I'll see you here the first Sunday of every month. And we will plan our lives. I need only three more months to earn the rest of the money. I want to be free to wed you in a chapel. You do agree, Remus?"

"Jean-Jacques, a few months mean nothing. But what is it you're not saying?"

His eyes pin shut, then open and he gazes to the stars.

In that instance, I know everything. "You don't know if he'll free you. Monsieur Duclos may say non."

Jean-Jacques tries to dance me about the bench. "He'll make the decision when he sees the silver. Then I'll have my wife and my freedom." He kisses my palm. "I must go."

It hurts to let him leave. I want to say his status doesn't matter.

But it does.

It matters where we live, where we can go, and it matters to our children's future. They would be enslaved, property of Monsieur Duclos.

"We are betrothed, Marie-Claire. That's all I can give you and be fair."

It isn't enough. I should be woman enough to tell him all this time away is too much. My mouth stays closed, for I must see him again.

"One day, my love, we will dance under our stars all night. I'll not leave."

"Wait." I run to the bench and take the pot of soup and the last of the kasav. "For your journey back, to nourish you. But I'll hold on to the calabash of water."

"My wife-to-be can cook more than kasav. I'm a lucky man."

With a final kiss to my fingers, he disappears into the bushes.

Dissuading my mother from coercing me to marry or move back to Léogâne will be difficult. But I will, knowing soon Jean-Jacques and I can dance under the stars, as friends, as man and wife, as free people, Affranchi.

Still, a part of me knows if he can't gain his freedom, I'll be forced to give him up. Those tortured and abused by Massa still come to the hospital. I'm not strong enough to turn from the safety of Place Royale and risk my freedom to be with an enslaved man.

16

Marie-Claire

1788
Cap-Français

The new year has come. My secret engagement is about to make me burst. This weekend I will bring my betrothed to meet my family. They should dance at my joy and help plan a wedding to celebrate. Yet they'll not hear any of it. They are too busy shouting and destroying each other in the halls of Hôpital de la Charité.

"Mamie, Maman, Elise." My lips tremble and my hands, too. "We should pray for the women they've brought in. Let us be at peace. It's the new year, La Saint-Sylvestre."

As always, none of them look my way. It's as if I've said nothing.

Maman's gold skin flushes red. "It's your fault. You killed him. You let him die, like you're letting these women. You closed your fist to Père and now those poor souls."

Mamie's whole body shakes. "Sainte, calm yourself before you say too much."

Elise flounces from the bench and crosses the white and gray tiles like she's a chess piece. "Both of you, stop it. We've all done this. We all played a part in Père's death. The sooner we admit it, the sooner we can heal. But our problems are nothing. Two women have been mutilated by a planter. There's a Grand Blanc in Saint-Domingue who has killed at will."

"Where have you been? Or is it not written about in your papers?" Mamie rocks on a bench. Her hands still vibrate. "A quiet war has been happening since '58. The Blancs' abuses have never stopped, so the poisonings continue. It will grow worse. The enslaved and the Affranchi see the injustice. The Code Noir lets anything happen on the habitations with no punishment."

"Poisoning is wrong." My maman's voice rings loud and clear like she's singing a piercing opera, the villain's part. "All violence is wrong. Someone must pay."

Mamie fans her hand toward her face. "Stay out of this, Sainte. The administrators will be here soon. Don't confuse things with your hate."

My grand-mère's skin is ashen. The poor woman has been closed in a room with the victims since they arrived. She's given them laudanum and prayed. Tired, her face drawn, Mamie sits with us but hasn't taken a moment to wipe their blood from her arms.

Taking off my apron, I expose my yellow gown to ruin, but I must mop the stains from her wonderful olive-brown hands.

She mumbles, then scrubs her fingers hard, as if to rub off the skin. "Their master didn't find any evidence. The Grand Blanc brutalized them anyway. Le Jeune is a monster."

"Evidence! Someone's guilty." Maman paces. "There are two women dying in there. Maimed. And you're out here choosing to let them die, just like Père."

Mamie doesn't look guilty. She looks hurt, stabbed through her heart.

Moans come from the room.

"I'll give them more laudanum." Holding my breath, I go to the patients. The door bangs as it closes behind me. The stench, the odor of death, slaps my face. It's not unfamiliar. I work the hospital floors. I clean beds and sores and prepare bodies to be buried.

But this is worse.

It's the stench of prolonged rot. The sheets on the first woman have slipped. I witness burnt limbs, chopped-off feet.

Her lips move, asking softly for something to drink. I dip the sponge Mamie has set beside the cot into a water basin and hold it to the patient's mouth.

She's weak, slipping away, but suckles like a babe.

The other woman is sobbing from pain. Before I can do anything, the room fills with men. The governor of Saint-Domingue, Vincent de

Mazade, has come. He and the physicians and others hover, lift sheets, and examine these women. Each man grimaces.

"Le Jeune has gone too far," the governor says. "This is terrible."

De Mazade has expelled planters for cruelties, but he often looks the other way, according to Elise's *Affiches Américaines*.

A big-nosed man swipes his sweaty forehead. "He suspected the women of helping with the poisoning."

I re-cover one of the dying women. "But he found no evidence and tortured them anyway." All the men heard my voice. They are looking at me.

The governor nods. "There were no poisonings on Le Jeune's habitation. The darn fool had a dream these wenches did this. He's killed two others. You see what's left of these."

"They're women, not wenches." For a moment, I cover my mouth. Then I shrug off the Blancs' stares and wipe the brow of this moaning soul. "I could get you soup. Would you like that?"

She nods, and I wipe a tear from her eye. "I'll feed you."

A man with a magnifying glass coughs and covers his nose with a handkerchief. "This is inhumane, but no jury of his peers will convict Le Jeune. The corrections to the Code Noir required by your assembly, de Mazade, specified no precedents will be set that restrict a planter's right to do what he wishes to his chattel. You can't punish Le Jeune."

"Even for murder?" Monsieur Lunic is here and is wearing more white than I've ever seen. "Gentlemen, the enslaved are railing against the harsh treatment," he says. "If Le Jeune is not punished, they'll rise up, this will be the start of revolts. The enslaved men number more than the fish in the sea. How will we withstand when they are morally right?"

The man with the looking glass stands up straight. "It's our way. We've dealt with rebellions before. We'll do it again."

The hungry woman moans. I touch her shoulder for she has no hand to hold. The look of death is in her brown eye. "No soup for you. But a hymn." I hum to her and pray for Mother Mary and St. Louise to feed this one when they welcome this sister home.

She's quiet now. I cover her with the sheet and back out the door.

Mamie's right. A war has been happening for years. It goes unnoticed because it's led by women. Lunic brings up male slaves, trying to use fear to stir the others, but I doubt those Blancs will ever think it wrong to kill any Black or Colored, whether man or woman.

My eyes lift to my family. Maman and Mamie are loud, still arguing. Elise is pretending to sleep in the corner, her way of getting away from their fighting.

Crossing to Maman, I put my hands on her shoulders. "There's nothing Mamie can do. One woman is dead. The other is unconscious and soon will be gone. Nothing will change that. Nothing can bring your father back."

Trembling, Maman looks lost. "She could've . . . He was alive until he ate my broth, broth she helped me make. She did it."

The veils from my eyes are torn away. Maman doesn't just believe Mamie refused to save Grand-père; she believes Mamie poisoned him.

My grand-mère says nothing.

Was my mother right? Is Mamie a soldier in the quiet war?

Elise stands up and glares at them, at me. She looks guilty. She must believe it, too.

Away.

I have to be away from them.

I run down the hall.

Elise chases and catches me at the outer doors. "Please, Marie-Claire, let me explain."

"Non. I don't want lies. I want something of my own that's true."

Ripping at the doors, I run from the hospital as fast as I can. By the time I look up, I've fled to the other side of Place Royale. Pacing faster, I pick up my weighty skirts. The sunny yellow stripes of the fabric bear mud, dust, and blood on the hem.

I stand in the middle of the rue and cry. I cry until I'm hoarse and I can't smell or taste death.

My day is spent. I head for the garden, and I might stay there all night. I can't go back.

Deep inside the grove, I run to my bench and bawl again like a babe.

"Marie-Claire? You're crying."

Jean-Jacques? "Did I dream you here? It's not the weekend."

"Everything is crazed. Fourteen enslaved people left their habitation and went to the governor's. They came to complain about torture. They want justice. Everyone wants to know what is to be done with a massa who—"

I rush into his arms, and he holds me tightly.

His face has a big purple bruise. Making my touch easy, I put my pinky to his cheek. "Jean-Jacques, what happened?"

He jerks back. "Like I said, everything is crazed right now."

"Sorry, my love."

"My face will heal. You talk. Tell me, what's upset you?"

How can I tell him one is deceased and the other will be dead before dawn and nothing happen to Le Jeune?

I can't.

He'll return to the habitation, which gives him no rights. This time he will join with others and kill the Blancs, like he told me in Notre-Dame de l'Assomption. Then Jean-Jacques will be beaten or burned or bludgeoned to death.

His wide eyes are on me and my hunger for him makes it hard for either of us to pull away.

With my palm in his, he eases our union to his chin. "Run away with me. Kouri avè m'!"

His Kreyòl sounds right, but I'm angry and scared.

His mouth vibrates as if he's thinking hard about something. Then he shrugs and turns his dark face to the sky.

It takes him forever to look back at me.

The knowing silence is the answer, but I need for him to admit the truth. "Say it, my love. Say it, then we can face it together."

"Duclos won't honor any price, not with the poisonings. He'll not free me, and I can't be without you." The pain in his face crushes my heart. "I've failed, Marie-Claire. Things took too long. It's never the right time for us . . . If you send me away, I'll understand."

"Never." I hold him, capturing him as if he's smoke rising and vanishing. "Our hearts are twins; our paths should be, too."

"You're my air, but Massa's cruelty—"

He stops and bites his lips, his beautiful lips. "If I were to die, I want to have us. That memory is what I want. Send me away forever with that wish."

"But we're not married, Jean-Jacques."

"We are. We are one. A hypocrite priest who has slaves working the fields cares not for an enslaved man's ceremony. Has it been too long? Have we lost our chance?"

I clasp his hand and lead him to the stream babbling in the distance. "Is that enough water for the Dahomey wedding ceremony?"

His smile returns. He helps me push the volume of my looped skirt out of the way and I sit in the jade grasses. On his knees, he locks his hands together and scoops them full of water. "Drink without spilling."

Cupping my hands beneath his to make sure nothing leaks, I put my lips to his fingers. The stream smells clean and fresh. It almost makes the scent of death go away. Only mangoes and the salt of Jean-Jacques's skin can push it from me.

The sips bring the cold to my tongue, like I hope the sponge did for the women. Then he lowers his head and drinks. Our foreheads join, and he slurps the last of the water.

His wet hands go to my face. "We are one. Married. Run away with me to the mountains. Tante Toya has trained me to live off the land. I'll teach you."

Escaping Maman, Mamie, and Elise sounds easy, but I've just begun as a governess here. My brown face has gained a little in this unfair world. "Non. The Brothers are letting me teach next month. It is the first time someone like me has been allowed. My grand-mère is able to be a nurse but has never taught Blanc students."

His eyes dart. "Perhaps I asked my questions out of order. We are married but still not going to be together?"

"I can earn money now to help free you. I can. Then our children will be free."

His fingers, still freezing from the water, are on my nose, my lips. "You're thinking of my children? Having them? Guess you are the right one."

Shivering, I blow on his hands to warm them, as if we could be cold on a boiling day. "What more is a wife to do?"

"Marie-Claire, the maroons live in the mountains. We could—"

My kisses draw him away from telling me things I don't want to hear. I don't want anything safe and proper. I've waited long enough. Jean-Jacques is mine. I claim him, as I claimed Le Cap, and my position at the hospital.

With my hands folding about his shoulders, I'll make him forget any plans he has but loving me.

The touch of his mouth this time is different.

He's different.

His fingers are urgent, with caresses that linger. I feel his cold hand slipping beneath my kerchief. His palms squeeze my bosom, then he fishes me out of ribbons—the ones on my stays, then the lilac ones in my braids.

His hands shift again to the laces crisscrossing my chest. I realize he's searching the layers to get to my heart. Doesn't he know he has it?

His tattered shirt falls away. The scarred muscles of a man are in front of me.

He lifts me to his lap and his fingers sink into the taffeta and clasp the satin, the garters holding my stockings.

His palms cup my thighs, his rough hand heats my silky skin. "J'adore, Marie-Claire. Love me, wife of my soul."

My face falls to his bare chest, my mouth resting on his scars, both old and new. "More suffering?"

"Every moment you're not close is a torture. My liberty and you— it's all I want. I'll do as you ask. You teach, and I'll keep saving, but I will dream of this every night."

By the brook babbling secrets, he's careful with my buttons and unwinds the bindings of my breasts. The storm that's always in his wide eyes rains. Unexpected tears leak when he presses close, joining my body to his. Clutching his back, I witness his mouth biting back his aches. Things tear and shift.

Pain and joy slip past each other until we move as one.

We are remade.

The newness, this union thrusts inside, pushing me to leap at the sky, which is now purple and twinkling for us. I'm completely his.

His breathing slows as he slips to my side. We listen to the calm waters. My head stays on his chest, and I promise myself to remember each beat.

He kisses my hand. "I'll go back and earn the last livre, and I'll visit my wife like she lives in another village in Dahomey. We'll be separate a little longer." His hand sweeps over my abdomen. "As long as this is home."

His voice is hoarse like mine and filled with questions.

He doubts my plan will work, but neither of us cares. We've lived too long without this love.

I sink my fingers into his tightly curled hair. It's wild and thick. "Yes, my husband, together there's nothing we can't do."

"Husband." His smile, one I haven't seen in ages, returns, brilliant and full. "And together sounds fine."

"A husband who listens to my voice." I kiss him, soaking in his eyes. As the tension in me returns, darkness covers our entwined limbs like a blanket. "All the stars are out, even the ones I first showed you, Romulus and Remus."

"Yes, the Gemini's constellation. One can guide troops by the stars. It's nice the gods gave us so many."

My arms wrap around him, and we let the night claim our lovemaking—every touch, every movement, every breath, his and mine swirling. It's all to be remembered and relived like it's the last.

I watch him become spent, breathing hard; I know he'll burst. He must know every time I send him away, he takes all of me.

"Our courtship of a lifetime started here. May we be happy beyond this garden, beyond all walls except the house we call ours. As loving as Romulus and Remus."

Jean-Jacques doesn't remember the story quite right. Romulus slew Remus over a dispute of a city wall. I don't want to fight with him.

Looking up into the eyes I've longed for forever, I know he'll never hurt me, not like the Lobelot women with their lies.

Rising to his love, I want our union to be stronger than reason or fear. The music of the garden demands that we dance again until everything is glistening with dew and sated.

His words are clear and slow—"Mwen renmen ou. Mwen renmen ou." And I answer with my love, "J'adore. J'adore."

In his eyes, I hope I see forever, and I try to forget that Jean-Jacques must return to a man who can kill him and all chattel at will.

17

Toya

1789

Cormier Habitation

Duclos had his man, the Brit, whip Janjak again. The fool commandeur giggled every time my boy's body convulsed. He'd tied Janjak to one of the whitewashed posts on the veranda, the newly painted hounwa of the grand-casa.

Decked in fresh white like the veranda, Duclos wore a waistcoat with gold thread and the expensive knee breeches he'd worn to church. Standing close to the flogging, he jerked as blood splattered on his stockings.

The crowd of enslaved murmured but didn't move. They were numb to Massa's cruelty. Like me, they were waiting for the right moment to rebel.

When Janjak returned from Le Cap, he confirmed that women burned and left tied to fences by Massa Le Jeune had died. Everyone knew the evil would face no consequences. This lit a fire under every person. They were ready to overthrow Duclos, even tempt the commandeurs who carried guns.

The Brit's cat-o'-nine-tails, formed of leather strips and shards of glass, cut deep into Janjak's flesh.

"What has gotten into you, boy?" Duclos said. "You're one of my best workers."

"I told the truth," Janjak gasped. "Le Jeune is a murderer."

The Brit reached back. The leather made a whirling sound in the air, then a snap when he struck Janjak.

Blood poured. The bits of his shredded shirt remaining looked like bandages from an amputation.

Couldn't stand this, not another moment. "Stop. He's earning money for his freedom."

Massa smiled. "No freedom. For you or him."

"I'm almost to four hundred livres." Janjak spat blood. "A hundred forty yet to earn."

Duclos must've forgotten he wore silk slippers, for he stepped into the red puddle. He cursed and said, "Well, the price goes up another hundred livres to buy me new shoes."

Janjak looked unconscious.

I took my walking stick and used it to tangle the straps of the whip. "Enough. I do the medicine here. I keep the enslaved strong. Your profit comes from their strength. A wise king knows when he's proved his point."

"Your king, huh?" Something changed in Massa's eyes. "Am I king to you, Toya?" He'd said the name I wanted with a half-smile, half-sneer, then waved off the Brit. "Untie him."

The man looked disappointed. "Yes, Monsieur Duclos." Garnier came from the back of the crowd, whispered to Janjak, and helped him stand before shouting to dismiss the crowd.

Duclos, who usually snickered at his own savagery, was no longer smiling. Maybe the hardened look on the Black and Brown faces frightened him. It would take little to spark violence, even a full revolt.

He walked over to me. "Am I savage enough to be like your kings? I hear they decorate their palaces with skulls."

"Do you want praise, Massa, or are you asking for forgiveness?"

His dark blue, almost black eyes narrowed. "You won't beg for your life or his, will you?"

"Why don't you strike me, Massa?" I shook my staff and slipped the whip to the ground. "That's what you want to do."

His head dipped to the bloody instrument. Wiping his sweaty brow, he looked again to the crowd of enslaved, not moving, waiting for a command to rebel. "The way you're revered on the habitation, what good would come from it? Probably get folks enraged and do stupid things like at the Le Jeune Habitation."

They hadn't started poisoning here, but it would happen. I could see it. The women were tired of losing their sons and daughters. Nosakhere would laugh at my stupidity then rally the people. Even without the great plan, I was ready to rebel.

"Is there nothing that will break you?" Duclos leered at the wounds to Jean-Jacques's back. "Maybe I need to keep torturing him until you find your voice—"

"To say what, Massa? Something to help you feel good? Nothing will. My voice, the will of my resistance, eats at you. More in the late hour when you try to rest."

His eyes zipped back and forth. "One day when I know I can control the outcry, I'll dump the hot slurry on you myself."

"That's too slow of a way to die. It needs to be quick, like the nephew whose funeral you came from. I suppose the gods did request one from your household after all."

He turned back, glaring at me like an inferno. "I loved that boy. He was good, and his chattel . . . someone poisoned him. They say he writhed for an hour, until he begged to die. That's not right. Shouldn't have happened."

There was pain in his voice. The loss of this one soul cut Duclos to ribbons. I felt his pain, for one unexplainable minute. Poison deaths could be agonizing, melting the insides . . . like hot sugar slurry on flesh. The massa who always seemed inhuman sounded wounded, but I offered him nothing—not a laugh nor a condolence.

"I've no successor, Toya." His voice choked. "No one to own the Cormier when I'm gone."

"Give it to your chattel. They've worked it and made it prosperous."

Growling, he went into his house. Tomorrow, he'd forget he spoke to me on his veranda like I was human.

When I got to my hut, Garnier had laid Janjak out on his bedroll. "What are you doing, boy?" he asked. "You're smarter than this."

"I need my liberty. I'll work for Duclos, but as a free man."

"Not going to happen. Not now." Head shaking, the commandeur strolled out my door, his gaze never lifting to me.

Taking water and salve, I cleaned Janjak's wounds. "Is she worth it?"

He winced as I washed the long cuts to his back. "Yes. My wife is."

"Your limbs will be stiff. Exercise them."

"Then I'll be stiff tomorrow. Did you hear me? I said my wife."

"Janjak."

"I have to be with her. Marie-Claire Bonheur Duclos is my reason for breathing."

"I've seen you with other girls. Why is this one worth dying for?"

"She believes in me and stars. Her eyes have hope. Nothing has taken it. My friend Fleur lost hers, maybe forever."

That was true. Fleur and so many others needed saving from the abuses.

He hummed softly as I bandaged his wounds. The tune was the old song of the poisoner Mackandal. With the wave of killings happening on the habitations, everyone sang it.

Two would come to change the world. Was it me aligning with Nosakhere? Had I rejected the gods' plan because of my pride?

A Gaou was meant to serve one of royal blood, but I'd sent the king's nephew away. We could've joined forces and brought redemption sooner. How many had perished because I was waiting for a sign?

I pressed on Janjak's bandages, the cloth soaking through with his royal blood. I prayed and replaced them with fresh ones.

Once he healed, we would leave and I'd begin to lead. It was time to make things right for Janjak and all the enslaved of Cormier.

THINGS STAYED TENSE FOR MONTHS, BUT MY SON AVOIDED MASSA, healed, and continued to visit his wife in Le Cap. Finishing my chores in the sick house, I marched back to my hut. Now that he'd recovered, we needed to discuss running off into the hills.

"Janjak—"

His bedroll was empty. Had he fled to Le Cap for his girl?

Monsieur Garnier came up to me. His ruddy face was pale. "Monsieur Duclos has sold Janjak. He's making an example of him."

I ran toward the grand-casa, but Garnier stepped in front of me and grabbed my walking stick. "Don't do it. I know you love Janjak, but Duclos will just make it worse."

Seizing my cane, I swung it like a spear. "I'll end this."

The commandeur's boots pounded behind me. "Toya. No. Toya!!!"

He caught up to my side. "When Duclos's nephew was killed, was it one of your curses?"

These fools who ran everything were fearful of their own shadows. If abused women coming to my hospital were shown out of *caution* the herbs that brought painful deaths, was this wrong?

No. And I kept at it.

"Toya? Toya, please." Garnier danced in front of me. "Think it through. The children, everyone here who depends on you to keep the balance."

"Maybe I don't want the responsibility anymore. No more appeasement."

He held up his hands and almost touched me.

I tripped him with my walking stick, then jabbed it into his throat. "You know better."

He gasped, but he was not the man I wanted dead. I charged anew toward the grand-casa. I made a picture in my head of the large house, with its wide veranda framed by the mountains. I'd keep it when I destroyed everything.

The screams.

The sounds of death.

Twirling my walking stick, I got close. I was prepared to end this.

A man was bound, his flesh torn. Like yesterday, blood coated everything.

But the prisoner was not Janjak.

I lowered my staff. "What is going on?"

Duclos put down the whip. "Ah, Toya, another one for your sick house. That is, if he makes it. He shouldn't have been late. No one has learned."

Then I spied Janjak, with his hands bound, on the back of a dray.

Before I could get to him, Duclos blocked my path. "That one is no longer any of your concern."

I towered over this man, but his commandeurs, even the new ones he'd hired, had guns in their hands. That was his answer to rebellions—bullets.

"Duclos, you know he's my concern." I went around him toward the dray.

Massa followed. "Well, he won't be for long. I've sold him off to the boilers."

At the boilers, the heat burned water out of the skin, the tongue. Men were broken and died in a year or less.

I caught up to the side of the dray.

"Tante Toya, take this money. Get it to my wife. She'll need it for the baby."

Baby? Duclos was going to destroy Janjak and his family.

Massa took the handkerchief from me. "This will pay for my new shoes."

The horse began to pull the dray up the palm-tree-lined drive. Running, I put my hand on its wall close to Janjak.

"Tell Marie-Claire. She's in the garden of Le Cap in Place Royale. Tell her I won't be back for her and the baby. Tell her she's the twin to my heart."

I stopped running and watched my seed be carted away to the blasted sugar boilers. Then he was gone, and I walked back to the hounwa.

Garnier untied the broken body of the poor man who'd died. The body fell to the ground with a thud.

Massa took off his hat and wiped his forehead. "Toya, I know the man who bought him gives no leisure time. He'll be worked to death soon enough."

"You're letting someone else do your dirty work, Massa?"

Laughing, he fanned himself. "Your curses only apply if I kill him. And you need to suffer knowing your boy will die."

After putting on his hat, he sat on a chair in his hounwa, putting his feet up on the rail.

My gaze went past him to the hills. They were calling me, calling me out of this misery.

But first, I had to complete a mission for Janjak.

That woman carrying his seed in Le Cap needed to know he'd never return. When I stumbled into my hut, I grieved on Janjak's bedroll. It was stained with his blood. I prayed and prayed.

I needed the gods, the twin stars, to remove my stubbornness. I was ready to bring revolution and liberty. I was ready to end Massa's reign. For Janjak, I was ready to fight to the death.

The Prophecy

One day gods from heaven came down.

The earth shook, dancing from the sound.

Zinsu, Zinsi will loose the bound,

And this hope made the world feel new.

Virgin wombs bore warriors tway.

Romulus and Remus, they say,

These Marassa battled always.

To find who's right and who will rue.

No forgiveness made heaven cry.

Brother against brother, many die.

Burn rues and chemins, death is nigh,

When the days are done, only pain grew.

—ANONYMOUS, STYLED IN THE FORM OF UTENZI

18

Marie-Claire

1789

Cap-Français

My heart beats hard within the corset. It needs to be loosened. The secret, this bundle of love in my abdomen, can't be hidden for much longer. But this is the least of my worries. I'm scared. In this garden of blooms and plantings and memories, I stand alone. Janjak has not visited in weeks.

Sitting on our bench, I close my eyes. Images of the humid day, the babbling brook, and him, him and me, we . . . that's all that's left. I must prepare for the possibility that he's gone. Duclos has killed him or he's fallen in a mountain pass or faced the anger of someone who does not like his face, his skin. Everything is against him, against us. All will soon target our baby.

The brush rustles behind me. I chide myself for getting worked up. Standing, I turn to greet my husband and the ache of a lifetime fills my chest. It's not him but a fierce-looking woman.

"Did you come for the hospital?" I point back toward the rue. "At the end of the rue."

She taps her long crook-necked staff. "Marie-Claire?"

My mouth dries. I purse my lips. "Oui."

"Brown-skin girl. Just as Janjak described." Her tone is deep. Her words are short, and her words are thicker than my love's tongue. "Janjak sent me."

That heart of mine keeps thudding louder and louder. I barely remember to breathe.

Her face stiffens, but her frown lines appear.

I say what she can't, what my heart has whispered in the night and every moment of the day. "He's not coming back. He said he'd send me word. How did he die?"

"Duclos sold him off to the boilers."

I exhale, grinning with relief. "He has a new owner . . . Tante Toya?"

"I am she."

Of course it's her. She's the vision of the strong woman Jean-Jacques talks about. And who else would he trust to convey a message. But she's not smiling.

My heart throbs. *He's not coming back.* "Madame Toya, are you here to say his new owner won't allow him leisure time?"

"No one returns from the sugar boilers. Enslaved men perish there, more than anywhere else. There you are sent to die."

My knees give way, and she lunges to catch me.

She helps me to the bench, the bench where I held him, where our love began. "What does Janjak see in such soft ones?"

Fanning my brow, I raise my gaze to hers. "I'm not soft. It's the heat, and I'm with child." His child—I want to scream this. "He almost had the money for his freedom."

"You and he trusted a Grand Blanc to keep his word? Maybe that's why you're drawn to each other, the need to believe lies."

Cradling my stomach, I close my eyes and relive my memories. Jean-Jacques took half of my heart. This babe will put a piece back. "I have something of him to keep. You've come at the right moment. You kept his promise. Thank you."

"Eghosa's handiwork, to choose a fragile vessel for our son."

"What?"

Toya leans on her staff. "With your wiles. Your easy voice. You swayed him. He kept taking great risks."

"Non." Tears leak down my cheeks. "Maybe. It's . . . I didn't take enough risks for him. He said he wanted to run away. We should have fled. Now he's gone, and I am to blame."

I swipe at my endlessly leaking eyes and put a hand over my stomach, as if it too will be ripped away. "I wanted our baby free."

Toya walks to the bushes, toward the stream where Jean-Jacques and I married, shared dreams, and conceived our secret.

I run, and catch her elbow. "Do you want something to eat? You must've come a long way."

This woman, deeply ebony and beautiful with the cut lines of her arms and legs, shakes her head. "I saw an ogbono . . . a mango bush, like the ones from my home. I picked a few. The skin is taut with a little give. They will be ready for my journey."

"I make soup to strengthen Jean-Jacques. He usually takes some for his journey back to Cormier. Kasav, too."

"I'm not returning to Cormier or Duclos's hands."

She didn't look lost or confused, but I was. "Where, then?"

"Gbowélé. The place I was me. I have to find me."

I'm frightened for her, but she seems calm and lifts her eyes to the cloudy sky. "I'll take some soup. I have a long way to travel."

"It will be my thanks for the peace you've given. Sit. I'll return shortly."

"There's no peace until there is freedom. There's only appeasement to a king, whoever he may be."

I understand her dialect and hear the beauty and truth. I also see that I am soft. I am a coward. I should've gone with Jean-Jacques and found our Gbowélé.

Once she sits, I begin to head to the convent's kitchen but she stops me with her staff. "Protect his seed. Let the babe know he descends from royal blood and great power. Let him know. Don't make him afraid to use it."

Her voice echoes as I hurry to get the provisions. I don't know what she means exactly, but I know this babe has to be protected. I'm a free woman carrying an enslaved man's babe. I need to figure out how to keep all I have left of Jean-Jacques safe from harm and chains.

IN MY TINY ROOM IN THE MONASTERY, PÈRE SITS STOICALLY ON A chair Monsieur Lunic has made for me. It was a surprise, something he'd worked on between his travels. It looks like a match to the ones he'd made for Mamie and the governor. My father's dark hand runs along the mahogany spindle; he seems royal and tired. I'm exhausted, too, listening to Maman, Mamie, and Elise arguing and blaming the pregnant belly I can no longer hide.

My aunt paces with my sheets in her hands. They bear no stains of my menses. It has been a long time since any have. She brought them for proof, but I'd already confessed.

"Marie-Claire," she says, "how could you? You have disgraced yourself."

"No disgrace. I married in secret, but the babe's father is dead."

Maman looks warm. She's pulled the kerchief from her shoulders and fans redness that's spread from her bosom to her throat. "Is that the truth or a lie? Have you nothing else to say?"

There's plenty to say, but she does not want to hear.

That I'm in the deepest love, head-under-water deep.

That Jean-Jacques's arms made me forget all the ways their fighting has hurt me.

"This baby is coming. I'll raise him and pour my love into him."

Elise's face becomes pink like the flowers on her printed cotton gown. "This sin cannot be found out by the Brothers. You have jeopardized my position and Mamie's, too. No Black girl will ever be allowed as a governess again. They made exceptions for you. I told them of your being good. You have made me a liar."

"I didn't make you a liar. You know me. You are like my sister, but I can't change the world for you and this babe can't be undone."

"But you are just like my sister. Sainte twists things up to suit her being the victim. You did this for lust."

Passing blame, all the women begin squabbling like noisy wayward hens.

Above their din, I shout, "We wed by his customs! The water ceremony. It was private and just for us."

Père glances at Maman. "He cannot be bad having a Dahomey wedding like our first, chère."

The anger in my mother's light eyes lessens. She offers him a smile, then turns to the window.

"Who's the Affranchi's family? I don't recall one mentioning West African roots."

My aunt has asked the question I hoped no one would, but it is inevitable. "Jean-Jacques was about to buy his freedom."

"An enslaved man? Non, Marie-Claire." Mamie wipes at her eyes. "That baby in your womb—"

"Will be Black and enslaved. The lowest of all things in this colony or the world." Elise covers her mouth. "I didn't mean . . . how it sounds . . . but it is true."

I'm trying to keep my face from breaking into sobs but this hurts as badly as if she'd slapped me. "That's not fair. It's not right."

She tosses the sheets to the floor and puts her hands to her hips. "But it is how the world is. Blanc, then Affranchi-Colored, then Affranchi-Black, then enslaved. Privileges are gained based on status and color."

"Elise," Père says. "This is not helping." He's been quiet. He seems much older. His foot still bothers him from his injury in the earthquake. Yet the love and hurt in his eyes gets to me more than the others. "You found love, Marie-Claire, and it was with a man you chose. I wish you had shared him with us. I wish you had not kept this love and marriage a secret."

Falling at Père's knee, I clasp his hands, his jet ones in my brown fingers. "I loved Jean-Jacques with all of me. Didn't care about his color or his status. He was beautiful. And he loved me."

Père sort of smiles, but there's pain in it. The crinkles, the lift of his lips, is forced. "But only you know this. Your actions say you are ashamed of him, his enslavement, and maybe his color."

Letting go his hands, I let his rebuke knock me flat on my bottom. The padding in my bustle keeps me from crashing to the pine planks, but even the yards of fabric forming my flowery print skirt are not enough to hide from Père's truth. I wanted Jean-Jacques free. I was ashamed and scared to tell my family. But I loved him, his scars, all of him.

His gaze goes to Mamie. "That's your problem with me, Madame Lobelot. Sainte and I sneaking away. I was fearful of you saying no and keeping us apart. I regret not telling you and facing your judgment or wrath head-on."

Mamie went to him. "You're the best man for Sainte. I've seen it all these years. You've made her path easy when I swore it would be hard."

She sticks her palm out to him. "Regrèt, pitit gason m'."

My grand-mère has said she was sorry and calls him son in Kreyòl. She's never done that before.

Père offers his signature smile with his dark eyes sparkling.

Elise and Maman are still mad and red. My aunt asks, "How do we fix things now?"

My father stands, but instead of talking, he whispers something to Maman. Dragging his leg a little, he grabs my aunt's arm and leads both women to the door. "Madame Lobelot, tell my daughter your story. Then she'll know what to do. Marie-Claire won't be pushed into anything. She can make a reasoned decision to protect the life of this babe."

They leave.

The door closes, and Mamie sits in Lunic's fine chair. "Marie-Claire, this is comfortable. More than mine. I'll have to speak to the cartwright about this."

Her easy voice soothes me. I waddle to her and put my hands onto the smooth, tight sleeve of her fitted caraco jacket. "He'll be pleased to make you something."

She pats my hand. "You know you must marry quickly. If anyone suspects . . . your Jean-Jacques's massa can take your babe. Having a child enslaved, subject to the whims of a cruel man, is intolerable."

I wrap my arms about my middle. "Non. That can't happen."

"Monsieur Lunic asks about you. He's concerned about you being poorly. I believe he'll ask for your hand. He's in love with you."

A little nauseous, I walk to the window and try to breathe. "He's a nice man, but I do not love him."

"Marriage is not always about love. Sometimes, it is for convenience.

Sometimes, it's for freedom." Her head falls back against the spindles of the high-backed chair. "Lobelot thought me pretty and sent for me on his habitation. The old enslaved women scrubbed my skin with sea sponges and wrapped me in a white sheet. They told me to enter the grand-casa to lie with my feet spread apart on Massa's bed."

How could the man my mother adored do that? "Mamie, no. Grand-père wouldn't—"

"It is the way of the massas. It is how they treat their wench chattel. Lobelot came to me, lusting for my flesh. And I began to shout, 'Non! Non! Non!' Some humanity returned to him. He stayed away."

"That's when he freed you?"

She laughs, but it sounds dry. "Non. He begged me to be quiet and tossed me out. He took his anger out on the old women for not preparing me right. The next week this happens again. I cry for mercy. He sees me as human. He does not touch me. I told him if he wanted me, he must marry me. He laughed and let me go."

Mamie's boldness doesn't shock me, but to know my grand-père is like the other Grand Blancs hurts.

"Every time he sent for me, I did the same thing. His humor is now anger. He wants to punish me, but I'm a hospitalière, a good one, and they are rare. He needs me. His slaves are healthy. He lets me go.

"The next time he brings up being his mistress. He'll give money and clothing, and even talks of the Code Noir. If I have a baby by a Frenchman and he claims the baby, then I'm instantly freed, my child, too."

That's the law Elise rails at. So, Blanc men tweak the laws to coerce women to indulge Massa's lusts, just for a chance to be free. "You gave in?"

"Non. He tried bribes and food. I knew my teasing drove Lobelot crazy with desire. But marriage was the only way to be assured he'd uphold his promises. Birth records must be correct."

"All of this won your heart? The gifts? The teasing?"

She shakes her head. "The poisonings on the habitations grew worse . . ." Her voice trails off for a moment. "Lobelot was afraid. He knew my cures were one of the things keeping people, even himself, alive."

"Poisonings, Mamie?"

"Yes, some women and men grew tired of the abuse. Many were raped, had babies, and weren't freed. They turned to maroon priests and people who knew herbs to make poisons. Some tainted the waters or served bad food to their master and his family. This time, when Massa Lobelot sends for me, he tries to convince me of the Code Noir once more. I'd be free if I had his child. I told him he could free me if he wanted. I didn't have to be his whore for this to happen. A Grand Blanc can do anything."

Mamie lifted the necklace she wore under the fichu lace beneath her jacket. The chain held a gold band, her wedding band. "He grew tired and came to my hospital on his habitation. He said, 'Fine. I'll marry you.'"

"He freed you. You married him and you were happy?"

"We had two fine daughters. A grand house in the center of Le Cap."

"Were you happy, Mamie?"

A sigh fled her lips. "I was at last safe. My daughters, too. I was happier with Lobelot than being enslaved. I was quite satisfied. If Lunic will marry you, then this child will be his. No one will say a word."

It seems like the hardest thing to do, to marry someone else. Toya called me soft. She's right. If I'd been brave, Jean-Jacques and I would be together in the mountains. He'd be alive.

"Marie-Claire, Monsieur Lunic wants you. As a mother, you do what you must, you become the devil to one, the protector of another. You take steps to be what your child needs."

Jean-Jacques had stayed to please me and legitimately buy his freedom. "Let me talk with Monsieur Lunic. I'll not lie about my situation. If he can accept me and this baby . . ."

Mamie hugs my neck. Her wedding ring on the chain feels cold against my chest.

"All will be well, Marie-Claire. You'll live past the hard parts."

Clinging to her, I vow not to be soft, but to be strong like Toya, like Mamie, and do what I must for this baby. Melting against my grand-mère, I hope her strength pours inside and fills me.

IN THE KITCHEN OF THE MONASTERY, I'M SITTING ON A STOOL WEAR-ing a gown of indigo, two sizes too big.

"Eat up, Monsieur Lunic," Maman says. She hands him another big bowl of my soup. The smell of pumpkin has finally stopped making me ill. I'm thankful for this.

"Mademoiselle Bonheur, this is the best soup I have ever had." Lunic slurps and smiles. He is a pleasant man.

Maman fixed a cup of tea. "You serve here in Le Cap, but also Port-au-Prince. That's close to Léogâne. You'll not be far from a visit, Marie-Claire."

"Port-au-Prince has excellent opera. I'll love to come." Elise is pleased. She has spread gossip Monsieur Lunic is courting me and ex-pects a betrothal any day.

My hand falls absently to my stomach. "Tell us about your city."

"My Port-au-Prince is beautiful," Lunic says. "There's a large hos-pital there helping the poor and the soldiers. When the earthquake—"

"Please, Monsieur, do not talk of the earthquake," Maman says, fanning her face. "I want none of those dreams. My husband almost died. I almost had to live without the love of my life—"

"Maman." I stand and head to the door. "I need air."

She nods and offers an encouraging smile, but Lunic comes to me. "Let's take a stroll, mademoiselle."

"That's not necessary, sir."

He offers me a waggle of his thick brows and a smile. "Indulge me?"

With a nod, I offer my consent. We walk down the hall. I stare at the things he's fixed or made beautiful—a pedestal for a crucifix. Shelves for hymnals.

Lunic places my hand on his arm. Since he always does this, it's not uncomfortable. His jacket is smooth and clean, his breeches tidy. I've seen him covered in sawdust, even in his graying hair. Through the years, we've become friends.

"You've not exactly accepted my proposal. Your mother and aunt, and of course grand-mère, have, but not you. I think it's important for the prospective woman to accept. Don't you?"

"Monsieur Lunic."

"Pierre, ma chère," he says and smiles like he adores me.

"Pierre, I do not love you."

His deep-gray-blue eyes find mine. "That's not a problem. I have enough love for two."

I'm blinking at him. "How? You don't know me."

"I've seen you caring for the sick in the barracks. You sing to one. Write letters for another. You make up a poem for a dying man, for him to believe his sweetheart still cares."

Lunic holds my hand, and we continue to walk. "Caring for the sick must be something I get from Mamie. She's a natural healer. Good with medicines and herbs."

"And the poetry? Where do you get that, Marie-Claire? Your mother has wicked lyrics about twins, or was it about Place d'Armes?"

Maman and the old rhyme she sings. I even heard Jean-Jacques . . . My heart stops, and I can't go forward, not another step.

"Chère, are you well?"

"Non. Oui! You're a wonderful man, Monsieur Lunic."

"Pierre, my love. Say it."

"Non. I'm with child."

He nods his head slowly, as if he's reassessing me. "Madame Lobelot mentioned surprises."

"Oh. Mamie has told you. Monsieur—"

"I want a family. I have none. I love my niece, Adélaïde, dearly. But it's not the same."

She's a dear. I've met her several times when she's visited Place Royale. He dotes on her.

Pierre starts us moving a little faster. "She and my brother and the whole family want to meet you. They do not live too far from Place de Clugny."

"Place de Clugny is where the gens de couleur live."

"Oui. My brother leases a fine house there. It's comfortable and affordable. He loves dancing and dining with his neighbors."

I know he says this to put me at ease. That a Petit Blanc will be happy with a Black wife. Somehow it feels true and natural for Pierre.

Marrying him doesn't seem tragic anymore. He's a good man. He's here and is free.

We walk past the garden. My garden. Ours—Jean-Jacques's and mine. "I love this place. I won't see this in Port-au-Prince. Does the hospital have a garden?"

"Nothing as fine as this. But at my cottage, there's plenty of room for flowers and a child, many children."

He lifts my hands and kisses my knuckles. "You cannot wait much longer. I have to return to Port-au-Prince in a few weeks. I want you with me, setting up our home and nesting."

His eyes are kind, but nothing like the ones of my love. "The hospital there needs good women to help nurse the sick back to health. That's the thing you're looking for, chère. You'll find all you need with me and have a new start in Port-au-Prince."

"Monsieur Lunic—"

"Pierre."

"Pierre." His face lights as if he'd waited forever to hear it from my mouth. "Pierre, how do you have such confidence when I have none?"

"I believe in you. I've heard the things you want. I'd like to be one of the things you need." From his pocket, he pulls out a carved horse, with delicate legs and a mane of wavy curls. "For you."

To touch, to take it, would be to accept Pierre.

There isn't much choice when he puts it in my palm.

"What say you, Marie-Claire? A marriage of convenience could lead to love."

There's not much choice in this matter, either.

I can't go home, can't stay in Le Cap as an unwed woman with a child. No one will hire a pregnant, wayward governess.

Yet I can't say the words. I can't let all my dreams of Jean-Jacques go. "Let me take a walk alone, Pierre. Then I will meet you, and we can go talk to the priest."

Closing my hand about his gift, he pulls me close and kisses my brow. "Do not take forever. Your mother frets. I'll head back and tell your maman, grand-mère, and Mademoiselle Lobelot."

With a wave, I send him back to the main building, then I go into the garden.

My eyes need to capture and remember every sight of this place, like the weathered bench and the prickly pear cactus that's grown taller than me.

Here, I remember all the dreams Jean-Jacques and I had. Then I let them go. Clasping the smooth wood in my palm, I run from the garden and catch Pierre on the rue.

"Mademoiselle? Did something frighten you?"

I look up into his handsome wise face. "Non. I think we should tell everyone together."

He kisses my fingers and leads me forward. Silently, I keep chanting, *This is for the best*, until we reach the chapel.

19

Marie-Claire

1791
Cap-Français

Hand in hand, Maman and I near the cathedral at Place d'Armes, Notre-Dame de l'Assomption. I want to continue along Rue d'Anjou and steer us back to Place Royale, but she's slowing.

Her gaze pins to the wood scaffold being erected.

"So much building," she says. "The tree-lined route into the city, Cours de Villeverd, is beautiful. Did they expand your gardens, too?"

When we moved back to Place Royale from Port-au-Prince, the gardens were the first place I went. "They added to them but left the stream and mango grove intact."

We keep walking. The rues are crowded. Le Cap is again changing. "My baby, Françoise . . ."

"Marie Françoise Célimène Lunic is a nice name." She steers us straight ahead, drawing us closer to the hypnotic hammering.

"Elise . . . She's not happy with me, is she?"

My mother looks at me with the sun making her cheeks extra rosy. "She's glad you had a healthy birth. She's thrilled you married Lunic."

That wasn't what I hoped she'd say.

Maman lifts my chin. "I'll not lie to you. You took risks with your life and reputation. My sister has become worse than me and Mamie. She'll find it hard to forgive. But you have to live your life."

I hold her close. Loving Jean-Jacques helped me understand my mother's deep love for Pére. I wished I'd discovered this sooner, not in his final years.

My father had a palsy in the rainy time last year and died this

January on La Saint-Sylvestre. Pierre and I and the baby arrived in time to say goodbye.

Maman held Pére's hand until he slipped away. There was something beautiful about that, looking into loving eyes and saying goodbye.

"Are you and Monsieur Lunic getting along?"

"Fine," I say with a nod, but I'd rather change the subject to how she's living without Père. How does she make it through the day when she remembers a joke they shared? I must keep my heart from breaking when I think of the garden or mangoes or see Françoise's eyes.

The hammering from the square gets louder. "Let's see, Marie-Claire, what's happening."

The venue is tight, packed with vendors. I grip Maman's palm. "We should find some ribbons for Françoise, then head back to the hospital. Mamie will have fun weaving lilac ribbons in Françoise's thick hair."

We turn down Rue Sainte Marie, the street of her old home. Her hands stiffen. "Bwa pele trees line the square now. Not as many elms as before. Place d'Armes looks older. I suppose it is."

As if someone has called to her, she leaves me and heads to the square. The bells of Notre-Dame chime solemnly. I walk faster to keep up to Maman as she weaves between the double rows of trees rimming the square. They have ashy brown bark that peels and splits to show fresh tan patches.

"They're talking of Vincent Ogé. Is he here?"

Ogé's a mulatto businessman who has visited the injured at Place Royale. I remember because Elise talked of him standing up for our rights, the Affranchi's. But Ogé and others truly mean just the free Coloreds, not free Blacks.

"Maman, let's find ribbons elsewhere."

She doesn't budge. "Ogé is bound like a prisoner. What are they doing?"

Soldiers with angel-white sashes hold guns on him and another man. If Elise and I were getting along better, she'd have warned me to avoid the square with news from her renegade papers.

"The death platform, Marie-Claire," Maman says. "They set it up for Ogé and his friend Chavannes? Chavannes is part of the Chasseurs. He's a hero in the American Revolution."

The Chasseurs—that was the army Jean-Jacques wanted to join to fight for his freedom. Part of me wishes he had, but then he could've been killed. I'd not have Françoise.

All the vendors, enslaved and free, run from the square. The crowd fills with more and more Blancs.

"It's happening again." Maman clutches her straw bonnet as if a strong wind will send it sailing, but it's hot with no breeze. Her eyes are focused on the platform. "Mackandal's curse said more would die."

"Maman, what are you talking about? You're scaring me."

"Ogé was in Paris for the French Revolution. He fought for the rights of the Affranchi to vote, to hold office. He swayed them, got the French Assembly to vote for it. He returned a hero. Why is he up there like a criminal?"

I didn't have an answer, and my gut twisted in knots. "Please. S'il vous plaît, Maman. Let's go."

My mother's shaking and clasps my wrist tightly. "They are making an example of Ogé and Chavannes. They aren't the ones of Mackandal's curse, Marie-Claire. They aren't twins bringing liberty."

A chant starts at the back of the Place. "Let them go! Let them go!" The Blancs up front yell, too. "They're starting a rebellion. Guilty! Guilty! Coupable! Coupable!" They drown out the Coloreds.

Absent from these chants are voices like mine, the Black ones.

But I'm used to it, and to condemnation. No one says it out loud anymore. It's in the eyes, the judging scowls. It's the whispers—the gossip in the halls, in the vestibule when I arrive to church with my Black daughter and Blanc husband.

The never-ending stares at the parties Pierre has me attend remind me of my status at the bottom of the free Affranchi world.

These quiet insults aren't as bad as the screams from my broken heart. It thumps that I'm disqualified, a fallen woman, a whore. I'm my worst critic. I have to remember I'm good, and that I deserve a new chance.

"Coupable! Coupable!" The Blancs have drowned the Colored voices again. The crowd keeps growing. Fighting will break out.

Maman slips away and goes to the front.

A man in a French blue jacket and red cuffs reads charges of insurrection.

"We were denied access to a lawyer." Ogé shouts this over and over. "Any free man can, but the Colored Affranchi cannot have representation."

De Blanchelande, the governor, a man who Pierre does projects for, is in the front. He motions to silence Ogé. He wants the crowds calmed as if this execution is just.

The platform creaks as the soldier with the most braiding on his shoulders steps between short Ogé and tall Chavannes. "The sentence of death is as follows. The guilty shall, whilst alive, have their arms, legs, thighs, and spines broken."

The people in the back begin to murmur. "Chavannes fought in the Savannah," someone shouts.

Another yells, "He bled for Saint-Domingue and the Americans in the revolution! Is this how you treat a hero?"

"The French stormed the Bastille for freedom," says a woman. Her voice is pitchy and loud. "Where's the promised liberty for Saint-Domingue?"

A soldier blows a horn.

Silence again covers the square.

"The two afterward will be placed on a wheel with their faces toward Heaven. There they are to stay as long as it pleases God to preserve their lives. Upon their death, their heads are to be cut off and exposed on poles, Vincent Ogé's on the chemin leading to Dondon, and Chavannes's on the rue to La Grande Rivière, opposite the estate of Poisson."

They can't merely die, they must be displayed. Is this where the massas learn cruelty? From the government?

Then I remember, the massas, those Grand Blancs, are the government. Jean-Jacques told me of the tortures on Cormier Habitation. The violence turned my stomach.

Wealthy-looking men in expensive bicorns with cockades of ribbons clap and chant anew, "Coupable! Coupable!"

I can't watch. I must get my mother and leave.

The soldiers begin hitting the condemned. My back is to the platform, but the crunch of breaking bones and their shrieks shake everything within me. "Maman! Maman!"

I see her bonnet and push my way through, pivoting and sidestepping. I look like I'm dancing as I dip under men's extended arms. My cotton caraco jacket fans and flaps at my thighs.

When I get to her, she's as stiff as stone. Her lips move. She's reciting a lyric, something she always hums. Didn't know there were words.

> *One day gods from heaven came down.*
> *The earth shook, dancing from the sound.*
> *Zinsu, Zinsi will loose the bound,*
> *And this hope made the world feel new.*

"Maman, you're scaring me." I touch her face and hope to clear the shadows filling her eyes.

"This happened before, Marie-Claire, the year you were born. I was in the dray. We were caught in crowds like this. And I watched Mackandal, the Maroon, die. The Grand Blancs decided his fate. The Blancs always decide when death comes."

"Let's be gone, Maman."

"Monsieur Lobelot was a Grand Blanc, a very important man. He could have stopped this."

No, he couldn't. My mamie's story made it clear. Grand Blancs only do what they want. "Maman, why would he help two men of color? How would it have benefited Grand-père?"

Her gaze sharpens, snapping to attention. "He could have done it if he wanted. Monsieur Lobelot did whatever he wanted, from marrying my mother when it wasn't quite done to planning to have Guillaume taken away and me sold off."

My mouth drops open. "No one ever said this."

She puts her hand to her temples. "He didn't mean it. He was angry. People say the wrong things when they're angry."

"Did he ever say sorry?"

"Non. He died." She looks lost, her skin pale and clammy. Then she hurries away.

It takes everything in me, even tugging up the hem of my round gown, to run and catch her. I sweep my arms about Maman. "It's in the past."

Soldiers beat the men. Ogé shrieks, then yells, "Last March, the General Assembly in Paris gave free men of color the right to vote. My punishment is for trying to gain my lawful rights. Let us go. Let my men go."

A soldier strikes him on his side. The blow makes Ogé spit blood.

The brutes in the white uniforms with their sashes tie the doomed man to a wooden wheel. It's as big as a cart's wheel. It looks like something Pierre built.

Ogé keeps shouting. "A prejudice too long maintained will fall. There should be no distinction to all free citizens, the right of admission to all offices and functions. That's my crime, trying to enforce France's wishes."

They strike him several times on the hands and legs. The last hit causes a deafening snap. The soldiers have crushed his bones.

Chavannes screams, "Fight, men of color! It is the only way to liberty. Liberty above all."

They pummel him, but he keeps crying out. "Nothing is obtained from the Blancs by their permission. Rise up! Rise up!"

I hate what is being done, but unlike Ogé, Chavannes is only calling for rights for the Colored, not Blacks, not all Affranchi. Even in death there is division.

A soldier strips him. Another makes cuts in his flesh.

Blancs fling their block hats. They shout at the tortured men like the condemned are animals, but those in power are the beasts. They roar as the air is scented with blood.

"Let the sun burn them! Laissez le soleil les brûler!"

"Brûler!"

Ogé and Chavannes's limbs are woven through the spokes of the wooden wheels as if they are yarn for a spinning wheel. Four soldiers pin each disk onto a pole, then lift it high.

"Crucifie-les!" The chant picks up in the crowd. "Crucifie-les! Crucify them, Ogé and Chavannes!"

A team of soldiers turns Ogé upright, like a top.

"Ask for *retentum*, Ogé."

The voice sounds familiar. Cupping my hand to my eyes, I hunt again.

It's Pierre.

The breath leaves my body.

"*Retentum!* Ogé," my husband cries out. "Let them strangle you. You die faster. Less suffering."

The wooden wheels, did Pierre make them? He's standing near the governor. Would he let his gifts be exploited by executioners just for advancement?

Why else would he be here?

Disgusted, I pull my maman. "Let's go. This is too much."

The woman cannot move. She's in a trance, like a Vodun Houngan has bewitched her. As sweetly as Elise, she sings in Kreyòl—my father's language, Jean-Jacques's, now mine and soon my daughter's—the haunting lyrics.

> *No forgiveness made heaven cry.*
> *Brother against brother, many die.*
> *Burn rues and chemins, death is nigh,*
> *When the days are done, only pain grew . . .*

That hum I've heard all my life. They never sang the words, for it's a curse.

Maman's face is different, not fearful. Something else. Her cheeks are red, but those golden eyes burn bright like a candle.

"Ogé and Chavannes, they're not the ones. And these Blancs, they don't know they are feeding the hunger for vengeance. Blood spilled will strengthen the twins. All of Saint-Domingue will pay."

With as much force as I can muster, I drag my mother to the trees. The garlicky smell of the shedding bark makes her cough.

Holding her again, I search for her spirit. I want to make sure it's still inside, not gone to be with Père.

She blinks a hundred times, then hugs me. "I'm well. Ogé and Chavannes are not the ones. They're not fighting for everyone's liberty."

Embracing her, with my chin on her bonnet, I cannot miss the scaffold. A soldier is twisting a cord about Ogé. He's chosen Pierre's way, the quick death.

"Fight the Blancs. They give us nothing by persuasion; we must take by power. Vengeance carry me." Chavannes's cry is loud.

The bells of Notre-Dame de l'Assomption ring. The church where Jean-Jacques and I said our first vows, where he told me of his desire to fight for the Americans like Chavannes, stands by as a witness. This is murder, sanctioned by the legislature, made true by the military.

If he'd gone, Jean-Jacques would have returned free. But would he too be caught by this mob?

"Marie-Claire . . . Marie-Claire?"

Now it is my turn to be silent. How do I answer Maman when my mind is spinning? I'm married to a Petit Blanc capable of building a torture wheel. And Jean-Jacques would be a rebel like Chavannes, but he'd fight for Blacks, all of them.

We say nothing, just flee toward Place Royal, the Hôpital de la Charité. It's our home again, but I'm not sure I want to raise my free Black daughter in a place that won't hear my cry for liberty.

And will kill without mercy or justice.

20

Toya

1791

Bois Caïman

White cotton clouds shrouded me as I walked north out of the mountains. Zinsu and Zinsi, the divine twins, had sent me visions of returning. My time in the wilderness was done. I must leave all my losses behind.

For two years in the wilderness, the gods had given me favor. No Blancs followed. No one threatened me. Maybe all feared a woman who had nothing to lose.

I was alone and at peace with the gods. Agé had allowed my spears to trap the bush anoles, the graceful lizards that roasted well over the fire. Avrikiti, the deity of fishermen, provided plenty of fresh carp from the fast-flowing rivers of the mountains. Then Okanu, the god of dreams, gave me good ones of my Minos, my warrior women. They thrived. They defeated the Oyo.

Nonetheless, dreams had no due date.

"Gaou Hangbé," I called up to the heavens, "I've separated myself again. I'm ready to be restored. Let my way be clear."

I didn't care whether it was hard or easy. At fifty-three, I merely needed the path to be righteous, and this place, Saint-Domingue, was where I'd planted my feet. Time to grow this spot into home and make it right for all.

Down the mountain, walking until the soil turned sandy, then dark, I'd marched across the Acul parish. Smoke rose from a nearby river. The trees here weren't pines but palms and figs. One of the oldest was gnarled and aged but abundant with green and brown jewels. I feasted on the figs and loved the thriving branches.

Though older, my time hadn't passed.

A solenodon—the little furry creatures with long noses and tails—peeked from his burrow.

Dinner. He chose the wrong time to make an appearance.

Slinging my walking stick in one hand and the knife Nosakhere had left me in the other, I gave chase.

Every now and then I thought of the counselor. I hoped he'd found peace. No other person would understand the way I viewed this world, one that needed to be conquered and made safe but him.

The solenodon was fast and led me to a meadow rimmed with palms, the spiral ones, with leaves like a lady's fan.

Noises, bits of conversations, sounded close. Had the gods led me to a trap? Knife firmly held in one balled fist, walking stick raised in the other, I charged.

Spreading leaves, hacking at branches, I launched into a crowded grove.

"Byenveni," a man said, welcoming me. "This is Bois Caïman."

A group of people with black faces, all shades of black—ebony, noir, blue-black, brown-black—stood around dressed in simple cotton dresses, tunics, and breeches.

I lowered my weapons. They looked like me. Some had to be ready to do what was right.

Then I saw the answer. Nosakhere.

He stood off to the side making spears.

My heart leapt, then fell down a crater. Zinsu and Zinsi intended to humble me, sending me back fourteen years, to when I rejected the chance to partner with him to bring liberty.

When his gaze came to me, I knew his thoughts mirrored my questions. Were we ready to start anew or finish yesterday's battle?

If he was the answer, so be it. A warrior seeking redemption needed a mission as much as she needed a war.

In Nosakhere, I had both—a sinner like me who had to make amends for our parts in enslavement and the unfinished battle of wills started at the walls of Calmina.

• • •

THE GREAT COUNSELOR STRODE TOWARD ME. HIS FACE WAS DARKER, his hair long again and twisted in thick braids. Had he become the priest's restored Sampson? Was he looking to bring down temples or to smash my stubborn head between his fists?

"Gaou Adbaraya Toya, you've come to hear the talk?" His stature remained strong. Fourteen years had diminished nothing.

"The noise drew me." My shoulders straightened. I owed him respect for leaving Cormier. If Janjak and I had followed, my son would be alive, alive with that girl, playing father to his own babe. "I will stay to hear."

"Tonight, there is much to learn. Dutty Boukman will unify us. He may have the plan you seek."

The crowd continued to grow. The noise of people consumed the night. I loved it—every word, every language, every laugh.

I heard tongues—some Spanish, some Kreyòl, bits of Twi and Kilong. A few spoke Fon, wonderful Fon.

Nosakhere pointed out a man called Jean-François who gathered wood for a big fire, then another called Biassou who lit it.

Flames grew and heated my cheeks as Nosakhere thanked me for the advice I'd given him. "You told me to go. I've been helping with revolts throughout Saint-Domingue. We've taken advantage of divisions."

Who was we? "What divisions?"

"The Blancs in Saint-Marc don't want to listen to the ones in Le Cap. Some are now royalists. Others call themselves patriots. They fight and kill each other. They turn on their offspring with the Blacks. The Blancs have killed mulatto leaders, but those Browns still refuse to partner with Blacks."

"What does it mean, Nosakhere? Like our people, there are many shades of Black. All should be one."

"No. All want power and someone else to kick," he grumbled, and this time, I saw more scars atop his royal ones. He'd not been sitting around waiting. For a moment, I was ashamed of my inaction. But I had needed my peace. Nothing else could prepare me for a time to act.

"Jeannot," Jean-François called out, "more kindling." The short fellow with rich noir skin went back into the woods. This thin new man groused but did as Jean-François commanded.

"That one is vicious." Nosakhere whispered this to me. "He'd kill a Blanc or Black, free or otherwise, if he suspects you want things to stay the same."

For the counselor to call a man vicious after what we'd experienced meant this Jeannot was one to watch.

"Gaou Toya, the joining of the enslaved on all plantations is the key. That's what we worked for in Mirebalais and Petite-Rivière. We controlled the land and held it until the French army came. Our force of over ten thousand met the resistance with honor. If all of Saint-Domingue can be organized, all the Blacks together can defeat the slavers, whoever they be."

He pointed to the people. "This crowd is hungry for action. Are you ready to act?"

Was this the way I'd begged the gods to show me? "Something will be said tonight to let me know this is my path."

His brow rose, but then he nodded before returning to the men with spears.

Pieces of oak added to the fire crackled and sent a sweet aroma into the air and I waited for flames to speak to my heart.

A woman came to the center of the ring. Her skin was light and reflected the orange and red of the blaze. Her hair seemed straight like the Blancs'. The glow of her eyes was green. This mulatto woman's presence spoke to the truth of what Nosakhere had said. All were needed, and all were uniting.

He joined me again and nudged my shoulder. "That is Cécile Fatiman. She's a Vodou priestess. She attends priest Dutty Boukman. Like a Minos."

Vodou mixed Catholic priests' words with the spirit deities of Africa. Vodou wasn't Vodun, but even I had begun to mix their gods with mine. Maybe this blending was the way for Saint-Domingue.

The priestess began to dance, then, bending on one knee as if holding a Minos's spear, she cried out, welcoming her priest.

Some bowed with their arms stretched.

Nosakhere leaned forward. Then I did, too.

"I will give respect where it's due," he said. "I'll show you the respect I've always had for you."

His face was earnest. The lines in his cheeks showed age. Maybe he'd changed in our time apart.

Lightning struck behind the clearing.

A tree snapped in two, sending limbs crashing to the ground.

The howling winds could be the beginning of a cyclone.

More knelt and whipped their hands, praising.

The sky, which had been beautiful today, gave way to a cloudy night where only two stars, twin stars, shone. They cast light on a priest who entered the camp wearing long purple robes. His braids went to his chin. And I thought of Da'mon, then Agwé and Janjak, even Fleur, who feared fleeing with sickly children—all dead or dying. This was the time for the young, the living to rise.

Another bolt from the clouds descended. It hit the ground, shaking the field. Cécile Fatiman lay prostrate in front of the priest. Her body convulsed. Her tongue sounded heavy and foreign, different from before. Then she said, "Share the message, Boukman."

The priest's eyes had rolled back. He appeared in a trance, stomping closer to Fatiman.

She could be hurt.

When I rose to protect the Minos, Nosakhere grabbed my hand. "Stand down. Dutty Boukman won't hurt the vessel who comes before. No one hurts the one who leads the way . . . or those who come to trust upon them. No one but a fool."

This admission of guilt—the woman who needed to hear it and the son were gone. "Our seed, mine and Eghosa's, is now dead because I had no trust."

Nosakhere looked away.

For a moment, I pitied that he didn't know what a fine man Janjak had become.

"The Good Lord," Boukman said, waving his arms, "who created the sun which gives us light from above, who rouses the sea, makes the thunder roar, demands you meet the moment."

The crowd grew silent when he jumped over Fatiman. "Listen well, all of you: The god, hidden in the clouds, watches us."

Boukman's preaching could've been that of a massa's priest. The seduction of Catholics was powerful. Pity their god didn't make the Blancs do better.

Nosakhere seemed to read my thoughts. He leaned near my ear and said, "Boukman's learned from the Blancs studying their Bible. He can now answer for all the gods."

Pointing at us, Boukman glared. "He sees all the evil done. The god of the Blancs demands from them crimes; ours, the true gods, ask for good."

"Wi. Wi. Wi." The chant, "yes," grew louder, followed by the Kreyòl, "Libète!"

Boukman just missed stepping on his Minos's hand as he went to the right. "Our gods who are good demand vengeance! An eye for an eye."

Pumping his arms like he'd been struck by lightning, he raised his palms. "Direct our hands; aid us. Throw away any god who thirsts for our tears. Listen to the voice of Libète!"

"Libète! Libète! Libète!"

The priest danced off his robe and it floated to the ground like a king's silk. His bare chest showed the scars of oppression, but none of the Dahomey scars.

"Throw off the shackles," Boukman said. "The Blancs must pay. Let us be instruments of justice."

My heart beat fast. Fatiman and Boukman, were they the twins of the enslaved tale, the song of gods coming down? The way people were praising this message, they might be.

Nosakhere helped me to stand, but his hands remained on my staff.

I wrenched free. "You're tempting fate trying to again touch what is the king's."

"Tegbesu is dead. You belong to no one but you. We are our own kings."

He was right, and I listened to the fire. I needed it to say "join, war, win."

The priestess rose. She twirled; her skirt of many colors flared. Then she stood at Boukman's side.

This partnering of dark skin and light, of man and woman, had to be confirmation of this new path.

"Now. The sacrifice." Cécile Fatiman waved forward two men carrying a black pig. The thing was fat and hairy, looking as if it weighed two hundred pounds.

She took a sharp knife and slit the animal's throat. Brass cups collected the blood. It was passed around the audience as communion.

"Drink," Boukman said, "This is our offering, our covenant."

Everyone drank. Then they got up and danced.

"Gaou Adbaraya Toya," Nosakhere said, "we must avenge the blood of the dead."

His dark eyes with smoke rings closed. When they opened, I saw raw pain. "Avenge him and her with me."

Before I could answer, he drank and pressed the cup into my hands. "We work together for now. You train them like Minos. They'll be disciplined in battle. I'll arm them. We are equals in this, Adbaraya."

The Dahomey water ceremony rumbled in my head and this moment called for the marriage of might and revenge.

I jerked the cup fully into my palms, spilled a few drops, then tasted the warm, salty liquid before passing it to the next. "I'm committed, Nosakhere."

The beating of drums took over.

Boukman wanted liberty.

Nosakhere eyed a nation.

Many called for all the Blancs to die.

Since the flames hadn't said what to do, I chose the goal of my soul, to build an army, head to Cormier Habitation, and bring judgment to Duclos's door.

21

Marie-Claire

1791

Cap-Français

Sitting at my grand-mère's bedside in the hospital she's served all these years is heartbreaking. Hôpital de la Charité is filled with injured planters and soldiers. Rebellions have exploded across Saint-Domingue.

Though Pierre wants to return to Port-au-Prince, it's not safe. I'm glad we've stayed. Mamie needs me. I hold her hand, and pray to Mary to return my grand-mère's strength. She's not opened her eyes all day.

Singing softly, Elise is on the other side. Her gaze is pinned to the door. "My sister won't come? This can be Mamie's—"

"Non. Maman says she just wants to be with my baby. She's fearful to leave Françoise with all the fighting happening."

Elise nods, but she knows it's not true. Having lost Père, Maman is lost. She hums the rebellion tune more and more since the execution in Place d'Armes. I've stopped trying to reason with her.

"Marie-Claire, go to your husband. I'll stay with my mother."

Shrugging, I sit, not budging. It's difficult to avoid him in our small rooms. He's angry I was at the execution of Ogé and Chavannes. I'm angry he was there, groveling for favor from Governor de Blanchelande.

Pierre made the wheels but says he didn't know they'd be used for terror. I don't know if it's true.

"Lobelot, forgive her." Mamie's voice is dry.

"She's speaking of Père." Elise comes closer. "He has. He knows you did nothing wrong."

My aunt wipes Mamie's brow. She wrings the cloth and pretends to ignore her mother asking my grand-père to forgive her for his death.

Though I believe it must've been an accident of some sort, this tragedy and unforgiveness has torn the women I love apart.

"Sorry, Lobelot." Mamie says it again, but this time it's not as clear.

Elise touches my hand. "It looks as if her fever has broken. This is good," she says. "I believe my sister is right. Maman will pull through, and we can all get back to our general feuding."

"No more feuding. We need to be happy for what we have. Maman finds joy in caring for Françoise and Adélaïde."

Elise pulls out a copy of *Courrier Politique et Littéraire du Cap-Français.* Her favorite renegade paper, *Affiches Américaines,* has closed. "Is your niece doing better? Have the nightmares fled?"

"A little. Adélaïde's frightened of noises and the dark."

Elise stretches and looks up at the high ceiling. The plaster molding is plain and white. Her voice carries. "I will read to Maman from the papers. The politics and gossip shall rouse her."

"Marie-Claire!"

Pierre calls my name from the door. This is the women's room. He's not allowed.

I wave to him to leave. He crosses his arms. "I'm waiting for you in the hall."

"Go on," Elise says. "Comfort him. Be a good wife to him. I'll take care of Mamie."

Her tone cuts through me. I married Pierre for my child to be free, to have a father. I said those vows because everyone made me believe I had no choice.

Pierre promised he had enough love for both of us.

He doesn't.

There isn't enough when he sees me crying about Françoise's eyes. They are Jean-Jacques's, and I still want him.

The Lobelot women were wrong about me marrying.

Now I am always wrong about everything.

"Marie-Claire, he's waiting."

Lifting myself from the chair, I smooth the cotton skirt of my round gown. The little tulip print in burgundy makes me seem cheery.

There are storm clouds in me. Something is going to crack and lightning will shoot from my heart.

Yet when I stand in front of my husband, I grow silent. I've lost my power to be bold. My voice disappears. It feels the mere scent of him, the fragrant cedarwood he works with, stifles me.

Pierre has no smile and holds out his arm for me to dutifully take it. "Come along, Madame Lunic. My family needs you."

Looking back at Elise, I see she's taken my spot stroking Mamie's hand.

"No delays. My niece is in trouble."

A quick glance at his face shows a tumultuous wave of emotions—fear, love, anger—all sweeping through him.

I clasp the sleeve of his jacket and feel nothing but the smooth weave. We walk and I steel myself to feel his hurt again. For what I can give Pierre in return for his love?

Nothing. I'm never enough.

PIERRE AND I ENTER THE TEACHING PART OF THE CONVENT AND pass through the corridors. My slippers patter ahead of his boots. "The students must be away."

He nods with his serious frown.

For a man who's rushed me from Mamie's bedside, he's oddly quiet. When we arrive at our rooms in the convent, I know why.

Maman looks frightened. "She won't come out of the closet. I've tried everything."

Picking up Françoise, I kiss my baby's head, right on her dark, dark braids. "I'll get Adélaïde out. Go get a cup of the tea Mamie makes for her."

Without asking how her mother is, Maman takes Françoise from my arms and heads to Elise's rooms.

The door closes.

Pierre paces. "Things were going well since her arrival. Adélaïde seemed happier."

How does he miss the dread in the thirteen-year-old's eyes? Or the way she clutches a blanket as if to hide? The memories of her family dying chase the girl.

Men must see only what they want.

He pounds on the closet door. "Adélaïde, I'm back like I said. I'm here with your new friend. Marie-Claire. She'll keep you safe."

The girl doesn't answer, but I hear shifting in the closet.

Waving Pierre away, I sit at the door and offer a light tap. "Your friend is here. Our birthdays are the same day, remember? This year we'll share a treat. What shall it be? A gateau au beurre? Your oncle gets the freshest butter. There's a priest who can . . . get the flavors right."

Mamie has sources for getting the best rums for the buttery cakes, between her old friend Monsieur Joseph and—

My heart stops. No one has told her dear friend she might die. He's been a faithful helper to her since the beginning, since they fled Le Cap when another man was tortured and killed.

Pierre nears. Eyes the door. "She screams something awful when I try to open the door. I should get my tools. I can take the door off the hinges."

"Non." My voice sounds weak and lost.

"What is it, chère?" Pierre put his palms to my face as if to check for a fever. The rough feel of his working hands, the salt and sweat of his fingers, only reminds me that he carves torture wheels using the same hands that cradle my little baby.

"Chère, have you made yourself sick watching over your grand-mère?"

"Non. I'm waiting on Adélaïde to let me in. I must give her time to not see us as monsters. Waiting is important."

His steely blue eyes assess me. Does he know I'm trying to hold on to seeing him as good, trying to find some comfort in our marriage?

"It's just her dreams. Dreams can keep you from seeing what's truly there."

I see the care, how he dotes on my daughter. Pierre's working his way into my hardened heart, but it takes time and trust. I'm low on both.

"Combien de temps vas-tu pleurer . . . how long will you mourn, chère, for things not there?"

That tone, sultry and low, slips through the shield of my ribs. He said this to his niece, but I'm struck.

"Not dreams. Real." Adélaïde's sniffled voice is muffled.

"She's speaking, Pierre."

He touches the door. "My lovely Adélaïde, it's your friends. Please come out."

"I heard the drums. Oncle Pierre, they can't find me."

Pierre's brow scrunches. "It's just the soldiers, our soldiers. The governor has put more here to add security."

Gone.

The illusive closeness I felt fades when he mentions de Blanchelande. That man gloated at the execution. He enjoyed the suffering.

I put my finger to my lips, then whisper, "I've brought comfort to other victims of the riots in Place de Clugny. The soldiers, the French soldiers, didn't take care. They assumed the buildings housed gens de couleur and burnt everything. Adélaïde saw her family destroyed. She hates that she's the only one to survive." I get closer to the crack under the door. "The soldiers are drilling. They'll not come inside. You're safe."

Pierre rattles the door. "Come on out. I have a meeting. Adélaïde?"

My head is shaking, and I point him to leave. "Go see about your governor and your important people. I'll take care of her."

He's dressed in his fancy onyx breeches and white waistcoat. Pierre wipes his hand through his hair, silver and black tied back with white ribbon. "But we are to go together. I want my wife at my side."

"Tonight, I'm at Adélaïde's side. Go on. All will be well."

"Will it?" Head hanging, he walks to the door. He changes out of his boots to evening slippers. Then he disappears.

The little girl comes out of the closet and into my open arms. I nestle her dark head against my bosom. She cries and I do, too.

"It will be all right, Adélaïde. You . . . we can heal."

I say this and want my words to be true.

But I must stop mourning. I come from a line of women who hold grudges and love repeating old fights.

"I promise, Adélaïde. We will heal." Rocking her as if she's small like Françoise, I dig deep inside my hard heart and hope to find the courage to make my words true.

IT'S LATE WHEN PIERRE COMES TO MY BEDCHAMBER. IN THE CAN-dlelight, he looks flustered, upset.

"What is it? The party ended too soon. Not enough politicking?"

Pierre closes my door, but is careful not to slam it and awaken Françoise or Adélaïde, sleeping in the next room. He tosses his fine coat to the floor. His graying hair is scattered and falling out of its ribbon.

The blue-papered walls make his eyes look darker. He crosses the simple yellow rug to my bed.

It's mine. He often sleeps in his workshop or in the sitting area out-side my closed door. He has let me go through my pregnancy and nurs-ing and a dozen other excuses to keep him from my pillows.

The excuses are dry on my tongue.

I can't taste them anymore.

"Tell me who was there tonight." I scoot out of the covers and meet him halfway. "Talk to me about the important people. I'll make us tea."

He catches my hand and kisses it. "The important person is here."

My cheeks warm from his compliment and the way he stares at my soft cream robe with a lilac ribbon about the waist.

We stand, half-intimate, half-strangers, in this bedchamber with furnishings he's built—the chest of drawers, a large bed with knurled posts for the bedframe. He's sculpted a life for us.

"You do love me, Pierre."

"Oui. But I need you to try, Marie-Claire, to love me."

"Did you know what the Governor de Blanchelande would use the wheel for? Tell me the truth."

His hands fall away from mine. "Now you'll put politics between us."

"Politics? Pierre, if we have a son, he'll want rights. He should be able to vote and hold office. The Assembly in France proclaimed it to be."

"One can only have a Colored son if one makes love to his wife."

"His Black wife."

"You're more brown. Delightfully brown, like the best gateau au beurre. And the kisses you have offered are like good rum—sweet . . ."

His fingers undo the knot of my ribbon, then he peels away my robe to expose my nightgown, my skin. "Luscious, full-bodied rum."

It's hard to swallow in the heat of his gaze as he asks, "Will you choose politics and make everything harder? And will you put your life at risk taking kasav and soup to brigands? The guards have told me you take my dray to feed people at night. They only let you come and go because you are my wife. They do not suspect that you, Madame Lunic, would do wrong or put herself at risk."

"People are hungry. The government has burned people, Colored and Black, from their homes. They've seized livelihoods. Blancs are hungry, too. I take what I grow in the gardens or the kasav I bake and feed people at night, when there is less scrutiny. I make sure my actions do not impede your rise."

"It's not safe," Pierre says. He's a large man, lean and tall, but with powerful hands. He's taken down trees between his palms. He slides the rest of my robe to the floor. "Oui. I built the wheel. I had a vague understanding of what they'd use it for. I had no idea Governor de Blanchelande would torture Ogé and Chavannes. I tried to talk him out of it, but de Blanchelande wants to be popular with the Grand Blancs. He's now struggling with the ones who are patriots who wish to defy France and the royalists who support Paris over him."

"Pierre, you let him use you for murder."

"The governor favors me. In his company, I can advance. We can advance. Our son will be beautiful and strong."

"And you'll love him, Pierre, even if his skin is brown like mine."

He parts my robe and kisses my shoulder. "I love you. I want us to have many children. I want you to be lost in their eyes and see me."

His hands slip possessively about my waist. "I'd like to think after all this time, I can please you. That our child will please you."

There's not much to say as he spins me and works away my laces, my caution, and my desire to resist.

The silks fall to the floor.

Then he helps himself to the ribbons on my shift.

I'm naked in front of my husband, naked and shamed.

Pierre puts his lips to my neck and kisses the arch. "Marie-Claire, you're beautiful. I love this skin. Can't think of a brigand or renegade soldier touching you. You must be protected. No more of these night runs alone."

Before I can protest, his mouth covers mine.

It's soft at first, but he's not a gentle man. His hands, rough and hard, seize my bosom. He's trying to coax me into feeling something. His hold is like a hundred arms. He's trying too hard.

"Mon amour," he says, "perhaps if you were with my child, a beautiful Colored child who'll have privilege, the very best of both worlds, this will keep you home. It would fulfill you. Oui, you should have two babies' mouths to feed."

"We have Adélaïde now. It's enough."

"Never enough, Marie-Claire." Pierre lifts me like a board, like a tree trunk he's ready to shape.

I drop onto the bed.

"Oui, Marie-Claire, try for us. Let there be us."

He wants to be easy, but his motions are wild, almost punishing. This man who sculpts the most delicate lasting things is hurried with me, unskilled.

My head keeps saying, *This is love, grown-up love. My husband adores me.*

But my body feels the difference. It remembers being treasured and held until all glistened.

Pierre who wants all, takes me anywhere but ecstasy. I keep hoping everything will feel like what I had, what I lost.

"Chère," he moans. Then he stills. "You have tears. Am I hurting you?"

Non. I have to stop mourning. I have to be a woman and not a child. My eyes—I force them open, wide and focused on him, the man who is here. I put my arms about his neck. I use my voice and say his name. "Non, Pierre. Love me."

Then I kiss him.

Everything slows.

I've taken control. Then I clutch his strong back and help him find a rhythm that's pleasant. Something that can be ours, that can grow. I've given away my first vows and fulfilled mine to Pierre. Two years after we married, we share a bed.

And I let him be with me, even as I cry.

Grown-up love, that's here. I say it and hum it.

And believe until it's done.

He takes me with him under the smooth sheets.

He sleeps without telling me his dreams. There are no stars beaming down on us. Pierre's pale peachy arm stretches over my shoulder, covering my brown breasts.

Light and dark. I weave my fingers with his. Compromises are the price a soul pays to be protected in marriage. And if I do all the things Pierre requires, I can utilize the color-free privileges of being Madame Lunic to feed hungry people everywhere.

22

Toya

1791

Massif du Nord

The morning air of Massif du Nord was crisp and made the lungs open. Marching, I led my troops around the camp. Spears in hand, we moved at a low speed, making our footfalls sure and quiet. At first, I pretended we were escorting the royal wives to the rivulet—too peaceful a notion. Then I imagined we were my fierce Minos on a hunt.

Advancing toward the stream, I saw a black anole sunning itself on the rocks. It wasn't an elephant, but it would do.

With a finger to my lips, I made everyone stand still and pointed to the target. Then I signaled for the attack and flung my spear.

Others did, too, but the launch was uneven.

I speared the anole. Two others were accurate, but the rest hit rocks or splashed into the water. "We need more practice."

"Nooooon." Their groans were loud, disheartening.

This was not a force to take to war. My own training to become a Minos—the tactics imprinted in my mind, all the ways of the Dahomey—I refused. I wouldn't take away their free will, but this left me a team who'd be compromised and die. "I cannot take you to war like this."

Pointing to Sara, the girl in the back, a tall one with hair cut low, I said, "Make a fire."

She had the best aim because we practiced at night, always before bed, throwing spears and learning about stars, just like I had with Janjak.

I motioned to the boy next to her to help. After a little squabbling, Sara convinced him of her way being right, then the two worked together. A fire soon blazed.

I took my speared catch and roasted it.

When it was good and charred, I tossed it to the group. They didn't work together. They tussled and fought. The delicacy was flung to the ground.

"That's not how we treat food." They didn't understand how to work together. These young of Saint-Domingue had been taught to scrape for everything. Nothing but pain was shared.

How do you restore humanity and dignity when they've grown up in a society offering none to Blacks?

I retrieved the trampled thing and washed it in the water. Then I tossed the good bits to specific trainees. The ones who had speared the anole, the ones who made the fire. "No rewards for just coming. You have to take pride in the mission. You have to want to succeed."

The sad looks on their young faces demoralized my spirit. I tapped my spear and summoned them. "Let's head back."

We took the long way to our camp, hiking slowly up the mountain. Music filtered to us, then happy chatter.

Arriving at the plateau, I saw life among the round thatch huts, like Gbowélé. No grand buildings or covered hounwa. No courtyards or kpodoji within protective walls. The welcoming Taíno people had bonded with the maroons here. Native to the mountains, they helped runaways recover from the abuses of the habitations.

It was surprising, Nosakhere being here, participating in the village as a blacksmith. No one mentioned Nosakhere's royal blood. He was a new man, a holy man, here.

"Gaou Toya, may we eat?" Pushed by the others, Célia, the youngest, a girl of twelve, came toward me with dust in her braids, wearing a torn tunic, a faded print of palm fronds.

"Wi. Dismissed," I said, watching them head to their bedrolls or to get a bowl of sweet mush.

Disgusted with my efforts, I sat down to meditate.

Nosakhere stooped beside me. "Harder than you thought?"

He handed me a bowl of labouyi bannann porridge. "You look upset."

I stirred the thick substance, the cooked-down plantains, but couldn't eat. "If I take these young to battle, they will die. We will, too."

I glanced at them, chatting about the fire. Thérèse, a woman in her twenties, got up and danced. "I'm at a loss for how to translate all their energy into battle toughness."

"Gaou, this is as free as they've ever been. It's difficult to change them from this, even to warriors."

He spoke truth, but it was no comfort. "They are young, Nosakhere. Why do I suddenly feel old?"

"Well, we are." Warm chuckles filled his face, smoothing lines created from seeing many suns. "These young born on this soil don't have the experiences we did. They don't understand. It takes more than discipline to prepare them. They are not Dahomey or born to our privileges. These are citizens of this island, Saint-Domingue."

He was right. I wanted them to all respond as I had without making them numb to killing. "Nosakhere, I was scared when the Dahomey attacked my village. They took Gbowélé in a day. Then I was flattered to be chosen by a king. I'd never been chosen before."

"Yes. My uncle knew you were special, the last of the village girls he spared."

I looked at him and saw the recognition in his face that he had helped destroy Gbowélé. If I wanted to be angry, I couldn't muster it. Whatever he had done, it was in service to the king.

"Axɔsu Tegbesu wɛ ɖÓ acɛ daxÓ é è nan ɖɔ lé é mì nan nɔn gbon é nu mì," I said, then he repeated it.

"It's obvious why we fail, Nosakhere. We need a king."

Laughter again filled his face. "No one wants a king. The French one and the Dahomey one are why we are here rebelling." He looked off in the direction of the highest peaks of the range. "Always a mountain. We solve this one problem of training and then move to the next, combat."

He stretched. "The Taínos say there is a new cacique, a new king is coming."

My gaze narrowed.

"Not me. The Spanish are after the island. They're beating the French, which means the Grand Blancs and the French king will lose."

"More people for us to fight?"

"Non, Gaou, the Spanish are winning because they've partnered with Biassou and Toussaint. Two Black men are making their forces win."

I remembered Biassou from Bois Caïman. "Why not Biassou and Boukman or Jeannot?"

"Boukman was arrested by a planter while he was trying to seize a habitation. Jeannot was shot by Jean-François for being too cruel to Blanc prisoners. This Toussaint is the son of the son of a military leader, Gaou Guinon. There are many myths about him. Some have even given him royal blood."

"Myths about a man from West Africa. Gaou Guinon's son was rejected by King Agaja, Tegbesu's father. How can he lead?"

"People have taken the title 'Gaou' to mean king, but I hear Toussaint is effective." He turned and looked at me. "Maybe you, Gaou Toya, are the true king we need."

His chuckles grew loud, then he disappeared, heading toward the high peaks to pray.

Nosakhere was a strange man. But somehow he'd become wise. I needed to figure out a way to instill pride in combat in these young ones, ones who've never been able to protect themselves on the habitations.

The chatter of Sara, the young woman with the best aim, caught my ear. Joy glistened in her eyes as she and Célia and two other girls picked up water pots and headed to the rivulet. Her gloating over her spearing-work encouraged me. Turning joy into pride had to be the way until the new king arose, one who inspired my troops to fight not merely for themselves but for this blended land of Saint-Domingue.

• • •

BRIGHT AND EARLY, I HAD EVERYONE WORKING, STIRRING THE BOIL-
ing pots. We needed to have the dyes ready for uniforms, good clothes
to bring pride to our fight. Nosakhere surely thought I'd lost my head
when I asked him to steal fabric. Many habitations had been abandoned in the valley. I was sure he'd find cotton or linen lying around
the grand-casas.

The man did as I asked without questions. He didn't complain about
anything at all. He trusted I knew what to do.

It was odd for us. He sat quietly watching my pots, the big wood fires
heating them. "Gaou Toya, what kind of chips must I get you now?"

"Bois de Campeche, the logwood. I don't have enough. It makes a
good black dye."

His brow cocked, but he went off with men and women eager to
pray in the mountains. He'd bring it on his return. I asked no questions about how or where; I trusted that they'd find more of the special
wood.

Sara bounced between pots, stirring this one, then that one. "How
do you know when it's done? No stars in the morning sky to guide you."

"The sun's positioning." I pointed to the boundless sky, at the shelf-
like layer of clouds. "When it is highest, the color will be ready."

This happy brown face that had never known enslavement peered
at me with anticipation.

Curiama, an elder woman of the Taíno tribe, brushed sand from the
long apron covering her waist. She said I should use the achiote pod to
make red dye and pointed to the markings on her eyes that looked like
rouge. "The inner seeds of the hull we use to decorate faces."

Her olive skin needed no adornment. Her smile, her inner peace,
was enough.

I was about to say no achiote, something about needing permanent
colors, when I heard someone screaming.

"Gran Toya, Tante Toya!"

Leaving Curiama and Sara to stir my pots, I went to the commotion. A new band of maroons had come to camp. Suddenly, a pretty

woman, pretty like the Krobo women, leaped into my arms. Dark olive arms swaddled my neck. "Gran Toya, you are alive."

I held on to Fleur.

She'd come alone, none of the children that she'd borne were with her. Didn't have to ask what happened. No mother would leave their young unless they had to. For Fleur to be here meant the Cormier Habitation's wet season or Duclos's cruelty had stolen her young.

Fleur cried. I did, too. Then I set her to work boiling marigolds for their yellow color.

WE MARCHED THROUGH THE NIGHT. OUR FORCES, MINE AND NO-sakhere's, were ready for our first battle. Tonight, we'd seize the Fla-ville Habitation at Acul.

This was a test to see if my discipline and strength training combined with the counselor's field assessments and weaponry would prove superior to the skills and guns of the men on the habitation.

Huffing a little, my fellow leader, the grand counselor, motioned to stop. "Time to rest. Flaville is over the ridge. We need to attack at our peak." His posture sagged a little. Our walk had been lengthy, but I suspected he was in pain.

I made the signal, the call of a vulture, a drawn-out lengthy hiss. My troops, especially my core of Minos, stopped in formation, three columns of four.

"We break here, then our forces are tested against Flaville's." After ensuring they were all seated, my three leads, my Minos, Sara, Célia, and Fleur, followed me up to the ridge.

"Get your eyes used to the darkness," I said. "See shadows and movement. You'll be scouts."

Sara, the tallest, plucked at the sash of her jet uniform. "But, Gran Toya, we don't want to leave you." The nervous but loyal young woman peered at me. "What if we fail?"

Célia, the boldest sprite, shook her head, her smooth braids flopping along her shoulders. "Never."

"She's right," Fleur said, nodding to youngest of our group, then she put her hand to her sash and shifted the holder for her knife. "We can do this, Gran Toya—I mean Gaou."

I smiled at the renewed strength in her voice, but I wondered if it would remain after she killed. I'd numbed none to death as in traditional Dahomey training. Yet maybe Fleur had, maybe all but Sara had become hardened, living with Massa's cruelty.

"Rest, Minos. The fight is ahead. It will be fierce. You'll be changed by it."

They began to sit and stretch, but Fleur stayed near me, her hands wound tightly about her spear. Her soulful eyes beamed, *I want change. I want to avenge everything.*

I put my arm on Fleur's shoulder. "You're good because you've taken control. That's better than anything."

Releasing her with a blessing, I sent her to our fighters. Then I looked out into the night, glancing at my past, the images of me and Eghosa leaping out of the Lama Forest, kidding around, making faces in the shining walls of Calmina.

The air stirred a little, like before a storm. The moon shone, but most stars hid behind clouds. Yet, the brightest two shimmered, boldly announcing they were here, watching.

Nosakhere approached. He wore a robe over short baggy pants.

"Still require your legs to be bared for battle."

"The way I was taught, Adbaraya Toya. The old ways. Not bee uniforms."

"Our group is proud. It's what they needed."

He peered up, cupping his hands to his jaw. "Then it is good."

Nosakhere's gaze was strong. Lately, we'd shared tactics and humor and now a sense of unease. At this moment, I saw him for what he was, a man who'd grown from his mistakes.

"I listened to you telling Sara last night about the twins in the sky." His smoke-ringed eyes centered on me. "The way you say it, it sounds like the slave prophecy. Have the gods come down?"

He began to hum the tune Janjak and the children of Cormier sang.

One day gods from heaven came down.
The earth shook, dancing from the sound.
Zinsu, Zinsi will loose the bound,
And this hope made the world feel new.

"Perhaps when we win tonight, counselor, we'll unleash Zinsu and Zinsi to the earth. Then they will tell us what's next. Taking one habitation away from the oppressor doesn't stop the oppression."

"Then we have to kill them all."

There was no humor in his voice. I heard nothing but sadness and truth. "How do we choose who lives and who dies? Which habitation is next? We aren't the king."

"Didn't you say we were all kings?"

"Nosakhere, the French or the Spanish won't allow it. They'll fight back. They have guns. We have to be sure of our next steps."

He eased against a tree. "Are you thinking we aren't ready? You want to back away?"

"No, Nosakhere. I want to win, but this is just one battle."

His glance warmed my face and fed me strength. Then he turned back to the sky. "Your old commandeur at Cormier, Garnier, once said the twin stars were his gods Pollux and Castor or Romulus and Remus."

He and Garnier talked of the night sky? "Didn't think you were the social type."

"When he drank the fool talked to anyone." Nosakhere puffed up his chest. "If Zinsu and Zinsi are up there, what magic do they bring? Do they heal us or finish our war?"

He wasn't talking about the habitations anymore. This thing called common purposes hung between us but so did Eghosa and Janjak and sorrow. Wasn't ready to fully forgive and let my anger go when I needed it to slay bigger dragons. "Let's get ready. We can't afford mistakes."

I glanced over the ridge and looked down at the habitation we'd strike. "Flaville's wife and children, are they away?"

"You care about the slaver's family?"

Some wives, like the always absent Madame Duclos, didn't seem to have much say. "Do the wives of any king, even a Grand Blanc, have a choice?"

Nosakhere laughed. "Our king's wives were protected, but they had power and influence. My uncle's mother was the reason he rose to claim the throne. And the Blancs have women slavers who are just as cruel as Massa, sometimes worse."

In the humid heat of the moment, I felt his story. The cruelty done to him. Emasculated and tortured when trying to redeem himself. "Did that happen here to you? Flaville is personal?"

He didn't answer, just stroked his chin and the beginnings of a beard. "The wife and children are in Le Cap. Massa Flaville rules with an iron hand. He's famous for sawing off limbs."

It was here he'd been punished. "If you want to lead this mission—"

"Non." He pulled at the bush in front of us, tearing at leaves. One smeared his fingers, but I saw my purity ceremony and the single one put on my lips.

I was innocent then, preparing for womanhood and my future. Then it was gone, all changed. "You sure? Killing can—"

"We stick to the plan."

Why wasn't he raging? How could he miss the chance to avenge his wounds?

"You look unsteady, Gaou Toya? Are you ready?"

I pushed all thoughts from my head as I took my cutlass from my sash and lifted the shiny blade Nosakhere had hammered, hardened, and sharpened. "I'm ready."

He pointed through the thick bushes. "My spy, the old cook, informed me of Flaville's numbers. Over two hundred enslaved. Weapons, flint-lock muskets, powder, and balls are in the hospital."

"Flaville put the killing tools where people need healing?"

"He thought no one would attack a hospital."

One glance and our eyes connected. "Nosakhere, he underestimated you. Anyone who does is a fool. Get in position. It's time."

Moving with our troops, the two of us, Gaou and Counselor, advanced on the habitation below.

• • •

DOWN THE HILL WE CREPT IN A FORMATION OF FOUR COLUMNS. AT the fence, the entry to the habitation, we split up. Half went inside, and to the left to surround Flaville's provision grounds.

The others followed me to the right to retrieve the weapons cache.

Moonlight glistened on the points of our spears. My sharpest shooters, Sara and Célia, had the two guns we possessed. These muskets were more for show than for use, with the wild way the balls shot.

I hissed like a lappet vulture, spread my arms, and headed to the sugar house on the right. One of our muskets fired. Luckily, the metal ball went forward.

Two enslaved men who'd been working ran out, yelping.

A Blanc man came out with a torch and a gun.

My spear sailed through him before he could load powder into the chamber.

We hit the house of the head refiner next. He was felled by Fleur's spear through the heart. Two other commandeurs had their throats slashed. We seized their guns and kept going.

Before reaching the hospital, I made sure we'd taken possession of the provision grounds and cleared them of the massa's drivers. We warned the enslaved to stay in place.

The gnawing feeling in my gut made me decide to take the grand-casa before the hospital. "Kill the habitation's king." Then there would be no quick reprisals for what we'd done.

Boom. Crack.

A Minos fired one of the captured guns, breaking a window of the large building.

"Massa. Massa. Brigands." A colored commandeur ran inside.

We fired. They fired, and the rest of the windows came down.

Smoke reached us, making the air thick and white. A similar cloud consumed the inside of the grand-casa.

We kept loading and firing.

Pop. Boom.

Boom. Boom.

At least three guns fired now.

If Nosakhere's report was correct, Massa Flaville would run out of bullets and try to make it to the hospital.

Boom. Whop. That empty noise, the hollow sound, was how a flint-lock belched with no ball, just powder.

Pop. Whop. Whop.

Seeing a man leaning out a window, I had Sara take aim and fire.

A wail escaped from his mouth.

Others ran out of the grand-casa.

My team rushed forward, slitting the Blancs' throats as soon as they came near.

"Don't shoot." The voice came from inside.

"Wi." Nosakhere had answered.

Lantern in hand, a tall man came out. "Don't butcher me. That's what you brigands did to over a thousand habitations. I heard you put a baby's head on a stake."

The shadow of a gun—I saw it strapped to his back.

His arm went back, reaching; I pitched my spear. I didn't miss.

He fell forward, but his gun discharged and struck one of mine, ten feet from me. Sara went down.

When Gaou Hangbé had fallen before my feet, I charged and slew her killer, then I went and protected the king. I didn't feel, I acted.

But this was Sara. Sara, my gun woman, my star gazer, lying in blood, with a wound to the head, not moving.

Giving the signal, I made everyone stand down. Many lit torches.

Nosakhere stood looking at the man I slew. His knuckles were white. I'd deprived him of this kill.

I wanted to say sorry, but you didn't do that to a soldier. He jerked himself forward. "I will go tell the people they are free."

He went back to the provision grounds, and I heard him, in Twi, Kikongo, and Kreyòl, say the words "Libète! Libète! Libète!"

I pointed to the hospital. "Fleur, take Célia and get everything, the weapons, the bandages, and the medicine."

Tears in their eyes, they nodded and did their duty. Soon dozens of muskets were retrieved.

The rest of my Minos stood guard over our fallen soldier, our Sara.

"We'll bury her the traditional way. It's what is due a Dahomey warrior, our worthy friend Sara."

Two rushed into the massa's house and brought back linen to prepare the body.

I glanced at this young sweet face, brown and round with eyes closed. It had been a long time since I'd felt this ache.

With the war we'd started, my respite from silent tears was done.

23

Marie-Claire

1791

Cap-Français

The rues smell of smoke. To the left and right of me, the cross streets are char. The uprisings have scarred the city and the people. In my dray, Adélaïde accompanies me as I turn on to Rue de la Vieille Jonallerie heading past Place de Clugny. Though that district has the most damage, Pierre's become fearful at the mention of going that direction. My young companion, my birthday twin, insists on helping with me. As I'd done with the Bazac, I intended to make these food runs alone, but Adélaïde didn't do well alone.

In one of my old gowns that's been taken in at the bosom, she grips the seat as if I am going too fast. "It used to have the prettiest houses, the Pearl of the Antilles, my père said. Oncle Pierre agreed. That's why we came." Her voice is sorrowful and angry but at least she's talking.

"God is with us, Adélaïde. We are feeding his people. It's healing doing for others. St. Louise, she teaches to help those with less. If you ever want to tell me what happened—"

"Look." She points at children playing.

I stop the dray near them, but I know this is one of Adélaïde's tactics to keep the bad bottled up. When I climb down, I offer the three of them kasav.

They take it and stuff their faces as if they've not eaten for days.

I stoop low, looking the tallest in the eye. "Are there more to feed at home?"

"Not much of a home. Burnt. Can we take food to our sister?"

I'm afraid to learn if they have a safe place to sleep. It's dangerous knowledge when I can't help. The guards at Place Royale won't let anyone through who doesn't reside at the convent or work for the hospital.

The smallest one gobbles another kasav, and she dimples like Françoise. That could be her without Pierre's protections. Rushing to the back of the dray, I gather all the remaining breads, a stack of twenty, and put them in their hands. "Take this to her."

They smile like I solved all their ills.

When I turn back, Adélaïde has the reins. "No more provisions means we can return to Place Royal."

With a nod, I climb on the dray and let her head back. It's enough that we fed one family today. Adélaïde seems cheered, but I only wish I could do more for both.

At the guard's gate guns are waved in my face. We stop as one soldier in French blues jumps on the back of the dray; others surround my horse.

MY HANDS LIFT. ADÉLAÏDE SCOOTS CLOSER TO ME ON THE DRAY. "There's nothing to find but kasav crumbs, Niece. We have nothing to fear." I say this with a calm voice, but I am frightened. With the assembly under de Blanchelande sending troops into Saint-Marc to confront Blanc patriots and Black brigands, everyone is on edge.

No one is trusted.

And none will accept that hunger has no side.

"Madame Lunic," the lead soldier says. His fingers smell as if he's found the remnants of the nutty kasav. "Where are you coming from?"

"From feeding the hungry near Place de Clugny."

This soldier knows me as Pierre's wife and knows that I always serve the poor.

He lowers his gun. "Madame Lunic, there's been a lot of trouble today. More executions are happening in Place d'Armes. Women shouldn't see it. Stay here in the convent for safety."

Can't flinch. Can't look disturbed about more killings. They must think I'm only concerned with loyal royalist colonists, but I will feed hungry rebels and any child I see.

"You can go, Madame Lunic. We must check everyone."

I revel in the magic of the name *Madame Lunic*. It allows me safe passage to and from the hurting streets of Le Cap. Retrieving the reins from Adélaïde, I head the dray past the guards and safely into Place Royale.

"Wait! Wait!"

My heart slams against me. Then it starts working. The voice is Pierre's. He runs to my dray. I see his tanned face, fresh from Guadeloupe's sun.

"Monsieur Lunic, you're back." My voice is happy. I step off the dray and into his arms. With a kiss to his cheek, I tell him I've missed him. "When did you get back? We weren't expecting you for three more weeks."

His face is bemused, reddening with anger and desire. "I need to talk with you and warn you again about driving into danger."

"Oui, my husband." I offer him another big hug. Pierre loves to feel me in his arms, and I've found that pleasing him cools his temper. Yet when he offers me another embrace, this one deeper, with his big hands caressing my back, I realize I've truly missed him and the safety of his embrace.

Offering a smile to the soldiers and to Adélaïde, he sighs and musses the curls peeking from my straw bonnet. "I want family every night this week," he says. "No night missions."

He leaps onto the seat and hands his niece down. "S'il vous plaît, madame and mademoiselle. I'll take care of this." Pierre will stow the dray in the shed, where he stables it and his tools.

Adélaïde shrugs. "At least Oncle is home."

It's good, but the uneasy look on Pierre's face tells me he has more changes in mind to keep us safe.

AFTER A LONG DINNER WITH MAMIE AND ELISE, WE LUNICS RETURN to our quarters. It's been a good week of everyone getting along. By our small burgundy sofa, Pierre plays with Françoise and the lion he's carved for her. It has wheels at the base.

Somewhere between Martinique and Guadeloupe, he has found the time to make it. Adélaïde talks to him about geography. All are laughing.

I'm standing at the threshold of my bedchamber, watching my family. For the first time in months, I'm happy. All is turbulent outside, but together here at Place Royale we're safe. I didn't know how much I loved this feeling until all of Saint-Domingue battled.

Though Pierre is smiling, he seems distracted. I don't want to argue about anything tonight. I just want to enjoy him, our family.

After an hour of songs, a quick knock on my door has my heart pounding. With the increasing number of soldiers and raids and rebellions, I'm fretful. I've fed people the Colonial Assembly hate. I don't want to be made an example.

But it's just Elise at our threshold.

My pulse settles as she enters and calls to the children. "Monsieur Lunic, I'm so glad you're back. Hopefully your work away is done."

His lips press into a line. "Most things, Mademoiselle Lobelot. But one can never solve all problems at once."

Nodding, she takes Françoise into her arms.

"Père!" my baby says with a dribble down her juicy lips.

"Oh, she said it again." Elise claps. "You'll talk in gobs soon. Maybe sing, too."

Pierre's face is a puzzle. One minute he's happy Françoise calls him her father. Then his eyes shift, and his smile fades a little.

"Come along, little one."

Françoise clutches the delicate kerchief of my aunt's dress. Adélaïde follows and smooths the yawning child's green-printed pinafore.

Elise and Adélaïde will talk politics and read more renegade stories. The *Moniteur General de la Partie Française de Saint-Domingue* is the current source. All the newspapers keep shuttering. Their owners must not be able to sort out Le Cap's politics, either.

When all have left and our quarters are quiet, I sit beside Pierre. "What didn't go well? I can tell something is wrong."

He threads his large hands together. "Nothing is wrong."

Pierre tugs at the ribbon in his hair. Dark locks with a spattering of silver fall. "Everything is great. What I have to say can actually wait."

He puts his arms about me and I hold him tighter. "The world has been crazy. Many are hurt and hungry. I miss having you here. Please don't be angry at me for serving my ministry."

"I understand chasing dreams. I've chased you for a long time."

Has he? The past few months it seems I exist only in the moments between his projects. Yet this has shown me I can miss him, miss him terribly. The regular sharing of a bed has become more than pleasant. I'll not deny the feelings he evokes when his hands slip to my hips.

He dips his head and teases my lips.

The kiss is soft . . . only a little hurried.

"There is much to discuss, chère."

With my mouth, I stop his whispers. I don't want to argue about leaving Place Royale in his dray, or his worries I'm feeding brigands. "I missed you, Pierre. Show me you missed me."

Those careless large hands grab me under the layers of my skirts. My limbs clench, then relax. Readying to go to our bed, he lays me back on the sofa. "You're the most beautiful woman. I'm sorry I'm not enough."

His words sting in their quiet truth. Yet his fingers are searching and finding me . . . here on the sofa, near Elise's hymnbook, near Françoise's wooden lion.

It's unexpected, the heat of those large hands on my hips, hips he's trained to expect him. He divides my petticoats, pushing at whalebone stays to free a bosom that's again mine, weaned from Françoise.

"Beautiful, and ready. My timing . . ."

We kiss and the world keeps spinning.

My garters, with their tiny brass springs, shoot across the room. Stockings fall as he sweeps the silk away.

He finds me and we unite, two souls who've let the busyness of life take away from building our marriage.

This is different. His strength and touch are different.

This rhythm is overwhelming.

It's deeper. So deep.

Those large hands cradle me with ease. They send me spiraling, crashing into him. For the first time my lips and mind, maybe even my heart, call out his name.

Clutching his shoulders, I need to keep him, but he withdraws, only to finish loving me in our bed. We lie together sweaty and sated with those large hands coveting my breasts.

He pulls my head to his chest. His half-undone cravat tickles my nose. "Where has this been?"

Maybe it was always there beneath my mourning. "Pierre, I've been silly. The time away has given me room to think."

"You needed room? I'd build you a castle. To know you love me, Marie-Claire."

I'd given him my pleasure like I loved him. This must be true. "Oui."

My husband is cursing under his breath. At first, I think he doesn't believe me. I have given a good impression of a woman pining for another since we wed.

"Chère, my timing is terrible."

"No. You've come back at the right time. Things are good. Or they can be better. Françoise would love a brother. Adélaïde is all the sister she needs."

Pierre groans again. "I leave for Paris in two weeks."

I sit up, pulling a sheet to separate us. "That's soon. I have to get someone to help Mamie. The hospital is overrun."

He tugs the sheet away and stares at me as if he's painting a picture. "I said I'm leaving, not us. The governor does not think you'll do well in Paris. The politics . . ."

"De Blanchelande does not want your Black wife to go?"

"You've not been one for politicking, and I'm representing the governor, to seek the funds to complete the arch for the entry of Le Cap. That's been my dream. You know this."

"But your Black wife and mixed family will keep you from your dream?"

He rubs at his neck as if his collar itches. "This is my dream. This is for us. We will be well off if I do this."

"And you'll return a Grand Blanc? Has de Blanchelande told you what has been happening while you're away? The patriots and royalists are fighting. The hospital is full of Grand Blancs and people of all stations, as well as colors. Everyone is finding themselves shot or burnt or even poisoned."

"De Blanchelande is using the soldiers for order. He's trying to rid those who undermine his authority."

Then I look at him and realize he does know, but his dreams are first. I've waited too long, mourning. Pierre has found other things to fill him while I withheld my heart.

He pulls from the bed, retying his white shirt, pulling on his white breeches. "Marie-Claire, this is a once-in-a-lifetime opportunity. I have to take it. I have to try. You can understand this."

If he gets the accolades he wants, he won't regret his choice of me. But I'm selfish. I don't want it to be too late to be happy and safe. "Stay. Stay and watch Françoise learn more words. Stay and let's build our family."

His eyes dart. I know he wants me to push him out the door. I won't. My voice won't cast him away. If things don't go well, he'll not be able to blame his Colored family or his mouthy Black wife.

It takes him a moment, but he sighs and sinks against the same threshold I stood against earlier thinking things had finally meshed.

"De Blanchelande says it is best for me to go alone. You were right about the acceptance of a marriage like ours. I'll be back as soon as I can, but with a fortune. And then I will build you a castle in Port-au-Prince."

He eases to the bedroom door. "If your feelings for me have truly changed, then we'll be more in love when I'm back and successful."

The man doesn't know he is enough, just as he is.

"I'll be back as soon as I can. Wait for me."

I remain silent until the door closes.

He's gone.

And I fall back shaking. Tomorrow isn't promised. Holding on to my first love may have ruined my chance to be happy.

24

Marie-Claire

1792

Cap-Français

Tugging the reins, I start my cart again. The soldiers still give us the typical warning about how dangerous Le Cap is, but nothing is new. The shortages, the burnt buildings, even news of the executions are commonplace.

Pierre has been gone for six months. Though he made sure my ministry had Governor de Blanchelande's blessing, it doesn't mean much now. The royalists have been drummed out of office. They say the governor has been sent back in scandal.

Adélaïde slumps. Her brunette chignon falls a little. "Has my oncle Pierre said when he is coming back?"

"He's busy working on his approvals." I hope there is a Le Cap when he returns. The affectionate notes saying he can't wait to return have stopped. With de Blanchelande out of power, I think he's too ashamed to admit he shouldn't have gone to Paris.

My dray heads down Rue de Vaudreil until I no longer see the guardhouse.

"The soup smells good. Mademoiselle Lobelot said we needed to go to the theater to give out food. She frets about the singers starving. The papers say the arts are at risk."

"That's farther than I intended to go."

My friend looks at me with such intensity, I must drive us there. "Elise is good at getting what she wants. We'll go but we won't stay long."

Clutching her scarf, Adélaïde nods, but her fingernails drive deeper into the seat platform until we pass Rue des Trois Chandeliers. That's beyond Place de Clugny, where her family last lived.

Her face seems drawn, more tense.

"Tell me what you're remembering?" I stroke a lovely dark curl that's fallen. "I want to help."

"Non. I'm well. Place de Clugny . . . I will always hear my maman's and père's screams. Then there are my screams." She peers at me, and I suspect the worst violation of a woman, let alone a mere girl. I want to hug her, embrace her against my bosom, and let her know she can heal.

"My twin, we end the day. We can give the food to the—the guardsmen. Then talk over mugs of hot broth."

"Non. We head toward the theater. I promised Mademoiselle Lobelot. She tells me everything that's happening. And she's fretful of the theater going away to New Orleans. If violence destroys the arts, everything is gone."

"You've been spending a lot of time with Elise. Do you talk with her about the past?"

Rubbing her arm, looking scared, Adélaïde points. "Look, Marie-Claire. An old woman is waving at us."

Carefully, I avoid a rut in the rue and pull to the side.

The lady with a blue scarf securing her gray braids holds up a baby to me. The boy is tan with large sagging cheeks, the first look of hunger.

I cradle him for a second and ache inside. My womb is still shut. There's no new child to solidify my family with Pierre and make him return.

The woman's Kreyòl is thick, but I understand what she says, and remember when I last spoke it, heard it. I give the hungry woman more kasav for the children huddling in the empty lot.

This hunger and devastation is familiar. This is Léogâne after the earthquake.

"Marie-Claire, we need to go."

Adélaïde is right. It's risky to stay in one place too long. Pierre added braces and tripods to hold my pots and calabashes in the dray. The vehicle is too valuable. Rebels or a poor mob might take it.

Handing the boy back, I give the old woman a whole kettle of soup. I've a feeling she'll feed many. To be begging, this Black mother of a Colored child probably doesn't have the protections of a Petit Blanc. I have them for now, but Pierre may never come back.

"Beni ou. Beni ou." She blesses us and says, "Mwen te yon lesiv men yo boule tout bagay."

Adélaïde clangs on a soup bowl like a bell. "We must hurry. I'll drive."

I wave to the mother. She walks away carrying the pot on her head and the babe on her hip. Adélaïde is right. We don't have time.

With her steady hand, she gets us moving. "It can be a trap. Mademoiselle Lobelot says the rebels are attacking people, innocent people. The rebels are going to burn Le Cap to the ground."

Some people aren't innocent, I know that. Looking at the dimmed streets where fashionable town houses once had life, I don't disagree. "My mother has written me. She wants us all to come to her in Léogâne, Mamie and Elise, too. She thinks it's too dangerous with your oncle away. She may be right. But then who will feed people like that woman and her children?"

"Marie-Claire, you're scared, too, for you to suggest running home to your mother."

I blink, then shrug, then give in with a nod. "My fear grows. This big, beautiful city I love is being destroyed by the soldiers, the rebels, the politicians. All ignore the needs of the poor."

One glance at Adélaïde with her clenched teeth and a wobble in her posture like she's cold in this sticky heat, and I know more is wrong. "What has happened? Tell me."

We pass Rue Notre-Dame, the street she should have turned left on to go to the theater, but she turns right and edges the dray closer to Notre-Dame de l'Assomption.

The noises of crowds sound like a military parade. "Why are we going this way? There's no church service. This is to Place d'Armes . . . the executions."

One look at Adélaïde with tears flowing down her reddening cheeks, and I realize we are heading to watch a rebel or brigand die. "We have to turn around."

She drips with sobs. "I must watch him be punished."

The bells of Notre-Dame toll, loud like my thudding heart.

Up high in the dray, I can see water bubble in the fountain and men being led to the wooden scaffold.

"Non. I can't watch another—"

Her hand closes about mine. She gives me the reins and jumps free.

Almost falling out of the seat, I'm reaching for her. "Adélaïde! Adélaïde, come back. We must leave. We can't—"

"Philémon, the priest, Mademoiselle Lobelot praises him for letting her sing. I will praise God when he dies."

She's pointing to the Blanc man with brown robes and bound hands led to the center of the scaffold. He stands between two men who are ebony like my father. One already has a noose around his neck.

Choking on tears, Adélaïde comes back and grips my hand. "You go back to the safety of Place Royale and the hospital and your aunt's hymns and wait for my oncle to return to you. Leave me to the streets and revenge."

"No. Adélaïde, that's not you. You're sweet and caring—"

"And one of Philémon's victims. My maman, too." She pulls at the kerchief that keeps her covered up, as if the truth is hidden on her chest. "He joined with the rebels to indulge his lusts. Then when he was done, Philémon pretended to the soldiers that rebels were inside our house. The soldiers laughed and burnt it down." Backing up, she's to the edge of the crowd. "All dead, all my family because of Philémon."

"I'm not leaving you. Come back, Adélaïde."

Like disappearing steam, the girl whirls away and becomes part of the chanting masses.

"Philémon!"

"Philémon! Mort à lui!"

"Mort à lui! Mort à Philémon!"

A fellow runs forward and tosses something—a tomato or a guava.

It splatters onto the platform and sprays red mush on the soldiers' whites. Even the hem of the priest's garment is stained.

"Minister of hell! Father Philémon, the noose is for you."

Adélaïde sings it.

"And Boukman! Boukman!" The crowd chants the rebel's name.

Snap. The man with the noose falls through a trapdoor. He doesn't dangle. The rope has broken and he's rolling on the ground.

The fruit thrower and his friends rescue him and pull him into the chaotic crowd.

I can't leave the dray to search for Adélaïde It will be stolen. "Adélaïde! Adélaïde! Come back."

Praying to St. Michael, the battle angel, to put his shield about her, I hope my niece will head to my arms.

A command is given. Boom. The platform drops.

Boukman and Père Philémon are hanged.

Their bodies, black and white, swing back and forth like pendulums.

The world slows as I see Adélaïde returning to the dray.

I think I can breathe.

A fellow helping the lucky prisoner escape passes my niece and runs toward the dray. He's yelling something that finally pitches above the reveling crowd.

"Marie-Claire Duclos! Marie-Claire Duclos!"

My name, my old name.

A ghost, my ghost, stands beside the dray.

Jean-Jacques Duclos.

My dead husband.

I never want to breathe again.

Adélaïde throws kasav at him. She must think he's trying to steal something. But what can he take that I've not already given him?

She grabs the reins and makes my horse flee.

We leave Jean-Jacques standing there calling out.

"Marie-Claire! Marie-Claire!"

My eyes try to drown me in sobs. I thought I finally had peace. My life had started over. He can't be alive.

Adélaïde's hand is upon mine. "The brigand knows your name."

Can't tell her, or anyone, that my first love, my Françoise's true father, lives. Not alive. Not alive. Figment! Ghost!

"Marie-Claire?"

There are no words that can come out with my heart lodged in my throat.

Right before we turn the corner, I glance over my shoulder, hoping for proof my fears made me see the impossible. That none of this is true.

The fellow who looks like Jean-Jacques stands there waving before turning to the freed rebel and helping him flee Place d'Armes.

The crowds chant, "Justice."

The soldiers who've left the white rebel whole hammer the decapitated head of the Black one onto a pike. Others toss his Black body to the flames.

Even in death there's no equality.

Adélaïde's quiet. Her face is wet. Her gaze is pinned ahead.

But I can't stop glimpsing toward Place d'Armes and questioning my sanity. I'm returning to safety while my city, my family, my world, are torn apart.

The Prophecy

One day the gods of war came down.
The earth shook, dancing from the sound.
Zinsu, Zinsi will loose the bound,
And this hope made the world feel new.

Of their callings, one craved power
The other sought peace every hour
To rid famine war made flower
Black, Blanc, and Brown—death had its due.

—ANONYMOUS, STYLED IN THE FORM OF UTENZI

25

Toya

1792

Massif du Nord

The morning sun warmed our mountain camp. The glow gave the round huts an orange sheen. Beautiful. Curiama waved at me as she headed to the rivulet to begin her bathing ritual. The Taíno have been oppressed for many years but here in the mountains they have peace. I prepared in my heart to not see this place again, but to take a piece with me. I'd store it with my memories of Gbowélé and Calmina. I'd tried to pull all these homes of my spirit into one, the one we the maroons, the runaways, were building below.

Nosakhere approached. His large eyes rested on me. "You've had your first victory in a long while."

"It's one habitation, counselor. This island is made up of many."

"Then we take another and another, until they are all are freed and cleared of owners."

"Until Célia and Fleur and the rest of our followers and the nice Taíno are dead?"

Squinting at me, he stroked his beard. "You've gained a heart after all these years?"

"I had one, but I put it away the day Gbowélé was destroyed. Then I buried it with Janjak and Eghosa. The empty space shouldn't be hurting again."

He put his hand on my elbow. The touch was tentative. Then his fingers curled into my muscles and turned me. "All those years ago, I was a fool who lusted for power. I felt entitled to it and everything I wanted. Now I can have nothing I want but freedom."

"You've touched the king's bride. That's worthy of death."

"I've already died twice. The first was when I saw a girl crying over the ashes of a hut my brethren set on fire and I did nothing to stop them."

My breath hitched. I swallowed and looked into his smoke-rimmed eyes. "When was the second? The mutilation?"

"Non. I was already dead when a woman enslaved my worthless ass. The second death was years ago, here in the wilderness when I realized you were right to do so. I deserved death for my treachery to Eghosa. It was why I could not meet the son, the only one I'll ever . . ." He coughed, then cleared dust from his throat. "I didn't want the image of his disappointment to stay with me when I see my sinful reflection in the water. Know this, Adbaraya, I fight not only to end enslavement but to make amends for the unforgivable."

His words met a spirit broken by Sara's death. "I'm no priest, no god to offer absolution. Why tell me this?"

"Anacaona was a female cacique. She led. You must lead."

"Curiama told me of her. The queen was hung after less than three years of ruling."

"In her time, she offered stability when the king died. Ours is gone." Nosakhere stepped back and bowed. "I'm redeemed in this fight, Adbaraya. I feel alive bringing freedom. Though I am unworthy, I wanted you to know I will follow you."

"One step at a time. Prepare. We take Cormier next."

He disappeared, and I looked to spiraled palms and the path of the rivulet that Curiama had taken. As a relic of the old ways, I wasn't prepared for a world with no king. I decided to go dip my heels in the water. An answer would come, something to take these small battles and unify the fight.

OUTSIDE OF CORMIER HABITATION, IN THE GROVES ALONG THE road, we waited for dusk. We needed the enslaved to be in their provision grounds to minimize casualties. Duclos's armed commandeurs would be the bloodiest combat yet.

Crouched beside me, Nosakhere seemed at ease. "Do not be beset with worries. My intelligence is faultless."

Rumors from drunken runaways weren't enough, but Nosakhere had been right in all our battles. He stared at me. "What is wrong, Gaou Toya?"

"Regrets. I've waited too long to act." I bit my lip and stared at the entrance of the habitation.

"Talk, Gaou. Only I'm listening."

"I came here as a hospitalière to heal the sick. I've returned to slay anyone who resists."

"We'll make their deaths painless. No torture or showiness. Second thoughts? We can fall back."

I put my palm up. "Our raids have provided guns for every Minos. We have plenty of bullets and powder. Shooting in a line, our forces will prove deadly."

"What about the greater war? Joining with other rebels to fight all the Blancs, Gaou Toya? That would be more weapons, and men to rival the French."

"Let's see how we do. If we rid Cormier of Blancs and hold it, we have a strategic position to Le Cap."

He nodded, or merely gave up arguing.

"Go. Get your team ready," I said.

He flipped me a salute as if I were a French solider and moved into position.

Quiet like mice, we began the assault, creeping through the grove, crawling through the brush.

Leaves crunched.

Everyone became still. But it was us, no commandeurs.

Minutes passed, and we began again.

As we'd practiced, our teams headed through the cane fields.

The Minos's yellow sashes exposed them against the jade stalks, but the women looked proud and strong. The shooters formed a line with the muskets drawn and pointed.

Nosakhere's men went to each hut, informing the enslaved to stay put or die. The hope was that they'd listen. We had no mercy for those caught in crossfire. We had to win.

When I arrived at the first commandeur's house, I found the one we called the Brit inside, eating his supper. Fury churned. I remembered how he had made sure Janjak's wounds were deep. Faces of the souls he beat to death flitted past my eyes.

I did nothing to stop him.

Fleur came to my side; she had a cutlass poised and ready. "Are you all right, Gran Toya?"

"Yes. Get back. Finish him if he makes it to the door." With my cutlass drawn, I went into the hut.

The Brit held up his dinner knife, but before he could clear his mouth, I struck. His body slumped to the floor. His severed head fell the other way.

I almost stooped to close his crystal-blue eyes, but his ghost needed to see the ants and the decay to come.

Fleur gasped when I came outside. She pointed to my cutlass. I hadn't cleaned the bloodied thing.

On the edge of replacing savagery with savagery, I wiped it down. "We have no room for prisoners. All the Blancs die today. They've earned it."

Her head scarf had fallen somewhere, exposing her wavy thick hair to the steam in the air. Fleur stared at the Brit's quarters and nodded. "All is not enough."

"Move out." I'd keep my eye on her. With Fleur staying longer at Cormier, I suspected she had many debts to repay, same as me.

Célia took the lead clearing the rest of the commandeurs' huts.

Once all were standing graves, we proceeded to the hospital. On the shelves, I saw jars I'd made like the ones my iya created.

Sending others forward to gather weapons, I lingered behind, glaring at the herbs and oils. The yellow one for mal de machoire looked untouched. How many babies died the past wet season?

Footsteps pounded behind me.

Spinning, I drew my weapon. My blade stopped an inch from No-sakhere's heart.

His gaze swept and tangled with mine. Then he backed up. "Your plan is working. I saw your handiwork in the huts. I remember why King Tegbesu felt powerful. He could do anything with Gaou Toya's protection, his greatest weapon."

"The king said that?"

He dipped his chin. "Now let's finish."

Célia ran inside. "There's men running to the grand-casa."

"Duclos has been warned. You think he'll welcome us with open arms?" My jest eased the tension building in my limbs. Our troops marched shoulder to shoulder until we reached the palm tree–lined majestic drive. I signaled to form columns.

"Forward." I led my team. Nosakhere's would follow.

The grove of mango trees had been planted in my absence. The sweet smell of the fruit reminded me of elephants, of Janjak, the boy, the eager student, the man who needed to live to see all our training being put to use.

Fleur motioned from the rear. "Garnier is missing. He wasn't in his hut or the fields."

Pop. Pop. Blast. Musket balls showered us.

We abandoned our columns and ran to the brush and began firing our spears.

Pop. Pop. Blast.

A man screamed, then fell from above. One of our spears had pierced him, flinging him from the high limbs.

Pop. Pop. Bang.

Célia fell hard to the ground. I went to her, shielding her.

Pop. Pop. Bang. Bang. Bang.

Nosakhere's forces had cut behind the grove and fired spears and muskets. My columns were bait, just as we'd planned. We knew some-one would tattle and prepare Duclos to counter our attack.

Pop. Bang. Bang.

Blancs and guns fell from the mango trees.

All dead. Our close-range shots were effective.

The ones still wiggling received a bayonet to the chest.

One man limped away.

Fleur broke cover, chased, and speared him through the back. The fellow's soul had departed before he hit the ground, but she kept beating and kicking him. "He shot Célia."

"Stand down, Minos. Fleur, she's alive."

"Wi. Just my arm," Célia said as I began using her sash to stanch the bleeding.

Sweat poured down Fleur's brow. She ran to us and took over Célia's care.

In silent prayer, I praised the gods my youngest Minos still lived.

Nosakhere flipped over the downed man. Tricorn rolling away exposed reddish-brown hair. Garnier.

Searching the body for bullets, the counselor asked, "This one special to you, Adbaraya?"

Killing an ambivalent soul who'd still ended up letting evil happen wasn't hard. "He chose his fate. We chose ours. On to Duclos."

As we'd mapped out our assault, our teams now surrounded the grand-casa but were about a hundred feet away, out of range of only the luckiest musket.

"Duclos!" Nosakhere said. "Duclos soti. Rann tèt. Duclos sort. Abandon."

The answer to our Kreyòl and French warnings to surrender was a muzzle leaning out of the yellow shutters.

Pop.

The musket ball landing at my feet.

My team formed a line, moved closer, and began shooting and reloading their guns.

Pop. Bang. Bang. Pop. Bang. Bang.

Our guns could fire three shots a minute. They belched heavy white fog.

The floating ash became too heavy to breathe. We withdrew and waited.

Duclos's guns stopped.

In Fon, I called for the enslaved inside the grand-casa to head out the door. I repeated it in Yoruba, Kreyòl, then Twi.

Men and women in server's aprons and a woman in sheets ran out of the grand-casa.

We held our fire as two men dressed in jackets and frilly shirts came out with their hands held high.

Our guns were trained on them. "Where's Duclos?"

"All dead! Tous morts!" the short one answered. Then he said a bunch of other words. None of it sounded like a location.

Must be visitors, they spoke too prettily and had clean nails.

"Do you own a habitation?" I asked. "Ou achte esklav?"

Sweaty red faces looked at each other.

"Do you buy slaves?" I asked again and raised my musket.

The taller fellow said, "Non. But we marvel at how you've trained yours. I'm fasc—"

A gunshot whipped past my head and lodged into the talker's throat. The other man had my spear in his gut.

The smoke cleared and I turned to face the shooter, Nosakhere. He wore the countenance of a man who fully understood the demonic system we Dahomey had participated in. "Never want to hear words about a sale of flesh again."

As my Minos checked the downed men, I went to the house. The air was chalky. Our bullets left dents in the stone walls. Three more commandeurs lay dead on the floor. Searching each room, I found no body of Duclos. Had he escaped dressed as a servant?

The girl in the sheets.

She had to have come from the bedroom.

I went to it. White walls. Small windows on each side of a grand bed.

Cutlass readied, I flung open the closet but saw only shelves, folded white shirts and waistcoats.

Burning with anger, I readied to slam the door when I heard a tiny shift, a creak of floorboards.

Hiding beneath the bed?

Throwing off sheets, I turned over the bedclothes. Nothing. Then I kicked at the frame. The thing shifted and exposed Duclos hiding behind the headboard.

"Get up! Lève! Lève!"

He tilted against the wall. "Thought I'd never get you back here to my bed. And tossing all my linens about like a wild woman. I remember you like linen."

With my arm raised, my cutlass ready to strike, I ordered him to move. "Lève! Rise, Duclos."

He did so, as slowly as a worm wiggling in the hot sun. "The prodigal has come home."

"This is not my home."

"Then why are you here? You're here because you have nowhere else to go. I'm your leader, your king, as Garnier said. You belong to me, Victoria, and you'll do nothing to me."

I slapped him with the back of my hand. He hit the wall with a crackle, the sound of splintering bones.

"My name is Adbaraya Toya."

"It's Victoria Montou. You're mine. And you know it."

Unable to control the anger in my soul, I put my cutlass to his neck. "I have no king."

Duclos shifted and the sharp blade drew blood. It pooled on his bright white nightshirt.

"Have you thought of what you'll do free? What all those slaves being free will want? They won't know how to handle it. You're children. You need a father. You need a king."

"Must you always talk and say nothing? Prepared to see your god? That's more kindness than what you gave to Da'mon, Agwé, Janjak, Eghosa, countless others."

His smirk dropped away. The man fell to his knees. "Toya, please. Don't kill me like this. Let me dress. Let me have some honor."

He reached out and clasped my tunic, touching my thigh. Spinning free, I swung as hard as I could.

My blade, sharp and gleaming, drew sparks along the wall. It sliced through bone and flesh and muscle as if they were butter. His face rolled to my feet. The white linen that washerwomen had scrubbed and beat upon the rocks to soften became fully scarlet.

"Never touch what's not yours. I'm my own king."

"Adbaraya." Nosakhere stood at the door. "You . . . you found him."

The warrior strode beside me and took my cutlass from my out-stretched hand. "I'll clean this."

He covered what was left of Duclos with the mattress.

"I avenged them, Nosakhere. I've avenged them all."

After swiping my blade clean, he gave it to me and put the tip to his chest. "Finish your judgment."

In his eyes, I saw the sorrow of all the wasted years and the reflection of my regrets—the pain and all the horrors I kept inside to keep my soul from shattering.

I dropped my cutlass, put my brow to his, and held his shoulders for an eternity before walking away.

26

Toya

1792

Cormier Habitation

Sunrise was beautiful from Duclos's hounwa, the lovely long veranda. The gold ball broke from the palm trees and warmed the earth. People worked the provision grounds for their own food. I saw them from the rocking chair, with my feet up on the rail.

Back and forth, with a cup of good rum, I sipped and stretched, and imagined I'd done this years ago.

Fluffing up the pillow under my neck, I relaxed. Maybe for the first time since stepping on Saint-Domingue's dark soil, I could.

Sure was comfortable here.

I could understand a little better why Massa had felt like he owned the world sitting here on his throne.

Taking the lacy fan Mrs. Duclos had left on her dresser, I waved air to my cheeks and waited for the next battle to come to me. Dèyè mòn gen mon. We'd cleared one problem, where was the next?

Fleur came to the veranda's rail, hanging on the post that had been used for torture. "Counselor Nosakhere has gone?"

"Yes, Fleur. He's returned to Massif du Nord. He and his team will wait for further instructions there. We will wait here. They've taken Célia back, too. She'll have the chance to heal with the Taíno."

She squints at me. "But she's one of our best shooters."

I trained her, but that didn't make it right. "I chose for her to be safe and free to grow older."

Fleur's small apple face frowned, but she must understand. War needn't be for the young. It was for those set in their beliefs, those who'd lived long enough to understand why they fought. It wasn't for someone barely old enough for a purification ceremony.

"I'm flame, Fleur. I chose for her to no longer burn."

"Splitting up from the counselor is best?" she asked.

My chin dipped in a slow nod. Nosakhere and I weren't Zinsu and Zinsi or any of the other celestial twins. We were two Dahomey warriors who'd found peace. Yet we each needed our own way forward.

Sitting here, I could wait forever for the gods to direct my steps.

DAY AFTER DAY, THE MINOS PATROLLED THE EXTENSIVE CORMIER land, circling it as if it had walls. I'd watch them from the veranda, my own hounwa, like the palaces of old. To sit and rock in the quiet had become my favorite thing. Today, I drank tea from a gold-rimmed mug.

Fleur ran toward me.

"Sòlda!" she said and waved her spear. "Attack! Under attack!"

I picked up my gleaming cutlass from the boards beneath my rocker.

In her jet tunic with yellow sashes, waving her arms, Fleur looked like an angered bee, but a proud one.

"How many soldiers?"

"Three on horseback, twenty on foot."

"Guns?"

She half bent over and gulped air. "Yes, but strapped to their sides. And they are all Black."

"The muskets?"

"No, the sòlda."

Sòlda Noir wouldn't be sent by King Louis. I blew into Garnier's conch, signaling the Minos to let them through.

"If this were an attack, the guns would be drawn. This is an emissary. They're bringing the king's message. Stand at the ready."

Flintlocks slung to their backs, the Minos took positions across the wide hounwa. The bulk of the soldiers waited at the start of the tree-lined drive. The three riders, two in front, one in back, trotted toward us.

One man rode a pewter mount, the other two sat on brown ones.

The three men wore uniforms—white breeches, white sashes, long white coats.

These weren't French soldiers.

With dark faces, darker than mahogany, they definitely weren't French.

Cutlass in hand, I stepped in front of my women and waited.

"Tante Toya! Tante Toya!"

That voice. It couldn't be.

Squinting, I saw my Janjak, my heart, alive and riding toward me.

"It is you!" the man said, then offered a hearty laugh.

I waved my Minos to stand down.

My boy, all dressed up in a uniform, swung his leg over his mount and leapt to me. "That is you, Tante Toya!"

He embraced me tightly. "I brought an army to free you, but it seems you've done it yourself."

"My Janjak. You live, but Duclos said . . . Why would I ever trust anything Massa said?"

He stepped back and bowed. "Yes, Jean-Jacques Dessalines lives, Tante Toya." He'd stretched the sounds of his new name, his voice booming.

Then I reached for him again and hugged him like the son he'd always been.

His limbs felt thin. Though he looked good on the outside, I feared for him and what these new clothes meant.

"Go with me up the hill, Tante Toya. I need to visit her. Come?"

I agreed and told Fleur to take command.

She flexed her spear-throwing hand. "Gran Toya, he could be used by the enemies, the sòlda. You should not go."

Janjak tilted his head. Then bowed. "Good to see you, too, Fleur." He crossed his arms behind his back. "Da'mon and Agwé would love to know you like this."

"Like what?" She glared at him, taking a step in his direction.

"With power in your arms and hope returned to your eyes."

She lowered her weapon. "It truly is you."

His words, her acknowledgment, stoked the flames in my soul for those who hadn't survived. At least some had survived Duclos's reign.

"We'll be back soon, Fleur." She and three other Minos held muskets on the armed men in white, all the columns of sòlda noir.

In silence, Janjak and I walked to the hills behind Cormier, the ones framing the grand-casa. Maybe with his mother as a witness, he'd tell me how he still lived and how he had come to wear a uniform that wasn't of France.

"IT KEEPS GROWING," HE SAID AND SMOOTHED HIS HANDS ALONG the bark and probably searched for his mother's marker.

Up in these hills, I didn't exactly remember the location of the tomb. I wished I could help.

Janjak circled the trees. The long white jacket flapped over his white breeches. He took off his blue hat trimmed in gold and made the sign of the cross over his head and shoulders.

"You *bested* Duclos. I would have loved to have done that. At least he won't hurt another soul." Fists balling, the boy . . . this man lost his grin. Those once-bound hands had freely killed.

"Don't waste another breath on that fool. Tell me how you're alive and who is your king. That uniform is not French."

He looked to the valley. "King Louis XVI does not recognize a Black soldier as free. King Charles IV of Spain has said there's no more slavery. He lets us be free if we fight for him."

"Saint-Domingue is France's colony. Her king is Louis."

"Part is French. More than half is Spain's. The way the fight is going, it may soon be all Spain's."

I leaned on my staff trying to make sense of it all. "You've traveled from the east of Saint-Domingue, on your enemies' land, to come here."

"Because of the Black troops, we control pockets as far as Massif du Nord. And no one knows the hills like me. I want to take it all."

"Let the Taíno be. Leave them to the mountains. Ayiti was once theirs. The Spanish took it from them."

"Ayiti?" He looked confused. "Mountains are not our mission. Ridding the cities and habitations of the French is." He kicked a rock with his glossy boots. "I hated soldiers. I'd see them in the marketplace treating women and enslaved like nothing. Would Mama understand my wearing these foreign robes?"

"You just said Spain supports our freedom, why would anyone disapprove?"

"They're using the Blacks to cause problems for France. I believe they want us to be nothing more than mangy dogs biting their enemy's ankles."

Picking lint from the red cuff of his white coat, I cast it to the wind. "Pretty uniform. A lobola for the marriage of Blacks and Spain, definitely not a bone for a mutt."

"Toussaint says so, but he will use the Spanish to get what he wants, freedom for all and autonomy."

"Toussaint? Gaou Guinon's grandson."

"You heard of Toussaint?"

"Biassou and Toussaint are much talked about. Has Spain married him, too?"

"Wi and Jean-François. Biassou is very proud, and sometimes envious of Toussaint's leadership and his bloodline. Is it true my friend is descended from royalty?"

Janjak's eyes, the ones I missed, big and brown with large yellow whites, glanced at me with such hope. He still needed a king and I'd let him have one until he discovered the one inside. We were all kings, now.

"Wi. His grandfather is Allada. He was a great leader, but the son lost the struggle for power. Guinon was sold into enslavement." I left out the Dahomey's hand in his troubles. "But tell me how you've come to serve Toussaint? How are you alive? Duclos bragged about sending you to your death at the sugar boilers."

His eyes drifted from me. He glanced down into the valley. "Duclos sold me to cruelty, but God purposed a good man, a free Black man, who bought me. Dessalines is a righteous mentoring father. He saved me from the boilers. I surrendered the name of the pig who killed my manman. I honor my redeemer and go by Dessalines. He is also Toussaint's brother-in-law and recommended me to him. Toussaint has employed friends and relatives in his ranks." He turned back to me. "Your training kept me. Your drills and teaching of military strategy have brought me notice on the battlefield."

I stepped to him noting everything—his smile, the dryness of his hand from holding leather reins. "The Spanish have talked to you and Toussaint."

"Biassou too, but he does what the high officers want without question. He gets drunk with them trusting nothing untoward will happen. It is unwise to trust Blancs and liquor."

"Sounds as if you chose the right king."

His laugh was full and rich. Janjak stooped and picked an emerald blade of grass and let it float. "If we help them and wrest control of Saint-Domingue from the French, they'll allow us to run it."

"You believe this, that those Blancs will let you rule an island taken from Blancs?"

"They have been good to their word so far." His arms lifted, showing off splendid brass buttons. "If the Blacks build up our forces at Spain's expense, it may not matter. We'll take Saint-Domingue from them. Toussaint says not to fret. He wishes us to be patient."

Now I chuckled. "You were patient when you tried to earn your freedom, but Duclos had no intentions of honoring his price."

His smooth face darkened. His wonderful eyes cut. "That was a mistake. One I'm paying for. Yet." He bit his lower lip. "How does one be still when the love of your life is within your grasp?"

This was a question I couldn't answer, for I never acted on my heart's desires. "You're pining for a girl on the Spanish side of the island? I do recall you had many girls."

"I've not been a monk, but my wife is alive. From what I have learned, she's married and goes by the name Marie-Claire Lunic. Her child, my child, calls a French Blanc her père."

"I'm to blame. I told her you were lost. She went on with her life."

"I never thought I'd see her or you again. And I've not been lonely. I have a son, César Jacques."

"Janjak, you've always been distracted by pretty faces. You once looked at Fleur."

"Fleur is like a sister, but Marie-Claire is my heart. Things would've been different if I'd been able to buy my freedom or if we'd run away." His fingers hooked on his coat between fancy buttons. "But then I don't think I'd be in the military. This profession feels right."

Restless, haunted by my own disappointments, I stretched and looked down to the grand-casa. "If I've learned anything, it's that time keeps moving. I told you before to try for what your heart wants, but that doesn't mean you get it."

"You're right, but I still want her and I like serving a king, whoever he may be."

For one moment, I heard Nosakhere's voice saying those words. Clearing my throat, I offered him the next lesson. "Know the rivals to the throne. Watch them, for they are watching you. And never forget your supporters. I did once."

Eghosa's son nodded like he understood, but no one but one man knew how much I wanted to turn back time.

Janjak took the lead and we started down from the mountains. "None of my rivals have you. With my Tante Toya's backing, I am unstoppable. That is if you wish to advise me."

Hearing this offer gave me a new purpose. Being an adviser would be good for me. I whirled my cutlass in the air, stopped its motion, and hitched the gleaming blade to my side. "As soon as it is clear who is the king, send for me. I have a team of fighters ready to do battle for you, Janjak. We'll serve you as you serve your king."

His adjusted one of the white sashes on his jacket. "If I said I didn't mean for you to be at risk or that you're too old—"

I leapt in front of him and put my blade to his throat. "Do you want to be buried with your mother?"

"Teasing and testing, Tante Toya. Who am I to deny you a battle?"

"No king goes into battle without his Minos guard. 'King Janjak' sounds nice."

His laugh bubbled and split his lips. "I'm no king. That title is not for me. Remember, it will be Toussaint or Biassou."

"There's royalty in you. You'll either be the king or an adviser to one. And I'll be an adviser to you."

The glee in his face melted. In its place was strong iron. "Be ready. The moment will come soon. Since you're secure and don't need rescuing, I can turn my attention to Le Cap."

We kept walking and I reveled in Janjak being alive, but not that he'd set his mind again on Marie-Claire, who abided in the heart of French resistance.

27

Marie-Claire

1792

Cap-Français

My grand-mère is on the far side of the hospital room, checking bandages. She comes to me, looking over my shoulders at the wrappings I'm applying to this patient's broken leg. "You're from a line of caregivers, Marie-Claire. I'm proud."

Peering up at her face, I can trace the lines beneath her tired eyes, and I see the lies. That the man I patched up was injured by a slave uprising. He's painted as the victim, but we know he, like the other Grand Blancs, has hurt people far worse.

"Hopefully Mr. Lunic will be back soon with good news from Paris." She's proud I married an ambitious Blanc who she thinks will become rich. She thinks I and my daughter are safe.

White is not safety.

Pierre's last letter tells of his important meeting. He speaks to none of the troubles de Blanchelande is in. The priests whisper that the governor's been arrested. That he'll not be back. That the man may face execution for being a Grand Blanc here and peer, a viscount, over there. They gossip Pierre can't come back. That he's under suspicion for the favor he sought. Skin hasn't saved him, either.

Oppression is striking everyone in Paris. None are safe. I doubt the five thousand Coloreds living there are.

Elise's renegade papers tell of the troubles, all the executions, which are as bloody as Place d'Armes. Boukman's and Père Philémon's deaths haunt, as does every injury of the fighting. My hands seem stained, by worse than the Le Jeune women, their murders. I've cleaned too many wounds of the innocent and the guilty.

"Marie-Claire? Marie-Claire?"

Hooking her arm about mine, Mamie heads me to the hall. Her gray hair is wrapped in white like an angel's. Her green-striped gown is wrinkled and half-hidden beneath a blood-spattered apron. "You're shaking. What is wrong?"

Wrong? I'm scared and angry and dirty, for I think of Pierre and hate his choices.

But I can't confess this. My voice dies.

She takes my hand and rubs at a red blotch under my fingernail. "You're working too hard, Marie-Claire. Go rest. Françoise, I hear, didn't have an easy night."

"She cries for Pierre. If I'd begged him to stay, would he have listened?"

Saying those thoughts that shouldn't be spoken, I clap my mouth.

She embraces me. "Marie-Claire, I'm so sorry."

"Mamie, deep down, I'm more Lobelot than Bonheur. I do not beg for anything. Begging is for food, not a man." Any man.

Her hold about my shoulders increases. "Things will work out. But go for now."

"Madame Lobelot, Marie-Claire." Adélaïde passes near us, entering the hospital room with a tray of bowls of hot broth.

She's not talked about Place d'Armes or why she never said anything of the abuse she suffered.

Like Mamie is comforting me, I want to embrace Adélaïde. I want it to be enough, but she floats away, silent, holding it all in.

"Marie-Claire," Mamie kisses my forehead. "Go sleep or walk. Go to the garden. Just go."

Ripping off my apron, I hand it to her and hope there is enough bleach to make it clean.

As before, as always, I run to the garden. Past the trees, past my bench, I kneel at the stream and scrub my hands.

Again. Again. Again. I'm Lady Macbeth, but these guilty spots are true. "St. Louise, how do I remove the guilt of those I couldn't help?"

With more vigor, I keep washing until a shadow envelops me, until arms collapse about mine.

CRYING, I CAN'T BUDGE FROM THE STREAM. THE SMELLS OF A GARden in bloom surround me as much as the starch of a military shirt. Jean-Jacques lifts me up and tucks me to his chest.

I don't resist.

I need something, something that isn't punishment or death.

Someone who won't judge me. I've done it enough.

My body relaxes against him, and I stay there, through the dusk, maybe to the dawn. The scents of cactus and mangoes dance in the air, and I suck it in as if it's my last breath.

The leather-and-wool smells of his boots and jacket are there, too. My body presses against his white sashes and long white waistcoat.

"You're a soldier now?"

"Wi. And you're another man's wife."

I push free. "I am, and a respected governess and missionary, too. How are you alive?"

His old smile reappears, the one filling his face, brightening and comforting like stars. "I kept breathing."

"But the woman, your aunt, she said you were dead."

His hand goes to his sides. His movements are slow, as if not to frighten, but how would I ever fear the twin of my heart?

"I was sold off, Marie-Claire. I was certain to be dead, sent to the boilers. But a good man bought me, redeemed me. Now I'm free."

"How long? And why is now the first time you've come to me? I saw you in Place d'Armes months ago."

"I've come. You just didn't see." He steps forward and turns the band on my finger. "There was no need to intrude on your life, Madame Lunic."

"She said you were dead. I was with child. To be disgraced . . ." Tears for the yesterdays we never had slip down my cheeks. "What was I to do?"

His brow cocks as he folds his arms over his brass buttons. "Love me forever. I suppose that's too much to ask."

It was, and I had. And now it was too late. "Pierre Lunic redeemed me. He has my faith."

Jean-Jacques's jaw clenches, then relaxes. Thunder clouds have rolled through him.

"Whose uniform? My aunt says every power wants Saint-Domingue."

"I'm fighting for the side that wants Blacks freed. That's the Spanish."

We were on opposite sides? "This is a French colonial hospital. Soldiers are here all the time."

"Since I said your name aloud and you, 'the feeding woman' of the streets, recognized me, I cannot put you out of my head." He steps closer and flicks drops from my cheeks. "It's the change of guard when I came. I took the risk. I still remember the way over the hills. I'll always know how to get to you."

He puts my fingers to his sashes. "I'm no ghost, Marie-Claire. I joined the rebellion in the Plain du Parish Nord. I fought with valiant men. I've followed them to fight for Spain."

"You could be caught, Jean-Jacques. Executed as a spy."

"You've always been worth the risk."

We should've run away together, but I was afraid. Now it's too late. I push away, half turning from the stream where we said our vows to the soft grasses where we made love. "I'm glad you're alive, Jean-Jacques. I must go back to my duties. My life is no longer mine."

He grasps my hand and forces our fingers to weave and lock together. "Maybe I've come to liberate you and take you over the mountains."

"I'm married. I made a vow."

"You made a vow to me first. Come away with me, Marie-Claire. Come away and let us live in the open, love me in the open."

"Non." My throat's clogging, but I have to say this right. "Just happy to know you're alive. I must go."

"I'm free. But without the woman I need, I'm shackled again. And there's the matter of my child. I hear she's a beautiful girl with my ebony skin who calls out for her Blanc father."

"Françoise Lunic is beautiful."

"Lunic?" The dimples and his smile go away. "Is the bastard good to her? Some Blancs are mean to daughters of color."

The angry way he says *Blancs* holds such venom. "Pierre Lunic is good to her. He loves her so. His letters . . ."

"The man is away?" His hand falls to the hilt of his sword. "The fool abandoned you and my daughter?"

Anger and possession entwine in his voice. He looks at me with a searing glare that burns through my muslin kerchief.

"I should go, Jean-Jacques."

"You should, but you're not safe from the man who is here and still loves you."

When he turns to leave, my world breaks again, and I cleave to his sleeve. "That's it? To say such things, then leave?"

His hand laces with my fingers. "Which husband do you love more? Who is it you think of when you look for our stars?"

I can't beg for what is not my bread. "You don't belong to me, and I don't belong to you."

"Decide whose wife you are, Marie-Claire, by the time I return. I will return." He walks deeper into the garden and is swallowed by the bushes.

And I run home before my foolish legs give chase.

IT'S DUSK AS I SIT ON MY BENCH IN THE GARDEN WITH PICNIC FARE. The note I received two days ago, written in the finest French, asked me to do so. Well, Jean-Jacques's note didn't ask for a picnic, just for me to meet him here on a Saturday evening like old times.

My shift ended early at the hospital, and I spent the rest of the day waiting. I feel silly. A hundred different things can stop him from coming.

A priest in dark robes enters the garden. They come more often as do the men of science visit.

My heart panics. What if Jean-Jacques shows? I can't be seen with a Spanish soldier.

The priest comes close. I expect for him to ask directions. He doesn't say a word for at least two minutes. He stares at the cactus.

To keep Jean-Jacques from being caught, I decide to pick up my basket and leave.

My slippers have only taken three steps when the priest says, "Sister, I'm looking for my birth-year twin." The shroud of the cassock drops. Those lovely wide eyes are exposed. "Have you seen her?"

It takes everything within me not to run to him. "I'm glad you're careful."

"I have too many responsibilities to be caught." He waves to me. "May I have a fatherly hug?"

Relief pours through me. I embrace him, but his touch is not brotherly. His hand slips to my neck, then to every fold of my kerchief.

I step away and tug at my layers to make sure I look untouched then put distance between us. "This is not fatherly or brotherly."

"Someone else's brother."

My cheeks burn. For there's no doubt how this would be if we were other people, the ones who trusted and escaped to the mountains. I open my basket, bringing out kasav and broth. "What a clever disguise."

"The priests are everywhere. I figured this will give me a chance to visit and escape." He does the sign of the cross over his chest.

"Your note was short and to the point."

He put a hand to his chin. "I asked a friend to write it for me. I wanted it perfect for you. Since this is an anniversary of our first wedding, it should be."

"Our first . . ." I put my palms to my fevered face. "How could I forget?"

Jean-Jacques looks down. He kicks a rock. The action exposes long white breeches and glossy black boots, peeking from dark blue gaiters. "I suppose I'm too sentimental."

He offers a brief peck to my cheek. "Happy anniversary."

The more he lingers, close enough for me to smell starch in his waistcoat, makes me wonder if his kiss is the same.

Dancing a little and humming, he moves to my basket. "I suppose it is the traditional wedding meal." He flips back the checked cloth and finds the warm kasav. In the calabash is warm soup. "This is a treat."

"Broth this time."

Picking a piece of the bread, he fingers it into his mouth. The pleasure of it makes him sigh. "The military doesn't dine better."

The banter in his eyes dies. "My next command is coming soon. The Americans and the British now play in Saint-Domingue's waters. Spain must defeat this advance."

"The sea is big. My father was a great fisherman, but he couldn't tell where the fish would be."

Pulling another long piece of the kasav, he again puts it into his mouth and licks the crumbs off his lips. "We'll know. My superiors want to make a big push to prove our worth. Once away, it will be a while before I return. But I will return."

"From what I hear, Toussaint and Papillon are wise. The French begrudgingly respect how Toussaint particularly keeps his troops disciplined. Many wish he fought for the French."

He flips the hood on, covering his thick, tightly curled hair, which he's cut to an inch high. "I want to see our Françoise. I want to see her before I leave."

It is such an earnest plea; I surrender with a slow nod. "Oui, but not today. She's with my aunt."

"Let's go, now. I won't make it a long visit."

"I can't take a man, even a brother, into the convent, not without permission."

"I must play a brother to see my daughter? Am I an oncle?"

My gut clenches. "With French soldiers about, it is a risk for you to be here."

"Lunic had special permission to be with you in the convent, before he abandoned you?"

His earnest gaze feels as if he's unwrapped a tightly held bandage and exposed scars. "He has not—"

"Gone for many months. Leaving you alone to raise his niece and Françoise."

Jean-Jacques knows too much of my life and I know none of his, not even where he lays his head. "But you'll be doing the same. Seeing my daughter, then leaving."

That smile and dimple collide. "I'll have double the incentive to return. I know what I've lost. Two days from now, let me see her."

He turns and walks out of my life. He'll be back to continue cutting away my excuses until he's skinned my soul bare.

28

Marie-Claire

1792

Cap-Français

I take my two-and-a-half-year-old daughter to the gardens. Françoise is in my arms, with lilac ribbons in her plaited thick hair.

She smells of lavender and coconut and milk.

Her eyes light up when she spots a flowering cactus. The bloom on the prickly green body is pink. I set her down, but don't want her to dirty her dress of gold and yellow.

Yet, this is where she was conceived—in love, in haste, in sorrow.

"Maman, flower."

I bend, letting my burgundy-print gown drape the fallen leaves. "C'est, bébé. It is pretty, but do not touch. It has spikes. It can hurt you."

"Not everything that looks good is good, my child." Jean-Jacques is here. His deep voice is melancholy.

"The father has come for you, Françoise. He's here to bless you."

Removing his hood, he stares for moment at me and at our daughter.

He must notice my child's eyes are his. "I should pick you up, to get a better look and give you the best blessing."

Nodding, I give him permission, but he does not move. He wants my voice to tell him it's fine, all is well. "Père, please embrace my child."

Scooping up Françoise, he sits on the bench. With our daughter in his arms, he rocks her and sings a hymn.

Yo sé que vive, mi Señor
Yo sé que vive, mi Señor

That was one of Elise's songs. I knew the tune.

Listening to the joy of his lyrics, I'm lost in the melody. The vision of the life we might've had intrudes.

Jean-Jacques lifts his gaze to me and in perfect French says, "Je sais que mon Seigneur vit." He knows his redeemer lives.

Yet the way he's looking at Françoise and then me, I'm not sure who he thinks will redeem him.

It isn't me.

I don't have enough faith in him or myself to restore a fly.

The years apart can't renew our love, but the friendship we had in the beginning, when it was a girl and a boy chatting on a bench, should live again.

FRANÇOISE AND ADÉLAÏDE HAVE FOUND ELISE'S STACK OF OLD NEWS-papers. Yellowed *Gazette de Saint-Domingue* from '91. Older ones, *Affiches Américaines* from '89, have all been cut into paper dolls.

I pick up the dolls and see Pierre's writing in the space around the print. Didn't know he read them, too. His marks are on an editorial suggesting absolute rule for white citizens of Saint-Domingue. What do the checks mean? Agreement or something to discuss later? Pierre never mentioned any of this.

I drop the pages and answer the knock on the door.

Mamie's there. "I brought you letters. One is from Monsieur Lunic."

Seeing the folded paper makes my pique cool. I'm getting upset over nothing. "Thank you."

She hovers, waiting for me to open it.

Breaking the seal, I scan Pierre's slanted cursive, looking for a return date. My dry eyes sting. I want to cry. But I have no tears left.

"Marie-Claire, what does he say?"

Crushing the yellowed papier ministre within my palms, I shake my head. "Pierre's not coming back, not for a long time, if ever. He sends me rubbish about staying to make himself a success. The man is sure I'm secure and safer in Saint-Domingue than at his side."

"I'm sorry, Marie-Claire. I thought he loved—"

"I'm strong, Mamie. My marriage was for convenience. I'm respectable and conveniently raising a daughter and a niece without a husband."

I yank off the thin gold band on my finger. It rolls across the table spinning.

Round and round, it falls and goes silent.

Before either of us says a word, Elise barges into my room. "May I borrow your . . . shawl? I'm going to the theater . . . What has happened? Lunic is dead. Isn't he?"

My heart collapses in my chest. "Non." The word sounds airy and lost. "Why . . . why do you say such?"

"Paris is raging. There are severe food shortages causing people to riot. The paper says the king is going to be arrested just like our old governor." She tugs the *Moniteur Général,* her latest renegade paper, from her reticule, and shows me.

My dressing gown, with curly bobbin point lace on the collar, swishes as I pace. The little bit of lace is expensive, but I made it a while ago expecting Pierre's return. "Chasing ambition has put him in harm's way. I'm to be a widow again."

"Non." Elise wrings her hands. "He loves you. He wouldn't be foolish enough to risk his life."

My gaze goes to the paper dolls and the evidence that Pierre stays informed, too. I'm gutted. "Was getting rich and becoming a Grand Blanc worth it?"

Mamie takes the copy of *Moniteur Général.* "Monsieur Lunic's life is here. You're here. He'll come back."

Now my head is shaking, saying non. "I didn't love him enough. And he knew it. That's why he took such risks. I'm not enough."

Moving to the window, I look past the blue curtains at soldiers marching through Place Royale.

"He's been gone over a year. His affairs are in order, and he left deeds to his property to take care of Adélaïde."

"That's how good—"

"That letter has no mention of Françoise. He's her father only when he's here and when he thinks it will melt my heart and let him into my bed."

Burning, I want to rip down the curtains, but I pull my hands to my sides. "It worked. And I wanted him and our family."

"What are you saying, Marie-Claire?"

"This marriage is a lie. And nothing can make it true. That's why he's away and in danger."

Elise rests a hand on my shoulder. "You need to calm down."

"And you need to listen. If singing in the theater was open to you, would you let anything stop you?"

"Non. You know I wouldn't."

"And that is the difference between us. I let you all persuade me to marry to get protections. I had protections. I was enough to protect Françoise. I was enough. I could've returned to Léogâne and made a way for myself. Then I'd have—I'd not fear for a man who doesn't think enough about me to stay safe."

Creases form on Elise's brow as she fumes. "You're respectable again. You're the wife of a good man."

"I was the wife of a good man before Pierre." I stare at my grand-mère. "Now, I'm just another woman of color, a Black woman who married a Blanc for comfort and was deserted."

"Elise, let's let Marie-Claire calm down. She has every right to be angry." Mamie tries to pull Elise from the room but can't.

"You make yourself sound like a mulatto mistress, using your wiles to entrap him. Marie-Claire, Pierre Lunic loves you. He worships the ground you walk on. Don't blame us if you've ruined things."

I smack my head with my hand and am glad my ring is on the table. "I cannot blame you or anyone for my being a fool. I don't hold grudges."

Elise's mouth opens like she wants to protest. Instead, she walks to the door. "I have to go, but Lunic will be back. Be patient and wait for your husband to return."

He has, my first husband, the one who truly loves me. I need to admit it and be brave enough to follow my heart.

• • •

THE DAY HAS FINALLY COME. I SEE IT IN JEAN-JACQUES'S EYES. WE are standing in the garden, me in an old blue gown with a small bustle, making my body, with the baby weight I can't lose, look curvaceous.

He's in priest's robes again. The brown fabric decorated with a white corded cincture hides the braiding of his promotion. "They've officially made me a colonel to Papillon."

"Not Toussaint?"

"Non. He's a busy man with no openings in his camp. I've learned to stay where I'm needed . . . and admired."

He moves to the bench, and I watch his swagger. Even in the costume, his gait is confident and bold. I want to tell him not to go, but I've offered no reason for him to stay.

"Marie-Claire." He takes my hand and draws it into the sleeve of his robe. The heat he's shedding is like a fire or the burning sun. "I'd like to see Françoise one more time."

Isn't there a different question? I see it in his eyes, can taste it in the fragrance about him, the smells of mango and musk.

"Would like to see her, even if I'm to be a brother to her mother."

There's no denying him, not when the war outside of Place Royale could steal him from my life. Keeping his hand, I lead him back to the convent.

We slip inside through the kitchen.

"Brother, dinner won't be started for a few more hours."

Pulling on white gloves, he fingers the clean table. "Is this where you make kasav and other goodies? I always like a wife who can cook."

I smile and tug him forward. "Follow me."

We go down the corridor. In a nearby room, my aunt sings her lyrics. "Elise's practicing for choir. Tomorrow."

Jean-Jacques tries to clasp our linked palms as if all were not at risk.

"Do you mind, Brother Jean—"

I bump into Adélaïde and almost leap to the roof.

"Sorry, Marie-Claire. I didn't mean to startle you."

Holding my chest, gasping, I wave my hands. "Non, I'm sorry. I frighten too easily."

She stares at me and the hooded Jean-Jacques.

"Brother Jean, the repair is needed in my room. It's around the corner. Third door."

Silently, he nods, makes the turn, and disappears.

I lock my arms about Adélaïde. "What is it? What has you cheered?"

"My oncle has sent me a letter, and it has a drawing of the Seine. A beautiful river."

Pierre has written to his niece, but nothing for me and Françoise. I want to ask if he's told her anything of the violence or if he's found a way home. I won't because I'm boiling.

"Marie-Claire, what is it?"

"I'm sad Monsieur Lunic has to keep extending his visit."

She shrugs her shoulders. She's a deflated strawberry. "Oui. I wish he'd come back sooner. He probably has a new project. He cannot stand idle."

"Oui. Never idle." My heart hurts. Pierre's silence hurts. "Let me get to Brother Jean. With Monsieur Lunic away, I must turn elsewhere to fix things. Can't let anyone think things are in disrepair and I want to replace my husband."

"Non. Non. We can't have that. Oncle will be back soon. You'll see. And Françoise is sleeping. I just put her down."

Adélaïde goes to her quarters down the hall.

Remembering how to breathe when my stomach doesn't feel kicked in, I walk as evenly as I can. Jean-Jacques is not waiting at my door. He's boldly gone inside.

I enter the room and bolt the lock. With his hood off, Jean-Jacques stands over the crib. Françoise is snoring. She's dribbling.

He bends and touches the braids I've made, nice tight ones in her wavy hair. "She has my mother's mouth, from what I can remember. But definitely your small nose."

"Well, she is three. Everything is small."

When he stands, he takes my hand and leads me about the room like he owns it. "This is where you lay your head."

"It is. It is a nice set of rooms."

"I don't believe we've ever been alone in rooms."

"At Notre-Dame de l'Assomption." I sniffle. "We were alone."

My eyes should be dry as desert sand, but they aren't. Watching Jean-Jacques pray over our girl is the sweetest thing.

"What is wrong, Marie-Claire?"

"Just seeing you and our daughter."

He hums Elise's song and spins me. For a heavy voice such as his, his whispers are light. He releases me.

"It's no use. I'm to go and serve in battle. I should do it with a clean heart. I still love you, Marie-Claire. I want God to forgive me for wanting another man's wife. But since I married you first, I'm not sure there is anything to repent for. What's your opinion?"

"Repent for something worthy." I step around our sleeping child and wrap my arms about Jean-Jacques and kiss him.

He's surprised, but it doesn't last. His lips fit perfectly to mine. I taste him and it is sweet like mangoes, just like I remember.

His hands whip off my kerchief and dip into the round gown's bodice. Those hands are rough, as I've grown to like, but this sensation is different against my bosom.

I lead him away from our daughter into my bedchamber. It isn't a good idea, but she cannot awaken to me being molested by a priest or kissing a man she doesn't know to be her father.

Jean-Jacques closes the door with a gentle push, then moves to the window. "A view of the gardens. And on the first floor. I have another place to visit at Place Royale."

"You aren't coming back, remember?" Dropping my face in my hands, I groan. "You should go, before I make a bigger fool of myself."

"For the woman I love and who loves me, I'll always be back."

Pierre claimed the same but won't return.

"This is rash. I'm hurt and still grieving us. We should—"

His hands are on me, caressing me like I'm delicate and precious and in dire need of affection.

Palms sliding to my cheeks, he captures my eyes. "You haven't thought, Marie-Claire. That is good for you. You're acting with your heart."

"Can't be. The thing doesn't work. It's too busy missing you."

When he leans into me, I don't shy away. I turn my mouth to his. His search to find me begins anew.

I let him, for I'm tired of hiding, tired of waiting for love, tired of all the things I think I wanted.

He opens the lacings of my tunic and plants kisses down my bosom. His robe falls to the floor, but he eases his sword beside it. His fingers undo the buttons and the wrapping until nothing separates us but my shift, his shirt.

As quietly as he can, Jean-Jacques picks me up and sweeps me to the bed. "I think we're too old for making love in a garden. A bed, it's a first for us, but I will miss how the stars fill your eyes."

I should say non, non. We can't.

I should remind him that this is holy ground, but my mouth is quieted by the taste of him, the salt of his throat, his Adam's apple.

His teeth rake the arch of my neck, then tease the valley of my breasts. "The scent of lavender here and here is as good as the garden. Better."

This feeling, this madness, covers me. His warm, rough hands smooth my skin, push me to joy. My legs cradle him, locking about him as if to keep him forever. I want someone to stay and love me.

But Jean-Jacques can't.

Yet, he's not leaving, not until this is done and I'm sated with memories that last, that will keep me from confusing love and desire with commitment.

Hot and wet.

Empty, then full. I burst and insist we start again.

Jean-Jacques laughs but his dancing hips oblige, and we make love like today is our last day on earth.

All the while he whispers, "J'adore. J'adore. J'adore."

And I answer, voicing nothing but my pleasure.

29

Marie-Claire

1793

Cap-Français

Sitting at my desk, I show Françoise letters. I made them big and blocky. I want her to have an education. With all the changes to Place Royale, to Le Cap, I'm not sure if it will be possible.

"Maman," she says with Jean-Jacques's grin, "better?"

I hug her tightly and wrinkle the long tunic I've wrapped about her limbs. She's a gangly thin thing, just like I once was. "A little, my girl."

Her tiny fingers pick up the folded note I've just received. Jean-Jacques has his secretary draft them often. He's been gone a few weeks, but after months of being together, it feels like an eternity.

I don't know if he sped up battles or the enemy merely surrendered upon seeing his forces, but he always hurries back. I didn't feel lonely. And he loves his little girl.

A knock pounds on my door. "Marie-Claire, Madame Governess?"

"Come in, Adélaïde. Why so formal?"

"You've taken over the head nurse position. Congratulations."

"It's a good position, but things change. Even with a new governor, the acceptance of the Affranchi here might not last."

Her brow scrunches. "I forget sometimes we are not the same."

"Of course, I'm older." I make her laugh and offer a funny face to Françoise, who giggles.

But that's not what Adélaïde means. Race now intrudes. Yet it always does in Saint-Domingue.

"May I ask you something? You don't have to answer."

The cherub has yanked on one of her curls that always flips into her eyes. Adélaïde's drawn face looks serious. She hasn't been sad like this in a long time.

"I want you to send me to France to be with my oncle."

Head tilting, I examine her. She looks shaken. "There's fighting in the streets of Paris. It's not safe."

"There's fighting in our streets." She clasps her arms about the bright blue sleeves of her pleated gown. Her gauzy kerchief frames the womanly body the young girl has developed. "Spain has every inch of the north but Le Cap. They'll be here next."

Adélaïde rubs her sweaty hands. "Skirmishes are everywhere. If it's not torches, it's bullets and cannons. A man had his whole leg ripped—"

I put my hands about Françoise's ears. "Please, chère, she's learning a lot. Let's keep her from wounds and war a little longer."

I've never said the word *war* before. *Battles* and *fighting* and *struggles* sound better and are shorter. My daughter pulls at my fingers as she dribbles down the front of her pinafore.

Françoise may lose both her fathers, one to the French Revolution and one to Saint-Domingue's war.

"After what I've lived through, Marie-Claire, I don't know how to keep pretending it's not happening."

When I reach for Adélaïde's hand, she scoots away like I'm poison. Offering her my sweetest, most patient smile, I say, "We are safe, Adélaïde. We live in safety with the best produce and gardens. The priests . . . the Brothers here are good."

"Beyond the guard gate, rebels and soldiers are still burning buildings. North of here in the Tannerie area, the brigands drill and have skirmishes with the French troops. We receive the wounded."

"Brigands? Non. Those are Spanish troops. They've allowed some of the *former rebels* to join the military."

Huffing, beet red in the face, Adélaïde groans. "You sound sympathetic to them. Because of your lover? Is he a rebel or soldier?"

My throat burns a little with vomit. "What did you say?"

"Françoise says *père* all the time. You have taken a lover and he has confused her."

Kissing my little tattler's brow, I sigh. "This is my business."

"Marie-Claire, I do the laundry. You're flushed in the mornings. Your cheeks are puffy and glowing. My oncle, your husband, has not returned, but you're with child."

Denying Jean-Jacques is the last thing I'll ever again do. "Oui, I'm increasing. Oui, this babe is not Lunic's."

"But you love my oncle. He loves—"

I pick up my letters, the two Pierre has sent since he left, and shove them at her. "Where's the love, Adélaïde?"

"That's how you justify infidelity? A poorly written note from a busy man?"

How does one share the freedom of living and doing what the heart feels is right? How to describe something as natural as breathing?

You tell the truth.

"Lunic and I have never . . . loved . . . we married for convenience. But now he and I don't want the same things. He's never cared for my charity work. And I never supported his dreams enough. We tried. It didn't work."

"He'll be humiliated. You don't want him back at all."

Non. I don't. I want nothing of him, not anymore. "I've written to him, confessed my condition, and asked him to divorce me."

"What does he say?"

"He'll not divorce me. He wants me to go to his property in Port-au-Prince before it's obvious I abused his trust."

Shaking, her lithe shoulders tremble; Adélaïde stares at me. "My oncle is merciful. How could you break your vows to such a good man?"

Her words are small, but they feel like a hammer driving my head onto a pike. "You've seen us, Adélaïde. Your oncle and I, we do not agree on much. He hates when I go feed the hungry."

"When was the last time you did that, Marie-Claire? It's been months. You're sitting around waiting on your lover. You don't obey your husband, but this man makes you stand still."

There's truth in her furious words.

I've stopped going for fear of missing Jean-Jacques in the unpredict-able moments he can sneak away.

"Look at you. You glow instead of being shamed. I thought we were the same. You've called us twins."

My gaze sweeps from her angry poked-out lips to her beautiful rosy cheeks then to her ebony slippers. "My shoes are dark like yours. But I walk out of these rooms in my Black face, and I have to prove I'm for peace. You just leave. We're not the same. Our journeys will never be the same."

"You've not suffered more than me."

"Non. I haven't. And I've never been chattel, though my face says I could be. You were rescued. Your abusers have faced death. Those who've hurt my family never will. There are hundreds of other things you and Pierre can have and experience, of which I might never be able to partake."

Holding out my olive hand, my Black fingers, I hope she takes the invitation. "But I still love you."

"You're different than what I thought, madame. I'm sorry about that."

I put Françoise on the floor with her toys. "The man who is my first love, the man I married and thought dead, Françoise's true father, is alive. He's returned for me when Pierre has abandoned me for France. I've a new position. I'm going on with life."

"Then send me to France to bring my oncle back. Then you two can love again and there will be no more differences. We'll be on the same side."

With all the fighting in Le Cap, colonists are leaving. But Paris is dangerous, too. "Non. You stay. We are still family."

Adélaïde stomps her feet and starts sobbing. "Send me to my oncle who looks like me, who knows which side is worth fighting for."

"Write your oncle and get his blessings. I do love you, Adélaïde, but I can also love a man fighting for freedom."

"A soldier? One of those rehabilitated rebels? He might've killed my family."

Tears soak her kerchief as if a pail of water has been dumped onto her head. She runs from the room.

I let her go.

Nothing she's said is wrong.

All of her indictments of me are true. The charges of the rebels who are now soldiers for Spain could be, too.

But I choose me. I'm a woman madly in love with a man fighting to change the world.

HELPING ADÉLAÏDE PACK IS ABYSMAL. HER ROOM'S SMALL. WE BUMP into one another crossing from the closet to her bed. Many months have passed, and we've not fully reconciled. The birth of the twins has softened things, the way only babies can.

"Marie-Claire, you need to go back to bed. Your confinement was early. Rest. Go to your family."

"You're family, too." I hold one of her gowns close to my chest. I smell the lavender of her soap. "You don't have to go."

"And become an arguing Lobelot? Non." She takes the dress from me and stuffs it into her bag, then stops, her reddened eyes gazing at me. "You can come. Oncle offered for everyone to come."

Pierre wants to reconcile. It takes a considerable amount of goodness to want to be forgiving. If it's sincere, I do not know. This time I know Jean-Jacques is alive. When all the battles are over, we'll be together.

That's my hope.

The war, the guns, the deaths are getting closer to Place Royale. Soldiers from the guard gate are patients in the hospital.

"Marie-Claire, are you thinking about it?" The hope in her voice, in her sparkling blue eyes, dies with a shake of my head.

"France is too dangerous. His old friend de Blanchelande is in trouble. The former governor has been tried and convicted. He'll face the guillotine. Pierre . . ."

Silence covers us. Paris is in chaos like Le Cap, but there the Petit Blancs are killing the titled Grands, any royalists.

Her face turns away to the closet. My rejection stirs the tensions anew, but Adélaïde has stood beside me, making sure each of my babies breathed air. Dark skin, reaching for the sun, protected in swaddling blankets—they were miracles. After watching Mamie and Maman and Elise work together for my children, I understand what matters.

Clapping my hands, I dismiss the sad talk. "Nonetheless, I've promised Lunic to get you ready and send you by ship. Paris, he says, can be cold. It's different from here and India."

Her lips flatten. "How has he forgiven you? How does anyone forget what hurts them?"

That I didn't know.

I brush a straight lock of brunette hair from her mistrusting eyes. "I wish I understood and could put it as an ingredient in my soup. Soupe de pardon, forgiving soup, has a nice sound."

Boom.

The walls rattle.

Adélaïde launches into my arms.

"The Brothers have arranged for you to join Governor-General Galbaud and the ten thousand others who are fleeing with him."

I close her portmanteau. "No matter what happens between Lunic and me, it has nothing to do with you."

When I open the door, I see people running.

Priests who have calmed parishioners flee as if Armageddon has descended. With the sound of cannon fire shaking the walls, maybe the end is nigh.

"Oh, Mother Mary, take care of us tonight. St. Michael be a shield."

Adélaïde grabs her bag and then my palm.

"No way on this earth I can let you out of my sight. I'll get you to France another way. Tonight, we find safety together."

She nods.

The next blast clears my mind. Hand in hand, Adélaïde and I run against the crowds to my children.

We fly into my rooms.

Maman is pacing and clutching her rosary.

All the babies cry—Françoise on the floor by the crib, the two little ones inside. My twins.

Elise picks up Jacques, the fussiest of my children. Adélaïde bends down and scoops up Célestine. This little girl has the prettiest eyes, like her père.

Mamie is sitting on my sofa, knitting like our world isn't on fire. "The wounded speak his name, Marie-Claire. Dessalines is a ferocious officer. They call him the tiger. If the French knew you had his children—"

Shaking my head, I silence her. "We have to leave."

My fingers are still linked to Adélaïde's. "Let's all flee out of the city."

"Oui. The babies must be safe," she says. We separate and she starts gathering things, stuffing clothes and a toy in her bag.

"The carriage won't be pulled round. I know of another way. Let's go into the countryside."

"We should head to Léogâne," Maman says. "It's always safest when Le Cap is burning."

Elise glares at her. "We were all getting along. Must you go back to the past?"

Ignoring them, I keep packing. My insides rip with the smell of sulfur coming through the window. Fighting is here inside my Place Royale.

Jean-Jacques hasn't met these babes. No letters will pass. The fighting has cut us off like a noose. His enemies will stab my children's hearts to drive their father mad.

My mother smiles with pride. "Dessalines is fighting to end enslavement and for the rights Ogé and Chavannes and even Mackandal died for."

That last name is like magic. It makes Mamie leap up, and Elise to shiver.

The window breaks.

A musket ball sinks into my cream wall. Black powder from the shot mars everything.

Maman sings her strange hymn, then says, "Judgment is here."

Something hits the broken shutter and catches it on fire. The curtains become engulfed. "The mob is coming. Françoise. Françoise!"

My four-year-old runs to Mamie and grabs her hand. Elise and Maman have the babies. Adélaïde carries the stuffed bag of clothes and some fruit. We go down a corridor. The Brothers, all the priests, are running. They're yelling at us to get out.

I hesitate. "They need help. My patients."

"Non. Maire-Claire, non. This time you protect family." Maman's voice is stern. "Save these babies."

I scoot Adélaïde close to my hip and lead them through the dimming passageways. Smoke is everywhere, as if this is a boucherie curing meat.

The door we intend to escape through is blocked. Many are pushing on it. A priest makes the sign of the cross and rams the door open.

We stay together and flow with the crowds. We are a sea trying to crash onto safe shores.

"They're coming." A man with bandages on his head runs as if he's being chased.

Maman sings her strange tune of two coming down. Elise sings it with her.

They are summoning death. It's here, with its putrid sulfur smell in the air.

"Our soldiers have retreated!" a lady screams, running in circles.

"We're doomed," another says.

Adélaïde looks small and frightened. I don't release her hand. We are different, but she's a part of me.

We fling open the kitchen doors and dash out to the grounds. Patients and physicians and priests pour out every door.

The explosions are deafening.

I lead us across the street and into my garden. Past the spices, and my bench and stream, I take them the secret way to the carriage house. "The dray's in here."

Maman climbs on the back of the dusty thing. She steadies the twins in her lap. Mamie has Françoise. Adélaïde and I hitch up the horse.

Done. We climb on board.

The route to Léogâne is long. I remind them all, "We'll have to fight to survive."

Adélaïde leans over the wall and holds up old calabashes, even my kettle for the big batches of soup. "We have a few things to help us and we have each other."

Her voice is a whisper, but it's strong in courage.

People yelling.

Guns. Cannons.

All the noises are closer.

I pull up the reins and direct the horse to Chemin du Port-au-Prince, the way to Léogâne.

My lover's forces are destroying the place I've called home.

Smoke begins to catch us.

"The gardens," Mamie says calmly. "They're on fire."

"No one can burn! No one!" Maman is rocking and holding my babies.

Rebels and soldiers in all colors of uniform fight along the way. This can't be Jean-Jacques. He'd not burn our special place.

With all my might, I tug the reins and make the horse move faster. We speed onto the chemin.

"Like soup runs, Adélaïde. You're beside me."

The babies are crying. Elise starts a hymn.

> *"Worthy the Lamb that died, they cry,*
> *To be exalted thus!*
> *Worthy the Lamb, our hearts reply,*
> *For He was slain for us!"*

Can't look back and see Place Royale, my safe haven, destroyed. I look ahead. I hope for tomorrow.

Passing the Bazac, I see more soldiers. Because of my confinement, I've not been here in months to feed the enslaved.

Then I hear gunfire coming from the provision grounds.

Shot after shot.

Bam. Bam. Bam.

Adélaïde and I witness the slaughtering of unarmed men, Blancs killing Blacks. It can't be unseen. I pray again to St. Michael to protect us and the poor enslaved.

Bam. Bam.

More slain.

More sin.

Maman sings louder. Her voice, her prophecy song covers Elise's hymn.

> *"Of their callings, one craved power*
> *The other sought peace every hour*
> *To rid famine war made flower*
> *Black, Blanc, and Brown—death had its due."*

A man in a uniform waves at us from the field.

"Arrêtez! S'il te plaît. Arrêtez!"

Yelling at us to stop. Never.

Adélaïde grasps the reins and our dray sprints past him. "To Léogâne then, Marie-Claire. No helping anyone. No soldiers. No Blanc, Black, or Brown."

Boom. Pop. Boom.

The shots, close and piercing, are the last thing I hear before my world shatters.

The Prophecy

One day the gods of war came down.

The earth shook, dancing from the sound.

Zinsu, Zinsi will loose the bound,

And this hope made the world feel new.

Of their callings, one craved power

The other sought peace every hour

To rid famine war made flower

Black, Blanc, and Brown—death had its due.

The twins couldn't see the world the same.

They broke it and blasphemed its name.

Then set the fool pieces to flame.

All believed liberty was through.

—ANONYMOUS, STYLED IN THE FORM OF UTENZI

30

Toya

1793
Saint-Marc

I sat at Janjak's table for dinner. We could relax. The heavy fighting ended. His forces controlled the north. His chef brought bowls of soup, steaming broth of herbs and onions. The crystal goblets on the large table held a shimmering red wine. It smelled like berries, not the harsh slave tafia.

Not exactly the meal to serve in a royal court, but with two princes, one arriving unexpectedly, it would have to do.

I'd been on this Saint-Domingue soil for thirty-five of my fifty-five seasons and I was again sitting with power, descendants of African power.

Gaou Guinon's grandson, the leader of the Black Spanish forces, Toussaint, sat across from Janjak, a descendant of Tegbesu's line.

I marveled at how they engaged in conversation. They were like old friends, but fluent in the language of battle. Where had they learned this ease?

Especially Janjak.

He was elegant whether offering a subtle joke or a decisive vision of a battle plan. Was this the nature of his blood, the influence of the woman he had loved and lost, or something greater—prophecy?

Toussaint's ebony hat with the large feather was on the sideboard. The red scarf he used to keep the sweat from pouring down his face was there, too.

"General Dessalines, I must say your troops have been drilled superbly. Godfather Baptista, a free Black, taught me French so I could read philosophy. He gave me a favorite book of his, by an enslaved man named Epictetus."

Janjak's bushy brows furrowed. "Doesn't sound French. But can his soldiers drill?"

"Non." Toussaint swirled his goblet. "Epictetus was a Roman who freed himself, went into exile, then gave lectures on life. He believed one should never possess worries about what one can't control."

Laying his spoon on his calabash, Janjak's gaze dipped. "Like who's killed on the battlefield or whether a hospital or church is burnt?"

Silence tied all tongues. The recent skirmishes had been very violent. Many innocents died.

"General, we cannot control what the rebel forces do, or the French," Toussaint said. "Except for Le Cap, we have the north and the west. That's a good job. Well done."

Fighting still broke out constantly around the city. The last revolt had overrun Place Royale, the place where Janjak's Marie-Claire lived.

Silent, even distant, he spooned his broth. The man had heard nothing from her in months. He assumed all was lost.

"Dessalines, we are accomplishing what we want. What Spain wants. That's good."

"You ordered it so. I've done my part to keep my territory free of the French and rebellions. The king of Spain should reward us for what his forces couldn't do."

"I agree." Toussaint lifted his glass. "Bravo, Général."

His use of French, not Kreyòl, *Byen fèt, Jeneral*, wasn't haughty, but I sensed it was deliberate, matching his changing sympathies. Our king wanted a new king, a French one.

Janjak, who always had a lusty appetite, stirred more than he ate. Perhaps his newfound Christianity taught him to put an imagined cutlass to his own throat, cutting one's hunger when dining with rulers.

Or was it the soup making him sad? His Marie-Claire made fine broth with perfectly caramelized bits. I remembered it from the one time we met and she sent me away with some and kasav.

Lowering his half-empty glass to the fine mahogany table, Toussaint tapped the wood. "I'm concerned. There's talk that once all of King Carlos's dirty work is done, he'll disband the Colored guards. They've yet to abolish slavery in the places we've taken for them."

"Their forces haven't gotten any smarter. They'll crumble and need us all over again."

Plinking the painted buttons on his coat, one of which bore an image of a crowned king, another a woman, perhaps his wife, Toussaint huffed. "I think we need to be wary. I don't think Spain understands how much they need us. Perhaps we should consider others who do."

"Change sides? But our weapons and uniforms are Spanish."

"Alliances can be changed like a uniform. The French are discussing ending slavery. They'll recognize the Blacks as full citizens."

"Blacks, or the Browns? Many interpret the forks in the French Assembly's mouths to exclude anyone bossale or congo. I've not risked everything for mulattoes to join with the French Blancs and then exclude the dark-skin soldiers, the ones who've won the hard-earned peace."

"France has learned this lesson and Spain has a time limit on our usefulness."

"What are you saying, Commander? Say it plainly."

"Dessalines, I'm asking if I have your support if we must do things differently."

There were only two other men at the table, Toussaint's aide-de-camp and Janjak's secretary. These men were probably the most loyal, but each sat squirming in their sparkling white Spanish uniforms.

Rising from his chair with his goblet in hand, Janjak offered a toast, clanking the side of his glass with his knife. "To the wisest leader who'll continue to lead the Black forces to permanent victory. Permanent victory is where my allegiance lies."

Everyone sipped.

I did and was thankful to be at the table, but shifting sides wasn't something a warrior did. It was confusing, and I hoped Janjak had Nosakhere's talents for strategy to understand what this new plan meant.

Watching the commander and my prince shake hands, I wondered if I'd seen the gods come down. These two men, Janjak and Toussaint, were bringing liberty to Saint-Domingue.

I toasted myself, too.

For I was prepared to fight to the death to bring Janjak's vision of freedom to Saint-Domingue.

TONIGHT AT JANJAK'S TABLE, HIS COOK ROASTED PHEASANT WITH mushrooms. This would've been good to serve Toussaint a month ago, but one never knew what ingredients the cooks would happen upon. Food was under tight control. Blockades came and went. Every force—British, French, Spanish, and perhaps the new Americans—wanted to conquer Saint-Domingue.

A lieutenant came into the dining room and shoved papers at him. "General, what is your opinion of Giles?"

"I'm considering the request and the punishment. I'll let you know in the morning."

Janjak's tone was distant. He picked at the bird on his plate.

I wondered why our leader wasn't addressed with his new rank, division general.

The officer saluted then left the room.

Janjak rose and moved to the window. He was well appointed in his new uniform—with a pristine white coat trimmed with gold braids on his shoulders and shiny gold buttons, lots of buttons. The scarlet cuffs and lapels were fine, too.

"What of this Captain Jean Giles?" Louis Boisrond-Tonnere, his new secretary, asked. He was tall, fair-skinned, handsome, but not haughty.

"I like his first name." Everyone around the table, mostly Black men, a few Brown, laughed and drank their wine.

Staring out the open window, he raised his glass. "I've not decided about his release or continued punishment."

"A week's imprisonment for being late to return on leave is enough servitude, General Dessalines." Boisrond-Tonnere refilled his glass.

That was the crime, lateness? Da'mon and Agwé—images of them playing with my boy in the Cormier provision grounds hovered before me . . .

And so did their horrid deaths.

"You must send a message, sir," Boisrond-Tonnere said. He was learned, given the privilege of education by the French, but despised them as much as Janjak. "I believe you understand a man taking leave to see about his love."

This hinting about the Le Cap woman was not kind and brought a frown to Janjak's face, one he quickly covered with a sip from his glass.

Boisrond-Tonnere pushed away his empty plate and pulled out his ink and quill. "I'm at the ready for dictation."

"I'm not. I said I'd give my opinion in the morning."

The man at the end of the table with a hooked nose slurped ale. "What type of message will it send to keep a good soldier locked away? We need Giles to have his battalion ready. We can't afford much loss of manpower."

"No man is indispensable. No one." Janjak returned to the table and picked up the notes his scribe had written.

To me it was a bunch of scribble, but this paper made them happy, made things happen.

"Gran Toya, what is it you're looking at?"

Now it was I who was caught off guard. I set my fork down. "Pride, Division General. Pride."

His characteristic grin returned. "Gentlemen, may I have a moment with my blessed aunt?"

The men did as their local king asked. Soon, it was he and I in a room three times as big as our hut at Cormier.

"You're proud of my strong leadership? They say I have an iron fist."

"I think they call you the tiger with the iron fist."

He pumped his hand, pushing up a sleeve, and I saw an inch or two of scars.

Knocking it back down, he almost seemed shamed. "I had Giles detained. He's a leader, and he was late from leave. It's a principle."

"It's Duclos."

"I remember. Da'mon and Agwé were killed for being late. Since rising in command, I've never violated my oath, even for Marie-Claire. Duty and liberty before love."

"There's nothing wrong with discipline, Janjak, but had Duclos shown any mercy, those two boys would probably be at your side like Boisrond-Tonnere."

His palm curled about his wrist. "If I had been selfish like Giles, I'd have my wife and the children waiting for me in my quarters."

"You're working for everyone's children. For all people to be happy."

He turned and peered out the window again. The sea was distant. The ships that used to cover the bay were few. "I wish I'd broken orders, left camp, and spirited away Françoise and Marie-Claire, with her womb carrying our next child."

"Your sadness is not about discipline or another life. It's this woman you've misplaced, but you've found others, like Thérèse, for comfort."

"Thérèse is an old friend. A man needs friends. How many wives did your King Tegbesu have?"

"As many as he wanted."

A sigh leeched. He closed his eyes for a moment. "The worst fighting is around Le Cap. She couldn't have survived, but I still hope for a miracle."

"You cannot possibly think of going. If Toussaint's right hand, his tiger, is captured, do you know how it would demoralize the troops?"

"Neither my happiness nor hers matters. Liberty is at stake. This is for all Blacks."

"Blacks and the one Brown, Janjak?"

"Boisrond-Tonnere? He's as Black as me under his light skin. We see the world the same." He drummed the windowsill. "I don't know if Marie-Claire had our new baby."

"Are you missing little ones? There are orphans everywhere who need a strong man to look up to."

"Tante Toya, what if I'm not strong? What if I've been lucky? What if I'm wearing this coat with the braids, all the trappings of a Spanish officer, and I should've farmed goats in the mountains and lived with the Taíno?"

Janjak came back to the table and tossed the papers. "And I can't read my own orders. I'm a charlatan."

"Under Spain's flag, you've secured the west and most of the north. It's why you get new big titles. Why read when you have an adviser?"

His laughter was slow but rising. Like the tide, the sound became full and sweeping, lifting his sad eyes.

"Janjak, I once thought those born on this soil enmeshed in French ways were soft, but I was wrong. Persistence is in your blood and in the bodies of those who breathe this air. Saint-Domingue will rise and be at the top of the world, the highest of mountains because of it."

"It's not wrong to mourn what could've been. I know you do. But if Marie-Claire lived, she would've gotten a message to me, somehow."

This time I had no ready answer, for I had regrets, many regrets, but I purposed to tell my king something to encourage him. "You and your love were born under the same turning sun. Your destinies are entwined. You'll see her again, and the babes of her womb, but only if you keep winning. It's your destiny."

"Destiny," he repeated. "We joked about both of us being born in '58, barely a month apart, as a sign." He pounded the table. "I'll send a letter for Giles to be freed. I need good men, especially ones who've learned lessons."

Janjak left the dining room, and I heard him speaking to his direct reports. "We must all rise together. Show mercy to Giles. Send a letter and remind all to take great care. I want no one taking unnecessary chances when the defeat of the French is at hand."

To the sounds of men hailing in agreement, I picked up my goblet. With my king's spirit cheered, I wouldn't let him dwell on which face of the sun he'd see his beloved again. With guns and fires raging in Le Cap, I suspected the dark side had already won.

• • •

THE YEAR CHANGED TO '94, AND EXCEPT FOR BRIEF BATTLES TO SET down rebellions or drive back French forces, Janjak's army continued in Saint-Marc. Rumblings about Toussaint's alliances continued. When I went to the dining room, I found Janjak pacing.

The open window invited cool breezes from the sea, scenting the room with briny, salty air.

The glass in his hand didn't have fancy red wine. When I stepped closer, the sharp and fiery smell of the tannish liquid burnt my nose.

My son looked disturbed.

"What's wrong, Janjak?"

"We fight under Spanish flags. We bleed and die for King Carlos, but he had Cabrera, Spain's commander in chief in the south and west, arrest Moyse. Toussaint's nephew is in chains."

Janjak downed the hard liquor.

"This is a struggle for power," I said. "The king of the white uniforms is trying to show Gaou Guinon's grandson is weak. Neither he nor his descendants can take the royal stool."

Janjak shrugged and went to the pitcher of tafia. "Want some?"

I shook my head. "That liquid can down horses."

"Horses." He gulped again. "But not tigers."

"This is another mountain, beyond the ones arising from beating the French. Gaou Guinon, the son, fought for power against his brother, Hussar. The older Hussar was wise enough to side with the Dahomey king Agaja, Tegbesu's father. Hussar was saved; the younger son was sold."

Janjak wore a blank expression. "Your wisdom is too much sometimes. Say it plainly. I've never read Epictetus."

"Be careful of your ally, and always choose a Dahomey."

A dimple surfaced, then disappeared. "This confirms Toussaint's fears. Spain will go back on its promises."

We were alone. This conversation was not the division general speaking to one of his corporals. It was mother and son. "What will Toussaint have us do?"

Janjak looked to the ceiling then gave me his goblet. "Toussaint says to stand by. Once Moyse is safe, we'll switch allegiances. The French National Assembly has again upheld Sonthonax's proclamation granting freedom to the enslaved and political rights to all Blacks and mulattoes."

"Didn't they do those things before and then refuse to uphold the edicts?"

"Wi and non. France only gave citizen rights to the free Blacks and Coloreds. They didn't abolish slavery. Ogé and Chavannes were killed trying to enforce it. They were turned over to the colonial assembly . . . by the Spanish." He rubbed his brow, clapping his palm against lines furrowing his forehead. "We are fools."

"Non. Janjak, you seized an opportunity. The Spanish king was the first to let Blacks be free and to join the military."

He grasped the table as if to shake it to pieces. "Is it too much to expect loyalty and liberty?"

"If the Spanish, whose colors you wear, can arrest Moyse, they can arrest Toussaint and you. And if the French prove to be similarly disloyal, make sure your king is ready to fight them all."

He patted his pocket and pulled out a little snuffbox. Janjak had taken up this nasty habit. "It will take a lot of bloodshed to do that."

This was the heavy burden of any leader, how to protect the herd, the young and old elephants, from the fury of lions.

"Tante Toya, I feel as if Marie-Claire and the children live, but I cannot look for them until this is all done. I must be ruthless. How am I to be Toussaint's sword, his tiger, if I cannot sleep thinking of her?"

"War is never safe, not for kings or queens or the children."

"A convent should've been safe. A hospital, too. Biassou had to rescue his mother from her nurse's position in the north. None of this is right."

Sitting beside Janjak, I offered him my best advice, something Tegbesu once told me. "In this war, you've always done what's right. My faith in you is complete." Then I added something to return his smile. "You'll look good in French red."

"I haven't decided, Gran Toya."

Moving to his hat, I picked it up and dusted it. "You have. You'll follow your king. You'll do what he wants. France is what he will choose, or he can select his own gallows if he continues with Spain. The message is clear."

"Janjak put the snuffbox into his pocket. "I'll follow the king when he decides. You may need to change the color of your battle garments if you choose to continue."

"French red will go with black and yellow. My team will be ready as soon as next week."

"We won't change sides that soon. The power of a hundred thousand Black fighters is hard to let go."

I headed to the door. When I looked back to say good night, Janjak pulled from his jacket the old letters his woman once wrote. No more have come.

If she was alive, I believed her smart enough to know she was a target; the families of kings or kings in waiting always were.

My opinion of Marie-Claire had grown. She wasn't soft and understood what Janjak must do. Creating a free and independent Saint-Dominique was worthy of sacrifice.

31

Marie-Claire

1794
Léogâne

Standing at the shore, as if I were waiting for my père, has me misty. The salt in the air stings my eyes. That's a good excuse for crying at the beach.

My père's been gone for three years. In the house he built, my family now stays. We are like a house of widows.

Thank the Heavenly Father for the children. Their love makes up for what's not there.

Françoise is with me. She's skipping along the beach. I watch her the way my mamie, my beloved grand-mère, watched me.

My daughter has a shiny shell in her hand. "Look, Maman. Look."

Her palm flattens, and there's a cowrie shell, gold and shiny and wet.

My tears fall harder. I kneel and hug her and hope to stay upright. But it's a terrible burden for a child to keep a parent going.

She stretches her five-year-old arms tighter about me. "I'll give you the shell, Maman, if that'll make you smile."

I snuggle my gangly girl. "You make me happy."

"You've not been since we left Grand-mamie to rest in the hills."

It was months and months ago when we fled Le Cap. My grand-mère had protected Françoise, taking the bullet that would have killed my child. My color-struck mamie died for my Black child.

She kept her calm and blessed her while she bled out.

On the side of the road, Elise sang as Adélaïde and Maman stayed back on the dray, holding on to the twins.

My mother never said goodbye or even sorry, not aloud.

A gull squawks, and my brow bumps Françoise's.

"Sorry, bébé."

"Non," she says, putting her sandy, salty hands to my lips. "Bird's fault."

"Non, Françoise. Sorrys need to be said aloud so all can hear and heal. Mamie loved you. Everything about you. Remember that. Run again. Let the cool air kiss your face, your beautiful face. That's Mamie's kiss."

Laughing, my daughter sprints away. I trudge in the wet sand to where the water licks the shore. People are fishing. Women have baskets on their heads and are walking toward the river to do their washing. Others have pots for water.

Cupping my eyes, I scan the shore. Houses are everywhere. Léogâne is in renewal and growing while people take in relatives from the crumbling north.

Out in the sea, the water churns blue with hints of foam. "Come on, Françoise, let's go. I don't see the boat we came to look for. Monsieur Lunic has not arrived."

"Maman, don't be sad. First Père will be here." Her eyes sparkle when she says this, as if I can make him appear.

We've written, Pierre and I. We've apologized on paper. Soon we'll say it in person. Voicing it and accepting forgiveness will be a new Lobelot trait. Then, we women can win at anything.

Readying to turn and walk back up Chemin du bord de Mer, I see him.

My feet plant in the brown sand. I wait.

Thinner, with more gray hair, it is Pierre. He waves, then lowers his arm like it's too heavy.

My heart does not skip, but I'm glad to see him. If we can live without hating each other, we can have friendship again.

He rushes to me. "Madame Lunic, it's good to see you."

His big old arms look like they will embrace me, but instead he stoops to Françoise. Pierre kisses her braids. "Let me look at you, chère."

He glances up at me. "I'm sorry about Madame Lobelot. She was one of a kind. A rare spirit."

Can't hold it in, all the ways I'm hurting.

He rises and put his hands to the points of my shoulders. "It will be all right, chère. It will be."

I'm sobbing down the front of his shirt. I don't know how anything will be the same again.

AT HER TABLE, MAMAN CHOPS VEGETABLES FOR MY SOUP. THE PUMP-kin I've brought her is as big as my aunt's head. The crowded house has made her happy.

Part of me wonders if she is freer because Mamie is no longer with us.

Elise unfolds her latest renegade newspaper, *Journal des Révolutions.* At least she found something to replace her missed *Moniteur Général.* "The Black general—"

"Who?" My stomach clenches. I wait and brace for the name Dessalines and the word *death.*

She flicks the paper. It makes a snap. "The Black general Toussaint Louverture, he went to Mass with the Spanish general Cabrera, then defected to France."

"To France?" Pierre's nose, which supports brass spectacles, wrinkles. "They were just fighting the French soldiers. Can they be trusted? And what do the Grand Blancs and the assembly say?"

I relearn to breathe. My stomach settles. "You've been away too long. The Spanish gained control over the west and north of Saint-Domingue because of the Black generals. France has agreed to everything, no more slavery and full citizenship for Blacks and Browns."

"Do women get rights, too?" Adélaïde peeks over Elise's shoulder. She loves these newspapers, too.

Pierre tsks with his tongue. "You've all become liberal in my absence. It's good I've come back."

The absence he caused; he says it like it was nothing.

With a hand to my hip, I glare at him. "Is liberal only good for Blancs throwing off a Blanc king? Is it a criticism reserved for Brown and Black when they end the stranglehold of corrupt governors and colonial assemblies?"

Frowning, Pierre folds his arms and sinks deeper into my grand-père's rocking chair.

There's something unsettling and yet à propos about a would-be Grand Blanc resting in the seat of the last one in the family.

"The system advantaged the Lobelots," he said, "and don't forget the privileges at Place Royale."

"One can look at it as privileges or the way a woman of color survives. The Grand Blancs created laws to benefit themselves. That's how they maintained power. No more."

Maman thwacks her knife hard on the table. "This is not the time to argue. After dinner, when all the children are in bed, is better."

Françoise is at Pierre's feet, frowning as her head shifts between us.

Adélaïde stacks Elise's fallen papers, then moves near her oncle. "I heard at the market that many of General Biassou's troops have disbanded. They will join Toussaint."

"Maybe now the Black generals will rid the British from Jérémie." Maman whacks another hunk of pumpkin to bits. "They will save us. No need to fear."

Was this barb aimed at Pierre or Mamie's ghost?

Françoise claps her hands as if to say *look at me.* "Tell us more of Paris."

Pierre's voice carries as he talks of rues and the Seine. He mentions nothing about the French Revolution—the hunger or the riots. Nothing of his friend the governor.

His eyes are dull. He becomes winded lifting Françoise.

"Such a good girl. And my Adélaïde is brave. If you'd come to Paris, I would have shown you the work I did on the friary for the Brothers in Drôme. The revolutionaries have confiscated it."

Françoise makes a fist with her little hand. "Horrible."

"It was beautiful. Drôme is set in the hills, like Le Cap." He sighs and puffs his chest. "Alas, nothing is like Le Cap."

"The revolution and the executions," Adélaïde asks, "did it happen as the paper says? Did they cut the head off of Louis XVI?"

"Adélaïde. That's not a question," Maman scolds, but Pierre lifts his hand.

"It's a question." He quiets for a moment. The way his eyes drift and his mouth draws to a tight line, I know he's remembering something difficult. "There was great hunger and people looked to the king and nobles for help. They questioned why the nobility and peers had things while others suffered. Violence became the answer. It was bloody."

"Sorry, Oncle Pierre." She put her hands over Françoise's ears. "I shouldn't bring up such things. You should tell more of your work."

"Adélaïde!" my daughter screeches. "I'm not a baby. I saw skulls on sticks as we drove deeper into the hills."

Pierre looks at me with the acknowledgment that it's all the same. "Seems all revolutions like chopping off heads."

"Dinner," my maman says in a voice that's light, as if nothing is wrong, as if we all hadn't seen so many faces of death up close.

It's time to nurse the twins. I'll go into the back room to be with the babies and pretend it's normal to talk of murder and abuse before supper.

Yes. I'm pretty good at deceiving my sad soul, too.

A WEEK HAS PASSED SINCE PIERRE'S RETURN. LYING ON MY MAKE-shift bedroll makes my back ache. The house in Léogâne feels cramped, particularly the back room where all the women and children sleep. We've ceded the front room to my husband. At night he rests on a cot by the rocking chair. Not knowing what he plans to do keeps my eyes from fully closing.

By marriage, he's the legal father of my children. He could take them or have me put away. Where he'd send me I'm not sure, since the convent in Place Royale and Hôpital de la Charité were destroyed.

Moving Françoise from the crook of my elbow, I prop myself up and spy Maman. She's whispering in her sleep. Elise and Adélaïde surround her, all crowding in the big bed.

The twins snore like little trumpets but are innocent and healthy. I'm happy I have them and Françoise. I need something of Jean-Jacques. I wish they had something of him, not just mentions in newspapers.

I hear movement in the front room. Tying on a robe, I pop up to have the conversation I've been avoiding.

Pierre is on one of my father's stools reading documents. His gaze lights upon me. "Oh, chère. You're up."

He stands and seems to lose his balance. I catch his arm.

"Thank you," he says. His voice is winded, like he's run a race. I help him to the rocking chair.

"Pierre, if I'm to be put away for my faithlessness, it will be a burden upon the children and my poor maman. Don't do that."

"Non. I won't." He takes a deep breath. "Talk to me. We were once good at that."

Clasping my elbows, I sit on a stool.

"Without your position at the hospital, what have you done for money?"

"Taken in laundry. Elise offers singing lessons. Adélaïde and I sell vegetables from the garden."

He looks distressed, with an ashen face, but this is honest work. I'm proud of what my hands have done. "Not quite what you expect of a wife of a Petit Blanc."

"You've not turned to harloting . . . for income. I suppose that's a blessing."

My gaze hardens. "You look thin. I hear the free love in Paris can lead to disease."

He laughs, then wheezes. "That type of love is never free." Rubbing his chin, he yawns. "Our letters have been friendly."

"I do not hate you. I hope you do not hate me, but I have always loved someone else."

"The twins? They are the ghost's?"

"My love hasn't died. He survived his enslavement. We found each other when you abandoned me."

"I was in France. You knew where I was."

"And you knew where I resided. You never told me you were coming home. I had no idea if I'd see you again." My voice is breaking. I didn't think I would, but I still have feelings for Pierre. "You knew my heart when we wed. You said you had enough love for both of us. You didn't. And when your dreams could take you from me, they did."

"I was a fool. I thought maybe you'd pine for me. Then everything went wrong, and I couldn't come back a bigger fool than when I left. I tried to make things work. When de Blanchelande was arrested on trumped-up charges, I stayed to help. I stayed . . . until they led him to the guillotine."

"Oh, Pierre."

"It was a perfect day, with the sun gleaming. They trucked de Blanchelande out on a cart, one with the kind of wheels I've made a thousand times. He bounced on a board with hands behind his back. His white coat was dirty and stained. No shave. He couldn't meet death like a gentleman.

"The gendarmes were all waving bayonets as the cart reached Place de la Révolution. The condemned man had to wait for his executioner to show. Can you imagine being prepared to die and having to look at the damned blade shining in the sunlight?"

His eyes close. A trembling hand pounds the chair arm. "It was quick when death came. The slice to his neck took less than a second."

I rub Pierre's back as he coughs into a handkerchief. "I do not have the clap or the pox. The sanitation of the rues of Paris is terrible. I have consumption. My lungs are no longer good."

"You're back because you're dying?"

"I thought the heat and the air would help. The air is better here, but I'm not."

His distant eyes sharpen, and I see a mask of pain wrinkle his face. "For a Petit Blanc, I'm amassing many Black children. The hurt is terrible when none of my seed has taken."

"Pierre, please."

"Where is he? Why is he not here giving you more children or providing for the ones bearing my name?"

"He's out fighting. I do not know where he is."

Pierre coughs anew and I get him a cup of water. Touching his hands, they feel so cold. "How long do you have?"

"Long enough to make things right. Starting with taking care of my family. We go to Port-au-Prince. You could've gone there directly. You're still my wife."

"Not a good one. I could not be there with how things are between us."

"My house is twice as large as this. We were there in the early days of our marriage. We were happy then, until I returned us to Le Cap to play at politics and build arches no will ever erect."

"Not everything is your fault. I should've—"

"Port-au-Prince is perfect. There's theater for Elise. More well-to-do young people for Adélaïde. And my—*our* house is big enough, with bedchambers for the family's comfort."

From my days at the hospital, I know how this sickness will ravage him. He'll need help. Someone to care for him.

He gulps the water, then sets it down and rocks in Grand-père's rocking chair.

I didn't think I had more tears, not after sobbing at the shore.

Half-blinded, I see him wave me forward. My head drops to his lap.

His fingers dip into my hair. "Adélaïde adores you. There's nothing for her in France. Our larger family should stay together."

"Pierre, you're offering to take care of our family. Can I be your friend and nurse? Will you let me do that?"

His thin lips hold no smile, but his eyes are soft and kind. "Oui. I'm making it easy for you to choose me again. But there is the matter of your risen lover. Will he visit?"

"Non." I grab a blanket and tuck it about Pierre's legs. "I'm not looking for him anymore. I have these young ones and you to care for. That will take all of my time."

"Sometimes fate finds you. He has found you twice. Can my last days be good ones, good and faithful?"

It's fair for him to ask. I don't want him ridiculed for having a promiscuous wife. "As long as you do not curtail my helping people, I can honor your request without reservation. We were friends before. We are friends again."

Gripping tightly to my fingers, he puts his head back, almost flopping against the rocking chair. "Good, chère."

"Would you like some warm tea before I go back to sleep?"

"Oui. Prepare us for the journey at week's end."

He releases my hand, and I warm the kettle over the fire.

Moving to another big city doesn't hold the excitement it once did, like when I first moved to Le Cap. But this move is not for me.

I'll put myself last and be what they need—nurse, mother, friend. As others have sacrificed for war, I look to St. Louise to help me nurture and spiritually feed my fated family.

32

Marie-Claire

1795
Port-au-Prince

Leaning on the sill, I look out the window of Pierre's bedchamber. His house is beautifully situated on the corner of Rue Dauphine and Rue des Miracles, blocks away from Port Marchand.

This is the capital of Saint-Domingue, but it feels tiny compared to Le Cap. There are buildings and a church. I'm sad there are no public gardens but I'm happy there are no scaffolds for executions.

Maman has taken the change in stride, helping with the children. Elise has found a small group of thespians in Port-au-Prince. They sing in homes. The big theater is closed because of continued fighting and the fear rebels or soldiers or spies might start fires.

Pierre coughs.

I move to his bed and help him sip water. "Do you feel well enough to go outside? The sunshine is warm. The little garden I've started has begun to bloom. Don't you want—"

His head slowly shakes. "Non."

Running my hands along the mahogany bed frame he's carved with fleur-de-lis at the posts, I feel the scratches I've made to mark the twins' height.

The bedchamber is where we gather since Pierre struggles to walk.

Taking the family from Léogâne saved us. Fighting now stretches from Jérémie to Maman's city. The united French forces under Toussaint are impeding British troops and stopping rebellions.

"Marie-Claire, you can go, go feed the people."

His face is too pale for me to leave him. "Non. Would you like me to read to you? Elise has found more renegade papers."

"Non." His chest rattles with coughs. His mouth opens and he pants. The doctor said it'd get harder and harder to breathe.

"The stones, chère, the marble will look good for the arches. Place Royale will be beautiful."

His fevers have made him forgetful. He doesn't remember that most of the buildings are gone and nothing will be built as long as the war rages.

Adélaïde comes with a cup of tea. "Marie-Claire, for you. You need to refresh yourself. You can't become sick."

My mouth has no thirst, but I take it. I'm at peace but still feel nervous for the coming moment he's gone. Caring for him is the glue keeping our family together. "Pierre, would you like some tea, too?"

"Non." It takes a moment, but he licks his lips. "Go out in the sunshine for me. Then return with the twins and Françoise."

Why should I go when he's lucid? These are the best times. He dreams out loud all the things he will build.

"Go. Get sun on those limbs."

Adélaïde comes and pushes me to the door. "I'll be with him. I can't bear to have you sick, too. No more losing people."

She holds her little hand out to me like it's a pact we can make, but war and sickness respect nothing. I tuck her fingers to my heart. "I'll go and then come back. Yell for me if I must hurry."

Outside, it takes a moment for my eyes to adjust. Françoise is with my mother and Elise, digging rows in the dark rich dirt. The knees of their muslin print gowns are dirty, but they are laughing until they see me.

"Is he . . ." Maman wipes her hands on her apron. "Is Monsieur Lunic—"

"Non." But it will be a matter of hours when he's gone. I look at her as if she and I are the only ones in this garden. I want to know how she handled knowing that Père's last moment was imminent.

Dusting off her hands, Maman stands. "Want to go to get water from the canals?"

Slowly, then more confidently, I approach and kiss her forehead. "For once I listened, just listened. Barely talked at all."

She hugs me, but I'm not sure she understood. I have peace because I exchanged apologies when Pierre was strong. All that's left are the good things to hear. I've nothing to hide or hold onto as a regret. "His time is soon, Maman. Be ready."

I scoop up Françoise. Her hands are covered in mud. "Let's leave the good Lobelots to gossip like sisters. I'll get my pretty girl cleaned up and then we'll say goodbye to Père."

Her brown eyes glisten, but it's time to show Françoise what it looks like to be brave and face truth.

CLOSE TO THE DOCKS, WE'VE SET MY SOUP KETTLES ON WOODEN tripods and have been serving food since ten. The briny smell arising from the close port called Marchand blends with the woodsy, lemony fragrance of thyme. I wonder if the line of refugees that reaches as far as Rue de Bonne Foy enjoys the scent, too.

I lead my household in this ministry. While Maman cares for the twins, I'm here with Adélaïde and Françoise. Today Elise is with us singing hymns with the crowd.

A few neighbors brought onions and potatoes to enrich the broth. Washerwomen, who've seen me feeding people these past ten months, have brought an extra vase of water to help stretch the soup and serve as many as possible. The locals have been kind. It helps my family grieve.

When soldiers pass by, my hands sweat, and I wipe them on the yellowing apron. Can't part with it. It's the only thing I have of Hôpital de la Charité and it does a good job covering my dress noir.

A woman and her child, younger than Françoise, are next and I fill their bowls.

She leans closer. "Mèsi. And do not be fearful of the sòlda. The Black generals control them. They won't harm us anymore."

My face must look confused because Elise whips out her papers. "It's true, Marie-Claire. Let me find the article."

"You're here to help, remember? You can find it later. Could you—"

"Now that Saint-Domingue," she continues, "and all the nations see what Black power can do, there will be no limit. Change is coming."

She sings scales, and I marvel at her change in attitude from wanting things only for Coloreds to appreciating Black people, encompassing Black as beautiful. It's amazing.

I won't call her a hypocrite, but someone who has, at last, learned not to fear someone else gaining rights.

Turning to watch Françoise playing behind me, I rub my sore neck, then I blink and the line grows. "How will we ever feed so many?"

Adélaïde dumps giraumon into the kettle. "I don't know how, either. This is the last of the squash."

Elise hums and keeps the order. Her church training has come in handy, but I wish she'd pick up a spoon and stir or help with preparations.

"Marie-Claire, I must leave soon."

"But Elise, people are still coming."

"You're going to have to send them away." Looking younger than her forty-three years, she raises her arms and dances about in a rust-color-print gown Maman has made from the cotton Monsieur Joseph has brought. He visits from time to time with news of Le Cap.

I suppose he's now a source for Elise's renegade news.

"Your kettles are running dry," she says in a singsong voice. "Tell them, next week, come early."

It's what I must do, but it sounds so cold. "Can't you tell I'm waiting on a miracle? I want St. Louise to see these hungry and fill these pots."

"I have a miracle. Well, almost one. Joseph says they may open Comédie du Cap again."

I nod and check the fire and look where my child is.

When I lift my head, Adélaïde's scraping one pot. Counting my fingers, I think we've fed as many as seventy people.

"You're not listening, Marie-Claire." Elise stoops and straightens Françoise's bonnet.

My child makes roar noises with the toy Pierre carved.

"Marie-Claire, my friends help me practice *Orphée et Eurydice* for my triumphant return to the stage. I've sung the part of Eurydice, the wife Orpheus tries to retrieve from hell."

"From hell, you say? For a dead wife? What some men will do." I shrug and point to the hungry people. "Please help us. The lines—"

"I will. And I've been helping. I talked to the priests of Eglise Paroissiale. If you can use their kitchen, you can make more food, even the kasav you used to take to the Bazac."

She says that place, and I see the soldiers executing the enslaved. My ears ring with the gunshot that killed Mamie.

I feel everything tangling up in my insides, but I come back to myself. I have people to feed.

And Françoise is watching. She has to see my persistence even in turmoil.

I spread my shoulders, take a breath, and then add new logs under the pot that still has soup before slowly adding water. "Later, Elise. I have to tend to the . . . well, it's broth now."

As if the curtains have closed, my aunt floats away, singing to the crowds before leaving.

"Vèv Lunic," an old man says to me as Adélaïde fills his bowl. "Bondye beni ou. Beni nou tout."

His words are kind, but Vèv Lunic, Widow Lunic, is bittersweet. Pierre is no longer in pain, but he died too soon. He still had dreams to fulfill.

"What did the man say, Marie-Claire?"

"'God bless you. Bless you all.' It's a little of the Kreyòl you heard when we ventured into the poorest neighborhoods of Le Cap. It's now the language of the free. Those who have had their chains broken by the military speak it. It's a pretty language. *Vèv* sounds so much better than *widow*. It feels less hurtful."

She grips my hand. "The tripods to hold these kettles, Oncle Pierre had them made for you. He's blessing your ministry."

For one moment everything seems possible, but then I look at the growing lines. I'm still waiting for that miracle.

• • •

WALKING TO EGLISE PAROISSIALE FOR THE MEETING ELISE HAS SET, I look for her. She should be on her way. Hopefully she hasn't forgotten. It's been difficult to get an appointment.

While I wait in the shadow of the church's steeple a Colored man with light gold skin, wearing a French blue uniform, steps into my path.

"Your mistress is wrong." His thin lips and chestnut-brown eyes appear to be looking my way.

"Excusez-moi, monsieur? I have no mistress."

He folds his arms and looks me over. "I saw you two weeks ago by the docks. You and your mistress were fawning over the Black generals, saying they ended enslavement. She's wrong."

My brow furrows, the feather on my bonnet droops to my eyes, and I see his condescending sneer in a haze of purple. "Good day, sir."

I try to move past him and enter the church, but he steps into my path. "She's very wrong. The Black generals are merely lucky. Perhaps they have been more savage in their attacks because of their bossale ways. Black will not keep winning."

He's standing in front of me as if the difference in our skin, brown and light gold, makes us different races. Color is a spectrum. "Don't you want the country whose uniform you support to win? Seems you were losing before the Black soldiers joined. Someone became wise and assigned the task of prosecuting the war to men who were up to it."

The soldier sputters, his mouth murmurs a curse when the deacon who prayed for Pierre comes out of the church and stops in front of me.

"Monsieur Tralier," I say, "can you help me? I'm being harassed by this officer. I have a meeting with Père Berlier."

Tralier pulls out his pocket watch. "Madame Lunic, Père Berlier can't meet with you today. Try back next week."

"But I have an appointment. It's been difficult to set. And the poor keep coming from Léogâne and Jérémie. We need a greater effort to help them. The parish's kitchens . . ."

This man with a high position sneers at me almost as openly as the soldier does. "I know you, Madame Lunic, and your situation. The church won't help with your endeavors."

"But the poor need help. The church is supposed to help."

"Is it right to take from Noah's good children and give to those cursed of Ham? I think we have bigger problems than feeding poor Blacks." The deacon's tone is horrid.

This man has been in my house near my children, all while thinking ill of me and my family. "Hunger does not discriminate, Monsieur Tralier. And I feed everyone, Black, Blanc, and Brown."

The soldier snickers as Tralier folds his arms over the fancy gray waistcoat gaping at his belly. This Blanc has probably never missed a meal, so he dismisses hunger.

Looking at his watch again, the deacon says, "Berlier is busy. Go home." He keeps walking and leaves me with the laughing soldier.

Hands on my hips, crushing the careful pleats of my jet caraco jacket, I glare at this giggling fool.

"Charity work is funny? Starving children are jokes?"

"No. I'd never laugh at that. I'm laughing at you, the famed Madame Lunic. I've heard of you. The Black woman who bamboozled an old sick Blanc into marriage and gave him plenty of Black children."

That isn't how . . . I can't breathe. It's like he's kicked me in my chest.

I turn to leave but the soldier follows. His mocking voice is loud. "What is it you truly want, Madame Lunic? For the likes of Toussaint and his motley generals, his dogs Dessalines and Moyse, to rule? Or do you wish to appear good to attract your next Blanc husband? Someone you'll probably give more bastard Blacks to."

If I slap this man, I'll be arrested. He's humbled me and mocked the name I haven't said aloud in four years. I'm stone, trying to find a way to fill my lungs, to live again.

The soldier is in front to me. "From the stunned look on your face, you don't know, either? Hopefully the French will wise up, put the Blacks in their place, and elevate brilliant, literate men like me or Rigaud."

"Hateful fool. Go find someone else to abuse."

People are walking by. He doesn't look ashamed of his treatment of me. "Go with your brazen talk. Let someone else see you have no manners. You're the dog. You're a beast in uniform."

He looks as if he would spit. "Rigaud, a true officer with education and foresight, a bold man of color, will fix things. Mark my word, bossale mulattress. Things will be fixed."

He leaves, going toward Place du Government, and I head the opposite way on Rue de Vaudreuil. Dazed, I'm lost until I am again at Rue de Bonne Foy.

My eyes sting. My steps become hesitant, but I keep walking until I see water, dark blue with waves. Forcing the briny air in and out, I stop at a ribbon seller. I stare at her wares—the shine, the grains, even lace. I'm silent, voiceless. The rejection I had from a vendor in Le Cap over lilac satin tumbles through me. That was a lifetime ago. Why do I still carry it? Why does the hurt stay lodged in my mind?

"Madame," the seller says, "may I help you?"

My throat is too choked with tears to say anything. I hold up a coin and point. The old woman's skin, much lighter than mine, shines with a luster of a pearl. She gives me it for free. "Gratis, li pa koute anyen."

I nod and blurt out my thanks for her kindness, but lift money to her.

She says again that it's free, no cost, and refuses to take my coin. "You're beautiful. You need this."

This woman complimented me without conditions—not "pretty for a Black girl." It wasn't a reward for showing my strength but something to honor my weakness. I can be weak and beautiful and Black.

Holding the ribbon high, I run to the battery. It catches air and sails behind me like the string of a kite. It looks free.

I'm free.

I must remember I'm not ashamed.

I've been forgiven.

I forgave myself. I'll not live in the shadow of another's ignorance. I won't apologize for my life—my family, my children, my choices. I'm free.

Confident and energized, I walk home ready to serve my way. That's my miracle. Me.

1798
Saint-Marc

From the fortifications of the hill in the north end of Saint-Marc, I looked out at the sea. The clouds formed a blanket ready to smother Saint-Domingue.

It would be something to do, to battle the sky. The fighting was light as of late.

Or perhaps Janjak was too effective. I'd never seen a military strategist as wise or as bold.

Then, when the battle was done and we'd won, he'd reward the fighters with dance and song and food. This blend of softness with the hard rigor of the battlefield amazed me.

Eghosa and Tegbesu would both be proud. Nosakhere, too.

I hadn't seen the counselor since he left Cormier. With all of Saint-Domingue rebelling, small breakouts here and there, I assumed I'd see him. Maybe I hoped he'd get the chance to look Janjak in the eye, man to man, warrior to warrior.

"Gran Toya," Fleur said with her hands held high, "how long do we hold this position?"

With my mind turning, I'd forgotten. "Rest. Then we start again."

One. Two. I pounded the ground with my new staff. The branch I'd used had been replaced with sculpted mahogany. The faces of Zinsu and Zinsi were scored in the grains. Janjak gave me this gift. He said it was me and Eghosa. Precious.

Must be getting old and soft to think of things as precious.

"Stretch." With our flintlocks lying beside our feet, I had them lean forward. "Keep the muscles strong, agile."

My wave of women numbered twenty. The next engagement, even if all we did was hold the land the demi-brigades cleared, we would be ready.

Hoofbeats echoed.

Looking over the stone wall, I saw Janjak and his close lieutenants coming down Chemin de Lartibomte. He waved, and I thought he would head to Saint-Marc's Place d'Armes or the small gardens and woods of Cours de Bellecombe. The way he always visited the grove of trees, I wondered if it reminded him of what he'd lost in Le Cap.

Janjak ordered his companions forward but dismounted and started toward my position. He was frowning. I wished he'd focus on the good. We'd helped King Toussaint save liberty. Spain ceded everything over to the French. And Sonthonax, one of the French commissioners, made Toussaint commander in chief of all the forces.

And my seed was his right hand.

"Minos, let us give our commander a good show. Pick up arms."

They did, slinging the new M1777 army muskets high. Different from the ones taken from the habitations, these guns used smaller firing balls and had better aim, making my Minos a deadlier force.

One by one, they snapped to attention.

As he climbed to our position, my Minos marched in lines, columns of four, like I had done for Tegbesu and all his advisers.

I clapped my hands. My leads, Fleur and Ponce, did a mock battle, leaping and jumping, swinging cutlasses. The display was magnificent. Fleur's silken black braids, beaded with baubles of her ancestors, bounced as she somersaulted out of the way of the blade and tripped Ponce.

Not one to be outmaneuvered, Ponce, a young woman of twenty seasons with skin of polished cedar, one of my newest additions, sprung up and cornered Fleur against the battery's stone wall.

Janjak clapped his hands. "Gran Toya, excellent." He clapped again. "Stand down. Stand down."

My leads stopped immediately and bowed.

They fell back into line, rejoining with my other bees in black tunics and yellow sashes.

"We'll start again tomorrow at dawn and patrol the fort's walls. Dismissed."

My Minos flitted down the stone steps and vanished to their quarters or to those alluring gardens. It was now just me and Janjak.

"Gran Toya, your Minos are diligent, but are you growing weary? You celebrated another season."

That was his polite way of saying I was getting too old for the fight. He was a good boy, fretting about me.

"Haven't killed enough people. Not enough to decorate your future palace."

Janjak bent, grabbing his stomach and releasing a high-spirited laugh. He needn't be concerned. I was fit despite my age of sixty years.

He sobered, then went to the outer wall. His palms gripped the stone of the battery worn smooth by pelting rains, even hurricanes. "Toussaint has promoted me over the Fourth Regiment."

This was well deserved. No one's district was more well ordered. When rebellions happened in the west, we were sent, and we quelled them. "The king is proud of you."

"Wi. Toussaint believes in me, but he's wrapped up in the French. He believes double-chinned Sonthonax's assembly will keep the proclamation of freedom."

Sonthonax, Polverel, Laveaux, and others were advisers who had been sent from France to help Toussaint, but they were only here to ensure the colony stayed French.

"How long will these advisers live?"

"What, Tante Toya?"

"France executes many even with no king. Do they put the skulls from the guillotine on the roofs of their palaces, too?"

Janjak offered another lusty laugh.

But I was serious. The Blancs liked cutting off heads as much as the Dahomey. I heard the people of France seemed to love slicing through necks in big ceremonies.

"They do execute people," he said, glancing off at the sea. "At least the guillotine is quick."

That was something to admire. Their killing wasn't slow like burning syrup. They had quick, humane decapitations. Just no making of skull lamps.

Janjak turned. His dark blue uniform looked better on him than the Spanish white one. "The Americans sit with Toussaint now that we evicted the British from Jérémie. I think they'll convince him to quit France and declare independence. Then Saint-Domingue would truly be free."

"No more threats would be good, but didn't we just switch sides?"

"I like this uniform, but the French assembly can vote and revoke their '94 law ending slavery any time they choose. There's talk they might do it next month. But there's always talk."

A trustworthy partner was always needed. I prayed the right ones would come, but my faith was in my king Janjak and his.

He rubbed his forehead, knocking his hat askew. The new hat was round, like a black stovepipe, with a cockade of swirled red, white, and blue ribbons. He'd started to wear the madras scarf on his head underneath, like Toussaint.

"Nothing will mean anything, if we lose liberty. What does a ribbon mean to little César?"

"You claimed one of your women's children as yours?"

His smile burst into a jaunty smirk. "The women come and go. No one is unhappy with this arrangement, but I'm sure he's mine. He's eight. I need to make sure César and any of my sons and daughters that live are left a good world."

I stood beside Janjak. "You've changed his world. They are free, fully free. Be cheered."

He nodded and clasped his hands behind his back. "I'm just out of sorts. Be prepared. If fights break out, Toussaint will send us to chase the next Romaine-la-Prophétesse from Léogâne to Jacmel and back."

Romaine-la-Prophétesse had tried to set up his own kingdom, something I'd accused Nosakhere of wanting. We'd stopped the prophet and cleared most of the island of rebels and insurgents.

Clapping his hands, he spun and looked down to the gardens.

"The king, Toussaint, has a wife and children living in his habitations. Maybe you should give this to César."

"Non. His mother has new friends. She gave up waiting. But beyond here in the Artibonite Valley is good land. I'll not be a man of war forever."

Nothing lasted. This was true.

I made sure to look strong in these moments. I wasn't ready for the pasture. "You lead your divisions well. No one can ask for more."

"Thank you, Corporal Gran Toya." He tipped his hat. "Good day, Gran Toya. Orevwa."

In his wide eyes, there was trouble. I wondered what he sensed.

As he left, I felt the sorrow in him. He'd sacrificed and suffered for the liberty we had now.

But my king was right. All could be lost in a moment.

THE SLIGHT CHILL IN THE MORNING AIR WAS AN ILLUSION. SOMEthing about the way the fog rolled up into the hills and loomed over the northern entrance of Le Cap seemed foreboding. I stretched these old eyes to Baye du Cap, the enemies only mode of escape.

Janjak said only one French ship was in the harbor.

That meant less cannon fire. The brass sixteen-pounder on land made a frightening sound. The larger twenty-four pounder from the ships shook the earth.

King Toussaint demanded the cannons captured and brought to us. Though they smoked as badly, worse than muskets, they were more deadly. One belch from the long bronze tube could cut down tens of men with iron balls called grapeshot.

"Gran Toya, are you good?" Janjak rode on horseback next to my marching columns. We'd followed behind legions of his men on the path to Chemin de la Bande.

"Yes, General."

He adjusted his hat and trotted forward.

We headed to Le Cap on a special mission for the king. Toussaint wanted the arrest of the devil governor, Théodore Hédouville. The foul man had inflated the head of our king's rival, a man named Rigaud. Unlike our Black king, Rigaud was the mulatto chief who wanted his light skin to be worth more than dark.

Many light-skinned men didn't see that the call for liberty was for all—Black, Brown, and fair-minded Blanc. They wanted it for a select few.

Fools like this didn't understand that under fire, bullets cut through all skin the same. Black and Brown in Sainte-Domingue needed unity to defend from the cannons' onslaught and win the peace.

"March!" My Minos and I drilled faster to keep up with Janjak's regulars. Closer to the city, I spied him on the edge of the casernes. From there, he'd direct the forces. I'd watched him twiddling his shining silver snuffbox until it was time to ride and join the fray.

The smoke hit our faces as we marched into the square, Champ de Mars. Lines of men fired at the government building.

The rhythm—load, pack, tamp—began. Then we waited for the call to fire.

The magic of the yell . . .

Our army's musket balls cut into Hédouville's lines. Men screamed. Bodies dropped in front of me. Unlike in our other fights, these uniforms were the same as those of our regiments. It was happening, our king Toussaint attacked a rival.

My muscles tensed, growing tighter, but I kept the rhythm, kept firing until the trumpet sounded.

The white plumes of gun smoke began to clear. Hédouville's men were running.

We led with our bayonets. The enemies leapt in retreat.

"Atak!" Our first sergeant blew his horn.

"Chaje!" I led my Minos forward.

Advancing down Rue Sainte Marie, we stabbed any Blanc wearing French blue.

The handful serving under a Black general were known. The practice of limiting the mixing of the forces made it simple. Even Hédouville's beloved Rigaud had only Black and Brown troops.

"Foule noir!" they called us. A Black mob, not soldiers.

"Cours! La foule noire arrive!" More turned and ran, but the rue was lined with bodies and guns.

We continued to advance.

Ash coated everything, even my tongue.

One man fell. Then another. The enemy became tangled limbs, dropping and knocking into the next man.

"Hédouville est parti! À la mer." One of our leads announced the fiend had fled to sea.

The last time I thought the man I hunted had escaped, I found him crouching behind a bed frame. "Let's search the gardens and grounds of the government buildings."

Brandishing bayonets, we entered one. Kicking open doors, running along marble floors, we searched every nook, every closet. Nothing.

In the last office, I heard the chatter of teeth. Pushing the desk out of the way, I found a man cowering.

He shifted his spectacles and smiled. "Only women."

I jabbed him with my bayonet. "Women who can kill. Get up."

His smile dissolved and his hands flew high. "Veuillez avoir pitié!" He begged for mercy. "Mercy! Pitié!"

My bayonet didn't move from his neck. "Where is Hédouville? Kote Hédouville? Hédouville?"

His lips quivered. "Échappé. Devrait être sur le bateau pour la France."

Boat to France? The single ship in the harbor. It had sailed. "Then Dessalines will have no use for you." I pulled back my bayonet to strike.

Turning ashen, he moved his hands. "Arrêtez, les informations! Stop, I have information! Sispann, enfòmasyon!"

Stalling tactic, even switching languages. I raised my weapon again. "Rigaud, enfòmasyon!"

Rigaud? I stabbed the desk next to him. "Talk."

"Dessalines needs to know Hédouville has unleashed Rigaud. He's gathering forces in the south to combat Toussaint. I have specifics and towns. Spécificités et villes."

The fool could be useful. Janjak ruled the west and north for the king, but Rigaud had the south, everything from Port-au-Prince down to Jérémie.

"You live for now. Tie him."

Smiling, he lifted his wrists. "Sois béni. Bless you! Bless you!"

Satisfied the government building was empty, I gave the command for my Minos to head to the docks with our prisoner.

As we marched, I saw more dead, but we arrived too late.

The boat was in open waters, now out of reach of our cannons. Hédouville had escaped.

Janjak rode to my position. "I don't keep prisoners, Gaou Toya. They don't keep ours. An eye for an eye, that's what every campaign has taught."

He sounded angry and disappointed, but I said, "I'd kill him now, but he says he has information on Rigaud, his movements and locations."

"And armaments," this fellow added. He hungered to live.

"I'll listen." He signaled to some soldiers to come for the prisoner.

They came and took the man away. I wasn't sure his chances of living had improved.

"Good work, Gran Toya. Head back to camp and prepare. I have a feeling I know what my new orders will be, to chase Rigaud."

High in his saddle, Janjak rode off. If he lingered in Le Cap, I knew he'd journey to the ruins of Place Royale. That place had his soul.

It would be good to be away from here. I needed my king focused. Rigaud was a smart commander, as strong as my tiger. Only a man with a clear head would win this battle, not one in misery over things no longer here.

• • •

APPROACHING THE DINING ROOM OF THE SAINT-MARC HOUSE SERV-
ing as headquarters for Janjak's divisions, I became enchanted, drawn
to the scent of yon bon sos mori, the savory dish of salted cod, a favorite.

Yet in the corridor between me and the onions and peppers on my
plate was a guard. An unknown man in a starched blue uniform, with
red collars and cuffs decorated with shiny brass buttons, stood in front
of me.

"What is happening?"

"Corporal Gran Toya," the guard said, "Commander Toussaint is
with the general."

Janjak's lusty laugh came through the thin doors, thin enough that
I could pierce them with my spear. Something was happening inside.

"I will relieve you, sir," I said. "Go on and rest. I'm sure duty will
call upon you soon."

The fellow swiped at his brow. He looked weary and tired.

The man saluted. "You do report to the general."

He moved. I took his place and appeared to be a stone statue, but as
soon as he left I cracked open the door and peered inside.

Tegbesu would hold meetings with the elders. I sat on his right side.
He'd look at me and ask my opinion.

It was shameful to be reduced to spying, but my king met with his.
I had to know.

Toussaint, his aide-de-camp, and his chief engineer, a Blanc soldier
named Vincent with mouselike eyes behind thick glass lenses, stood
on one side. Janjak and his trusted secretary, Louis Boisrond-Tonnere,
who'd joined the army fresh from the streets of Paris, were on the other.
Educated, refined, but dedicated to his boss, he'd translate anything
difficult or peculiar Vincent might say.

The secretary's friendship with Janjak had grown. I liked him, except when drink made his lips loose. All manner of gossip and conspiracies spilled out.

Wiping his fingers on a cloth napkin, Janjak rose from the table.

The way he laid the white linen flat mimicked the mannerism he'd picked up from Boisrond-Tonnere and the Blanc French officers.

"Commander Toussaint," he said. "I didn't expect you until morning. I'm glad we can share a meal, but you should go straight to the news bringing you to my table."

"General Dessalines." Toussaint flexed his hand. It seemed stronger, much improved from the damage done when a cannon fell on him a year or two ago. His hair was grayer. The wrinkles in his brow had deepened, mirroring the weight of his increased responsibility.

"Your informant was correct." Toussaint leaned against the wall. His buttons—some were brass, others cloth, painted pictures. "Reports say Rigaud is organizing in the south. He's splitting the island we've just unified. I want you in place. If he attempts it, you can capture him and drive all disloyal forces into the sea."

Janjak took up his wine. "I will, but this could have been sent by dispatch. Commander, it's always nice to see you, but a wise person has taught me to get to the heart of the matter. What is this visit about?"

King Toussaint, the private man, sighed. One of Janjak's complaints was that few knew the man's thoughts.

Our leader dropped the fine round hat with a feather and a red, blue, and white ribbon cockade to a chair. "You're right. I've been negotiating with General Maitland directly. All British forces will withdraw from Saint-Domingue. He has agreed to this and if necessary to provide support. A blockade to starve Rigaud and his followers out of their entrenchments."

The look in Janjak's wide brown eyes said he was not impressed with this information. He fiddled with the white cuff of his shirt, the buttons of his open silk waistcoat. "Just admit you missed dining at my table."

Toussaint laughed. "Yes. I do, but the point. Lines of communication have been opened with several governments. If Saint-Domingue wanted to be free of France, I believe we'll have British support. I believe the Americans will aid us, too."

With his thumb, Janjak pinged his glass. "Funny how the two countries can have a war and still work with one another on a common goal."

"I think it will be like this for Saint-Domingue and France."

Rolling up a sleeve exposed the old massa scars on Janjak's arm. "You're looking for a war to gain this goal? You must be certain. One might consider it treason if we failed, since we're working under a French flag. Failure could mean hanging for all and reenslavement for most at my table. Not pleasant dinner conversation."

Toussaint's face blanked again. "Vincent is loyal and has been privy to conversations."

Oh, the king was too trusting. I turned away, looking to see if more Blanc spies had come to hear.

The hall remained empty, and I kept my ear attuned.

"Dessalines, if we make this move, we won't fail."

"Well, the French flag can always be improved to make something new. It's not a favorite. Saint Dominguans can come up with something." Janjak's hearty laugh filled the room. "Sit and have wine. There's always food at my table."

He came to the cracked door and gave me a look, confirming he knew I'd overheard. Instead of reprimanding me, he drew me in and called to his servers.

A few chairs from his, I eased into a seat and settled in to see the politics of eating.

Servers in bleached aprons brought more food. Onto my plate and Toussaint's for second helpings, they dipped out the fish, drizzling the heavenly golden sauce on top. Then they added big spoonfuls of plantains and potatoes—all nicely caramelized.

Toussaint took a few bites, then pulled his long fingers together. Again he pumped the one hand as if to improve its mobility. "Edward Stevens was chosen as the consul general of the United States. I have word he'll be sent to me in Le Cap. Stevens works for President Adams's secretary of state, Pickering. This is America's stamp of approval."

The young Vincent cleared his throat, then said, "Stevens and Pickering have given assurances to their commitment for commerce, arms, and in some cases direct defense of a free and independent Saint-Domingue."

Toussaint drank from his red wine, then paused for a moment as if he struggled to say something. "They have Washington's man behind it. We have his full support."

"Please don't mean Jefferson?" asked Louis Boisrond-Tonnere. "We all know you revere Washington, but I wouldn't trust his old secretary of state, diable blanc."

Toussaint shared a look with Vincent then took up his glass, swirling red wine as if it divined secrets. "Washington deserves praise. He formed a nation, but do you know Jefferson?"

"He was there when I was in Paris. The statesman who drafted a Declaration of Independence, then fled the war for safer shores. He partied and such while others died for his alleged principles." Boisrond-Tonnere shook his head, his mouth frowning as if his drink had soured. "Jefferson will never be for an independent Black state."

"Come now, my heated friend." Janjak set down his fork. "What? You met him once or twice and have such strong opinions."

"My community knew all about him. All the Black servants of the big houses tried to convince James Hemings to stay and keep his sister in Paris. They were free there. But Jefferson confused his sister. The fourteen-year-old was scared and pregnant. Poor Sally feared Jefferson would take the baby. That's the reason she went back. James went to protect her."

"Never had a sister," Janjak said, "but I can understand wanting to protect someone." He looked at me, and I felt Eghosa's presence.

Boisrond-Tonnere poked at his cod. "Jefferson's bold words of freedom and every man being created equal are lies. He hates the Negro, every Black. Yet, he had to possess the poor slave girl he nightly abused."

Everyone quieted. Some looked my direction. I tightened my fingers on the knife I used to cut the potatoes. If I ever met this Jefferson . . .

Janjak pleaded with his eyes, and I calmed.

Toussaint waved his hand. "Settle, gentlemen, Corporal. That's not the one I speak of. Hamilton is Washington's man. He's assured Pickering he will help frame our constitution and assist anything else we need to be independent."

"The bastard from Nevis turned gentleman?" Boisrond-Tonnere smoothed his thin mustache and harrumphed. "But isn't he out of power? That Callender piece in the newspapers about an affair and embezzlement ruined him."

"Callender is one to watch for American scandals," Vincent said, "but Monsieur Hamilton is wily. Never to be underestimated."

"Here's to never falling prey to whispers of power." Janjak toasted the air. "Lively discussions, Commander Toussaint, about my table."

"Spirited," Toussaint said and finished his meal. "But I'm confident we have reliable friends in America."

Janjak glanced in my direction. Well done, I said with my eyes, to engage the king at this level. Once we subdued Rigaud, we'd know if our forces were ready to break free of France and if our alliances would keep their promises. For Saint-Domingue to be free and officially led by Black power, we had to keep winning.

34

Marie-Claire

Elise and my mother will leave tomorrow. They are giggly like young girls, acting as if they are twins.

Maman is at the table Pierre made, chopping vegetables. Elise is humming, sitting on a stool watching, not helping. Typical.

But Adélaïde's there shredding manioc for kasav bread. She's nineteen, with big, gorgeous blue eyes. She's always covered up, even in the heat of summer. The mobcap covering her brunette curls steals her youth. I don't know how to help her live her life, but I'm grateful she's in mine and a sister to my children.

Five-year-old Célestine is in my lap as I twist and braid her hair. My hands smell of coconut, not the liniments and peppermint I use at the hospital. With the war at our doorsteps, I had to volunteer.

"Ouch, Maman," she says. "Too tight." The braids must be this way to survive how hard she and her brother play in the yard.

"Sorry," I say and snuggle her neck. Her hair is long and thick, longer than Françoise's.

My son, Jacques, plays with the wood soldier and the cart Pierre made him before he grew too weak. He hums, his voice sweet but lower than Elise's.

The tune, though, is not a hymn.

It's the old poem my mother sings sometimes. Very odd he knows it, but they spend a lot of time together.

"Oh, I will miss the love in this house." Maman wipes at her eyes.

"Then don't go." Françoise lifts her head from her newspapers.

"Chère, your mamie is going on an adventure with Aunt Elise. We must wish them well."

"Non." My daughter jumps up. "They're going back to the city full of fires. It killed Grand-mère. Poor Grand-mamie."

"Françoise." I put Célestine down, to her delight, with a half-done head of coiled braids. "That's not fair. They have dreams, and they have been a blessing to us for a long time."

"Non," my daughter says again. "We left her in the middle of nowhere. We never speak her name. She was brave and funny and deserved better."

Scattering her papers, Françoise runs from the room.

"I'll go to her." Adélaïde wipes milky manioc liquid from her hand and shoots across the pine plank floor to the room they share.

The door slams.

And we are left quiet, because Françoise is right.

Tomorrow, these women who have been pillars in my life will take a dray and head to Le Cap as if a war weren't going on.

But I won't say a word. That's what Lobelot women do. We are quiet when we hurt, when we love, when we hope for our dreams.

I go to Elise and kiss her brow.

Then I step to my maman and put my lips to her forehead. "Two sisters going to live to the fullest. Thank you for everything you have done. Go with God."

There are tears. But no one mentions Mamie.

These two left Mamie in 1758, and they've done it again. The war shouldn't have made us forget to honor her.

The sisters start chattering again.

Plopping back to the twins, I start twisting the rest of Célestine's braids.

And I close my eyes, listening to Jacques sing, and hold in all the injustice. One mistake, one sin has erased this woman. And I wonder which one of my wrongs will do the same.

• • •

FATHER BERLIER, THE BUSY PRIEST WITH NO TIME FOR THE *IMPROPER* Widow Lunic, stops in front of the hospital room I'm readying for patients. His priestly robes are pristine. Not a drop of blood splatters him, unlike my treasured apron.

Shifting my pail of supplies, rolls of bandages, ointment bottles, I curtsy to him and wish he'd be on his way. The church had been central to his life, but now I shun it and all its artifices. I rarely take my Black children to sit in the whitewashed chapel.

"Madame Lunic." He whispers as if he's afraid he'll wake the dead. There are too many bodies to be buried to fear this.

He doesn't go away.

I glare at him. "What is it you want, Holy Père? As you can see, I'm busy preparing for more injured soldiers to be brought from the Chemin de Léogâne."

"Was it a surprise attack? I heard it was bloody."

"Pretty sure the army didn't willingly walk into an ambush."

His head bows. "I wanted to say, it's not unnoticed how you're serving the poor and the good work you do here at the hospital."

"Please go down the hall and offer your blessings or whatever it is you do. I'm of an age where shallow praise no longer matters."

"Madame Lunic, I'm sorry."

With his dull blue eyes looking dour and small, maybe he is. It matters not. "I'm doing what I've been called to do. God has allowed my hands to serve."

I brush past him, leaving his face as red as the cap on his head. The lady who wanted others to hear her words has nothing else to say.

A woman is in the hall carrying another woman.

My breath catches a little. Every time I see females injured, I say a silent prayer for the Le Jeune martyrs. Then I wave the soldiers to the room I've just readied.

The ambivalent priest stands there with his hands on the crucifix hanging about his neck.

"Sir. I need you to go. The women need privacy." With the back of my hand, I shoo him away like a chicken.

Then I turn to the fighters. "Place her on this bed. Can you tell me what's wrong?"

The older one opens the cowrie shell vest of the injured.

Poking at the makeshift bandage made of a yellow sash, I see the problem. "Musket ball to the arm."

I start cutting the cloth away, exposing more of the wound. "Looks like the bullet shot straight through. You're lucky, no poisoning, but you've lost a lot of blood."

"Poisonings are bad. Are you the hospitalière or a mountain houngan?"

"Non. I've worked a long time in hospitals. Particularly in Le Cap, Hôpital de la Charité."

The older woman steps back. "The smells of hospitals are unforgettable."

The doctor steps into the room and looks over my shoulder.

A cutlass whips the air. The older warrior whirls the weapon, forcing the doctor to back up.

Eyes big, like moons or twin stars, he adjusts his spectacles. "What's going on here?"

"That's the physician, madame." I keep my voice level to try to calm everyone then switch to Kreyòl and repeat. "Nonm sa a la pou ede. This man is here to help."

From the corner of my eye, I see the cutlass lower. My pulse slows.

"Madame Lunic, keep cleaning the wound. Bandage it. Then let's get ready for soldiers." He leaves the room.

The one woman's gun looks like the weapon of a French soldier. The blood on the tip of the bayonet seems fresh.

I stop staring and return to cleaning the wound, sprinkling tafia on it to stop infection—another tidbit from Mamie.

The warrior woman comes closer and rubs my patient's cheek as if to rouse her from a faint. "Hold on, Fleur. Kenbe la."

"Since there's no metal in there, this should heal nicely. Geri byen."

When I pour the tafia again onto her arm, the patient whimpers and thrashes. I try to hold her still, but the commotion rips at her vest.

A lone shell hits the floor.

Ping.

It bounces and lands near my feet, then rolls to the sandal of her friend.

I turn and catch the warrior's gaze. Recognition hits like lightning. Everything in me trembles as if the earth is quaking.

The doctor sticks his head back inside. "If you've dressed the injury, I need you down the hall, another patient. More soldiers."

"In a moment." I begin wrapping my patient's arm with bandages from my bucket.

"Fine. Hurry, Madame Lunic." The doctor's footfalls move away.

"I thought it was Duclos." That voice—I'd heard it once, long, long ago, telling me Jean-Jacques had died.

I ignore the draw to ask questions. It's obvious she's one of the women fighting in the war, fighting with Dessalines.

"It's been years." Gran Toya's voice echoes. "Fleur is good with a musket. The kings . . . Commander Toussaint and General Des—"

"Done. Your friend will be fine." I take up my pail and toss my scissors and my bottle of tafia into it. "Once she awakens, you can take her back to Toussaint."

At the door, I stop one last time and let my gaze soak in this woman who is fighting with the troops commanded by the Black generals. "I'm going to send two bowls of soup to this room. Eat before you head back to your camp. It'll give you strength."

"Should I take a message with me?"

"Rekonesans. Gratitude to you and all soldiers who are fighting for a better Saint-Domingue."

Then I run from the room before she tells me about the man whom my heart never forgot, whom the war took away.

. . .

MORNING COMES BEFORE I'M READY. FRANÇOISE CURLS HER HEAD against my thigh. Célestine and Jacques have stolen my pillow. When I came from the hospital, they'd all been frightened by the cannons.

Troops have set up camp along the chemin surrounding Port-au-Prince. It has taken three days to patch up those who could be made well and we let the gravediggers handle the rest.

Adélaïde appears strong, even unemotional, but I know her. Sounds of war stir her worst memories.

Mine are pretty bad, too.

And I have an assortment of sounds to trouble me—cannons, muskets, fiery mobs, Mamie's shrieks.

When I sit up in bed, little Jacques tugs on the scarf wrapping my hair. "Don't go, Maman."

His voice is light and filled with the garble of a dry mouth. But I hear him.

The hospital will make do without me. I'll spend the morning in this big bed with my children. Then Adélaïde and I will make kasav, and she'll read me the latest in the renegade paper and more about the French war going on. Mulatto against Black. Both wearing France's uniforms.

Cannons pound in the distance.

The walls shudder.

If the Blacks win, does it mean the power struggle is over? Everyone is equal? Or does it mean the Blacks will be treated the same as Coloreds?

Boom. More grapeshot is dropping and scarring the land.

I count and listen, but I hear nothing else. Snuggling in the crisp linen sheets, I look at my nightstand and Elise's letters. She and my mother, those sisters, have survived two months in the renewing city of Le Cap without arguing.

Miracle. Maybe warring sides can make peace.

Lifting up, I stretch and still hear no guns.

"Don't go, Maman." Jacques's sighs are full of yawns.

Circling my fingers in his wavy hair, I lie back. "Oui, mon garçon, mon petit homme." He's my little man of the house.

This is my family and we've survived the war even as it rages closer.

Closing my eyes, I rest and allow my mind to think about my beautiful children and only a little about the general commanding troops near my city of Port-au-Prince.

A WEEK HAS PASSED AND THE FIGHTING SEEMS TO HAVE MOVED ON. Father Berlier has sent a note. He wishes to talk to me about the food program. I'd rather be a stubborn Lobelot, but my children are growing older. They have to feel more welcomed in the community. They need to worship in church.

Walking the long way down Rue des Fronts Forts, I head to Place de Linton, the way to Eglise Paroissiale.

The hair on my neck tingles. A scan of the left and right reveals nothing. No soldier to taunt me is near. No one is behind me. No one is watching.

When I get to the church steps, Father Berlier is there.

His cheeks redden, and he makes a quick sign of the cross. "Madame Lunic, I'm glad you've come."

"You sent for me, sir."

"Not exactly. She did."

From the shadows of the vestibule, Gran Toya steps out. "Good, you're here. You don't keep regular hours at the hospital?"

"I volunteer. Is Fleur well? Has she lost her strength?"

"Much better." She sets down her spear with a thud. "I've orders from General Dessalines to bring you to the government building."

I put my hands on my hips. "I have responsibilities I must see about."

Taking a note from a pouch tied to her sash, she hands it to me. "He said you'd be difficult. And to give you this."

My pulse speeds, but I refuse the paper. "I don't need this, thanks."

"He said you'd say that, too."

The ebony woman has aged, but the strength in her muscles shows as her hand tightens about her spear. "But he ordered me to bring you, Madame Lunic."

"Tell him I declined. If you'll excuse me."

I try to step around her, but it is impossible to assail a wall. I give up. "Good day, Gran Toya."

When I turn my back, I pray the warrior won't run me through with her spear.

She does not.

Instead, she hoists me over her shoulder and heads away from the church.

AT FIRST, I FLAIL DOWN GRAN TOYA'S BACK, BUT THEN I GIVE UP struggling. It's broad daylight and she's carrying me like a sack of flour from the church. "You intend to carry me to Dessalines's hideout?"

"Civilians." Her low voice sounds filled with contempt. "He's a part of the French army. The general is in the government building. The lair is not far."

Gran Toya is huffing, working too hard to do this.

This isn't fair to her. I don't want her injured. "Put me down, Gran Toya. I willingly come."

She walks another hundred paces before setting me on my feet. "No tricks."

Smoothing my apron, leveling my turban, I start walking with her down Rue de Condé. "You can trust me, though I can't return your trust . . . using a priest to trick me." But in this act is there a message? We've used the deception of one before, in Place Royale.

The warrior woman looks as if she wants to protest but decides against it.

The square with the government building looms closer. "Tell me how he is."

"Busy."

"Then why are we bothering him? He should send for me when he's not busy. Perhaps when the wars are done."

Groaning, Gran Toya stays at my side. "The general ordered me to bring you. And you've delayed enough."

"Has it occurred to you that I'm busy, too? There are people to feed, people displaced by these continued battles."

Gran Toya does not respond. She shows no emotion at all.

"At least tell me of the danger he faces."

This makes her stop. Her gaze burns.

"He's a soldier. There are many dangers. Often, he is the right hand of power. And now, he's distracted because he knows you're alive."

I swallow hard. "And you wish I wasn't?"

Her fists pump. "I wish you no harm. But the general is trying to win a war and bring lasting liberty to Saint-Domingue. You're a distraction."

Her voice carries both sympathy and anger. I want neither.

"You'll see him in a few minutes. It's not my place to advise him to finish the war before he sets up his kingdom."

Kingdom? "It sounds as if you're advising me to tell him this."

"You're the one asking me questions. You're the one unsure."

My steps slow, but one withering glare from the warrior makes me hasten.

It is awful to be transparent in front of a stranger.

Up two steps, we go into the government building.

Officers in deep blue coats with brilliant white waistcoats and breeches move in and out of the hall.

She takes me to the biggest doors. "Go in."

Gran Toya folds her arms and I hesitate.

"Madame Lunic, he sent for you. That should tell you all you need to know."

For a moment, there's warmth in her tone. Then her dry voice booms. "Go on."

She pounds on the thick panel of the solid doors.

"Come in." His voice, Jean-Jacques's.

Holding my breath, I open the door.

He's there. A group of men in uniforms is gathered about him. Paper is everywhere on a big oak desk.

"Aw, Madame Lunic, we meet again." He hasn't looked up. Instead, he has written his signature on the document in front of him.

"It seems you're busy. I can go—"

His chuckles start. "It seems one of us is always going. Gentlemen, excuse me. Madame Lunic will give me a personal account of the hospital situation."

Once they scoop up the signed documents, the officers tip their hats to me and leave.

The door shuts.

It's only him and me and our memories.

Rising from his chair, he comes to the front of the desk and teeters on the edge.

His wide palms grip it as if he needs to hold on for balance or sanity.

"My condolences about Monsieur Lunic. I hear he passed away a few years ago after a long illness."

I nod. "Oui. He was a good man."

"You're again down to one husband. That's a pity. I hear he was good to the children, my children."

It isn't his prideful voice ripping into my chest. It's the wetness of his wide eyes, eyes that soon match mine.

35

Toya

1799

Miragoâne

The fight led our forces from Port-au-Prince, putting down rebellions and those sympathetic to Rigaud.

I thought the progress would be good, but it's made Janjak quiet. That woman has changed him again. I didn't know if this made him better. I hoped it didn't affect his leadership.

Janjak rode to the side of our troops. "Over this next hill will be a pass, a channel. This leads us to the lake, d'Etang de Miragoâne."

The ground beneath my sandals was a carpet of emerald. The uneven terrain demanded shoes. I refused boots. At sixty-one, twice the age the average slave lived, I was fit, in my sound mind, and loving every bit of soldiering in Saint-Domingue.

At the top of the ridge, the sky broke open. Clouds fell away. Pure radiant sunshine beamed down. The freshest air in the world greeted us. For a second, I was following in Tegbesu's procession as we took the royal journey from Abomey to Calmina. I missed Africa. I missed it all.

No one in the military knew this feeling. The one man who did, Nosakhere, I hadn't seen in years. I feared his luck had run out with the rebellions. He was the type to die in battle, not to sit around waiting for it.

I kicked a rock and it tangled in the grasses. Our old African world was mostly flat. Here, as in all of Saint-Domingue, one was always on a hill.

Dèyè mòn gen mon.

There were always more mountains.

I looked at my king, Janjak, on his gray horse. He gazed at this vast land, frowning. His mountain was leaving this woman and their newest baby behind.

Down the channel, the Minos and I headed toward the crystal-blue lake. Off in the distance was a small town, maybe Miragoâne.

"We break for camp," he called out. "Get a good night's sleep."

People shuffled and found positions. Tents went up. I grabbed my bedroll, but my eyes stayed on Janjak. He stood at the water's edge. He flipped the silver snuffbox in his hand.

Slowly, I approached, but his commanders beat me to him. Their whispers, their boasts were loud. They took him off to the tents.

Soon a big fire burned, and Janjak held court in front of the orange flames.

I picked up my fancy stick and walked near the lake. The dusky light fell onto the water.

"Gran Toya."

Janjak followed me. He was without his black hat and his jacket. I saw stains of sweat on his shirt.

"It was a hard path, Gran Toya. Your women are impressive."

"Well, now you should believe women are good for something other than amusement."

He pulled his hand flat to his chest. "You wound me. You know I have a great affection for women. I love to love them."

"Too much affection, Janjak. From city to city, you have a woman, sometimes many. The fame of Dessalines makes sure they are in endless supply unless we shelter in Port-au-Prince."

"That widow I have loved the longest." He stooped, picked up a rock, and skipped it over the water. "You don't approve of Marie-Claire."

"Tegbesu had many wives. Many females admired him. He did whatever he wished. He was the king. He had nothing to prove."

With his arms folded behind his back, he turned away. "I still haven't proven myself to you, Gran Toya. I suppose finishing this war and winning it will do."

He'd learned a lot since our time at Cormier. The way to take the hills, how to choose the best paths. My pride in him expanded. "You've bested the enemy already. Nothing more to prove. You're a great warrior."

"But not better than Tegbesu?"

"Perhaps. I'm not the one to tell you how to lead beyond the field, but a concubine in every city is not good. How do the king's children inherit if they are kept in the shadows?"

His mouth opened as if he had an excuse, but there was none. His treatment of women was shabby. I was his mother and I thought I'd taught him to respect women.

"This ground is rotten toward women, but we're here to help you win. We've taken casualties and killed. Yet men still treat women as amusements."

"I love women. I wouldn't be here today without you and Manman."

"Janjak, Eghosa would be proud of your battle tactics. And I am, too. You'll help Toussaint break the yoke of every enemy. Everyone is counting on you to support Saint-Domingue's king."

"Ah, that's where you're wrong. This is a republic. Neither Toussaint nor I will be king. France did away with Louis many years ago."

"There will always be a king. One man will hold power. Always."

He looked out on the shimmering lake and maybe even to the ring of mountains and the purple sky. "You and your Minos get some sleep. We take the bridge into the city tomorrow. Once we cross, we will claim Miragoâne for Toussaint, then we'll again be on the hunt for Rigaud. Everything is matching up with your informant's information, including the way he's reinforced Jacmel."

Slapping my hand to my brow, I offered Janjak a hearty salute, but my arm was a little stiff and it was clumsy. "Yes, sir."

He looked at me the way he often did, like a protective son to his mother. "The fighting will be intense. Cannons tear through my best men . . . and women. I've a different assignment for you."

"Yes."

He thumbed his lips. "Get Madame Lunic and all of my family

from Port-au-Prince. Bring them closer. Her mother has a house in Léogâne. Take them there. It's close to our next campaign. Having her there should cut down on my popularity."

I balled my hand into a fist. "You're sending my team to nurse-maid duty?"

"The Minos protect the queen for the king, do they not?"

That was true. It was one of our functions for the king, but I loved prosecuting the full war.

"It's an order, Gran Toya."

It was. My king commanded it.

After saluting, I pivoted and headed to my Minos.

But my heart was heavy. I didn't want an easy assignment. I wanted to keep making a difference.

"Gran Toya." His voice hit me. It was soft, as on the day Eghosa died. When I turned, his wide eyes were thoughtful. "Yes, General."

"Thank you. My mind will be at ease knowing you have her, that my family is safe."

This plea stirred my heart. He'd chosen a fine time to prove he revered women. But Janjak's being focused, not worrying about Madame Lunic or me, benefited his army.

A loss now would doom liberty for the Blacks.

My thirst for the fight was not bigger than the fight.

I repeated this, assuring myself that this was an important mission, not a judgment from Janjak that I'd grown too old for the battle.

THE JOURNEY OVER THE HILLS WITH JANJAK'S WOMAN AND THE children wasn't miserable. The babies had stopped their whine, their little fusses when they looked over the side of the dray. We were high up. The mountain views were magnificent.

The sky was white and dove into the bluest water.

It wasn't Gbowélé before the invasion.

It wasn't the Lama Forest before fighting lions.

It wasn't the groves and waters surrounding Calmina.

It was mountain after mountain, and I felt I could fly. After all these years, this was home, Saint-Domingue. And even in this small way, I was doing my part to bring her liberty.

"It's beautiful, Gran Toya." Janjak's woman had their newest in a sling. Jeanne Sophie was the name she sang with her hymns.

The dray guarded by the Minos had all the things that would make us a target on the chemin to Léogâne—pots and pans, a bedframe, and a rocking chair jiggled with each bump.

The woman checked on our supplies and her twins and the first daughter often. It was a beautiful family.

She caught me making eyes at the babe.

"You do care." Marie-Claire smiled for a moment. Then her lips flattened.

"Are you sad the Blanc servant girl didn't come?"

She scowled. "Adélaïde is not a servant. She's my niece and my friend."

"If you say so."

Marie-Claire cooed at the baby. "Adélaïde is. She's making good money doing embroidery for dresses and wants to keep our feeding program going. Now that the church will help it will be easier. I hope they are not offering just to impress General Dessalines."

The look on her face changed from hostile to sadness. "Madame Lunic, you don't want the general impressed?"

"Non. I'm looking at the guns your armed women bear. You call them Minos."

"Wi," I said and hoped her questions would end. But her lips pursed. There would be more.

"Tell me about the Minos. I see they are strong and rise early every morning for exercise. They're smart. I hear different languages but also unifying Kreyòl."

"Wi. They're here to protect you and your family and take you to Léogâne to your mother's."

Walking at the side of the dray, Marie-Claire looks back at me. "How did the general know I needed to return? I only received my mother's letter last week. She left her sister in Le Cap to return to Léogâne. They were getting along well. Now Maman says she misses my father's house. I wondered when she'd begin missing him again."

"Hiding in the flames."

"What?" She peered up at me, stumbled a little, but recovered. The baby was barely jostled. "What about flames?"

"My iya, she chose to hide in the flames to protect me, to give me a future. It took me years to forgive her. But it was her way of making mine easier. It was all she knew to do."

Marie-Claire looked away. "She's hiding something?"

"No one runs into the flames or an empty old house for themselves. They are convinced it's best for the ones they care for. When they realize it's not, it can be too late. But it's a choice. Everyone gets one, even if it's wrong."

She pumped her arms a little. "I'm in the flames then. I want to be with the general, but I fear those who learn that these are his children will use them as targets."

Now her eyes were soft and wet.

Mine, too.

I tried to give her peace, but the woman returned me pain. Remembering how I felt when Duclos threatened Janjak to control me cut deeply into my flesh. Four babies provided a whole lot of opportunities to hurt.

36

Marie-Claire

1799
Léogâne

In the place outside of L'Eglise Sainte Rose de Lima, I tend to the community garden with the young women I've recruited to fight hunger.

I wipe my brow. The heat and labor of cleaning garden beds have made me sweaty. My flower-printed cotton sleeves stick to my arms.

Gran Toya has inspired me to encourage more women to help. Sharing this burden and watching volunteers come is amazing.

Françoise is with me. Maman has said she can handle my young ones for a little while. My mother wants to lavish them with more love. Whatever happened with Elise was big. She refuses to tell me.

As Gran Toya advised, I'll let her hide. Maman is safe with me. If I need to know, she'll say.

The line for food has already started. The refugees keep coming from Miragoâne; even people from as far as Jérémie have heard of the soup lady.

"The fire is getting low, Maman." Françoise stirs and will ladle our rich broth. She's such a great help, like my missing Adélaïde.

"Maman?"

"Oh, oui." I add kindling and elm. The scent of sweet ash becomes as good as cologne water.

Swiping my brow, I adjust my mobcap, which keeps the scent of cloves and wild scallions out of my braids.

With my mighty spoon, wonderfully carved of neem wood, I scrape the best bits from the bottom.

In another hour, everything is ready. One glance at the smile of the woman filling her calabash is all the comfort I need.

A young man limping with a cane, leaning like my father did, is at the end of the line. I hope my pot holds enough to feed him.

More minutes pass. The soup is getting lower.

I hand my spoon to Françoise and I bang a pot. "Ladies, you've been most generous today, helping in the community garden, but we need a little more. Every mouth needs to be fed today. Does anyone have something to give?"

My voice doesn't seem loud enough. I clang the side of the pot. The wop-vibrating sound shows how hollow it's grown. "Does anyone have something to make our offering stretch? I know we have many strangers today, but they who only do good to those who they know, that's not genuine affection. We're called to love all the people."

"Keep going, Maman. Tell them." Françoise holds my hand for a moment. "There are more who might help."

Clearing my throat, I begin again. "It's our great duty, the saints teach us, with benevolent affection to feed the people. While the spiritual interests of our fellow man are important, our care for their welfare starts with a bowl. A warm full belly is the start to peace."

My heart is beating hard.

The level of the soup goes lower. I'm praying for someone to hear me. "He who gives for nothing, who helps without the hope of a reward—that's true kindness. It will bear the most fruit."

St. Louise, I'm giving them your message . . . our message. Send—two young women come running with a big pot full of cooked chicken and more carrots and potatoes. They pour the contents into mine and add rosemary and thyme. The fragrance warms my nose.

My eyes close. I bless God and the saints. St. Louise has come and helped me serve the people.

The man at the end has come at the right time. His calabash will be filled with meat.

There are tears in his eyes when I give it to him. "I was hungry. I heard there were angels in Léogâne."

He places the bowl to his chapped lips, and I feel his joy as he slurps. "I almost didn't come," he said as he wiped his mouth with the back of his hand.

"Where are you from, sir?"

"Jacmel. The hunger is great there."

"Is it bad? I hear the fighting is bad."

He nods. "Lots of shooting and the famine, it's killing all the people in the city. They've eaten the cats, madame."

When everyone who is in need has had a bowl of soup, my daughter and I douse the fire and wait for my pot to cool, but I remember the young man and pray for Jacmel. "The work is never finished, Françoise."

"It is today. And we made a difference." Lugging our pot and tripod, we head home.

Pushing through the door, I find Maman humming with sweet Jeanne in her arms. "Get cleaned up, and I'll show you how this one crawls."

I was dirty with soot on my skirt, on every finger. "Don't have the strength for all that, but I will get low to watch."

On all fours, I wipe my hands on my soiled, humbled hospital apron. "Come on, Jeanne."

She starts and toddles and begins to topple, but a shadow towers over us.

Big dark hands stretch and pick up my littlest girl.

"Ah, Jeanne Sophie, you're the prettiest of my small ones. Jacques, Célestine, and Françoise, and now my little Jeanne Sophie."

Dirtier than a dust rag, I turn and see Jean-Jacques's smile. He's handsome and neat, wearing a uniform with more braiding and fancy stitches than ever.

CLEAN AND DRESSED IN MY FINEST LINEN DRESS, I ENTER THE MAIN room. Jean-Jacques is rocking in my grand-père's chair. He looks comfortable as the girls sit around him, listening to his tales of the Dahomey.

Seven-year-old Jacques stands off a bit. When he moves closer, he says, "Tell us more of the war. I want to know where you are when you leave my mother to make her own way."

"Jacques," I say in what I hope is my gentlest tone, "you know your father is fighting for liberty, for all the mothers."

"He's always gone. And everyone says the general has no wife. At least Papa Lunic claimed you. He didn't disgrace you."

I look to my maman and wonder if she has filled his head with such. Sainte Lobelot was always the model of the perfect wife. She had the perfect union with a husband who did come home.

Jean-Jacques stands. "You're the man of the house, son. It's obvious you protect your mother and sisters. When I was your age I protected my mother, then my Tante Toya."

How is he protecting Gran Toya if she is in the fight?

He shakes my son's hand and then walks to the door.

My heart falls. I don't want him to leave, not like this. "Jean-Jacques?"

He turns with the smile that always melts my heart. "Aren't you all coming?"

Curious, I follow. The children, too.

A soldier who has been waiting on horseback dismounts.

"Madame Lunic, this is Louis Boisrond-Tonnere, my secretary and dear friend. He'll be my witness."

"Witness to what?"

Refined and stately, he turns to me and dances down the rue like there's music.

His breath smells rich, like my mother's broth. Not tafia or any other strong drink.

"What are you doing, Jean-Jacques?"

"Celebrating." Grabbing my arm, he whirls me down Rue de Croix until we are close to the church.

Then it's clear.

He wants to marry me, to formalize my waiting on him. "You wish to marry me again? To make me Madame Dessalines in public? Non."

I spin from his arms in my own dance, one of independence and pride. I head back toward Maman's house. "Children, Maman, let's go home."

My mother's face falls. "He wants to marry you and make a good woman of you."

With my hands to her cheeks, I lean in close. "I'm a good woman, just as I am. A widow with a mission for feeding and healing. I take after Mamie."

Her golden skin reddens. "I see. She didn't think well of me, either."

Shoulders slumping, she carries Jeanne Sophie, gathers the twins, and Françoise, and walks toward the house.

Tall Monsieur Boisrond-Tonnere backs up. "General, seems you have more convincing to do. I'll see madame's family to her dwelling."

His light face has sympathy painted in his high cheekbones.

"Very good for a military man to know a wise retreat." I soften my tone. "Come eat something, then be on your way to wherever you need to be. The next battle awaits."

Jean-Jacques whips off his onyx hat and fans. "Seems like the rebellion I must quell is here. What has happened?"

"It has been a long day. I fed a great many. I must feed myself. I'll sit and rest in my grand-père's chair."

Arms folding, then shifting, he taps his chin and asks, "You don't want to marry twice or a third time?"

His hand slips to my waist. Strong and possessive. "Or is this something else?"

In his eyes, his wide eyes, this act was to claim me now forever to the world, not just in a private garden or sneaking about abbeys or government buildings.

But when he's gone, my children and I are open targets. Targets that are expected to behave in certain ways, ways befitting a general.

With my hand to his lapel, I shake my head. "I see you, Jean-Jacques, always have. I know you have to fight. But do you see and hear me? Do you know what it is I want? It's not to be waiting for you to have a spare moment. It's not to have our children on display for one of your enemies to hurt in order to punish you."

His gaze wavers. His arms drop to his sides. "I want the world to know my heart. That you have it."

"And the other women, the others who share your spare moments, will they know this, too?"

The grin I can see in my dreams springs from his lips. It launches to his eyes. "You're the only one I want to marry."

"But you're popular. The rumors are said in the lines of the hungry, from here to Jérémie."

"I'll not lie. There have been many arms I have found solace in since we were torn apart."

"And some in the in-between times, when distance separated us."

He offers me a tilt of his head with his joyfully parted lips. "Guilty. Is that what you want me to say?"

"Truth, always the truth." I pat him away. "Now, here's mine. I need you to go and win the war. I need you to do it in haste. When it is time to be together, it will be forever."

"What?" His brow scrunches. He rubs the high collar of his blue jacket. "I thought this would please you. Your mother said it was what you wished."

Shrugging, I head to the house.

"Marie-Claire?"

"My mother believes love is all that matters. It isn't. Don't misunderstand. I love you more than myself. That is why I give you fully to the war effort."

I look away a moment to the mountains and remember how we had to go through seldom-used passes to avoid being seen. "I don't want to hide. I cannot live as a target. I'll not have you upset at what's happening here or let our beautiful babes distract you from the war."

He swoops me into his arms. His lips demand submission. His arms sculpt me to him with hands seeking, pressing palms to my skin.

We are moving to the side of Maman's house. In the shadows, he's trying to ignite my soul. He has me against the wall with hips ready to move with him for pleasure.

Clothes part.

Things fall out of the way. If I surrender, I'll have a memory to last until . . .

His kiss fills me. My mouth is hungry for him. His hands are on me, burrowing, caressing, promising me release.

I want this.

Hot and trembling like an earthquake. That's how it is when it's fevered and illicit and secret.

But this is only physical.

And only for a moment.

The next minute, I'll be empty and alone with another of his children to rear.

I can't fear the people I am to help, thinking one of them wants to make my children pay for Jean-Jacques's war.

Can't let my lover have everything and give up my children's safety, my mission, my soul.

"Non." I push away. "Jean-Jacques, I give you to the war effort, but not me, not again. I won't share you anymore with Toussaint or Toya or that uniform."

He's panting, pulling up the fall front of his white breeches. "I'm listening. Though this is an inconvenient time to talk."

"That's not listening. It never is. It's all flames. I can't be burnt again. I've run out of places to hide. Please go. Say goodbye to the children."

Picking up his hat, he bites his lip. He moves, then stops. "Is there nothing you want? Nothing that will change your mind?"

"Bleach. It's hard to get right now."

"Bleach is what you want, Marie-Claire? Yes. I'll have some sent." He bangs his hat against his hand, knocking off dust. "My wife won't marry me a second time?"

With a shake of my head, I point him to the door. "Let the children know you love them and will see them when the war is done."

"That could take a long time."

"I know. General Dessalines, Godspeed. When the war is won, we will see about us and our family."

"Wi, Madame Lunic. Until we meet again." He bows and heads around the corner.

It takes ten minutes before I hear the hoofbeats of horses trotting away.

Then I let the air leak from my lungs.

Relearning how to breathe, how to live without his touch, I let my resolve dissolve. Sobbing, I slip down the wall.

The Prophecy

On the day the great gods came down

One shook the earth and split the ground.

The other great twins fed the bound,

And served the broken healing stew.

In the final hours of the battle,

The twins unite, free the chattel.

They declare peace, share a saddle.

They have a world that is now new.

Darkness, light, truthful twins conspire.

Wars end with forgiveness and fire.

Yet the cost, the blood toll's higher.

Then Zinsu, Zinsi say adieu.

All was freedom's price to pursue.

—ANONYMOUS, STYLED IN THE FORM OF UTENZI

37

Toya

1800
Jacmel

Janjak chatted with his secretary and aides at our post along Chemin de la Grande Rivière. He should have been happy, but he seemed tense, hands folding, shifting behind his back. His new shako hat and decorated jacket with gold braiding didn't cheer him. You'd think we were losing.

We'd chased Rigaud here, to Jacmel. His forces were hiding behind the walls of the city. After several days, it looked more and more like his side was waiting for ours to quit.

I picked up my musket and led Fleur and Thérèse around the wall. The way the sun gleamed on the fortified battery rimming the city reminded me a little of Calmina. If the structure of bricks and wood had been mudded smooth and oiled to make it shine, it might have doubled for the place I missed the most.

Jacmel's tile and thatch roofs didn't have the heads of victims lined on top. Rigaud's forces had put some on pikes along the chemin but not on roofs. I supposed I would never understand the choice. There were enough dead for both.

Janjak came to me. The fury in his dark face was worse than a cyclone. "The people of Jacmel are starving, but Rigaud refuses to give up."

"Concerned about your enemy's meals?"

His brow rose but his signature smile didn't appear. "Hunger is a bad problem even for an enemy, I'm told."

My king's mind was on the woman who had said non to him. His advisers went to their horses, readying to go to outposts, but they didn't look well, either. The wordy secretary, the drinking aide-de-camp, and the rest seemed deflated.

"What has happened, Janjak?"

His gaze flitted past my face to the high walls. "Toussaint is depending on other voices."

"The king has many advisers. Is this wrong?"

Janjak shrugged. "Stevens, the new U.S. consul general to Saint-Domingue, and his boss, Pickering, the secretary of state, have gotten President Adams to promise trade, to defend our waterways by all legal means."

"You believe this?"

"Do I believe what a Blanc says? Non. Toussaint believes they are more frightened by France gaining power than Blacks. We are a check to the republic. Blancs will stop other Blancs from having too much and will use us to hammer Paris."

Why would a French colony . . . be a problem for France? The look on his face said the rest. "Your king wants independence."

"If the First Consul Napoleon keeps consolidating strength, it could be bad. The man has ambitions of conquering the world."

"What Blanc doesn't?"

This ushers a laugh from my sad king. "Napoleon's slaveholding wife has needs that only the sugar trade can meet. It's easy for a man to be swayed by the bad influence of a woman."

"The right one can lead you to the light. A good man knows the difference."

He dips his head, agreeing with his heart in his eyes. Marie-Claire's turning him away has made him think.

"They call this battle of Jacmel the War of the Knives. Toussaint is one blade and Rigaud is another, both fighting under French flags. Each wants to be the one Napoleon seeks to be his leader here."

"But you said Napoleon can't be trusted?"

"That is everyone's dilemma. Toussaint wants independence and Napoleon's respect."

"You don't believe we can have both."

"A wise man said it is better to be feared than loved. Boisrond-Tonnere has read me Machiavelli's *The Prince* and *The Art of War*. Better words inside than Toussaint's Epictetus. Better sentiments, too. For only fear will keep people unified and wanting to be led."

My head shook. The beads on my helmet rattled. "That's what the slave masters have taught. Fear is control."

He didn't answer. His head was on the other side of the wall, the clouds, or back in Léogâne.

"Carry on, Gran Toya." He doffed his hat and caught up with his men.

My cane with the twin gods reminded me of two coming together, not this split of allegiances. I sought prayer to bring clarity of purpose to Janjak and an end of this war. As with the Oyo, there was such a thing as fighting too long.

THE WIND WAS ROLLING DOWN FROM THE HILLS. IT HOWLED IN THE quiet of the night. Guns and cannons added periodic rattles to the darkness. I left Fleur and Ponce on patrol in front of the entry to Jacmel. I and my trusty cane went to Janjak's tent.

He sat at a table studying maps. The lines and circles with numbers held meaning for him. "Is there something you need, Gran Toya?"

"I came to see about you."

"As a soldier to her commanding officer."

"As a Minos to her king, as a mother to her son."

His wide eyes lifted. "Is that so?"

"You're not sleeping. I remember in our hut at Cormier how things bothering you made you restless."

Humming the old slave tune, he sat back fumbling with his snuff-box. His hat was on the table's edge along with his coat. "Rigaud and Pétion are brilliant French officers. Their men fight valiantly. Too valiantly. If all my men were so brave, I'd never lose."

"You've not lost. We've won, battle after battle. Miragoâne has fallen. Grand-Goave and Petit-Goave. Your leadership has done this. Only Jacmel remains unbroken."

"They'll more likely starve to death. I heard they're eating horses now. That's a waste of men and beasts."

At the sound of cannons, I moved to the entrance. "The big guns are erupting from the Baye de Jacmel." It drummed and drummed. The sky sparked and lit like stars.

"Ah. The Americans have arrived." He joined me at the opening of the tent and looked out toward the walls of the city.

More fire streaked and crashed into Jacmel.

"Captain Perry of the USS *General Greene*. Toussaint's bon ami, President Adams, has kept his word. Pickering, too. Perry will use his frigate to keep the British from supplying Rigaud. When they run out of ammunition, maybe then they'll surrender. Then the two sides, Colored and Black, should unite and look to the true enemy."

"Your king has convinced you France is the enemy. It might be Britain."

Janjak shrugged then stretched as if all the weight of the armies, the world, the stars were on his shoulders. "What if Toussaint and I are the twins, the promised ones in Mackandal's song? What if this is not just to stop enslavement here but to build a new world?"

The slave curse frightening the Blancs, Janjak still thought it true? Him and Toussaint? Could be.

"The stars are falling again, Gran Toya, like they did when we fought in the hills bordering Léogâne. Mountains rimmed everything like a bowl. The cannons moaned. The earth shook like it would be torn apart."

He sighed, but his hands hooked behind the lapels of his dark jacket. "The heavens were on fire that night."

It was awful. Our troops panicked. Men broke lines, running, even dropping their weapons. My Minos stayed in place, but we weren't enough to keep order.

"Half my men thought it was a Vodun judgment."

"What of the other half, Janjak?"

"They knew it to be. It was a sign, like the fabled lightning strike at Bois Caïman."

"I was there. It's true. Bois Caïman was true."

"Well, it showed me we're not prepared to fight France. This prolonged War of the Knives says it, too. I must convince Toussaint. There are a lot of voices in his ears." Janjak's loud sigh steamed the silver snuffbox in his hands. "He won't listen to a loser. Pétion almost won today."

This was true.

Janjak had used his demi-brigade to assault the batteries of the city. The Minos and I were caught between them and the wall we'd breached. Surrounded, we'd used our bayonets and literally stabbed our way into retreat. We slipped past the guns of Fort du Gouvernement to a position near the walls of Jacmel at Fort du Léogâne.

More cannons pounded.

The grapeshot would push back Rigaud's forces and keep them pinned down.

Clasping his neck, Janjak looked up. "I tried to rush and bring an end to the fight, Gran Toya."

"The Vodun priest would say the Marassa have judged us. We're guilty of trying to end this too quickly for Toussaint, or France, or the widow?"

His posture stiffened. "Can the answer be all three?"

As when he was little, when he'd go up into the hills and scour the sky, I pointed out the two brightest stars. You could see them beyond the smoke. "The Marassa, the divine twins, will hide their faces sometimes. Yet they still control justice and timing. Why wrestle, Janjak?"

"I'm a good Catholic now, as Toussaint wants all his officers to be." His brow cocked as he spun to me. "But a shower of fire and stars shooting over my troops doesn't quite seem to be like an edict from Pope Pius VII. Nor does waiting on Americans to slow my enemy."

Gripping my staff, I held it close to my cowrie-beaded breastplate. The shimmer of gold from the shells reflected in his troubled eyes. "I don't think your pope wants us to depend on anyone but him."

Janjak flipped open his snuffbox and put a pinch to his wide nose. "It is silly to think any man has influence over skies, popes, or happiness."

He took another whiff of the fine tobacco. "I'm not the first man to try to take Jacmel and fail. Romaine-la-Prophétesse tried and freed over ten thousand enslaved. For his efforts the French captured his wife and daughter."

"But we are on the side of the liberators. Has Paris taken our freedom?"

"Non. But Toussaint won't listen to my caution. He'll definitely not listen if I fail Jacmel."

With my hand to his shoulder, I tried to remind my king of who he was. "Why are you telling sad stories when you have defeated so many? You're wonderful and skilled. Most of Saint-Domingue fears your name."

With a small smile and a little nod, he walked back inside. "Someone told me I needed to think of living beyond the war. Or was it that life begins after the war?"

He rolled out his map of the city. "These things are a mishmash in my mind. Colonel Christophe will be here soon for the plan to take Grand Fort and Fort Talavigne."

"You will win the buildings, the battle, and the war." And the woman, if she was what he wanted.

His noted smirk returned. "Someone has faith. Go rest. We mount a new surge soon. Gran Toya, when this battle is done, I intend to make changes. You'll stand down. You've served long enough."

"We are not done. There is plenty of fight in these bones."

"As for you and your Minos, you all will rest with honor." He glanced at me with his wide eyes. "You were almost killed today in front of Fort du Gouvernement, in front of my eyes. It's a miracle you got out."

"That's the risk of war."

"Well, the risks are too high for me. I couldn't protect Manman or Marie-Claire, but I can save you."

His gaze had always been respectful, yet he looked at me not as a soldier but as an old woman whom he wanted to see sewing on some veranda.

I wasn't too old for the fight. Women started the fight. We'd kept the fight going until new armies could be born. Women shouldn't be made to stand down now.

"Get rest," I said, then left, holding in all my complaints.

The next morning the sun appeared as usual. I gathered the Minos for exercise near the chemin and the Grande Rivière.

Fleur, who'd been on duty, charged toward me, cutlass raised.

Taking my musket off my sling, I aimed behind her.

She reached me and lowered my gun. "Not the enemy. Women in white are coming. Ghosts. Led by twins in white."

Squinting, I saw them coming in the distance, then prepared for the judgment. The gods had sent the Marassa to decide the battle of Jacmel.

38

Marie-Claire

1800
Jacmel

After offering medical aid to the injured at the military camp Pasquet, miles from Jacmel, I headed our mule train of mercy down the chemin. The fast-moving waters of the Grande Rivière cry for us, for the dead lying along the banks. The land is curvy with green hills and emerald fanning pines.

The thunder of cannons announce we are minutes from the blockaded city.

"Ready, Marie-Claire?" Adélaïde sits beside me in our trusted dray.

Though my fingers grip the seat tightly, I nod. "Oui. The hungry of Jacmel are Blanc, Brown, and Black. They are innocents and soldiers. Are you ready?"

"The mission is stronger than the missionary, Marie-Claire. I've seen too much. When you said you'd do this, I had to, too. Like always, side by side." She takes her hand, chafed and tanned by the sun, and clasps it about mine.

Then I ask the others—

the mère whose child was killed by grapeshot in Petit-Goave,

the fille whose parents have died of starvation in Jérémie,

the sœur whose brothers died in violence on a habitation in Miragoâne,

the grand-mère who's buried too many of her sons, her daughters, her grands—"Are we ready to war on hunger? To heal above strife?"

"Wi. Oui. Lanfè wi."

Woman to woman, we send each other a blessing, then I motion the mules forward.

Adélaïde tugs at her white turban, which matches mine. "Dr. Duperoy of Jacmel wrote the hospital in Port-au-Prince. No one is helping here. All others have fled. He can't do it all by himself."

"No one can, Adélaïde."

The foggy air begins to roll across my face as we pick up speed. "Yippee."

Our white garments flap in the wind as if we're gliding down a long corridor.

Halfway to the checkpoint, I see soldiers, then people hiding in a small grove of bushes. Refugees.

Adélaïde notices, too, but we continue toward the wall.

We have to appear neutral to all sides, fearless to the soldiers, whether they fight for Toussaint or Rigaud. Both sides have left the people to starve.

Looking at the women who've joined us, I pray none of these disciples are hurt.

At the bend in the road, we have to stop. Soldiers are in our path aiming guns.

MUSKETS WAVE IN MY FACE—I REMEMBER THE GUARDS DOING THE same at Place Royale. The safety of being known as Pierre's wife is gone. I must be brave for me and my angels in white.

Soldiers bang my soup bowls as they crawl all over my dray.

I will the terror away and lift up my voice and sing.

> *With angels round the throne;*
> *Ten thousand are their tongues,*
> *But all their joys are one.*

"What do you intend to do?" The soldier does not lower his weapon. It smells of the sulfurous gunpowder. It has been fired today.

"To feed the people."

Then I sing Elise's song as loudly as I can.

> *Worthy the Lamb that died, they cry,*
> *To be exalted thus!*
> *Worthy the Lamb, our hearts reply,*
> *For He was slain for us!*

Women approach. My heart almost leaps through my white tunic. They'll know we've come for mercy.

"Lower arms," the lead says. Gran Toya, with her walking stick, comes down the path.

The soldier does as he's commanded.

Rejoicing, I fly down from the dray and lead my girls in bowing. "We've heard of the great suffering. The shortages of medical supplies. We're here to help."

Her sullen ebony face is unmoved. "Turn and go back. War is happening. I cannot guarantee your safety."

"If I feared for that, I'd not be here."

She pounds her staff even as she ensures all soldiers keep their guns at their sides. "You can go no further. Go home."

"Fine," I say. "Unpack, ladies. We'll feed the people from here." We set up our cookstoves and tripods to hold the kettles. Our packs have everything, even loads of wood.

"Madame Lunic." Gran Toya shakes her head. "You have a family in Léogâne. They need you. Return and raise babies."

"Babies here need to eat, too."

I ignore her grousing and have the medicines and bandages unpacked. Others are chopping pumpkins on white sheets.

"Madame Lunic!"

"I'm a widow, Vèv Lunic. My husband is God. He directs me. With this calling, I know He'll watch over my little ones. Excuse me."

Her Minos have wide eyes. They may never have seen anyone

defy her. Gran Toya drags me by the arm. "What are you trying to prove?"

"That no one should starve. Keep cooking, ladies. Adélaïde, lead for me."

My friend nods. The music of our pots and chopping continues.

In the bushes, I see civilians; they look thin and weak. "The War of the Knives has stuck too many guts."

"Marie-Claire, you cannot go through the gates."

"I don't mean to be disrespectful, Gran Toya, but there's famine behind those walls. Hearts are hardening against Toussaint and Rigaud. All the work of unifying Saint-Domingue will be lost."

"Can you hear me above your own voice? If you die, Janjak's children will be motherless."

"Better motherless than to have a mother who is soft and a coward."

Lifting her arms to the sky, Gran Toya looks shaken. "Children . . . daughters don't understand when a mother chooses to die. They just know she's gone. Their lives will never be the same."

When our eyes meet, she must see the tears in mine as I see them in hers. "Better to die fighting than sitting and watching dreams wither. They'll know I did this for them and all the children."

Her face softens. She understands my truth.

"I understand the risk, Gran Toya. Let me get to it."

She lets me walk away, back to my singing women . . . in time to see Jean-Jacques and his officers dismount.

THE STICKY HEAT OF THE DAY IS NOTHING TO THE FLAMES IN JEAN-Jacques's stare. I've never seen him this furious. Never.

"Is this your battle face, General?"

His breathing sounds rough, as if he has to bottle himself up. "Did you come to embarrass me?"

"Non. To feed starving people."

"Well, this is quite embarrassing. The mother of my children, who has cast me aside, shows up at the battlefront like a nun."

"You once dressed as a priest."

"But that was to get to you. Who are you trying to get to, Marie-Claire?"

"Refugees. They're streaming to Léogâne. I've seen so many hurting. We had to come. We had to help. This is my calling."

His expression doesn't change, but before he can begin another diatribe about how reckless I am, I bow my head and go back to my food line.

Adélaïde has things well in hand. Her apron has spots of broth, but nothing else is out of place.

I slip on my treasured apron and start stirring. I gaze at Jean-Jacques. He's standing in the same place, wearing a new uniform with splendid gold trim. The hat he rotates between his palms is also adorned in gold, too.

A young boy runs from the bushes. His cheeks are rosy. "Soup, madame, s'il vous plaît."

I fill a bowl with hot broth and chunky cut vegetables.

Then more people from the woods come, running and stumbling to get to my pots.

Infantrymen run from the outposts. Guns are lifted and readied to fire. And I look to Jean-Jacques, the man with the power to help, to Gran Toya, who has his ear, and I pray. "St. Michael, shield us to do God's will."

The soldiers get closer.

Jean-Jacques blinks and raises his hand in a fist. His soldiers stop moving.

The general marches to me. "I see now why you needed bleach. Had you been planning this, to be in white and put yourself at risk, when you refused me?"

"No. The refusal was for me. The decision to come to Jacmel is from seeing the starving refugees."

Gran Toya and others clear the grove of men and women—all in rags, all skin and bone. A few are Black, most are Blancs. The rest are trapped behind the walls.

"Let them go, Jean-Jacques. Feed the people. Let us take the medical supplies to the hospital inside the city."

He slaps on his hat, crowning himself with all its authority. "Do you think you can just walk into Jacmel?"

"I came by mule train."

"Madame Lunic!"

"Look at the hunger, General." I take his arm and turn him to the people slurping my soup. "Toussaint's top man can announce what we are doing to open Jacmel for a little while."

Gran Toya came near. "Janjak, we found over a hundred refugees in the grove. We rounded them up. But you have no use for prisoners."

"Non," I say, with my hand still on his sleeve. "Have mercy on them, they are fleeing the famine."

"General?" His aunt fingers her musket. "What say you?"

Jean-Jacques glances at me with angry and yet hurting eyes. "Make them form a line, an orderly line for madame, Gran Toya. That's the best way Madame Lunic can serve them."

Her breath releases. She nods and orders the Minos to organize the people.

His secretary, the one who came to Léogâne, steps to him. "They could be spies. They could be soldiers in disguise."

Jean-Jacques sighs. "If so, we'll meet them again on the battlefield. The angels of the war need to see we're about controlling the insurrection, not slaughtering the people. She must see my passion as I see hers."

"Thank you, General Dessalines. Thank you for listening."

"Don't thank me, Madame Lunic. Though you've proven how incredibly brave and foolhardy and committed to people you are, you've embarrassed me. You've disobeyed and put yourself at risk—"

"Jean-Jacques. I'm—"

"If you live through this day to repay me and soothe my battered ego, you'll marry. I'll personally take you back to Léogâne and get the deed done. Then I'll return and finish this fight with Rigaud. Then you'll marry me again in front of my commander. Toussaint needs to meet the woman willing to defy his top officer."

He walks away before I can protest or agree. His voice is monotone, without his usual smirk or laugh. I'm not sure if this is all jest.

He climbs to the top of a wooden structure that refugees are calling Fort du Léogâne and yells into the city. "Let the angels of the war inside to feed the people. They have medicines, too. It's no trick. Cease fire for two hours."

"Oui! Oui, deux heures de cessez-le-feu."

The gates open. I leave Adélaïde but take four others with kettles and medicines and head inside Jacmel.

I'll know whether Jean-Jacques is kidding about marrying if I survive.

39

Marie-Claire

1801
Saint-Marc

The first time I wed Jean-Jacques was in Place Royale's garden. The second was in April 1800 at the chapel where my parents wed, L'Eglise Sainte Rose de Lima, in Léogâne. This third is October 1801, as we celebrate the end of the War of the Knives.

Rigaud has sailed to France, disgraced. Toussaint and Dessalines have conquered the Spanish side of Saint-Domingue. All the island is one, under France and Toussaint.

My hands are moist beneath the simple lace gloves my mother has made for me. Delicate in white threads, the point de gaze lace has tiny flowers and is trimmed with lilac ribbon. "It's the prettiest thing I own."

"The shawl I made the gloves from," Maman says, "was your mamie's. I took it the night I left her in '58."

She looks like she wants to confess something, but I hold her. We have peace, finally all is peace. I truly understand what hopeless love is. I'm hopelessly in love with Jean-Jacques. He ended the war. I want to think it was for me, but it was for Saint-Domingue.

"But that night," she says, "I heard the prophecy of two coming down to change the world. It has to be you and Dessalines."

She kisses my cheek, then leaves me in the vestibule to take her place in the chapel with my children.

This old wooden structure in Saint-Marc has shutters for windows, no glass at all. Grapeshot has made dents in the wall, but the whitewashed building is the house of God and all his saints. It can unite us. It can unite our world.

My heart races waiting for things to start. I rub my palms together, the lace catching a little with each pass.

Each of our ceremonies has been different—from forbidden love, to celebrating living, to being crowned Madame Dessalines, the wife of Toussaint Louverture's highest-ranking and most successful general.

In a quick glance, I see Maman in her baby-blue gown and all our children dressed in fine linen—the girls in white dresses with yellow flowers, Jacques in cream pantaloons and a garnet-colored jacket.

My Jean-Jacques stands at the altar in an onyx jacket with gold epaulets. He wears a fine jet hat blocked and embellished with a cockade of red and blue ribbons.

Elise sings at the side, near the baptismal. She's come from Le Cap, full of glee and is starry-eyed at the generals and their wives, whom she's only read about in her papers. For a moment I think she's brought a copy for Jean-Jacques and Toussaint and Christophe to sign. General Christophe is a very tall man who fought in the American Revolution.

Peeking again, I see him sitting with his wife. They're a lovely couple. Much in love. Marie-Louise is stylish, with her long hair up in a colorful bonnet.

Monsieur Joseph, Mamie's dear friend, came with Elise. He'll walk me down the aisle for this wedding. He looks older but is still strong. His brown eyes take me in. My gown is cream with pink and green flowers and vines. The pleated train is pressed and Adélaïde has embroidered petals about the hem.

She's also sitting in the back with the children. She won't stay long after this ceremony. She'll head off to Port-au-Prince. My friend is ready to restart her life. The city . . . our whole world of Saint-Domingue has finally claimed peace.

Suzanne Louverture, Toussaint's wife, sits close to the Christophes. She's elegant, with a blush-colored gown wrapping her full figure and a matching turban. Two small children sit at her side. I'll ask their names later.

Beyond the door of the church, Gran Toya and her Minos march. They look resplendent, with new brass cuffs.

But why are they on guard?

In fact, I see more people in uniform these days. Isn't the war over?

Each breath comes faster and faster until my lungs seem ready to pop, but Monsieur Joseph squeezes my fingers. "You're a Lobelot. You've nothing to fear. Just put on a smile and show the world they can't break you. That's what Madame Lobelot did every day, even when the worst came."

His dark face is wizened, but his topaz eyes are lively and bright.

I raise my chin and lean on him. We enter the chapel, but I stare at my beloved Jean-Jacques's grin then turn back to the worrisome look on Gran Toya, who enters the sanctuary with her spear.

THE RECEPTION HALL IN SAINT-MARC IS LARGE—WHITEWASHED limestone walls with arches supporting the ceiling between mahogany beams.

Tables are adorned with gateau au beurre with a rum sauce and platters of fruits, all on white linen. Rum with sweetened milk is served in goblets for guests.

I take one and enjoy the flavor, like vanilla and molasses. The music is lively, and even Elise favors the crowd with a song from the musical she's practicing. Now that things are calm, she's starring in plays. Not as the lead yet, but she tells me it's only a matter of time.

I finish my milky rum and spin to the tempo.

My husband, who likes to dance, has disappeared. Where is he?

Suzanne Louverture stands alone. When I approach, her hands shake. Her goblet jitters, perfuming the air with vanilla.

"Madame Louverture, are you well?"

With a blink, her countenance changes to a happy smile and she embraces me. "I'm glad you have caught Toussaint's tiger."

"Well, we sort of caught each other."

Her regal profile in the blush turban turns sad. "Support him, them. I fear this world wants Black men to fail." In my ear she whispers, "It's not over. The war is not over."

I can't believe the struggle that began before Jean-Jacques and I were born, raging since Mackandal in '58, keeps burning. Forty-three years is not enough?

My insides are screaming. They're raging. Why can't we all be left alone?

I have to say something.

Seeing Toya with her spear and shining cutlass, I move toward the door where she hovers.

"I need—"

She moves out of my way without complaint.

When I enter the side hall, I quiet my footfalls on the tiles, for I hear the echoes of Toussaint's and Jean-Jacques's voices coming from a nearby room.

"We took the eastern part of the island, Spanish Santo Domingo, in January. Months ago. You're telling me today, the twenty-first of October, that it was against Napoleon's expressed wishes?"

Jean-Jacques sounds panicked.

The sound of a fist hitting a wall booms.

"Calm down, Dessalines. It was against Napoleon's purview, but it had to be done."

"Pur-what? You should've shown me a direct order from the First Consul. Now we've disobeyed. Toussaint, you're forcing Napoleon's hand. We just found peace. The whole world is at peace."

"The Spanish side of the island was always a threat. You can't have free and enslaved colonies sharing a border."

"The same can be said against every English island sharing our sea. Or what of the slavery-loving United States? Liberal Adams is gone. The new president hates Negroes. Jefferson thinks the only good one of us is a dead one or one in a chained collar, or light-skinned enough that he can pretend she's his dead wife."

"Dessalines, we are a trading partner to the United States. We have treaties in place. All that won't go away. They'll step in again as a way to balance France."

Another punch shakes the wall.

"Ouch." Jean-Jacques must've hurt himself, but the shouts continued.

"Toussaint, your Hamilton helped you write your constitution, but he's no friend of Jefferson. There's no influence left in America's government who believe enslavement is wrong. And you sent this document to Napoleon without sharing it with your generals."

"We've worked hard to free the colony, the whole damn island. Dessalines, we have to be strong and show we can lead."

"You didn't give us a chance to understand this or advise about this. Toussaint, you told no one. You just acted."

"It's what I felt was right. I abolished enslavement for the whole of Saint-Domingue. The twenty-eighth of January will be revered. Our independence gives us the right to dictate our terms. Us alone."

"We fought, but you decided."

"As your Gran Toya says, there's one king."

"But we are brothers. We fought together."

"Dessalines, we are still brothers. Brothers fight sometimes."

"Like Romulus and Remus? I suppose we know who is who, since I have an arrow through my heart."

"We still fight for Saint-Domingue, but as a free independent country. Dessalines, I need your support. Do I have it?"

"I . . ." Jean-Jacques stares at me as I enter from the shadows.

Toussaint comes to me and kisses me on the cheek. "You have an elegant, calm bride, my friend. She'll be an asset to settle you down and help you build upon the land in the Artibonite."

He's taller than Jean-Jacques. His tongue possesses a good command of French, but his dark brown eyes, almost black, say the truth. He's fearful the peace we've just won is temporary. The visionary man has pushed too hard for change.

I put my hand on his. "My husband is passionate about Saint-Domingue. You know he'll do what he must to protect it for the children. All the children."

My voice is clear.

These men are human and ambitious. I'll not criticize when I can see they're already weighed down in doubt.

"Toussaint, may I have my husband alone? Can you find one of the other generals to instruct tonight?"

"Of course. General Dessalines, I'll see you at week's end in my offices at Saint-Marc."

Jean-Jacques nods and his commander leaves. I wait to hear the thud of the closing door before I put my gaze on my husband.

"You heard?"

"Yes, Jean-Jacques."

"The man thinks Napoleon won't care about what we've done. The up-nose slaves think they can take on the French. Napoleon will send every battalion to come at us. The Americans . . ."

I step to him and put my finger to his lips. "You married me in a time of peace."

"I married you a few times. Should get one right."

Again I silence him, this time with a kiss.

My mouth fits perfectly to his, with lips that are soft and malleable and hungry.

"Marie-Claire, peace won't last."

I weave my hands beneath the warm wool of his jacket and the smooth lines of his waistcoat to the soft linen below.

We need to make up for time lost and the time we might never have.

Peace will end.

War will rage.

I know it.

The way his heart trembles beneath my palms, he feels it, too.

His jacket falls to the floor.

Waistcoat. My turban and dress go away.

Petticoats and garters and medallions drop.

My braids, his breeches.

We tumble onto a sofa.

It's small. The cushions are hard, inflexible. But we are used to making do, making the best of stolen moments.

I want to feel nothing but his love, his skin, every scar on a chest screaming for my warmth.

War is coming again. With our public marriage, our acknowledged family, this time the struggle can take everything away.

40

Toya

1802
Crête-à-Pierrot

Readying to leave for the fort at Crête-à-Pierrot, I stood guard at Janjak's office in his grand-casa at Habitation Frère.

I stretched my limbs and took deep breaths, but the shouting between the general and his aides was harsh. Words like *cut off, the hard-fought south,* and *fallen* made me cringe.

The door opened. Men filed out. I went in.

The fancy bottles of wine on his sideboard were untouched. On his rich mahogany desk was an open glass jug smelling of fire. Tafia.

In a shirt and white waistcoat and dark breeches, I saw a man drinking lava readying to explode.

Resting on my walking stick, I sighed. "Is everything bad?"

"Gran Toya, I never truly understood how fast time could move until a king or a consul for life decided I must die."

"Blanc men have wanted you dead for a while, some Brown and Black, too. This is not new."

"It is when Bonaparte sends his brother-in-law, General Leclerc, and thousands of elite Blanc soldiers to do so. Add over half of Toussaint's army, the many mulatto and Blanc soldiers who have defected to France. I'll be fighting the men who just fought with me in Jacmel."

"What's the plan? There has to be a plan."

He took a swig of the tafia from a crystal goblet. "General Christophe, under Toussaint's orders, took a torch to everything. The rebuilt Le Cap was burnt to the ground: the town houses, the barracks, everything but a few churches. Barely got my wife's aunt out of there.

"Leclerc's forces came ashore to nothing."

Wish I'd been there to watch, to see the frustration on those faces, entering the same port where the slave boats used to disembark and seeing flames. "That won't make them leave, will it?"

"Non. The defections have made their numbers swell. Toussaint wants to wait them out and hope the wet fever season kills off the troops coming from France. Yellow fever kills many."

"That's a whole lot of trust to put on the gods, to kill the right ones."

He put his face in his hands, rubbing his temple. Tafia left a nasty headache. "Leclerc and his number two Rochambeau, son of a hero of the American Revolution, shall be surprised."

"I have the Minos prepared."

"No, Gran Toya, I need you here."

"I'll have part of my team here on nursemaid duty. They can handle the chaos, Janjak."

"Chaos?"

"The running children, the sad mother-in-law, the sour singing aunt who cries every day over Le Cap's destruction, and your poor wife. Another set of twins wars in her gut."

The mention of his children to come made him sit back with boots up and a more arrogant smile than before.

"I'll make sure nothing happens here. But you need me. You need my women. You won before with us at your side. With your numbers cut you need us more than ever."

"Gran Toya. You've been out of active fighting for two years."

I twirled my stick and knocked his feet to the floor. "Unlike you, we've trained every day. Not one of mine is idle or slovenly."

He rubbed his face. "I don't know. To risk—"

"Janjak, think like a commander. You have an able, trained team but won't use them because you think me feeble, or worse, you think like the French and believe women are good for nothing but harlotry or housekeeping. And Black women are no good at all."

He chugged from the jug, then wiped his sleeve on his lips. "Promise me not to get killed, then we have a deal, Lieutenant Gran Toya."

In the French army, I was given a title and a low rank. In the people's forces, I am promoted. "Women are the key to helping you win. And you know it."

"Vive les femmes!"

I snatched up the jug. "Go to bed. Check on your wife. You'll be gone for a while."

He stood, taking the jug as he passed me. "I know."

Janjak left, and I went out to my Minos to prepare them for this battle and the ones to follow. The French wouldn't give up, and I'd die before we let their forces win. Given the promise I'd made, I had no choice but to break the enemy.

LEAVING MY MINOS THÉRÈSE AND PONCE TO WATCH OVER JANJAK'S household, Fleur and I and the rest of my team marched to our latest assignment, to slow Leclerc's advance at the fort of Crête-à-Pierrot.

We gathered between the clay walls of the redoubt deep in the Artibonite, close to Marchand, where Janjak had settled his family.

Wasn't so sure that was wise, but they were his orders. Toussaint felt the mountains were strength. From the old days, the myths and fears would work on the massas and those born on this soil. Climbing the sides of the high redoubt, the channel we'd cut, I felt more confident that this position was out of reach of the ship's cannon. We only had to fear the ones on moving carts. No one was secure when iron balls and grapeshot fell.

"Gran Toya!" Fleur ran up the redoubt huffing and puffing. "The general is coming."

In the next instance, Janjak and his closest advisers rode past. He tipped his hat, which was black but with no trim. His jacket was ebony with gold braiding. No more French blue, now and forever. They entered the fort.

After an hour of being on watch Fleur came to me and presented my cutlass. "Sharpened, Gran Toya."

I took the blade and held it high. The way the sun gleamed on it, shining bright, it was ready for use again.

Fleur was my most faithful Minos. So many battles we'd fought side by side. Most of the cowrie beads on her breastplate had fallen away. She'd mended it with red and gold wooden balls. War should only last as long as uniforms.

Movement at the bottom of the hill caught my eyes.

"Gran Toya!" a soldier shouted. "They're coming. The horses, the French army."

Waving my cutlass, I whipped our teams forward. "Run to the fort!"

Forgetting formations, all sped to Crête-à-Pierrot.

Bracing, waiting for the last soldier to come inside, I listened for the closing of the gate.

I heard nothing.

I saw Janjak with his hand on the locking beam. He refused to secure it.

All quieted for him to speak. He cleared his throat. "For those who do not feel themselves courageous enough to die, while there is yet time, go. Leave!"

No one stirred.

He yelled "Leave!" once again, but no one moved. He flung the gate open wider. "Let the friends of the French depart; they have nothing but death to look for here."

Again, not a soul blinked.

The noises of the advancing army reached us. I knew they were probably at the bottom of the redoubt.

He took up a keg of gunpowder. Stepping back, he spread a trail of it right to the gate. Then he grabbed a torch, lit it, and waved. "Since you all intend to stay, you must fight, for I will blow up this fort if you do not defend it. It won't fall into French hands."

"We will stay. We will fight." One fellow pounded the end of his musket to the ground.

"Fight!" Fleur and I shouted this at the same time. "Goumen!"

Man after man, woman after woman, we all gave our allegiance.

Janjak slammed and bolted the gate. "Man the cannons. Let us greet them with grapeshot."

People started running to their positions.

Pistols fired outside the gate.

Through the windows, the loopholes cut in the stone walls for cannons, I saw a man on horseback. The medals on his chest sparkled like my cutlass.

He waved a letter. "By orders of General Rochambeau, I order you to surrender Fort Crête-à-Pierrot or prepare to die."

Janjak took a pistol from his aide-de-camp, aimed through the window, and shot the man.

The herald slumped forward. His horse ran down the redoubt.

"Surrendering is death." Janjak moved back to the center of the courtyard.

Men and women, some dressed in uniforms, others in rags, waited with their weapons drawn.

Fleur had to tap me, to draw me from the loophole to our position on the far wall.

I was stunned by Janjak's eloquence. This was Marie-Claire's influence. The accuracy of his shot was mine.

Then this old body took its position. Holding my musket felt right. This war would probably be my last, but soldiers, warriors, male or female, hated being away from the fight.

THE DEATH TOLL AT CRÊTE-À-PIERROT WAS HIGH. A MONTH OF fighting had filled the redoubt with French bodies.

Our bodies lined the fort. Our twelve hundred men and women fought their fifteen thousand. I thought we could outlast the French, but Rochambeau was stubborn and kept bringing reinforcements.

We lost two hundred. They lost fifteen hundred. Janjak said he made them suffer.

I sat on the mountain of Cahos, looking down at the smoldering fort. Janjak evacuated us through the night.

My king had been distracted. His grimace was thick. He went for a walk to clear his head. Pity he didn't go alone.

That was a nice way to say he gave his special attention to a woman in a soldier's uniform. They returned hours later.

It could be innocent, a soul to talk with since he and Marie-Claire weren't getting along. She struggled with Janjak having to again return to war and the sickly nature of her pregnancy. I feared for the babes in her womb.

But when I looked at him his wide eyes told his shame. Didn't he know his wife would see what I did?

Janjak moved to the plateau above where his officers stood. High up, they could probably see all of Saint-Domingue. I wondered if Janjak could see his grand-casa at Habitation Frère and his pregnant wife praying in their garden.

Pushing on my staff, I left my soft patch of grass and climbed up to his group. Lamartinière was there. His Blanc face held such strain. He was one of Janjak's chief officers, a mulatto with the whitest of French features, but his insides were Black. He wanted our side, not Bonaparte's, to win.

"You took every measure to secure the fort, oui? I know you did. We've cut into their numbers. The more dead Frenchmen, the better for us." Janjak's voice held the vigor of a warring Tegbesu and the comfort of Eghosa roasting ogbonos.

"General, Leclerc's Rochambeau does not care. He'd have all the French dead, thousands and thousands for one of us."

"There's no more strategic reason for this fort than any other." Janjak looked again toward the fort. "He wants to intimidate us, to make us quit."

"Like rats, they swarm in pairs. Lat, you did your best." Monpoint, whose skin was dark like Janjak's, didn't try to outdo Lamartinière or imply his incompetence.

This gathering was the first I'd seen where the colors of African blood were not at odds. They all acted as one.

"Rochambeau is Leclerc's new dog. He takes pleasure at chewing on our bones." Janjak took out his snuffbox, a habit he seemed to be indulging more and more.

"As you instructed, we abandoned the fort last night, leaving only prisoners and our wounded. Six hundred men I've brought to you, Dessalines."

Janjak glanced at me. "Gran Toya, did you need something? Is all well—"

Bam.

Bam. Bam.

More shots rang out.

Handing me his treasured box, Janjak stumbled closer to the edge of the plateau. From an inner pocket he whipped out his scope and studied the fort below.

He made the sign of the cross. "They're killing our wounded. Shooting some, bayoneting the rest."

His finger made another cross, his hand shaking. "This wasn't how the military taught us to engage with wounded."

Janjak had had a no-prisoners policy early, but as his rank rose, he followed the French ways of battle. "This isn't right."

His scope went into his pocket, and he swiped his box from my palm.

"What were you going to say?" Montpoint asked. "We should've abandoned the fort sooner? Gotten the wounded out?"

"Non. Of course not. The French keep coming. Not sure they'll run out of rats by the rainy season."

Muskets sounded. The bleak noise echoed.

I touched his arm. "Janjak, the point of the bayonet is intentional. Doctors will skip those wounds for bullet holes. Marie-Claire, your wife, and her nurses are the only ones who'll try. Your wife is a good one."

I should be more subtle in bringing up his woman.

He looked away, hiding his telling eyes. "She's not herself. Some wounds, some fears are too deep, never going away, even if we want it."

The mask on his face was the same as when Duclos sold him off to the boilers, when he believed he'd die. One defeat didn't destroy everything. He'd taken the blame for this fort, these deaths.

I hadn't been able to understand Eghosa's weakness and punished her for not being perfect. Yet through her mistakes and mine, and even

Nosakhere's, the people of this island might be saved. "We still have fight in us, General. We believe. I believe."

He said nothing more and went back to his officers.

I trotted down to my Minos. I prayed our mistakes would show us the right way. And we'd be ready and brave enough to do what had to be done. Crête-à-Pierrot must be a beginning, not an ending.

41

Toya

1802

Habitation Frère

We returned to Petite-Rivière de l'Artibonite in the dark. Janjak's habitation was pitch black and quiet as if the land was mourning. It was an omen.

Within days, word arrived from Toussaint. Seeing the continued onslaught of the French, he decided to lay down arms before all his followers died. He would surrender to Leclerc and Rochambeau in Le Cap, giving them his sword in Champ de Mars.

He must've chosen there instead of Place d'Armes, the place of death for all the rebels before him. *Rebel* would be what they'd call him now, not king. Toussaint had reached a deal with Leclerc: his generals would keep their rank and enslavement would never return to Saint-Domingue.

In my gut, I knew it all to be lies.

How do you fight when the king says the battle is done?

FROM THE SCOPE, THE POCKET LENS JANJAK GAVE ME, I SAW HIM AND his aides riding in from Le Cap. Gray and brown mares were saddled beneath them. His uniform had changed to blue, French blue. The people hated this color.

I knew Janjak did, too. I wondered how long he'd labor under it. He needed to fight.

I often thought of my mother these days, these days of not fighting.

When others surrendered, my iya remained calm. She draped the last of our family beads—white, green, red, and ebony, all laced with golden cowrie shells—about my neck. Her hands smelled of sweet, sweet aloe and felt smooth like the silky flesh of coconuts. Her jet face was silent, no tears. But I heard her say my name, Adbara, Adbara, like a chant, a prayer.

She sent me away with a kiss, blocked the hut door, and let herself be consumed in the blaze.

My hands swiped my cheek. I hadn't remembered the kiss before.

Or her chilling calm.

Or her strength.

She knew what was happening and chose to give me a chance to live. My mother chose me. She did.

Water from the cloudless sky dropped onto my hands, my walking stick.

I wiped my face and saluted Janjak and the others. They passed, hooves kicking up clay, horrid, horrid red mud.

He wore this blue uniform to stop the killing. I wondered when he'd realize that when one king bowed down another must rise. While I had strength in my body, I'd help him do what had to be done.

TWO MONTHS HAD PASSED SINCE THE LAYING DOWN OF OUR ARMS. I stood on the hounwa and looked out at the mountains surrounding the Artibonite Valley.

Built in the city of Marchand, the grand-casa of Janjak was similar to Cormier—same framing, same brown shingled roof, same long wraparound veranda with poles, poles a Grand Blanc would have used for punishment. If Janjak had constructed a long drive lined with palms it would be Cormier's twin. If he found lise trees it could be Tegbesu's kpodoji.

Marie-Claire stepped out of the house. It was the first I'd seen her without a babe locked to her bosom.

"Will there be more dancing tonight, Gran Toya? My maman said you would know."

"Wi. There will be. The locals must come hear what's next."

She nodded, but I knew she was lost.

Her gaze went toward the tents and huts spanning their acreage. "More workers for Jean-Jacques's fields?"

"More coming for his vision."

"Maman will love to cook for all the hungry mouths."

"What of you? When was the last time you cooked?"

"My maman will do it."

Janjak's mother-in-law, Marie-Sainte Bonheur, had come to live with us. She was an odd quiet woman. But she doted on him and was good to all the children.

Someone had to be good to them during this time of loss.

Marie-Claire looked fragile and didn't understand my insistence that she give her husband attention or share her grief at the loss of Pierre-Louis, the oldest of her second set of twins. She walled herself off from Janjak. And now the other one, Albert, was sickly, too.

Prayers and salves didn't help sometimes.

"Gran Toya, why can't Jean-Jacques be like Toussaint, retired to his fields, planting—"

"You want your husband imprisoned?"

It was brutal to tell her the truth others had hidden. But we needed her to bless this path for Janjak, for all of us.

She hit at her chest. She seemed to be choking.

I dropped my walking stick and pulled her into my arms. "Let the good and bad in, then out. That's how to breathe."

Her tears wet my vest. "He can't be. Jean-Jacques followed him in surrendering to France. Leclerc penned my husband's commission. I've seen the letters."

"Toussaint and his wife and children have been sent to France as prisoners."

She stepped back, clutching her head. "No, Madame Louverture is in Saint-Marc. She came to our three-day wedding celebration. We ate ice cream in my garden. She would have told me."

I touched one of her hands, wanting to draw her back to the present.

"The wedding, the last one, as you joked, was two years ago. Madame Louverture was here three months ago." I hesitated, then for a moment I touched her stomach, which no longer protruded. "She was here before you gave birth, before you lost Pierre-Louis."

"This is a cruel joke. Jean-Jacques would have told me."

"No, he wouldn't. He's terrified of losing more of you."

"Non. My aunt. She has all the renegade papers. She would know."

"The fool went back to Le Cap the minute some theater reopened. The French love their amusements. Rochambeau, who enjoys productions, is entertaining people in Place d'Armes and feeding Blacks to dogs."

"Elise is not silly. She wouldn't . . . risk all for a moment in the sun." Her eyes flickered. "I have to get her back from Le Cap. I'll talk to Jean-Jacques."

"If you ask, he'll risk all to save the foolish woman again. He'll do anything for you. But what will you do for the people, the ones you claim to love? The ones you risked your life to feed?"

"What are you asking me, Gran Toya?"

"Release Janjak to his destiny. King Toussaint sacrificed for peace, but the French devils want blood, our blood. They say they are torturing his wife and children to make them give false statements. Their king, Bonaparte, imprisoned Toussaint on a mountain. He'll die there."

Marie-Claire's hand clasped her mouth. She half turned to their habitation's vast land, the place she may have thought was safe. "Why am I just learning this? Why hadn't Jean-Jacques said . . ."

I've been told my face speaks the truth before my lips move.

Marie-Claire became silent. Her eyes shut. She had finally heard.

"I'm not soft, Gran Toya. Wanting peace is not easy. Sometimes it's harder."

"Then don't be deceived anymore. You know what has to be done. When one king falls, another must be elevated."

She turned to me, anger flushing her dark olive cheeks. "Jean-Jacques is not a king. He's a general. A general."

"He's a general wearing liar's colors. This is the moment for him to claim power, to show the world we can lead, that Toussaint's example of Black power was correct."

Rubbing her temples, Marie-Claire looked as if she wanted to disappear, but there was no escaping destiny.

My throat filled with a lump watching this woman break down and sob. I knew she sobbed for Suzanne and Isaac and Saint-Jean, Toussaint's family, as much as for her own lost Pierre-Louis.

I went to her as if she were Eghosa. Seizing her by the shoulders, I shook her, then I held her and blessed her forehead with a kiss. "Be the king's conscience. Make him do right for the people. Give him the strength to bring liberty back to Saint-Domingue."

Her eyes glistened. "We'll lose him again. He should know one of his children as a babe, to see how Albert changes each day."

In Marie-Claire's face was her truth. She feared losing both father and babe.

I accepted that I wasn't Eghosa, not soft or soothing. I was a soldier, blunt and hard. "Toussaint is gone. Janjak must lead or all the children will die—the fast death by a musket ball or a slow one, reenslavement."

"You know what you are asking? Remember how many years the fighting has taken him from me, from our children?"

"This is for all children. For the benefit of them. That could be one of your speeches when you were whole and doing your calling. Be her again. Send him to his calling."

Gasping and crying, she walked toward the garden. I prayed she found the good soil to ground her. She needed to support the king or we were all doomed.

42

Marie-Claire

1802

Habitation Frère

Sitting on my bench in the middle of the garden, I watch the malachite butterflies spread their lime and yellow wings and kiss my flowering shrubs. They seem to like the red passiflora. The bright petals splay about the belled centers like petticoats.

They sound like the outrageous tulle skirts Elise wears onstage. Her latest letter makes me laugh. She sounds happy.

But I'm fearful Le Cap will burn again, and that all of Toya's fears will come true.

Yet worse, I'm fearful of me, the soft coward I've become.

I want Elise's joy.

She still hasn't sung a lead part, but merely being in the atmosphere of the theater is enough for her now. I love that she's found peace. Yet she's ignored every one of my letters asking her to return. Maman spoke little to my aunt when she was last here when Jean-Jacques evacuated her from a burning Le Cap.

In matching straw bonnets, my mother works with Françoise and Célestine in the herb garden. Jeanne Sophie is beside them and has sent hers sailing onto a trimmed bush.

Jacques drills by the cobblestone path leading to my mango tree. "Un, deux, trois. Un, deux, trois." He's marching and counting. His father would be proud.

But Albert is with the nurse inside. I've gone to the nursery six times to make sure he still breathes.

Maybe I should check one more time. I rise from the bench and head toward the house.

"He's fine, Marie-Claire."

My mother's voice stops me midstep. I put down my foot and smooth my check-print skirt. I turn to her, noting the serenity in their faces. No hint of dread. "I just want . . . want to hear his voice."

She wipes her hands on her apron. "I know how important it is to hear your child's voice. Or to miss the ones telling the truth."

The winsome sorrow in her tone makes my broken heart hurt more. "Write to Elise. Tell her all is well and ask her to come."

Maman digs in the dirt. "Go inside, Marie-Claire. Check on Albert, then come back out here with us."

I give up. She's set in her ways as much as me.

"I won't be long." I walk through the double doors and let my slippers glide down the tile floors.

As soon as I enter the hall, I see Jean-Jacques. He's coming from the nursery.

His face is unreadable, then I realize he's been wearing masks, one for the French, one for people who've come to hear his thoughts, and one for me.

Sucking in my tears, I go to him.

"He's sleeping well. You were right to bring your Adélaïde here."

"You don't mind a Blanc French woman in your household?"

"I do, but if it brings you comfort, what am I to say?"

Had his fears for me, my sanity, made him go quiet? "I've chased your voice away. I'm sorry."

"What? Marie-Claire?"

I take his hand and lead him into his office. The walls are warm, a solid yellow. His desk gleams and smells of orange oil. Maman or Adélaïde might have seen to that.

His fingers are linked with mine, and I tow him to his cluttered desk piled with maps.

"What do you wish to say, Marie-Claire?"

"Non. I want you to speak. I need you to tell me what's in your heart."

He breaks free, pushes papers aside, and sits on the desk. "What confession do you want? It is obvious I've done something."

I lift his chin, rubbing my hand along the shadow on his jaw. Then I rip the blue and red jacket from his shoulders. I take it and toss it to the ground.

"If I had a match, I'd burn it for what they did to Governor Louver-ture and his family."

A half grin takes over his round aged face. "I see you hate this as much as Gran Toya."

"They will treat you like Toussaint the first opportunity they can. They'll take the children we have left and torture them, too."

He reaches for me and puts his arm about my waist. The hold is tighter than the ones that made me feel like delicate clay.

"I know what must be done. Are you telling me I have your blessing to go to war?"

"You would go whether I wanted or not, but I want you to have peace, knowing I support you. I need you to keep Saint-Domingue free. End this war that's been raging for decades once and for all. Better not quit until it's done."

"Is that an order from Madame Dessalines?"

"It's an order from every Black mother to the man who will save the children."

"Only if you are there to feed them."

My hand slips from his waistcoat to his cheek. "Yes, I'll make enough soup to feed all the world, and I'll start by getting my husband a bowl."

I start to leave, but he grasps my hand. "Non. I just need my wife to hold me and to keep talking about soup or family or anything she wishes. I miss your voice. I miss your laugh. I miss knowing you'll be here when I return."

My arms thread about him and I keep him safe in my bosom. I must give Jean-Jacques to the world, then he can make it safe to be Black and Brown and excellent.

His being the king will change us forever. We'll never simply be Monsieur and Madame Dessalines. We'll be father and mother to a hungry nation, one that must live beyond infancy.

OUT ON THE VERANDA, I READ ELISE'S LATEST LETTER. A MONTH has passed since the last and again she mentions nothing of how the world is changing. She's performed onstage for Rochambeau and his generals. She says Leclerc would've come but was feeling poorly.

I crumple the paper.

Maman follows me. "Are you well? Your cheeks are red. Too much sun?"

"It's Elise. She's loves the stage. She sees nothing else."

My mother sighs and smooths her apron. "That's my sister. Only wants what she wants. She's gotten it, too."

One could say the same of Maman or Mamie or even me. She shrugs, takes a dust rag from her apron, and swipes the rail. "How much time before war starts?"

"It has never ended. Remember Mamie saying that. I know what she means now." I fold my arms and look out at the tents. "The French revoked the laws abolishing enslavement in Martinique and Guadeloupe and Sainte-Lucie. It's only a matter of time before they do the same to Saint-Domingue. It will be soon. Make up with Elise. Get her here."

Maman grimaces and maybe grunts. "My sister never takes responsibility. Rochambeau is operating like he's Nero. Ordering performances, demanding mulatto women entertain him. She's flattered."

"He's Caligula holding court. Letting spectators watch beasts eating the flesh of Blacks." I lower my tone and grip my mother's hands. "Do whatever you must. Even apologize. Bring her to safety."

Her light eyes move from side to side like they've been attached to a pendulum. She's weighing her options, how much saying sorry will cost her.

I truly give up. Lobelot stubbornness be damned.

Before I turn, I see Jean-Jacques riding with his pistol raised. He's alone. No guards follow.

Not thinking, I run to my husband. "Are you all right?"

Out of breath as if he's run from Le Cap, he jumps from his horse. He has no jacket, just a waistcoat over his shirt and breeches.

"They know. They know I plan to rebel."

With my hands to his hot face, I try to get him to calm. It takes minutes for his pulse to slow. Closing his eyes, he holds me.

"In Le Cap, I met with Christophe to confirm his loyalties. He's for rebellion. All will again fight together for our mutual liberty. Then I was to see Leclerc, to continue my ruse of support. But before the dinner . . . a priest . . . his servant . . . made a sign of my wrists being bound."

"Jean-Jacques, they were going to arrest you?"

"I took the warning, left, and shot my way out of there. My guard and I barely escaped. He's heading to the hills to inform the maroons and the Taíno. All of us need to come together."

"Was Christophe in on this?"

He squints at me, then shakes his head. "No, but the French are coming for the Black generals. Anyone of color who's worn an epaulette won't be spared."

Even if I had second thoughts, I have none now. The French want to slaughter the resistance before it begins. Non. It must thrive.

I gaze into Jean-Jacques's eyes and give him my strength, my soul. We are united in this fight, a fight he must win.

THE NIGHT IS TENSE, BUT NO TROOPS SHOW AT THE HABITATION. For the next three days, Jean-Jacques meets with his men into the wee hours.

They come up with a plan. There's no looking back. I stand on the veranda watching people gather.

Drummers take up positions around the yard, taking the rum barrels stretched with goatskin and begin to beat a dancing tune.

This rhythm, a marching drill, helps the columns of men and women organize. It makes my mood lighter.

I peer up at Gran Toya, who watches from a two-story guard post. I think she'll see troops coming and can give us enough time to repel them.

Jean-Jacques kisses my hand and then says to the crowd, "The drills look good. Now everyone dance. Then eat the feast my wife and mother-in-law have made."

He still wears the resplendent hat of the French, but also the black coat he had made years ago for our wedding.

In a blink, Jean-Jacques leaves my side. I see him dance and cut through the crowd, heading straight for the outpost, and I follow.

"Gran Toya, how is the land?" he asks with a hand cupping his eyes.

"As good as ever."

"Come down. Join the dancing."

"A celebration? Wi. For you to let women of any age come fight is a victory."

With arms open, he glances up. "I want to win. I'll agree to that."

"Good, my king," she says. "Women know how to win."

"It's best you call me General. Some may get the wrong idea."

That wrong idea has given everyone hope. People he's fought against, like Pétion, whom he beat with Rigaud at Jacmel, are coming to join my husband. Then there is Christophe, a onetime rival for Toussaint's praise. I still wonder if he was involved with Leclerc's trap to arrest Jean-Jacques.

The Taíno and maroons have come down. They want a lasting peace, too.

Jean-Jacques takes Gran Toya's staff and tries to get her to dance.

Maman steps out with baby Albert in her arms. I weave my way through the crowd to them and see his smile, his wide eyes. He looks good. His coloring is a healthy olive brown, not jaundice yellow.

"Françoise," Maman calls. "Take your maman out to your père, then she can get some of his wiggling before he's all spent."

My daughter, pretty and tall, pulls me into the crowd.

We move toward Jean-Jacques's voice. "They come for the music tonight. They will stay for the dream. Like at Bois Caïman, I want my vision to catch fire."

I stare into his wide eyes. He believes we can do this.

Bump. I stumble a bit and a man with strong hands rights me. For a moment, maybe a few seconds, his eyes look the same as Jean-Jacques's, same wide brown with big yellow circles, the same shape.

"Sorry," he says and keeps moving.

"Come on, Maman. Père's over here."

Jean-Jacques has climbed the tower. "Like the people you trained long ago, Gran Toya. Our brothers, the maroons, from Africa, men and women born of this place, and the Taínos, the original people of the island—all arriving here to find true freedom."

The music starts up again with singing. The echoes call out.

"It is time to rejoice," Jean-Jacques says. "We have seized guns from Fort La Crête-à-Pierrot. You'd think the French wouldn't forget we know how to get to our forts, even ones we've given up." He claps his hands. "Enough weapons to arm my ten thousand troops. We'll soon be ready."

He swings down and drops in front of me. "Madame Dessalines, do you feel up to dancing? It's a shame to waste a song when there's someone to dance with."

"General, I think your daughter will join you."

As suave and as debonair as I know him to be, he links my hands and Françoise's. He dances to the center of all the people.

Yet my eyes go to Toya, who's using her lens to scan the crowd. What can she be searching for when her dreams of Jean-Jacques leading are coming true?

My husband whirls me and my skirt flares and catches in the air.

Françoise swirls, too, in her orange skirt that looks like the flowers tended by Monsieur Descourtilz, a botanist Jean-Jacques has coerced into making mangoes grow in my garden.

Coerced is a nicer word than *forced*. My husband, smiling and laughing and dancing, doesn't trust many Blancs. None are here dancing, not even Adélaïde. I hope Jean-Jacques realizes the new Saint-Domingue must be for all.

43

Marie-Claire

1802

Habitation Frère

Unable to sleep, I arise from my bed and walk in my garden. Then, in the moonlight, I see it and seize it, the perfect mango. The months Monsieur Descourtilz has been here have helped me grow one perfect fruit.

Gardening takes my mind from the revolution—how often Jean-Jacques has to go away, the wounded men and women who return, the ones who don't.

I juggle the mango in my slick, sweaty palms. It's unusually warm this October night. This beauty of my garden keeps me from fretting about little Albert. He isn't better or worse. The sameness has become good to me.

The smell of the mango and its taut skin promises it will be tangy and sweet. My mouth waters as if I'd walked from a desert.

My garden shows many colors and shades—green, yellow, and aubergine—and is healthy despite my husband's chasing the botanist with a sword for laughs with his secretaries.

I hope it was for laughs.

Jean-Jacques's been a little erratic lately. He's leading the revolutionary forces all across Saint-Domingue. Distance and time have come between us. Yet he's returning before a final push.

My stomach clenches. This may all be over soon. We could win.

A world without war.

To look at my husband and children and know they are safe—safe and Black and thriving. And not targets to someone who wants enslavement to win.

Toya stands guard on the veranda. That means he's here. And I have a mango meant to be shared.

Entering the grand-casa and feeling brave, I begin to sing. My tune is one of Elise's old songs. I listen to my voice carrying in the corridor, tumbling on the tiles, bopping on the burnished beams framing the walls.

> *Your husband weeps,*
> *begs the gods for you*
> *and asks for you among mortals,*
> *yet scattered to the wind*
> *are his tears*
> *and his laments.*

That's from an opera, *Orphée et Eurydice*. My last letter from her says she's gotten her wish. She sang the lead, but these lyrics, lyrics she's practiced through the years, rise in my head as if I were sitting in the audience, in the front row.

The words are sad to me, a woman who's mourned too much and for a man who is mourning now.

In the nursery, Maman is with little Albert. She's singing the strange old hymn from when I was born. Then she whispers, "Your père is the one, the one who's come down to bring liberty. And you will do something great, too. You are his son and a twin. I know it."

Leaning at the doorsill, I listen to her and smell sweet lavender and the mushroom scent of palm oil in the room. She's silly and wonderful and encouraging. I don't know how I'd survive without her. I see a stack of newspapers near the foot of Grand-père's rocker but no letter from Elise. Come to think of it, it's been a few months since I've received anything from Le Cap.

I turn and go to find my husband.

Light filters from beneath his door. I prepare to knock, but the strong words being said inside makes my hand rigid.

"The blockade is working. Nothing is coming in or going out. No weapons, nothing. We are crushing them. We will win soon."

"What of the people, Boisrond-Tonnere? They must be suffering."

Something is said, but the sound of a chair moving blurs it.

"Port of Petit-Goâve!"

"The American schooner *The Federal*."

A ship in a port? Is that what has us winning soon? I put my ear to the door and listen to Jean-Jacques.

"Who's the captain? Was he unharmed?"

"He's fine. Captain Barr is fine." Another voice, perfect French.

Jean-Jacques laughs. "There's no such thing as a fine Blanc, gentlemen."

"General, we don't need them. Our stranglehold will do what we want."

". . . you know he had mulatto women come to a dinner just to show them their husbands dead in coffins . . . monster."

"Ignore the theater, General. The Americans will see from our handing over of Captain Barr we mean them no harm. But you must write and convince their president of this."

"Non! Non! Non!" Jean-Jacques's voice. "The leech slaver won't listen."

"We are about to win the war, General. We must also win the peace."

The tones I hear are separate and distinct—the squeaky voice of an aide, Juste Chanlatte, talks of peace.

Perfect vowels taught by the finest French tutor—Jean-Jacques's personal secretary, Boisrond-Tonnere. Soulful, resonant—Diaquoi, his aide-de-camp.

They are trying to convince my husband of something he is resistant to.

My knocking silences the chatter.

Boisrond-Tonnere opens the door but stands there blocking my entry. "Madame Dessalines, may I help you?"

"I've come to see my husband. You have him every day. I want him now and I have a mango."

"Madame, there are—"

"A mango?" Jean-Jacques interrupts Boisrond-Tonnere. "Let my wife enter, gentlemen. We break until dawn. This matter won't go away, but a ripe mango can ruin. It is ripe?"

"Of course. What do you take me for, sir?"

The gatekeeper bows and moves out of the way. All the gentlemen scatter, leaving me and the man running the war against the world a few feet apart.

"Yes, Marie-Claire." He thumbs his lips. "Are the children well?"

"They are, and they miss their father."

He nods and shifts his maps. "And I miss them."

"I miss you."

He puts down the paper he's been holding and waves me forward. "I'm here and I'm tired. I don't have the wherewithal to match wits with you. Just give me the mango."

"When did we become a battle?" I come to him and kneel at his side. "When did things become hard? We can talk of anything in the garden."

"There's a list of my faults. I'll start with the last one, my deceit to Leclerc."

I twiddle the mango between my fingers. "Since he tried to arrest you and send you away like Toussaint, I think that's an excuse for deceit."

A little bit of his smile peeked. "That's a generous attitude. Then there is the matter of the Belairs, the rash husband and wife duo the French executed. Some say he was my rival and I aligned with Leclerc to have them shot."

"The truth, Jean-Jacques?"

"That he was my rival? Wi. That I worked with Leclerc? Wi. That he was sloppy and tried to start a revolt before we were ready and would doom what we have now? Wi."

"Leclerc had his wife arrested, Jean-Jacques. They shot her in the bosom."

"The brave woman asked for it. She had no fear." He put his head down for a moment, then sat back in his chair. "I had to turn them over. Leclerc was suspicious of me. I tried to encourage Charles to flee, but he insisted on going to Leclerc. Trusting any Frenchman is like trusting a Grand Blanc. Like Toussaint, the naïveté got them all killed."

"All?"

He bit his lip for a moment. "Toussaint is dead. Napoleon kept him in a cold prison on top of a mountain. He died of consumption in his lungs." He picks up a note and hands it to me. "Toussaint, il est mort."

Consumption. Pierre was in great pain when he died from it. I bat away the letter and put my arms about my husband. "Toussaint was your mentor. A father figure, or as Toya would say, your king. I'm sorry."

Jean-Jacques pulls me into his lap and caresses me like he did long ago on our bench in Place Royale. He's tender, this man who has so much blood on his hands.

With all my heart, I hold on to him, his humanity, his humor. It's all escaping smoke.

"Come walk with me. In the garden." I wave the mango at him.

"Marie-Claire."

"In the garden, Romulus. You've built a wall about Habitation Frère. We're safe here. We are on the same side, but we've never shared a mango."

"Yes, I stole them."

"I'm asking you to share this. I couldn't have a garden without this fruit tree. And you didn't kill the botanist who helped. Thank you."

He slips his hands into his jacket and pulls out a knife. On top of his important papers, he stands the mango up with its point in the sky. "Cut on one side of the seed. Then the other."

Leaving the middle alone, he takes the two sides and cuts a grid, squares like the rues of Le Cap.

"This is the magic." He presses on the skin and it pops up the cut mango chunks. One can enjoy the pieces by pulling them like porcupine quills. "Half for you. Half for me."

Rising from his lap, I sit in a close chair and eat the tangy mango pieces.

"The perfect gold, Marie-Claire, but did you have to leave me?"

His smile is coy. I want us to be friends and lovers, whatever he needs to be the good man I know him to be.

"What has put Boisrond-Tonnere in a mood?"

Jean-Jacques gobbles up mango. Juice leaks from his lips. The old feeling to lick them stirs. "Brandy. There are shortages with all the blockades. We'll have more wine when the war is done."

"Our tree must grow another. I can taste the ice cream from it. Put salt on your list of things to get for me."

"I will. I still provide you bleach, but you'll not be donning nursing white."

If I ask why not, another of our old arguments will stir. I do not want that tonight.

"Talk to me."

He looks to the ceiling, then to his sticky hands. "We were discussing whether to write a letter to President Jefferson, the leader of America, and beg for help. The Blacks are enslaved in America. Jefferson owns people. He doesn't care about Saint-Domingue throwing off our shackles."

"Adams did with Toussaint. He helped with Jacmel."

"Different war, different president. They only helped us to bring pain to Britain and Spain. I need them to go against France, their big trading partner. Blanc men don't do anything to hurt their money. Black, either."

"Remind President Jefferson of his country's long-standing friendship in Saint-Domingue. That Blacks and Coloreds helped their quest for freedom."

"To remind a man who was partying in France while his country fought for independence? I doubt America will help."

"What happened to Pickering or the trade man, Brunel, with the Colored wife? What of Hamilton? There are many men in the United States who can help."

Jean-Jacques licks his fingers. "Pickering and Brunel were Monsieur

Hamilton's friends. Hamilton is out of power. And the reporter who brought him down, Callender, is now writing about Jefferson's Colored concubine."

My brow scrunches when he laughs, then sobers. "It's ironic. An affair with a Blanc woman brings down Colored Créole Hamilton, but the Blanc man Jefferson has not been harmed by the knowledge that he owns a Colored woman who has his babes and he won't free her."

"Colored enslaved women are no concubines. She has no choice but to accept his rape, like Grand-mère long ago."

He's breathing hard. "Sorry, Marie-Claire."

I don't want to think of the horrors of enslavement. I plop the last piece of fruit into my mouth.

Then I mumble, "It sounds as if Boisrond-Tonnere likes renegade newspapers, like my aunt Elise, but he's right about writing Jefferson. If we can make a friend in America, it might dissuade others from helping France."

I put his sticky thumb in my mouth, then pop out the wet digit. "Let them know America has a friend here. Let them know we want to have a relationship."

He wipes his fingers with a handkerchief. "What if I write that we will follow the example of the wisest nation and throw off the yoke of tyranny and expel our torturers? Boisrond-Tonnere says that will get to him. I don't know."

With a shrug, I take his cloth and wipe juice from his lips. "I'm not sure about those words, but you must try writing to Jefferson. Send him a letter. If he responds, you'll have an opening. He must respect Saint-Domingue's chief general, Dessalines, the man bringing peace to the colony."

"Respect is important. And a long-standing friendship is better." He tugs off my mobcap. My pins fly and my braids come down. He tugs my braids and pulls my lips to his. The motion is quick and jittery, a snap decision.

But I have thought about it, him and me, long and hard. I'm not a girl of whims, but a woman, one who needs to be heard and desired and who must encourage the man with the weight of the world on his shoulders.

His mouth becomes more demanding, and his fingers find all the openings of my gown, every button.

A shriek shakes the house.

Jean-Jacques puts me to his side, takes up his sword, and rushes through the door.

FUMBLING WITH MY ROBE, I FOLLOW JEAN-JACQUES FROM HIS STUDY into the hall.

He's waving at me to stay back, but I'm right there at his side.

It's Maman. She's jumping up and down. The woman sees us and heads in our direction.

Jean-Jacques shifts his sword to keep her from being run through.

Gran Toya and her three Minos flood through the garden doors. My eyes move from the bandages on her arm to my mother grabbing my husband's shirt hem, one he hadn't quite stuffed into his breeches. "You have to help, Dessalines. You have to go get my sister."

"Maman?"

"Please, Dessalines. Please, my son." Her voice echoes. The proud woman is begging. "Save her. Get her out of Le Cap."

Jean-Jacques bites his lip but utters nothing.

Gran Toya looks to me and then to him. "General, go rest. We'll handle this disturbance."

He glances at her, then nods to me and retreats to his office.

But I saw how their eyes met. They're in accord. They know something that's secret to me and even Maman.

His office door closes with a thud, and I tug my mother to me. Rocking her. "Explain."

"Elise has written a note in the newspaper."

"What? You must mean an advertisement like a playbill. She's been singing lead. That's all she ever wanted."

My mother is shaking her head fast. It might unscrew. "Non. The last page. She found a way to cry for help in the paper. The blockade has cut off food to Le Cap. She's starving to death, starving with all the singers and actors. No one can leave."

"Starving?" I cut my eyes to Toya.

Gripping and loosening her hand around her staff, the woman nods. "Rochambeau is cornered. His forces are caving. Le Cap will fall."

"Cornered, nothing can get in. But they have gardens. They grow . . ." Then I remember fires have burnt them all down. "There's no food on scorched earth. What about fish from the sea? My father fished those waters all the time."

"No one fishes. Rochambeau has drowned ten thousand Black men in the waters. He plans to kill any Black over age twelve. He and Napoleon plan to reinstate enslavement."

Gran Toya's tone is even and more unfeeling than ever, but maybe that's how hard truths must be said.

"Rochambeau thinks Blacks that know freedom will never accept enslavement again. He's right. We won't. So, he plans to kill us all."

"Kill all?" My stomach hurts as if her staff has plowed through me. "Drowning men, then? No one is that cruel. He—"

"Hands bound. Some are gagged. Rochambeau and his officers don't realize there's not much screaming when there's no air."

I'm sickened. This can't be. "Gran Toya, there's a lot of people in Le Cap. He can't kill them all."

"Some escaped. But now Rochambeau won't let any more go. Some have been shot for not carrying on as though they weren't starving. Imagine being a cook feeding the general roasted quail while you eat paper to live another day."

"He's a monster," Maman says. "How is this allowed? Aren't there rules to war?"

"No rules for those who don't think their opponents are human.

The French general and his officers stay on boats, dining on all types of delights while the people starve."

"My sister should be let go. She only loves music. Anyone who looks at her should see she's harmless. She's not a rebel."

"Why, Madame Bonheur? Because her skin is light? Rochambeau blames Colored women for the fall of the colony. He's crueler to them."

No! Elise is suffering.

And Jean-Jacques knew.

That's why he's not been sleeping. He loves my aunt, but he also knew of the Belairs, people he served with under Toussaint and did not save.

"Dessalines is the leader," Maman says. "He can do anything. He can save my sister."

Gran Toya shakes her head; her tired grimace sharpens. "Should he risk the whole war to rescue a stubborn Lobelot? One who thought her privilege would make her exempt from how Rochambeau would treat his enemy?"

Maman's fists are shaking. "You unfeeling monster."

"He held a reception just to show mulatto women the husbands he'd murdered. Who's the monster? And who is responsible? Warnings to leave have been in those papers you read, but she ignored them."

Sobbing, with hands flailing, my mother crumples to the floor.

"Gran Toya, you and your soldiers should rest." I help Maman to stand, but she pulls away from my arms and waves the renegade paper like a flag. "Elise and I . . . I have to tell her I forgive her for the past. She has to know."

My mother rambles—more nonsense of the past. None of it matters.

Gran Toya bows her head; it drops as if she's bone tired. "If the war ends soon enough, maybe your sister will be saved. Pray for that."

Maman presses her hands together to beg again. "We should go now. While there's time."

"Sometimes it is too late." Gran Toya's eyes lift and drift to the right. "It's like saying goodbye to ashes. The one you love is already gone."

Gran Toya walks away and I let her.

The warrior needs rest.

"Marie-Claire, go to your husband. Get him to—"

I lift my mother's chin. "Don't bother the general. This is not a mission for him. He has to save Saint-Domingue. Feeding people—that's my mission."

Eyes wide, she grasps my arm. "Non, Marie-Claire. I can't risk you, too."

It's too late. My mind is made up. Once a Lobelot woman decides something, there's no changing her path.

44

Toya

1803

Habitation Frère

We'd returned to Habitation Frère to rest before marching to cut off Rochambeau at Vertières, near Le Cap. Between politicking with his war counsel and now the bickering of his wife and mother in-law, how would the king stay focused?

Shaking my head, willing my aching bones to move, I walked to the bench behind the grand-casa in the middle of the garden. I watched the lights of the house die as they were snuffed, one by one.

I prayed that all slept.

A torch shone behind me.

I almost pulled my cutlass, but I'd been expecting this meeting. "Nosakhere, you've decided to say hello."

"We've seen each other every week as I man the cannons. I like those weapons. I take pride in firing them and helping defeat the French strongholds in Les Cayes and Jérémie."

He marched to me, wearing half a uniform—the top half, the coat and shirt, over his short pants. His gray hair was full and feathered out like a ball. His beard was thick, curly silver.

His weathered hands held the M1779 musket I'd issued him. "Where the fight is, Gaou Adbaraya Toya, you'll be at the center of it, serving the king. You found one after all."

"You're not dead, Nosakhere. That's good."

"It is. Been lucky." He paused, his wide eyes reflecting the fire, maybe even stars. "Curiama and Célia send greetings. They're alive and well. Célia is starting a family. Both women send their prayers for liberation." He put the torch in a holder. "Good that you have not slowed."

"Wi." And I was glad he'd lived, that we'd lived to see change. I glad Célia had a chance to grow up.

"Then why do you seem glum? All the talk is we're winning. The French forces are a third of what they were. Insurrection is everywhere. Farmers are rising up in the south as far as Grande-Anse, Rigaud's old stronghold."

"Good." I snorted a laugh, thinking of Jacmel. "Rigaud had his generals slowly killing the city. He should've surrendered. Then the French might have goodwill from the citizens."

I glared at this man I'd known forever, who'd been away just as long. "Nosakhere, I thought you'd find a mountain and be your own king."

"Dèyè mòn gen mon. They are everywhere." Now he chuckled. "I travel a few places causing trouble. But all can see it, feel it in the air. Dessalines will do it."

My brow cocked. "I think so, if he's focused and all aligns."

"He's been pretty lucky. The old leader Leclerc, Bonaparte's brother-in-law, has died of yellow fever. The sickness eats up many of his troops. Others wish to leave. Our brawn and luck took the rest."

Nosakhere sat beside me, slipping his arm under my hurt one. "Hesitation is death. You never hesitated to kill, Toya."

"I did a few times. Always with you."

"In Calmina? And then Cormier? I thought—"

"There were others, particularly when you left."

The grin that was Janjak's appeared. He sat back with my hand still in his. "He's going to do it. Bring liberty. Correct the wrongs I and others—"

"That we, that Tegbesu did. The king was wrong. I was wrong. In a few weeks, we set all right."

"The boy, Janjak, Eghosa's son . . . the man, he will do it."

"Would you like to know him?"

Drawing his shoulders back, Nosakhere blew hot air onto our joined hands. "Let's let him win the war. Then we will see what pieces can be put together."

"But I never told him. If I die or you—"

"Win the war, Adbaraya. That's important to two Dahomey soldiers. The war. Nothing else."

We sat like this, quiet. Touching. Breathing. Waiting.

The torch extinguished.

The stars gave way to the light.

When my awakened eyes fully comprehended the hour, Nosakhere was still at my side, staring at the mango tree and its clusters of pink blooms.

A WEEK PASSED, THEN WE MARCHED FROM HABITATION FRÈRE TO the north. Janjak was sure if we won today, we'd defeat the French for good.

Twin stars twinkled in the brightening sky in the mountains above Le Cap. We'd followed Janjak's old paths to gain the advantage. At dawn, we'd head toward the southern entrance and capture the first firing position, Barrière-Bouteill.

Janjak stood at the top of the ridge looking down with his scope. His coat was rich garnet, his hat fully ebony with a plume and gold trim. This was different from all the uniforms of the French and Spanish.

He called all the divisions together under armor bearers waving triumphant red-and-blue-striped flags. These were like the old French ones but with the white silk sliced away.

It hit me.

This battle wouldn't only end enslavement forever in Saint-Domingue, it would establish a kingdom. It should be different. We had to become different together.

Taking a flag and waving it, Janjak said, "Today, we fight to end the war. Today, we give the nations an example of our zealous nature.

Libète! Endepandans! This is our rallying cry. We've dared to be free, to be by ourselves and for ourselves."

They roared, and Janjak, who was once uncomfortable with his speech, became a tiger with his words. Tearing off his hat, he whipped it to his chest. "Let them tremble when they approach our coasts. Let us never forget the cruelties they perpetuated, and the souls lost."

Staking the flagpole in the ground, he stopped and looked out at his army. "They divide, but we are consolidated, one family. And this gives us victory over our butchers."

The troops roared.

Janjak waved them quiet. "Toussaint Louverture, I've been faithful to the promise which I made to you when I took up arms against tyranny. I shall keep my oath. Never again shall a colonist or a European set his foot upon this territory with the title of massa. Enslavement will never be on our shores."

Then he gave the signal and pointed us to the hills. "Onward! We will win!"

The battle cry of Nosakhere, "Mì nan du déji! We will win!" was music to my ears.

Women and men cried out in all the mother tongues of the people born here and those stolen from Africa.

"Yebedi kunim," Twi.

"A yoo ṣẹgun," Yoruba.

"Nou pral genyen," Kreyòl.

"Nous gagnerons," French.

"Mì nan du déji," blessed Fon.

I looked at my Minos, all dressed in our jet-black tunics and yellow sashes. Everyone's beaded breastplates were redone in red and gold beads. No more cowrie and the old.

Every battle, the French soldiers chanted hate. They called us women witches, but they feared our Black bodies and that we now had control over ourselves.

Today, I will watch them cower.

I lifted up my rifle with the sharpened bayonet. "Eghosa, my sister, today is for you!" My shout was for me, but it drowned in the joyful cries of *we will win.*

"Forward! We won't be stopped." General Capois rode ahead encouraging us with his raised fist.

Our lines looked good. Many were dressed in waistcoats and breeches Janjak had liberated from blockhouses in Jérémie. As with everything, we were a mixture of everything and united above all.

My walking stick remained at Habitation Frère. My hands were full, with a cutlass hooked on one side and an oiled musket on the other.

General Capois circled back. "March!" He was diligent and hungry for the fight.

The cannon cart rumbled to the right of our column. They would be positioned at Butte Charrier. From this hill, our forces would strike. Janjak had taken every lesson of divide and conquer and all my tales of routing enemies to make a decisive plan. We'd conquer the south, at Fort Bréda, to the west, at Fort Pierre Michel, and to the north, at Vertières.

Nosakhere sung out another battle cry as he manned the cannon cart and helped steady the big brass sixteen-pounder over the uneven land. Though he'd donned the uniform, he wore a sash belt across his hips. He had on his short pants.

But on the inside he fought, like me, for liberty, for redemption.

We stood down and stopped near Charrier. The sun was higher, above the horizon. From here, I could see the blue, blue water, the very sea that separated me from Africa and brought me here to help birth a nation, to mother and war for my sister's seed.

Nosakhere looked at me.

To me, and only me, he whispered, "Forgive my trespasses."

My chin dipped to him, but before I could ask the same our lines shifted and separated.

His section headed down toward the entrenchments of Charrier. That plateau seemed flat, with no trees, just brown dirt and grasses.

My last sighting of Nosakhere was of him handing the loader a rough osnaburg bag filled with grapeshot. When the sack made from the slave cloth exploded, lead balls would rain terror, killing or maiming anything in their path. If any of the enemy were slavers, I hoped the flaming bits of cloth would burn their clothes, tools, and anything made from entrapped labor.

Janjak, on his silver horse, rode near.

The sight of him in his resplendent red coat, sitting proud, uplifted my soul. "Gran Toya," he asked, "are you well?"

"Anxious. The fight will restore me." It always had.

I straightened and held my gun out, for the first time appreciating how much I had become accustomed to leaning on the staff. Janjak had wanted me to stay at Habitation Frère with the children and Marie-Claire. But he had enough guards there, and with her friend Adélaïde coming to support her, I wasn't needed. I was meant for the fight. I'd die for it.

He rode up the hill.

Lifting my head, I searched the sky again. It was now full light, and the day exposed clouds rolling like thunder. Rain could delay this battle.

No. We'd come too far from where we started to have our fire doused.

As we neared Vertières, the sweet air of the mountain changed. The wind coming from Le Cap covered my face with death.

The stench devoured the breeze.

The taste of it, sour and thick, coated my tongue all the way to the back of my throat. I swore to my gods this would be Rochambeau's day to fall. Ten Frenchman for every one they had drowned in the sea of Le Cap.

"Halt." Red coat flapping, General Capois returned close to my position. "Habitation Vertières is below."

I peered around the soldiers and saw a masonry building, not a fortified blockhouse. This had wattled walls and cut-out loopholes for shooting.

"My good men and women," Capois said, "you must gain control of the hill. The army's salvation depends on it. Forward!"

Draped in a bloodred blanket with gold and black trim, his ebony horse leapt and galloped toward Vertières.

We followed.

Gunfire. Shots hit all around.

One man fell beside me.

Then one of my Minos. Thérèse, but she stood and rapped her sash about her arm.

I couldn't stop, but she knew what to do. I had trained them to be prepared.

A big cannon fired from a loophole that poured smoke. The black ball struck the beautiful horse, knocking it flat. General Capois leapt off and kept charging.

When I heard the blast from behind, then cheering, I knew our side had started firing.

Drive the devils to the sea.

Under a wave of bullets, we marched forward, wounding the men coming at us from the house.

Then their guns stopped. They ran at us with their bayonets drawn.

We shot. A line of bullets hit.

Blood spattered on the ground. Lead balls thwacked skulls.

We kept going.

General Capois led us as we swarmed and kicked in the walls.

The sound of our cannons roared again.

Some of the enemy held up their hands.

Others ran out the back like ants.

When I started to give chase, a Blanc rejoiced when his bayonet pierced my side.

ON THE GROUND, I HEARD MY NAME, MY TRUE NAME.

Slowed motions blurred my vision.

Boots stomped past.

My name sounded again. This time the fire had given one.

"Adbaraya Toya! Adbaraya Toya! Get up."

Eghosa?

I saw her face. She was beckoning me to come along with Gauo Hangbé.

King Tegbesu said rise.

"Well done." He clapped.

The shine of the impaler—the stick the enemy placed heads upon—waved over me.

I was the prize today. The French would display my head.

Failure.

"Adbaraya Toya! Adbaraya Toya! Gaou, get up."

I rolled when the shiny point came down again.

The blade lifted.

This time it was aimed at my face.

I wouldn't squirm. I would see death head-on.

My iya told me sit, then whispered to choose life.

My blinking eyes revealed to me the enemy. From his uniform, a colonel. He reared his arm back. "The witch will die."

Then the man fell at my feet. A spear with the sharpest point ran through his innards.

"Adbaraya Toya! I said get up." Nosakhere took his sash and tightly wrapped my side. It hurt to breathe, but I stood.

Leaning on him with musket in hand, I retrieved his spear. Then we both witnessed flames erupt from Vertières. Men inside burned, caught in hell's fire.

"To the doctors for you," he said and led me, him stabbing the enemy, me bayoneting them as we went.

Janjak rode down from Butte Charrier. "Victory. The French are retreating. Victory. Let us take Le Cap."

He stopped in front of us. "Well done, Gran Toya. Everyone, well done." He looked at Nosakhere. "Take her back to camp. Thank you."

Nosakhere saluted our commander, our king, the seed that changed things. "The angels in white have arrived. They are back at Fort Bréda."

"The women in white, on a mule train?"

"Yes. Adbaraya, you saw them?"

No, but I knew them. That crazy, brave Marie-Claire had come. She couldn't miss the fight, either, not that I blame her.

A shot.

A last salvo of grapeshot soared.

I spun to Janjak but he was fine. He'd been protected by trees.

Nosakhere gave me a big embrace, tight, lasting, sticky, sticky with blood.

He slipped to the ground. Nosakhere hadn't hesitated. He'd been struck shielding me. One ball had ripped through his side, another his neck.

I sank beside him, angered at how his throat refused to stop bleeding.

He wouldn't let me undo the sash. Instead, he kept holding my hands, holding me. "Gaou, you taught her son well. Her son, your son." His wide eyes became slits. "Long live Dess . . . Long live you."

My fingers stayed enmeshed with Nosakhere's until his lids firmly closed.

I made myself remember the feel of him—the roughness of his palms from working metal for spears and banding for cannon barrels. In death, he'd gotten it right, the way to hold me and fire.

THE RAIN STOPPED ITS PESTERING SPRINKLES. THE SKY CLEARED, leaving a path for the mango-orange sun to set.

"Hold still," Marie-Claire said. She cleaned and bandaged my wounds.

"You're not supposed to be here." I gritted my teeth, and she smiled back with hers.

"Gran Toya, you know why I've come. You've brought liberty. Now I can save my aunt."

"No. The streets of Le Cap aren't safe. Dead and deserters are there."

"Bandage done. Take the dray and return with the wounded to Habitation Frère. It'll be back soon, and I've more women there to take care of the injured. Your Minos Thérèse is well and already on her way to her tents."

"That's why you had your Blanc niece return to us. Your partner in this farce."

"Adélaïde is with the children. She loves them and will be with them

if something goes wrong. My maman is my partner today. She had
to save her sister."

The mother-in-law came, too!

Madame Bonheur looked frail and haggard.

This was not a good plan. But who could stop women on a mission?
The war was won. My duty to serve was almost up. I needed to make
sure Janjak had help preparing the peace. He needed a live queen with
a conscience and love for people. "I'll take you two, but this violates
Dessalines's orders—"

Marie-Claire made fists of her hands. "He can't stop me. I have to
do this."

I laughed. I wasn't dead and could probably throw her over my
shoulder and haul her back to the habitation. "You'll owe me a favor.
Something you must agree to without hesitation. Otherwise, you and
your mother are going back to the children."

Her eyes darted for a full minute, but she nodded. "Oui, Gran Toya.
I give you my word."

Good. When my debts were paid, I'd come back and honor Nosakhere.

I retrieved mules and called to my closest Minos.

Ponce and Fleur grabbed two of the other pack animals.

"Non, you don't have to go—"

"We go to Le Cap," they said, almost in unison.

On our own mule train, two women in white with three in black
rode toward town.

Slow and easy, we headed down the route we'd marched, where we'd
fought to the death.

The bodies of our brethren lay on one side. I recognized many from
training.

On the other side—in the trenches, near a small bridge—lay the
French, white men turning gray. Blood was everywhere.

My mule was at the rear, following, looking for trouble.

Marie-Claire took the lead. She knew exactly where she needed
to go.

Nearing the burned habitation of Vertières, I searched for No-sakhere but he'd already been moved. The army would bury the dead in a mass grave or burn them.

None of this was acceptable for a Dahomey, one who'd died with honor. "I should've seen to it, made sure the earth received his body with dignity, given him a proper burial."

"Who are you talking about?" Marie-Claire looked back at me.

"Someone I knew a long time ago. He did wrong, but now all has made been right. That happens sometimes."

"Like letting a city starve to defeat the French."

Couldn't respond. Wouldn't. War had created a free nation, one Marie-Claire would ensure thrived when it was my turn for the earth to receive my flesh. Janjak couldn't rule alone.

I knew this mother, this warrior with a heart for the people would keep a promise to support the king even when he did wrong.

45

Marie-Claire

1803

Cap-Français

We journey the longer way to Le Cap, to the northern entrance, via Chemin de la Bland du Nord.

My old city is rubble. What isn't charred or marred with grapeshot has a suffocating stench.

Our mules cross onto wide streets. Decaying bodies are everywhere. Carts, like the one Pierre made, are overturned. Bit and pieces of businesses, of lives, line the sides of Rue de la Providence.

"A tragedy," my mother says. "A tragedy."

Gran Toya's mule catches up to mine. "We must hurry. Rochambeau has retreated, but his forces have not surrendered."

"Not formally. Look at this!" I wave my hands and point. "The war is done."

She nods and slows her mule, again taking the defensive position at the rear. "Lead the way to the aunt, Marie-Claire."

The warrior slumps in her seat. Though she's strong, she should be in bed. I pick up my pace, urging my animal forward.

"This was the Paris of the West Indies. My père, Lobelot, he loved it here till the day he died. Your mamie loved it here, too. Her angel must be crying today."

My ears almost explode like cannons, pounding and jolting my spine. Maman has never said a kind word about Mamie. Now she calls her an angel, the woman she blames for her père's death.

Not caring about the old feuds, I lead us to Rue du Lion, then cross to Rue Sainte Marie.

It's late in the day, about the time people gather for dinner. The fancy town homes should have candles burning, but there's no semblance of life.

The houses of the Grand Blancs are empty. They've made it out. Elise could have left sooner or stayed with us after the last wedding or after the evacuation when Le Cap burned again. Stubborn Lobelot. She always had to come back here.

The trees at the government park at the corner of Sainte Marie and Rue Espagnole are missing. In their place are spikes with shrunken dark heads. It's impossible to look away.

Gran Toya mumbles something about roofs or lamps, but the impaled skulls remind me of the evil Janjak has been fighting. My wavering spine stiffens.

The last part of the way along Rue Espagnole seems like miles, but we've arrived at Comédie du Cap. Maman dismounts. The two Minos take a guarding stance about the mules.

An old man sits on the steps. He's disheveled and thin. Yet those dark sunken cheeks are familiar. "Monsieur Joseph?"

Toya takes her musket off its sling and holds it out with the bloody bayonet raised as we approach the steps.

"Joseph?"

I run back to the mules and get a calabash of coconut water and give it to him to drink. "It has nutrients. It will make you feel better."

He guzzles like he's not drunk in weeks.

Maman stoops to him and rubs his cheeks. "Where is Elise? Where's my sister?"

He drops the calabash. Nothing is left to spill.

"Elise Lobelot. She has played the lead again. This time, Molière's *Le Dépit Amoureux*."

Maman puts the calabash in his hands. "Where's my sister?"

"She's wonderful. The generals, they overworked her. They wouldn't let her rest. Night after night she had to perform. The poor girl, she's finally resting. I just left her to get some air."

I have him by his thin shoulders. "You left her where, Joseph? Answer me."

"Madame Lobelot won't mind. Hope she won't. She's my dearest friend. She hasn't minded anything since I helped her. Elise was young. She didn't know what was in the jar I brought. The herbs killed Monsieur Lobelot. Elise only wanted him to stop fussing at Sainte. She was scared the man would sell her sister."

His words mesh together. He's disoriented, but I think I understand. I release him then look at my mother.

Her gold face is cherry red, but she doesn't look shocked.

"Elise poisoned my grand-père. You thought it was Mamie. Maman, you hated her and blamed her when she was protecting your sister. Did you know this?"

She mops at tears. "Elise confessed when we moved from Port-au-Prince to Le Cap. We were getting along well. She trusted me to know the truth. Elise thought the spice would take away Père's anger. She hoped it would calm him so he wouldn't sell me off. She didn't know it was poison. Maman never exposed her. She protected her. My beloved sister tried to apologize, but I blamed her for the anger I had for our mother. Things could have been so different between us. It can't be too late for me and Elise. She has to know I forgive her."

I shake her until Gran Toya pulls me back. "If you'd forgiven her, she could be safe at Habitation Frère. We all could be."

"It's not too late." My mother dashes up the stairs and yanks the playbill on the door. "See? Elise Lobelot, she played Lucile, in Molière's *Le Dépit Amoureux*. Lucile, a lead character and not a maid. She's playing the lead regularly, like she always wanted." Maman claps. "She has her heart, and I can apologize. We'll all be better."

I trudge up the steps and take the handbill. "The date says October 27. That was a month ago."

My mother looks panicked. "Monsieur Joseph. You said you just watched her perform."

"Yes. She was brilliant, and in the end as the generals left, she lay down to rest."

My heart sinks. I shift Maman from the doors and start to wrench them open. Gran Toya blocks me.

"I have to see. I have to know."

Bang. She stabs the doors with her bayonet. She pries them open as if they are the nailed lid of a coffin.

The stench escaping rips up my lungs. The darkness inside prevents us from seeing, but no living thing is inside.

Toya orders her women. One of her Minos brings a torch, which I take from her. "I've seen death enough. I'll go."

She bows and holds the doors open. I ascend into the theater.

Empty box seats are to the left and right.

The aisle is strewn with rotting bodies. I step over them to the stage.

I see something with pink tulle and lace, lots of lace, and a dried-up face with teeth missing. The hair is long, and the skin, I can tell, is gold. Everything I know of medicine from my years at Hôpital de la Charité confirms to me that this is my aunt, Elise Lobelot.

I make the sign of the cross with shaking fingers and then turn and leave. Stepping out of the theater, I close the door.

"Where's Elise?" My maman looks hopeful, until I shake my head.

"No living person is in there."

She sobs and falls to pieces.

I look at Toya, lower the torch, and blow out the flame.

46

Toya

1804
Habitation Frère

I stood on the hounwa looking at the place where troops once camped. The new year had come and gone. Everyone celebrated La Saint-Sylvestre and the surrender and removal of all the French forces.

Rochambeau was gone. His terror was over.

The foolish soldiers who supported him died; the ones who wanted to live retreated. Over fifty thousand of their fighting men fell to yellow fever or our guns and bayonets.

Rochambeau sent capitulation documents to a British ship on a Sunday. Eight days later, Janjak and Christophe and other leaders signed a Declaration of Independence. I'd like to think it was similar to the one the first father, King Toussaint, had crafted, just a little too soon.

Getting ready to sit and put my feet up, I saw Janjak ride in with his secretaries. He made a point to travel about the entire country checking on all who had fought, dispensing justice to those who still supported annihilation of the Blacks.

Marie-Claire's mother stepped out with her lacy shawl and stood beside me. "Monsieur Joseph's doing better. I think he will live. We saved one."

"That's good, I suppose."

"Should we tell Dessalines what has occurred, Gran Toya, or let him settle inside to a dinner and some sleep?"

"The commander . . . our new governor would want to know. Then he can help Marie-Claire."

She wrung her hands, still frightened of the temper he had displayed when he found out I'd led them into Le Cap. He'd fussed and stomped, then left. That wasn't true anger. No one lost a head. But he may have taken it out on others. I feared for him and all the rage he bottled up inside.

"Seems a shame, Gran Toya, to not give him a moment of peace."

Gripping my walking stick, I almost wanted to strike her. Picking and choosing, when to listen, when to be angered, when to forgive, had ruined her. "Kings don't get the luxury of choosing when bad things happen."

Janjak stopped his horse, leapt down, and offered the reins to a servant. The governor's black boots needed polishing. They were covered with all the dust of the island, the free island.

"Gran Toya, Maman Lobelot, the Taíno people send their greetings."

"Good trip, Dessalines?"

"Wi," he answered to his mother-in-law. The Taíno call Saint-Domingue, or old Hispaniola, Aytia, meaning mountainous country. "I think Hayti is a good name for a new country."

"Dèyè mòn gen mon. It's true." Madame Bonheur looked nervous. She mumbled, "There are many mountains."

He took his black hat off and stashed his gloves inside, but he seemed to be assessing us. The cheer in his face became weariness. Then his lips thinned with fear. "What has happened?"

The mother wrung her hands. "We tried to break the fever."

His gaze slammed into mine. "Gran Toya, be direct."

"Your son has passed. I'm sorry."

"Albert." He rubbed his mouth. "Where's Marie-Claire?"

"She's in the garden. Been there since it happened."

He started to move and I stopped him. "She needs to be heard. Let the pain come out. That will help her."

"I'm still angry you and the Minos led my wife and mother-in-law into Le Cap. It hadn't been cleared. It was dangerous. She should've been here adding months or years to Albert's life."

"It doesn't work like that. You know this." I bowed my head, then lifted it. "I heard her. She would've gone on her own if I hadn't accompanied her."

"She embarrasses me when she does not listen and appears as a battlefield angel."

"Angels have to be somewhere; the place of war is warranted."

His folded arms went to his sides. "She's a brave and reckless woman."

"Your match, Janjak, your twin. I wish you each could see that."

The sadness in his eyes said he did, but he had too much blood on his hands to love an angel. He plucked the buttons of his fiery-red coat. "You and the Minos are now permanently assigned to her protection. No more going with the military. You two will stay here, where you're needed. Marie-Claire needs you."

"I thought that was a husband's job."

A heavy lump went down his throat, bulging and slowly slipping his neck. "My duty is to Saint-Domingue, the new Hayti, first."

"Janjak, she's the one to help you. The war is done."

"Is it? How many times have we thought we'd found a lasting peace only for it to be threatened again?"

The mother-in-law lifted her hand. "She knows of your action to prevent a future war. The executions. She still gets the renegade papers."

His face dimmed and he stuffed his hat tighter under his arm. "Her hands are too clean for the work that needs to be done. She won't understand. One who's never worn shackles never will understand."

With shoulders blocked and straight, he went into the grand-casa.

I wasn't sure if a guilty king knew how to heal a hurting queen.

47

Marie-Claire

1804

Habitation Frère

Sitting on the bench in my garden, I'm comforted by the shade of my mango tree. It's all leaves again, no fruit.

There's commotion coming from the house. I hear a horse. My husband must be home.

I don't move. My actions in Le Cap trying to save Elise had him fuming. He's been away for months. He's come home too late to say goodbye to Albert.

Arms folded about my shift, I close my eyes and pretend I'm young, readying to discover the world of Le Cap.

When the bench sways, my gaze lifts to Jean-Jacques. He sits beside me, blocking my view of the tree and the mountains surrounding our home.

I no longer see forever, not even the peaks.

"Marie-Claire." His voice is thick. I wonder if he stopped in the nursery, if he sat in the empty rocking chair and stared at the empty crib.

"Marie-Claire, forgive me. You should've sent for me."

"Where? Send for you where? I hear you've been all over the island."

He picks at lint on his red jacket with the pretty gold braids. "All over the country, the new country that's been liberated."

"Liberated. It's done? Good."

He rubs his hands together as if they'll never be clean. I know that feeling.

"Marie-Claire."

"My Adélaïde wants to return to Port-au-Prince, but as she's not a priest, and she's not American or British, and she refuses to ever marry, she meets none of your criteria to keep her life. My friend, my Blanc friend, is afraid of my husband and the military he has built. She believes you'll murder her."

He closes his eyes for a moment. "Everyone who is a danger to our liberty is gone. Our new nation, Hayti, is truly free."

"Free of Blancs? Petit, Grand? Does size matter?"

"Marie-Claire, we have a son to mourn. Let's do that."

"There are many mothers with souls to mourn. You had their sons shot. Over three thousand, Jean-Jacques. They'd laid down their arms. You could've had compassion."

He leapt up. "They have no compassion, not for Black skin. We've been at war for over ten years. More if you count the first uprising, the poisonings."

"That was wrong, too. Poisoning or shooting people with no weapon—"

"They have weapons. Their belief that they are superior, that they can abuse or terrorize at will—that's a weapon. And it will be wielded any time they feel threatened or want to show themselves strong or the mood strikes on a Tuesday."

"Non. People can be reasoned with."

"Marie-Claire, ingrained hate cannot be reasoned with. It must be destroyed."

"You hate them. Does that mean you must be destroyed?"

"I am. Every time I look in your eyes, I see a monster reflected in them."

"I don't think you're a monster, but three thousand people, Jean-Jacques?"

"Three thousand have been shot at my orders. It's a third as many of the Blacks Rochambeau drowned in the sea. It was less cruel than the dogs he trained to devour Blacks in his theaters. Ever watch a soul fight to breathe being burnt in hot sugar? Do you know it takes days for the ants to eat a man to death?"

My heart goes out to Jean-Jacques for the things he's witnessed. And to Elise, starving Elise, made to perform for the French monster.

"Rochambeau is cruel, but you've tried to best him. You don't have to be like him."

"You don't know his cruelty. I've shielded you from it, so you could be here for the children. One of us needs to be alive for them."

"You can't shield me from suffering. I've seen torture, women with limbs burnt off. And Elise's teeth had fallen out. Do you know how long you have to be hungry for that to happen?"

He holds me, and it is not enough. I needed these arms supporting me when Albert stopped breathing.

I thread my fingers with his, folding them with mine as if we were praying. "Do you think God didn't hear my pleas for our son because too many Blanc mothers were on their knees praying for theirs?"

His hands drop away. His neck cranes to the blue and white sky. "Marie-Claire, please."

"You've shown yourself to be Rochambeau's equal in cruelty. No, a third of his cruelty."

Jean-Jacques puts a palm to his lips, then drops his arms to his side. "You win. I'm a flawed man. I'll admit it was revenge, revenge for the hundreds of thousands the Blancs have killed in the cities and habitations everywhere. I witnessed . . ." He bites his lip then rubs at his neck as if it aches. "You've never been enslaved. You don't know how their sentiments will fester. The Blancs will plot and strive to put chains again around our necks. They'll invite more war. They'll not stop."

"Are you done killing, Jean-Jacques?"

He shrugs. "You don't understand. Don't think you ever will. Safety means nothing to you because you have always had it."

"Ha. I loved you. There was nothing safe about that."

Now his lips form a mirthless smile. "You have a grandfather who was a Grand Blanc. That gave you the privilege of being born free. You married a Petit Blanc. That gave you protections to move about in safety. I was born in chains. I saw what Blancs do in power. If there's ever a moment of instability, they will side with anyone but the Blacks."

He is right about me.

I've never been enslaved.

Mamie had; she married a man she didn't love to gain freedom. I had privileges because I was a Lobelot. My mother and Elise always had more because of their light skin.

None of this was fair.

"Lilac ribbons." The words and the memories fall from my lips.

"What?" His brow scrunches like I've gone witless. His gaze, which has been on my bare feet, lifts to my face. "What, you want ribbons?"

"Non, but I couldn't have any. The Le Cap vendor didn't think I deserved any when I was small, but I did get some for free when I was older. Both vendors were Black. Some things are ingrained, but some things can be changed."

I lift my hands to his. "Minds and hearts can be changed."

He kisses my palms and then pats them away. "Françoise and Célestine and Jeanne Sophie can have all the ribbons they want. Jacques can have whatever he wants, because I led an army that broke the back of the French. I'm insuring none will again rise in war. No more war."

"But what do I tell Adélaïde?"

"Tell her she's Black because you love her. All the citizens who are left are Black. We all start at the same place. We all can have lilac ribbons."

A slight breeze redolent of mangoes, of the lush honey of passifloras, tries to soothe me, but I'm lost.

"Marie-Claire, I need you. You must help me lead. Use your heart to feed every soul and find ways to keep the people unified. France may not be done. They can come back and start another war."

"You have friends in America, and the British helped blockade and strangle Le Cap."

"Blanc friends, Marie-Claire. The British have too many enslaved colonies to care about helping the Black state. Jefferson has never written back, not even an acknowledgment. He's making deals with France and Spain. A Blanc slaver in the presidency will always side with other slavers."

My husband looks as if he wants to spit. He's angry, but he turns to the mountains.

Then it happens.

Tears roll down one cheek and then the other. "I was away doing what I thought to be right, and Albert, he went to his mountain."

I curl onto the bench with my feet up. "Jean-Jacques."

He joins me, but with a space between that could be a mile. "Albert was always sickly, but he loved high places. I would take him and Jacques up into the hills. They picked places for me to build forts."

To judge from the wetness on his face, the emotions are true.

"You didn't send for me when Pierre-Louis lay dying. I would've come. I loved him, too. I would have flown back for Albert."

My eyes feel sticky. They shouldn't be. I've cried enough to fill several soup pots. "The nation is still mourning the loss of her sons and daughters. I cannot be selfish."

"But I am." He lifts his hand before I agree. "I know I am. I'm flawed and I've strayed in anger, in lust, in emptiness."

"Jean-Jacques, I don't want to do this. If you want the words 'I forgive you,' I forgive you. I've learned it can be too late to say those words."

He gets up and kneels before me. "I need you, Marie-Claire. You're the mother of our new nation. Will you also be a mother to Serrine?"

"What?" My heart and head are pounding. I've heard of others. I hadn't . . . I hoped. "I can't think about this now."

"You have to. I want you to love all my children. César and Francillette, they are from before we found each other again."

The way he said it, I knew there were others. "Tell me of the ones after we married when you said I was enough."

"Innocent is a fine boy, he's a year old. And there's Angèle, also a year."

"Oh." It's all I can say. The rumors are true. And when I put distance in our bed mourning Pierre-Louis, our first lost twin, he found other arms for comfort.

Jean-Jacques has my hand, but the touch is cold. "I will bring her . . . Serrine. You will love her. Her mother is dead. She needs a mother."

This was what I did to Pierre, forced him to love children that weren't his. How were my lies any different than Jean-Jacques's?

"Marie-Claire," he says, rising as if a weight has been pushed from his soul.

But I'm crushed.

I don't know how to go on with him, knowing what he has done.

He points to the blue and white sky and Albert's mountain. "I have charged Christophe to build fortresses about the nation. Forts around here and across Hayti. Up there, I'm building one for you, Fort Madame, others for my children."

Jean-Jacques spins back. "Tell me you'll love all of them, that you'll mother Serrine."

"Oui. Children are not responsible for our problems. And Serrine should not be an orphan. Bring her. I will love her."

He smiles like the world is wonderful. "My generals will be here tonight. Will you make your soup and kasav?"

"You crush my world and now you want dinner? Are we to pretend all is well?"

"Wi. I need you to do this. We write the constitution for Hayti. The soup, it is a symbol of things coming together. Of caring for the people."

"Maybe it is a symbol of independence. Ask my mother, she knows my recipe. I'm not needed. I shouldn't be on display for the generals."

His lips frown, and he pulls his hands behind his back and walks toward the house. "Make it all, s'il vous plaît. And the kasav. It's all needed. You're needed."

He offers me a final fretful look, then enters the house. Gran Toya doesn't glance at him. She comes straight to me. "I'm sorry, Marie-Claire."

I nod, numb, now a mother of more as I mourn mine. "I must thank you. You disobeyed your king to take us into Le Cap. You've given me and my mother peace."

Plodding forward with her staff, she sits beside me. "I must collect on your promise. You said you'd give it to me, no matter what."

"Oui. Oui, Toya, whatever you want."

"I'll not be at Janjak's side forever."

"Yes, Gran Toya. Forever is hard to see. Wait, are you not well?"

She shakes her head. "I've been his guide for war. We must guide him for peace."

In an instant, I knew what she wanted. "No. Don't say it. I'm working on accepting what he's done in the midst of losing my child. Ask nothing of my dealings with Jean-Jacques."

"Timing, my queen, can't be controlled, not when there are more mountains. My request is for you to forgive him and be at his side now and forever. Be his soul. Stir him to peace. Save him from his worst notions. Hayti needs you. He needs you."

"No, Toya. Give me another thing to promise. Something to bring to you."

"It's all I want. And you are a woman of honor. You gave me your word."

I did promise Gran Toya before I knew of the extent of his adultery and the massacre of three thousand. "Let me grieve. Leave me with my bare mango tree, my mountains, and my memories."

She bows to me as if I were royalty and returns to the house.

Can I close my eyes to it all? How can I help Jean-Jacques? His heart is crowded with mistresses and liberty. There's no room for me.

MY MOTHER PACES ON THE CORAL TILE FLOOR AND SHOUTS AT ME. "Marie-Claire! You cannot be serious. You must go to the coronation. He's your husband. You must do this for him. He loves you."

"I'm not sure what that means anymore. The idea of a long-suffering wife, is that what he cares for?"

"Marie-Claire," Maman says, "this is the bargain you have struck by taking his name."

I rock baby Serrine in my arms. She's beautiful and quiet, with light bronze skin. Her complexion matches the paint of the walls of the newly constructed palace. Jean-Jacques is on a building spree.

But I'm sitting with this babe with copper-colored eyes shaped like her father's. "This is what I have for his name. Mothering one of his many children. Serrine is lovely and healthy. I've seen the new baby boy. I'm sure others will come forward."

"Marie-Claire, I'm sorry."

"I love Serrine with all my broken heart. At least Jean-Jacques is here to see her as a babe, to learn the amusing things she does as she grows. I will have to see if baby Innocent can visit often, too."

Waving my finger over Serrine's face, I watch her eyes move. "Maman, look at how alert she is. She follows me. I hope she comes to love me."

"Marie-Claire, you're not answering me. You can have such influence. You can—"

"Did Père ever disappoint you like this? Did he do things you could barely stomach?"

Maman flutters in her pale pink gown of silk. Britain has begun trading with Hayti again. We can purchase goods like Mamie did when I was little.

If I could go back, what would I change?

Never going to the garden? Never talking to a boy with wide eyes? "Answer, please. Did Père ever break your heart?"

"Non. Your père was never cruel to me, but he didn't bring a nation out of enslavement. Their roles are different."

"As are ours, Maman. You have fought to honor your marriage above all else. I fought for my children and to feed God's sheep. I don't know what to fight for now."

My husband comes into my room. He stands at the door with a big box in his hand. He offers his warm smile with dimples, the old one that used to melt my heart.

Maman scoops Serrine from my arms. "I will take her to Adélaïde." Cooing, she runs from the room. She's intimidated by Jean-Jacques's power.

"My niece will stay and be a governess to the children, provided she is safe." My gaze bores a hole in his garnet military coat with yards of gold braiding. I want to pierce his chest and release all the poison puffing him up. Then maybe only love will remain.

He tumbles the box in his wide hands, round and round. "General Christophe says he has sent salt. His wife craves your mango ice cream. They'd like you to have some made for the dinner after the coronation."

"You have asked me to entertain the ladies during the coronation celebration. I'll fulfill my duty."

"You are elegant and lovely." The package fumbling stops. "I hope they do not bore you."

"Non, Marie-Louise is a lovely girl. She and Christophe do well together. He loves her completely."

I turn back to my desk by the window. "Is there something you need?"

"You were right, the Americans seem to have forgiven my actions and are employing secret diplomacy like Toussaint. My jeweled crown was financed by a private shipper from Philadelphia. They put it on the frigate *Connecticut*." He holds out the box, slipping away the bright white ribbon. "These coronation robes are made by a tailor in London. They don't see me as bad."

"Jean-Jacques, you made choices. You have brought liberty and it seems to be holding." I clap for him. It's an empty and hollow rhythm. "I suppose, well done."

"Doesn't feel well done." He puts the box on my bed. Opening the top, he pulls out magnificent purple robes with a fur edging. They look expensive and suited for a different climate. Something in Europe, not the West Indies. Something Blanc, not Black. But when had Black been royal outside Africa?

That promise to Toya is in my head. It's bumping into my skull. This is the old Janjak, the one wanting my encouragement. Then the crowds or the generals or time or something else will separate us.

He will change. He'll go back to being puffed up.

For the promise I've sworn, I swallow the lump of pride caught in my throat. "You'll look well tomorrow. All the festivities will go well. I'm sure of it, encircled by all your generals. Their voices and their fidelity you need."

"That means you'll not be coming?"

"I'll be here with the children."

"Will you be here when I return? Marie-Claire, you spend a lot of time at Fort Madame."

"It's the one you dedicated to me. Near the fort you built for Innocent."

"You do not like my son?"

"I love your son. He's a fine young man. As is your new daughter Angèle, who will visit next week. And then there is the new woman in Le Cap you are fond of, she seems quite spry and willing to have more of the emperor's children."

"You know all of it," he finally says.

This pretty room feels thick and sweaty. The tension of my wanting either to be aloof or to box his ears is at odds with my promise to Toya. Everything about Jean-Jacques and I is too crowded. "We should've always lived in a garden."

"What? What did you say?" His head tilts to the side. He didn't hear my whisper.

I toy at the thin sleeves of my robe. "I hear everything. I just believe the rumors now."

He comes near and takes my hand. "Hear my apology. And I want you . . . need you to come to the ceremony. You must be there. You are the empress."

"I will stay and care for Gran Toya. She's not better."

"But she's coming. She'll see me crowned. She knows the importance of this moment. She has forgiven me. Please, the nation must see us united."

He folds his arms behind him. "I'd not be the man I am without you and Gran Toya. I'll not order you to come. You know me better than that, but I do command you to think on it. Hayti needs its mother, the woman who will raise her right."

He leaves my room.

The need in his voice twists about my heart and draws me from my chair. I want to go to him and say let's try again.

But it's the old trap, the old pit. If I drop into it, I'll be caught and eaten alive.

Instead, I sink on the bed, lying on the crisp white sheets, and put my hands on the box.

My fingers swirl along the soft pelt of the fur.

Not sure if I'm crying or laughing, but I definitely find myself singing.

It's Elise's hymn, her favorite.

Conspire to lift Thy glories high,
And speak Thine endless praise!
The whole creation joins in one,
To bless the sacred name
Of Him who sits upon the throne.

Six of the finest horses in all of Hayti will be at our grand-casa tomorrow, leading a gilded carriage. They'll pull this English-made contraption all the way to Le Cap. Down Chemin du Port-au-Prince and through the formal entry of Cours de Villeverd, the carriage will pass through the assembled crowds of free people.

It will whip past the ruins of the Place Royale, the spot where Pierre's arches were supposed to be installed. The horses will prance down the fully paved Rue Espagnole.

I'll have to hold my breath as they near Elise's theater and breathe again when we arrive at the center of Champ de Mars.

People will be celebrating liberty, dancing.

Artisans and blacksmiths, coppers, even ribbon sellers will line the cross streets cheering.

Then Jean-Jacques will make his way through the crowds, past an altar bearing his name, sit on a mahogany throne, and be crowned emperor.

To bless the sacred name
Of Him who sits upon the throne.

Humming this softly, then thinking of Maman's old tune about two coming down to change the world, I decide.

I'll wear this robe, hold his hand and my head high. I must see the completion of what we started—the dream of a young boy with wide eyes who told a young girl with stars in hers about a better world.

No one has to know I'm there for Toya and Hayti and liberty.

Fort Madame

Sitting on the edge of the mattress, I mop Toya's fevered head, then I place on her tongue a small cube of tangy mango.

She sucks on it, gathering its sweet juice, then spits it and blood onto a napkin. "Thank you for bringing me here. The smooth walls remind me of Calmina. Use palm oil to make it shine."

"Yes. You told me." My head nods as if her words make sense. I've made my fort a small palace, complete with the best furnishings. "This is my place to get away from everything. To escape the political dinners and diplomatic wrangling, and now you're trying to escape me. Toya, this isn't right."

She smiles a little, and I adjust the garnet-and-black scarf to her head. The fever has matted her short gray locks. "Don't know if you're tender headed. Françoise is. Célestine, non. Serrine, oui."

"No fixing on my hair. Agé and Zinsu and Zinsi will have to accept me as I am." Her deep brown eyes open. "I see you as you are. Your passion and heart. I accept you, too, Marie-Claire. I've always heard you."

A tear leaks down my face.

Her words mean more than any. No two are more different than us. Darkness and light, both graced from above. Jean-Jacques needed us both to move liberty forward. We did what we were called to do.

Toya squints at me. "How do the Minos serve you, Empress?"

The news makes me smile. "Your women and mine—"

"They are yours now."

"Gran Toya, we feed the poor. We teach cooking and help with nutrition. No one shall starve in Hayti again."

She nods her head. "Soup now. I know you brought some."

Of course I did. "It has healing powers." May it work and save my friend.

Very gently, I bring the bowl from the small table.

Toya catches my hand. She holds it for minutes. Smooth and rough, but both palms still have vigor. Our fingers slip together and cradle the spoon. We work together to feed her the healing soup, drop by drop.

"Marie-Claire, I want the burial of a warrior. Janjak and my Minos know what to do. Make someone tell you."

"I will but save your strength. The emperor will be here soon."

"He needs you, Marie-Claire. He will always need you." Her throat is dry. A cough rattles her chest.

Looking into her closing eyes, I want to tell her the truth. I cannot be Jean-Jacques's guide, maybe not even a friend. We are bound by the children and Hayti. Nothing more.

We missed our moment in the sun when the new war, Bonaparte's war, put us on the paths we were meant to follow.

Yet my stomach twists. I hate that I cannot honor her dying wish. Toya risked her life for me in war-torn Le Cap, all to save someone who was already dead. But that was Toya—brave and loyal and fierce.

"Your face has lines, Marie-Claire. What's wrong?"

Toya has to know the truth. Not another soul in my life will go to the grave without hearing my regrets, without us exchanging forgiveness. The Lobelot curse needs to be broken, today.

Wiping her cheek, I touch her face, trace the lines of wisdom, of pain. "Toya, forgive me for every time we've been at odds."

"Nothing to forgive. You fight for your voice. Keep at it."

That would be enough, but I owe her a full confession. "Toya, you asked me before to help him . . . Jean-Jacques. To advise him, be his conscience, and I thought of it—"

She touches my lip. Her finger silences me. "I relieve you of this request. The king is wrong sometimes. His warrior, too. This queen has power in her heart, her own sense of righteousness. Do what your heart tells you. Nothing else."

Drenched in sweat, Jean-Jacques runs through the door. "Gran Toya! Gran Toya!"

Her eyes glance at him. She offers him a full smile, then turns back to me.

Then her lids close forever.

The emperor of Hayti falls to her bed and grips her hand.

I move from the bed, giving him space to grieve, and head to the door.

He cries out to God, calls to the doctors. "They were to treat her as if she were me. Marie-Claire? Marie-Claire, don't go."

My slippers have not crossed the imagined line at the threshold.

His voice warbles. His plea for me to stay—it's fast and garbled.

Something in it vibrates my spine, pulls on all those old memories trapped in my heart. I could be on a bench in Place Royale, in the garden, waiting for Wide Eyes to talk.

But I do not stop. I step over the line and leave him to mourn alone.

My place is not as a tender wife but as the empress, the empress of Hayti, and I have duties to perform for Duchess Adbaraya Toya.

I, Marie-Claire Bonheur Dessalines, must go to the Minos and learn to prepare a traditional Dahomey burial to honor my sister, the most noble woman I know.

Fort Madame

June 15, 1805

Everyone has gathered at Fort Madame for Toya. Generals in red coats and white breeches; grand ladies in flowing gowns of pink, green, and gold; and the good people of Hayti have come for the state funeral for Gran Toya, who shall be known forever as Duchess Adbaraya Toya.

My friend Monsieur Joseph has made it, too. His mind is not sharp, but I take care of him. His wild gray hair tied back in a lilac ribbon, he's sporting a new coat of jade. I told him he gets to stand up top with the family to represent my grand-mère.

I look out my big window where the cannon sits. Jean-Jacques says it's the sixteen-pounder used in Toya's last great battle, the siege of Vertières. It should be shot for her, but too many have been fired in the land.

Françoise and Adélaïde come and hug me. I embrace them and tell them how much I love them, everything about them, every day.

"Look at the people," my daughter says. "They've all come for Gran Toya."

Adélaïde cradles baby Serrine. My niece's eyes smile. She's not fearful anymore. The new constitution makes her, like me, Black. Jean-Jacques has kept his word. We are all now Black.

"Look at the flag, Empress," she says. "They are waving the new flag."

Last month, Jean-Jacques designed a new flag, different than the revolutionary one, the red and blue one Catherine Flon had sewed. This one is black, symbolizing all who died, and red, to represent the blood shed for freedom. No more blue of France at all.

The fluttering Hayti flag stands out against the gray-blue sky, the emerald grasses and palms covering my mountain.

Watching people waving makes the day feel festive, less sad.

Little Jeanne Sophie has a flag in her hand, twirling it. The lilac ribbons adorning her thick braids make me smile, but I pull her back from the window. She's fearless, a little too fearless, sometimes. Fort Madame sits very high.

The emperor comes with all his sons—Jacques, César, and Innocent.

"Thank you for doing this, Marie-Claire." Even in his red jacket with white sashes, he seems lost. That look with his heart in his eyes tugs at my chest.

Maybe he's weighing things, regretting what has kept him from spending more time with Gran Toya and the family.

There will always be a draw to him, a pull for what we've shared. No one can slice a mango quite like Jean-Jacques. He's the father of my children, the man who brought liberty to Hayti.

And he's my emperor.

I still believe in the good in him. I'll help him when he truly wishes to listen.

But we are darkness and light.

We are not the same. Never will be the same.

But we can work together for Hayti and live separate lives.

"Marie-Claire," he says, "I have eight sergeants of my elite guards to carry her coffin behind you."

"But her Minos will lead the way. That's the way it must be."

"Yes." Jean-Jacques puts his hand on my shoulder. "You should wear a crown. As the empress of our new nation, you should have one."

I reach for his cheek and flick away a tear.

Old habits, for both of us.

"One was never made for me, Emperor." I don't mean it as a slight but as the truth.

He looks fragile, but I'm strong and confident. I know who I am and what I must do, but more so what I need.

"All know me. I'm the emperor's wife. I forgive us, Jean-Jacques, for not being enough. And I'm grateful we are enough for Hayti."

My voice makes his dimples show. He needs to hear I'm letting the bitterness go. All curses have to be broken for our children and the next generations to remain free.

Smoothing my black crepe gown and its lengthy train, even beads, red and blue about my collar, I stoop to adjust Jacques's ebony coat. All the boys have white breeches like their père, but black, black coats.

When I stand, I catch my mother's eye. She's pushing for reconciliation. I'm not sure she'll ever understand my choices. I don't know if she'll honor them, but she hears me. That's our new start.

"Jean-Jacques, I had Gran Toya's body prepared, curled over and wrapped. Even if she's in a wooden box, it will be as close to the Dahomey way as possible. The burial chamber has been dug. It's ready. I'm ready."

He nods and fiddles with his snuffbox, then he remembers himself and shoves it into his pocket. "Thank you. You're a tower of strength, Marie-Claire, my beautiful Marie-Claire."

"I was a girl who listened to a boy in a garden and helped him dream and let him know he was worth more. That was my duty, Emperor. But Gaou Adbaraya Toya made Hayti possible."

He looks at me as if he doesn't understand.

But I do.

In 1758, Toya's choice to protect a king ended up creating one, one able to break the yoke of the island's bondage. Years after my birth, this warrior came to me, down from the hills. She taught me to claim my power and to create my own.

Toya and I, war and peace, darkness and light, are forever joined in loving Hayti and giving more of ourselves than we ever expect to receive.

"Jean-Jacques, I'll follow her legacy and expand my training of young women. That's what I can do for our nation, train them to be nurses and to feed and defend the people."

His eyes beam. He doesn't comprehend, or maybe he does. I won't press. It's time to begin the public ceremony.

Alone, I walk to the barracks. The sergeants are in position about the flower-strewn casket. The white ranunculus and hibiscus from my old gardens at Habitation Frère contrast the rich dark mahogany kajou. Two men in front, two in back, and four at the corners, are ready to lift my friend to take her rest.

The Minos stand tall and proud, ten of them in their signature jet with yellow sashes.

The procession starts.

We pass our emperor, friends, and family along the steps of my fort.

Singing a hymn, I listen to my voice echo in the still air.

I lead the casket all the way down from the mountaintop to the valley below.

My head is up, and I shed tears for Hayti, beautiful, liberated Hayti. And I know without regret, this is the proper way to send my sister, the best mother and warrior, home.

Author's Note

Sister Mother Warrior was an honor to research and write. My search to reclaim the stories of powerful women of color has led me to Adbaraya Toya and Marie-Claire Bonheur. We often hear of the men, the Black generals, but not the women. This is a shame. Women were instrumental to winning the Haitian Revolution and fought on the battlefields and streets and towns alongside the men or in their stead.

The task at hand was a bigger challenge than I first imagined. What's often taught in American schools of the protracted Haitian Revolution is very limited. More often than not, the texts oversimplify the narratives—pushing versions of this side good, this side bad. Very few do justice to the accomplishments of a brave and lucky people. The inhabitants of an island formerly known as Saint-Domingue or Hispaniola, most newly freed from enslavement, overthrew a world power and set back a dictator bent on world domination.

Before his defeat at Waterloo, the pattern of breaking Napoleon's hubris and military might started on the shores of Le Cap . . . by Black folks. Of course they had help. The Americans and British, and at times the Spanish, all played roles or foils against the French, but this is not to take anything away from the strength of the local people, particularly the women, who decided they wanted liberty or death.

Many women fought alongside the men for independence. Sanité Bélair, Catherine Flon, Cécile Fatiman, Marie-Jeanne, and Suzanne Simone Baptiste Louverture are just a few. The torture of Suzanne by

Napoleon's forces to get her to incriminate Toussaint could fill a whole book.

Nonetheless, my account focuses on two women, Adbaraya Toya (also known as Victoria Montou and Gran Toya) and Marie-Claire Félicité Bonheur (also known as Madame Lunic and Madame Dessalines). To a lesser degree the story includes the women of her family—Elise Lobelot (her aunt), Marie-Sainte Lobelot (her mother), Madame Lobelot (her grandmother), and Adélaïde Lunic (her niece).

Madame Lobelot is a composite of the myths surrounding Marie-Claire and Diana, the mother of the revolutionary fighter Georges Biassou, who worked in one of the charity hospitals in Cap-Français.

Adélaïde Lunic is a composite character of the white women and men whom Marie-Claire befriended, protected, healed from victimization, as well as those who decided to stay and fight for independence, too. The Blanc priest Father Philémon was executed for being in league with the rebels and was alleged to have assaulted women, particularly white women, during the rebellions. A few other Catholic priests, like Father Cachetan, joined the side of the rebels and were jailed or executed for their participation.

There are so many stories within stories, and I had to pare down and simplify the threads to weave a tightly focused fabric of the revolution, which spanned more than forty-five years. Women were central to the war. They were part of regular forces and often heroic in battle. They rebelled and kept attention on the plight of the enslaved long before the rise of the Black generals. I wonder how many women prosecuted acts of resistance but their sacrifices are unknown because their names weren't written down.

THE LANGUAGE, THE FLAG, THE SOUP, AND OPERA

The language of the book was chosen to reflect status, stature, or education. Those with education spoke French. The Affranchi spoke both French and Haitian Créole, known as Kreyòl at the time. The enslaved spoke Kreyòl. Enslaved Africans spoke the languages of the Gold Coast.

My goal is to make the book feel of the period but to be extremely readable for today's reader.

The Haitian flag changed several times, twice under Dessalines's control. It has continued to change. The present-day country has returned to a version of blue and red.

Soup Joumou is a long-standing tradition, served on New Year's to remember the revolution. One myth is that Marie-Claire made it. However, it was made differently from current recipes with noodles. Noodles weren't introduced to Haiti until the twentieth century.

Now that I've watched the Netflix series *High on the Hog,* I suspect it was likely served with cooked rice, rice from Africa grown in America or the West Indies.

Lastly, Saint-Domingue was a cultural and world leader in theater. I had to include operas and hymns. This is part of the colony's rich history. Operas performed in Le Cap and Port-Au-Prince are included.

MY MADDENING METHODOLOGY

Haitians have a saying, "Dèyè mòn gen mon." It means beyond mountains there are mountains, which speaks of persistence amidst problems. On a literal level it's lots of mountains. When it comes to the history of Saint-Domingue, one must persist through mountains of generally agreed-upon, well-documented facts, differing opinions, alternate history, differing versions of fabled history.

Why so many differing time lines and perspectives on the Haitian Revolution? Competing forces are trying to spin the narrative to suit their prerogatives. From apologists to nationalists to extremists to sexists to religious fanatics to the common everyday Créole Facundos et Fabiolas—everyone wants to have their say in shaping this vital story.

Haiti is the first nation to throw off the yoke of enslavement in the western hemisphere. It's the second democracy in the Atlantic. It's the beginning of the first Black kingdom in the nineteenth century. Everyone wants to have their piece of the story, and these arguments fall into the following buckets:

1. Recasting history in favor of French pride
2. Reshaping and/or deifying with Vodun elements
3. Reshaping and/or deifying with Catholic elements
4. Reshaping and/or deifying with Voodoo elements
5. Recasting history in favor of African pride
6. Modifying elements to favor the reputations of Dessalines and Toussaint
7. Altering elements to detract or debase the reputations of Dessalines and Toussaint
8. New scholarship that casts doubt on old scholarship
9. Dessalines and Toussaint, themselves, enhancing their backgrounds to meet the visions they wish to portray

While everyone should weigh in, there needs to be more scholarship that separates fact from legend. There came a point, after translating my second or third French account of the burning of Le Cap or the Battle of Crête-à-Pierrot, where I decided everyone was right, and I'd use these variations to craft the best narrative and to explain what happened through multiple eyes of unreliable narrators.

For my sanity, I favored the writings of C.L.R. James, Thomas Madiou, and Edna G. Bay to help construct the broader narrative.

James, the famed Trinidadian historian, has done exhaustive research on Toussaint and the Haitian Revolution from a global view and the perspective of a person of color and a West Indian scholar. The cerebral nature of Toussaint, the loyalty and mutual admiration of Toussaint and Dessalines, and the duplicitous role Dessalines had to take on after Toussaint's surrender to Leclerc and prior to the last phase of the revolution is based on James's work. James settled for me how to handle, in context, accounts of infighting. From Madiou's version of Dessalines, I agree that Toussaint and Dessalines admired and respected each other and that differences arose out of distrust of France (Dessalines was right) and the betrayal of Toussaint by Leclerc.

Madiou offers an exhaustive moment-by-moment, battle-by-battle accounting of the revolution and interviewed people who were still alive at the time he wrote, like Dessalines's widow, Marie-Claire. Madiou presents Dessalines as a man given to dance and laughter, one who loved drums. That man seemed more worthy of marrying Marie-Claire than the savage Dessalines often portrayed elsewhere. Little tidbits in Madiou's presentation also helped color Marie-Claire and Dessalines's relationship.

Bay is an expert on the Dahomey people and the Minos, the warrior wives of the African king. The Dahomey story is a foundational pole in the tent of enabling the formerly enslaved people to rise up and have great battle acumen. Yet this strong warrior people also plays a primary role in the slave trade. (See my note on Africans as Slave Traders.)

Nonetheless, the importance of women in Dahomey society mirrors the importance they take in Saint-Domingue. Dahomey women are fearless, and they take roles in leadership. This scholarship characterizes for my novel how women were viewed on Saint-Domingue's battlefields and the respect Dessalines has for Gaou Adbaraya Toya.

GAOU ADBARAYA TOYA

My editor asked me a fateful question: How does Adbaraya become a Dahomey warrior? All my research narrowed down to a sentence or two about Adbaraya, that somehow, she was abducted and sold into enslavement.

In my mind, her capture had to be some kind of battle or huge snare to entrap a Minos, a woman whose mere presence struck terror in men. The Minos were fearless. They took down lions and elephants. They were trained to kill without a thought. They were toughened through physical trials and what we modern folk might call brainwashing. Success was achieved when they felt no pain.

Gaou Hangbé is modeled after one of the only female rulers of the Dahomey. She's credited with starting the Minos, the female guards. She was also a twin, the sister of Akaba, the king she succeeded.

With more research, I learned about the process of becoming a Minos. If you were one of the lucky women saved during a Dahomey raid and not sold, you were given the opportunity to train as a Minos. *Given* is a euphemism. You had no choice. The training could kill you. If you refused to train, you could be killed or sold. They did love skulls and decorating with them. Yet, when you look at the bloody French Revolution and its avid use of the guillotine, and French colonists' enthusiasm for putting the heads of the enslaved on pikes, one could see the Dahomey assimilating well in Western culture.

This is great information, but it didn't answer the question. How did Adbaraya become a Minos? Desperation set in and I took part of her name, Adbara, and found it had Northern African, Arabic roots. It means to separate. I had less luck with *Toya*, though I found the surname in Benin and West Africa. One Indian root for *Toya* meant door or water. Putting the pieces together, I got potentially a migratory family, like a Yoruba tribe, that came from North Africa. Then I studied Dahomey raids under Tegbesu's conquests and found a good candidate in Gbowélé. This city is close to the Lama Forest and has plenty of potential to serve as a place to ground the genesis story for Adbaraya, a child whose village and family are destroyed by the Dahomey. Most of the inhabitants of Gbowélé were killed or sold into enslavement.

Adbaraya fought in the revolutionary army and the preceding versions of Dessalines's battle divisions. She commanded her own troops, fought in the most critical battles of the war, and defeated three French soldiers in hand-to-hand combat while in her mid-sixties. I personally feel her military acumen made Dessalines, the boy she raised, into one of the top battle strategists of the era. Adbaraya is a legend. Her praise is overdue.

MARIE-CLAIRE FÉLICITÉ BONHEUR DESSALINES

Marie-Claire was born August 12, 1758, to Guillaume Bonheur and Marie-Sainte Lobelot, a poor but free fishing family from Léogâne. She was educated by a religious order in Le Cap, primarily the Brothers of Saint-Jean de Dieu; her aunt, Elise Lobelot, worked as a governess for the order. I traced the order to near Place Royale, where a major charity hospital, Hôpital de la Charité, was located.

Here, Marie-Claire met and married a French Petit Blanc, Pierre Lunic, who was a master cartwright for the Brothers. She was widowed in 1795. There's very little information, much of it conflicting, on what happened to Lunic. He became in the manuscript a foil of the tensions between Petit Blancs and Grand Blancs and a way to highlight the other freedom movements happening at the same time.

Many accounts say Marie-Claire had eight children, all with Dessalines. Others said she had none and was barren. Others said she took in all his children. However, Madiou (her contemporary) and others talk about her raising young children and her mad dash to protect their son Jacques and leave the capital after Dessalines's assassination. Jacques is the boy twin in the set of surviving fraternal twins, Jacques and Célestine.

There are dozens of stories or myths of Marie-Claire that are delicious but don't truly fit her or her mother's lives. I added these tales to the grandmother's story of how she becomes free and marries Grand Blanc Lobelot. The white-sheet process of massa sexualizing and raping their female slaves is one of those horrifying details I included.

The mule train, preaching on the battlefield, Marie-Claire's interaction with the botanist Descourtilz, being sent fur robes for coronation—all are true. The advocacy for feeding and healing and keeping people safe speaks to Marie-Claire's character. To me, it also confirms the long-term nature of her relationship with Jean-Jacques. She wasn't a starry-eyed miss when they formally married but a grounded soul and widow. Just meeting a general on the battlefield of Jacmel and agreeing instantly to wed doesn't seem right for her, or for any two people who are strangers. A longer relationship in which indelible bonds are built seems closer to what they had, and I reflect that in the narrative.

Nonetheless, as the two have two weddings/wedding dates on record—April 2, 1800, in Léogâne's L'Eglise Sainte Rose de Lima and October 21, 1801, near Saint-Marc—it seems a fitting theme to their larger courtship. The latter wedding, Toussaint and his wife attended.

Dessalines was a known philanderer and at one point was rumored to have mistresses in every quadrant of the island. Euphémie Daguilh, one of his most influential mistresses, had her expenses paid for by the state. She is said to have helped the wounded in battles circa 1805.

Yet, Dessalines was politically astute, working deals with various governments. I can't help but think he was aware that the sentiment of his onetime allies had begun to turn against him. I suspect in those times he may have drawn closer to Marie-Claire, wanting her encouragement and guidance. On August 12, 1806, he planned a big birthday celebration for her. It was grand, with dignitaries attending.

Dessalines was assassinated on October 17, 1806. Marie-Claire became a defender of his legacy and had nothing to do with the generals she believed murdered her husband. She lived in poverty but continued advocating for nutrition until her death in 1858. Her courage on the battlefield, her capacity for compassion and to live by her heart, should be commended.

Marie-Claire should be given credit as one of the first battlefield nurses. Before Mary Seacole and Florence Nightingale, Marie-Claire Bonheur's name should be added for her mule train outreach to help the sick and injured in Jacmel and other places during the extended Haitian Revolution.

THE THEME OF TWINS

I love a good theme, but this came barreling toward me as I assembled my historical timeline. The year of Dessalines's and Marie Claire's births, 1758, seems like a magical astronomical year. It's the clear start of the documented battle for freedom in Saint-Domingue with the killing of Mackandal. It's the year of the crowning of Pope Clement XIII, whose reign is known for Jesuit suppression and expulsions. This religious battle further limits Black and Brown participation in worship in the West Indies colonies.

Then there are strange facts that map to the theme of twins. One of Jean-Jacques's nicknames is Romulus, as in Romulus and Remus, who founded Rome in Roman mythology. It's also one of the names of the twin stars (Castor and Pollux) of the constellation Gemini. The

Dahomey are one of the few tribes that celebrate twins as good, not evil. Zinsu and Zinsi are semi-divine gods known for exploiting magic. Marassa are divine twins of Vodou responsible for justice, and they control people through their stomachs. Very fitting for a narrative with minor themes on hunger, poisonings, and Lobelot's soup.

AFRICANS AS SLAVE TRADERS

There is no doubt that African tribes along the Gold Coast willingly sold captives to European slave traders: English, Spanish, French, and Portuguese were the main buyers. To support the white gold, sugarcane, in the West Indies, European powers bought millions of people from Africa to populate plantations or habitations in all their colonies.

In the Dahomey culture, when a village was raided, anyone who was not deemed useful or assimilated into the tribe was sold or executed. The apologist argument of tribes not understanding the extent of the horrors might be true, but let us not kid ourselves: I believe these sales were about money. Just as enslaved labor enriched European powers, the wealth made from the sales was significant to the tribes that participated.

COLORISM

At times, reading of the power struggles in Saint-Domingue among people of color and Blacks is heartbreaking. Colorism stems from the view of power. The closer a person's skin is to white, the more perceived power and privilege that person is thought to have or could attain. There is no way to tell the story of Haiti and not include this.

1. If free mulattoes and light-skinned Blacks had gotten the right to be full citizens with the ability to vote or hold office or have a say in taxation in Saint-Domingue, I'm not sure full abolition would have been sought or achieved.
2. It is my humble belief that if the French had not been duplicitous and had treated mulatto and light-skinned people better, as in

not having been as outwardly racially prejudiced, this population wouldn't have joined with the Black generals to defeat the French.

3. If free Blacks had never been made to fear white rule or the subsequent return of enslavement, many massacres wouldn't have occurred.

4. If free Blacks had trusted mulattoes in joint rule and vice versa, the War of the Knives and the starvation of Jacmel wouldn't have occurred.

5. The subsequent breakdown of factions two years after the revolution can again be traced to the mistrust of mulattoes and light-skinned Blacks for darker-skinned Blacks.

DESSALINES'S BLOODLINE

The facts of where Dessalines was born and who his parents were are disputed. Some have him as a Créole Black, meaning born on Saint-Domingue. Others describe him as bossale Black, meaning he was born in Africa and transported. At different points in the retelling of his life this shifts; a woman named Elisabeth may appear as his mother. New scholarship suggests that the creolization of Dessalines, the making him more adjacent to white power, comes from a shame some have had aligning with an African identity.

When I leaned about scarification, I split the myths—conception in Africa but physical birth in Saint-Domingue. His "tribal" scars have sometimes been reported as marks on his face, other times as more intricate scars on his chest. It is also reported that Dessalines was often severely whipped on his arms and chest during his enslavement, leaving many scars. I have no doubt that he and other men were brutalized. Saint-Domingue habitation owners, the Grand Blancs, had a reputation for being the cruelest masters in the West Indies. They perfected all types of horrendous ways to inflict pain and to cause slow, malicious deaths.

I chose to center Dessalines's scars, not only as a key to his African identity but to give him access to a royal lineage. Novels involving enslavement have to cover a lot of painful ground. I chose to use these scars as a source of pride. Again, more scholarship is needed, but I wouldn't be surprised if this becomes new mythology, a new mountain in the tale of Dessalines.

Nosakhere is invented to be Dessalines's path to Dahomey royalty. He is used to highlight more Dahomey culture and a vehicle to illustrate the cruelty done to enslaved Blacks. He is also used to show the revolts that continued during the extended revolution.

THE PROPHECY

Funny thing happens when you hang out researching Northern Africa and migratory Yoruba: you fall in love with the poetry. I began a frantic search for a poem or reading I could use as an epigraph. Somewhere in the middle of my research, I started hearing a beat. Then the beat turned into words, which retrieved a lost memory of my father.

Dad used to tell me stories of his childhood in Trinidad. With his thick accent and pulsing rhythm, he would break out into song or a poem one could drum to. I'd like to think he was the first accountant beat poet before it was cool.

The prophecy in *Sister Mother Warrior* is that remembered rhythm but set to Utenzi style, which is found in Northern Africa. For the words, I'd like to think I received an assist from a latent childhood memory, one I'd forgotten, and my father. I'm thankful it has been returned and could be used on this journey.

Acknowledgments

Thank you to my Heavenly Father; everything I possess or accomplish is by your Grace.

To my beloved editor Rachel Kahan, I love the way you think and push me to write the best books. Thank you for believing in the power of story. I am so proud to share *Sister Mother Warrior* with you.

To my fabulous agent, Sarah Younger, I am grateful that you are my partner. You are my ride-or-die friend and sister.

To Gerald, Marc, and Chris—Love you, bros.

To Denny, Pat, Rhonda, and Felicia—Thank you for helping me elevate my game, the gentle shoves, and every challenge.

Adjoa, love your gifts. I always learn something.

Dr. Albion Mends and Isabelle Felix—Thank you for the riches you bring.

The Writers of Me and My Sisters, The Divas, and my friends in Black Authors in Residence.

To those who inspire my pen: Beverly, Brenda, Farrah, Sarah, Julia, Kristan, Alyssa, Maya, Lenora, Sophia, Joanna, Grace, Laurie Alice, Julie, Cathy, Katharine, Carrie, Christina, Georgette, Jane, Linda, Margie, Liz, Lasheera, Alexis R. and Alexis G. and Jude—Thank you.

To those who inspire my soul: Piper, Eileen, Rhonda, Angela, and Pat—Thank you.

And to my rocks: Frank and Ellen—Love you all, so much.

Hey, Mama. Can you see this one, too?

Thanks, Pa. You know why.

Bibliography

Accilien, Cécile, and Jowel C. Laguerre. *Haitian Creole Phrasebook: Essential Expressions for Communicating in Haiti.* McGraw-Hill, 2011.

Alpern, S. B. "Dahomey's Royal Road." *History in Africa* 26 (1999), 11–24. https://doi.org/10.2307/3172135.

Bailey, Gauvin Alexander. *Architecture and Urbanism in the French Atlantic Empire State, Church, and Society, 1604–1830.* McGill–Queen's University Press, 2018.

"The Battle of Minden—1 August 1759." *Journal of the Society for Army Historical Research* 7, no. 28 (1928): 126–28. Accessed April 25, 2021. http://www.jstor.org/stable/44232580.

Baumgarten, Linda, et al. *Costume Close-up: Clothing Construction and Pattern, 1750–1790.* Colonial Williamsburg Foundation, in association with Quite Specific Media Group, New York, 1999.

Beckwith, Carol, and Angela Fisher. *African Ceremonies: The Concise Edition.* Harry N. Abrams, 2002.

———. *Faces of Africa: Thirty Years of Photography.* National Geographic Society, 2009.

Bellegarde, Dantès. *La Nation haïtienne.* J. De Gigord, 1938.

Bellin, Jacques Nicolas. Carte des environs du Cap François et des paroisses qui en dependent. [Paris, 1764]. Map. https://www.loc.gov /item/74691147/.

Bello, Bayyinah, Marleine Bastien, and M. J. Fievre. "The Queens, Empresses, and First Ladies of Haiti." Panel discussion, Miami

Book Fair, Nov. 21, 2020. www.miamibookfaironline.com/static /9fcc58d873a08c8ed96b0fb989bfcd25/Queens-Empresses-and-First -Ladies_SCRIPT.pdf.

Bernard, Marie Jose, et al. *Haitians: A People on the Move.* Board of Education of the City of New York, 1996. files.eric.ed.gov/fulltext/ED416263.pdf.

Buckridge, Steeve O. *The Language of Dress: Resistance and Accommodation in Jamaica, 1760–1890.* University of the West Indies Press, 2004.

Buyers, Christopher. "HAITI: STYLES & TITLES." *The Royal Ark.* www .royalark.net/Haiti/haiti2.htm.

Cale, John Gustav. "French Secular Music in Saint-Domingue (1750–1795) Viewed as a Factor in America's Musical Growth." 1971.

Chartrand, René, and Ray Hutchins. *Napoleon's Guns, 1792–1815.* Osprey, 2003.

———. *Napoleon's Overseas Army.* Osprey, 1989.

Chartrand, René, and William Younghusband. *Spanish Army of the Napoleonic Wars.* Osprey, 1998.

Coates, Carrol F. "Dessalines: History in the Theater." *Journal of Haitian Studies* 2, no. 2 (1996), 167–78.

Cole, Emily. *The Grammar of Architecture.* Barnes & Noble, 2006.

Cristini, Luca Stefano, and Jacques Marie Gaston Onfroy de Bréville. *Uniforms of French Armies 1750–1870, Vol. 3 (Soldiers, Weapons & Uniforms GEN).* Luca Cristini Editore, 2019.

Daut, Marlene. *Tropics of Haiti: Race and the Literary History of the Haitian Revolution in the Atlantic World, 1789–1865.* Liverpool University Press, 2015.

Dayan, J. "Codes of Law and Bodies of Color." *New Literary History* 26, no. 2 (1995), 283–308. http://www.jstor.org/stable/20057283

Dayan, Joan. *Haiti, History, and the Gods.* University of California Press, 1995.

Debien, Gabriel. "Night-Time Slave Meetings in Saint-Domingue (La Marmelade, 1786)." Translated by John Garrigus from *Annales historiques de la revolution française* 44 (Apr.–Jun. 1972), 273–84. s3.wp.wsu.edu /uploads/sites/1205/2016/02/voodoo.pdf.

Dubois, Laurent. *Avengers of the New World: The Story of the Haitian Revolution.* Harvard University Press, 2005.

Easton, William Edgar, et al. *Dessalines, a Dramatic Tale: A Single Chapter from Haiti's History*. BiblioLife, 2009.

Fernández, Eladio. *Hispaniola: A Photographic Journey Through Island Biodiversity/Biodiversidad a Través de un Recorrido Fotográfico*. Belknap Press of Harvard University, 2007.

Fick, Caroline E. *The Making of Haiti: The Saint-Domingue Revolution from Below*. University of Tennessee Press, 1990.

Fodor's Essential Caribbean. Fodor's Travel Publications, 2019.

Forbes, F. E. *Dahomey and the Dahomans*. Cass, 1851.

Freeman, Bryant C. *Eighty-Eight Historical and Present-Day Maps of Saint-Domingue/Haiti, Its Sites, Towns and Islands*. University of Kansas, 199AD.

Gaffield, Julia, ed. *The Haitian Declaration of Independence: Creation, Context, and Legacy*. University of Virginia Press, 2016.

Garran de Coulon, Jean-Philippe, and Marguerite-Élie Guadet. "An inquiry into the causes of the insurrection of the negroes in the island of St. Domingo. To which are added, Observations of M. Garran-Coulon on the same subject, read in his absence by M. Guadet, before the National assembly, 29th Feb. 1792." London, Printed and sold by J. Johnson, 1792. France, Assemblée Nationale Législative, Pre-1801 Imprint Collection, and Miscellaneous Pamphlet Collection. https://www.loc.gov/item/03006338/.

Garraway, Doris Lorraine. *Tree of Liberty: Cultural Legacies of the Haitian Revolution in the Atlantic World*. University of Virginia Press, 2008.

Gazette Politque et Commerciale D'Haiti, Nov. 14, 1804.

Geggus, David Patrick, and Norman Fiering. *The World of the Haitian Revolution*. Indiana University Press, 2009.

Girard, Philippe R., and Jean-Louis Donnadieu. "Toussaint Before Louverture: New Archival Findings on the Early Life of Toussaint Louverture." *The William and Mary Quarterly* 70, no. 1 (2013), 41–78. https://doi.org/10.5309/willmaryquar.70.1.0041

Gunsch, Kathryn Wysocki. *Benin Plaques: A 16th Century Imperial Monument*. Routledge, 2020.

Haitian Historical and Cultural Legacy. depthome.brooklyn.cuny.edu/habetac /Publications_files/Haitian-Historical.pdf.

Herskovits, Melville J. "A Note on 'Woman Marriage' in Dahomey." *Africa: Journal of the International African Institute* 10, no. 3 (1937): 335–41. Accessed April 25, 2021. doi:10.2307/1155299.

James, C.L.R. *The Black Jacobians: Toussaint L'Ouverture and the San Domingo Revolution.* Penguin Books, 1989.

Jenson, Deborah. "Jean-Jacques Dessalines and the African Character of the Haitian Revolution." *The William and Mary Quarterly* 69, no. 3 (2012), 615, doi:10.5309/willmaryquar.69.3.0615.

Kentake, Meserette. "Marie Claire Heureuse Félicité Bonheur: Empress of Haiti." *Kentake Page,* June 8, 2020. kentakepage.com/marie-claire -heureuse-felicite-bonheur-empress-of-haiti/.

Le Port Au Prince. [1750] Map. https://www.loc.gov/Item/74692171/.

Madiou, Thomas. *Histoire d'Haïti.* H. Deschamps, 1985.

Mama, Raouf. *Why Monkeys Live in Trees and Other Stories from Benin.* Curbstone Press, 2006.

"Marie Claire Heureuse Félicité ~ Biography: Photos: Videos." *Alchetron.com,* May 13, 2020. alchetron.com/Marie-Claire-Heureuse-F%C3%A9licit%C3%A9.

McClellan, James E., III. *Colonialism and Science: Saint-Domingue and the Old Regime.* University of Chicago Press, 2010.

McCloy, S. T. "Negroes and Mulattoes in Eighteenth-Century France." *The Journal of Negro History* 30, no. 3 (1945), 276–92. https://doi.org/10.2307/2715112.

Mckey, Colin. "The Economic Consequences of the Haitian Revolution." Robert D. Clark Honors College, Department of Business Administration, University of Oregon, 2016. https://scholarsbank .uoregon.edu/xmlui/bitstream/handle/1794/20330/Final%20Thesis -McKey.pdf?sequence=1&isAllowed=y.

Merkyte, Inga, and Klavs Randsborg. "Graves from Dahomey: Beliefs, Ritual and Society in Ancient Bénin." *Journal of African Archaeology* 7, no. 1 (2009), 55–77. doi:10.3213/1612-1651-10126.

Morton-Williams, Peter. "A Yoruba Woman Remembers Servitude in a Palace of Dahomey, in the Reigns of Kings Glele and Behanzin." *Africa* 63, no. 1 (1993), 102–17. doi:10.2307/1161300.

Nash, Gary B. "Reverberations of Haiti in the American North: Black Saint Dominguans in Philadelphia." *Pennsylvania History: A Journal of Mid-Atlantic Studies* 65 (1998): 44–73. Accessed April 25, 2021. http://www.jstor.org/stable/27774161.

North, Susan. *18th-Century Fashion in Detail*. Thames and Hudson, 2018.

A Particular Account of the Commencement and Progress of the Insurrection of the Negroes in St. Domingo Which Began in August, 1791: Being a Translation of the Speech Made to the National Assembly, the 3d of November, 1791, by the Deputies from the General Assembly of the French Part of St. Domingo. Printed for J. Sewell, 1792.

Phelipeau, René. *Plan de la Ville du Cap Français et de Ses Environs . . . par le Sr. René Phelipeau . . . C. J. Chaumier, Sculp. Échelle de Deux Cent Cinquante Toises = 205 Mm*, 1784.

———. *Plan de la Ville et des Environs de Léogane dans Lisle St. Domingue a. p. d. r.,* Chez Le Sr. Phelipeau Ingenieur géographe Rue de la Harpe près Celle du Foin, 1785.

———. *Plan de la Ville de Jacmel et Ses Environs pour en Faire Voir le Blocus Commencé le 28 Messidor an 10 et Terminé Par L'évacuation Le 21 Fructidor an Lle*, S.n., 1803.

———. *Plan de la Ville de Léogane et des Ses défenses*, S.n., 1800.

———. *Plan de la ville de St Marc dans l'isle St Domingue*, 1785.

Ragatz, M. P. *A Guide for the Study of British Caribbean History, 1763–1834: Including the Abolition and Emancipation Movements.* U.S. Government Printing Office, 1932.

Ramgahan, Kavita. Fon translation. Translation-Services. 2021.

Ramsay, T. W. *Costumes on the Western Coast of Africa*. Scholar Select.

Rey, Terry. *The Priest and the Prophetess: Abb Ouvire, Romaine Rivire, and the Revolutionary Atlantic World.* Oxford University Press, 2017.

Satterfield, S., and G. E. W. Carter. *High on the Hog: How African American Cuisine Transformed America*. Episode 1: "Our Roots." Netflix, 2021.

Satterfield, S., and G. E. W. Carter. *High on the Hog: How African American Cuisine Transformed America.* / Episode 2: "The Rice Kingdom." Netflix, 2021.

Schiebinger, Londa. *Secret Cures of Slaves: People, Plants, and Medicine in the Eighteenth-Century Atlantic World.* Stanford University Press, 2017.

Serbin, Sylvia, et al. *The Women Soldiers of Dahomey*. Collins/UNESCO, 2015.

Sowell, David. Review of Karol K. Weaver, *Medical Revolutionaries: The Enslaved Healers of Eighteenth-Century Saint-Domingue*. *The American Historical Review* 112, no. 5 (2007), 1579–80. doi:10.1086/ahr.112.5.1579a.

Stowell, Lauren. *The American Duchess Guide to 18th Century Dressmaking*. Page Street, 2017.

Street, John M. *Historical and Economic Geography of the Southwest Peninsula of Haiti: Report of Field Work Carried Out Under ONR Contract (222) 11 NR388 067*. Department of Geography, University of California, 1960.

Thwaites, Reuben Gold. *The Jesuit Relations and Allied Documents: Travels and Explorations of the Jesuit Missionaries in New France, 1610–1791; the Original French, Latin, and Italian Texts, with English Translations and Notes; Illustrated by Portraits, Maps, and Facsimiles*. Burrows, 1896.

Timyan, Joel. *Bwa Yo: Important Trees of Haiti*. South-East Consortium for International Development, 1996.

Tucker, Phillip Thomas. *Gran Toya: Founding Mother of Haiti, Freedom Fighter Victoria "Toya" Montou*. Lulu.com, 2020.

———. *Marie-Jeanne*. Lulu.com, 2019.

White, Ashli. *Encountering Revolution: Haiti and the Making of the Early Republic*. The Johns Hopkins University Press, 2012.

About the Author

In addition to being a novelist, **Vanessa Riley** holds a doctorate in mechanical engineering and a master's in industrial engineering and engineering management from Stanford University. She also earned a BS and MS in mechanical engineering from Penn State University. She currently juggles mothering a teen, cooking for her military-man husband, and speaking at women's and STEM events. She loves baking her Trinidadian grandma's cake recipes and collecting Irish crochet lace. You can catch her writing from the comfort of her porch in Georgia, with a cup of Earl Grey tea.

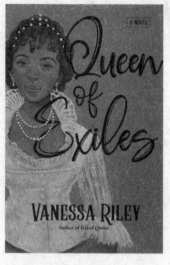
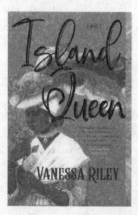